Praise for Michael M

"A mythological cycle . . . highly relevant to the twentieth century . . . The figure of Elric often resembles many purely contemporary figureheads from Charles Manson to James Dean."
—*Time Out*

"Elric is back! Herald the event!"
—*Los Angeles Daily News*, on *The Fortress of the Pearl*

"[The Elric] novels are totally enthralling."
—*Midwest Book Review*

"Among the most memorable characters in fantasy literature."
—*Science Fiction Chronicle*

"If you are at all interested in fantastic fiction, you must read Michael Moorcock. He changed the field single-handedly: He is a giant."
—Tad Williams

"A work of powerful and sustained imagination . . . The vast, tragic symbols by which Mr. Moorcock continually illuminates the metaphysical quest of his hero are a measure of the author's remarkable talents."
—J. G. Ballard, author of *Crash*

"A giant of fantasy."
—*Kirkus Reviews*

"A superb writer."
—*Locus*

ELRIC
SWORDS AND ROSES

ELRIC
SWORDS AND ROSES

CHRONICLES OF THE
LAST EMPEROR OF MELNIBONÉ

—— VOLUME 6 ——

MICHAEL MOORCOCK

FULLY ILLUSTRATED BY JOHN PICACIO

BALLANTINE BOOKS · NEW YORK

A Del Rey Trade Paperback Original

Copyright © 2010 by Michael Moorcock and Linda Moorcock
Foreword copyright © 2010 by Tad Williams
Illustrations copyright © 2010 by John Picacio

Published in the United States by Del Rey, an imprint of
The Random House Publishing Group, a division of
Random House, Inc., New York.

DEL REY is a registered trademark and the Del Rey colophon is a
trademark of Random House, Inc.

The stories contained in this work originally appeared in various
science fiction magazines and books, as noted on the
following acknowledgments page.

Library of Congress Cataloging-in-Publication Data
Moorcock, Michael.
Elric : swords and roses / Michael Moorcock.
p. cm.—(Chronicles of the last emperor of Melniboné ; 6)
ISBN 978-0-345-49867-0 (pbk.)—ISBN 978-0-345-51898-9 (ebook)
1. Elric of Melniboné (Fictitious character)—Fiction. I. Title.
PR6063.O59E459 2010
823'.914—dc22
2010039723

Printed in the United States of America

www.delreybooks.com

2 4 6 8 9 7 5 3 1

Book design by Julie Schroeder

The Revenge of the Rose was first published in the UK by Grafton Books in 1991. "Stormbringer: First Draft Screenplay" appears here for the first time.

"Black Petals" first appeared in *Weird Tales* magazine (edited by Stephen H. Segal and Ann VanderMeer) No. 349, March/April 2008.

"Aspects of Fantasy" (conclusion) first appeared in *Science Fantasy* magazine (edited by John Carnell) No. 64, April 1964. The introduction to *The Skrayling Tree* was first written for Borders, Inc., 2003. The introduction to the French edition of Elric first appeared in *Le Cycle d'Elric,* Éditions Omnibus, France, 2006.

"Elric: A New Reader's Guide," by John Davey, appears (in this form) here for the first time.

———

Grateful acknowledgment is made to the following for permission to reprint previously published material:

La Revanche de la Rose, Pocket Books, cover artwork © 2006 by Marc Moreno; *La Forteresse de la Perle*, Pocket Books, cover artwork © 2005 by Marc Moreno; and *Elric et la Porte des Mondes*, Fleuve Noir Books, cover artwork © 2006 by Guillaume Sorel. Reprinted by permission of Univers Poche.

"Империя Мелнибонэ" ("Empire [of] Melniboné") map by Н. Михайлов, 1992, appeared in *Хроники Элрика / Призрачный Город* (The Dreaming City/The Sleeping Sorceress), Terra Fantastica, 2001. Artwork reprinted by permission of Maureen Bell on behalf of James Cawthorn.

The Sailor on the Seas of Fate, Yanshuf Books, cover artwork © 2005 by Yael Bar-Dayan. Reprinted by permission of Yanshuf Publishing.

Cover artwork by Howard V. Chaykin, for *Elric*, self-published portfolio, © 1975. Reprinted by permission of Howard V. Chaykin.

Elric portrait for *Star*Reach Greatest Hits* cover © 1979, 2009 by Frank Brunner. Reprinted by permission of Frank Brunner.

A page from "The Green Empress of Melniboné," by Barry Windsor-Smith and Roy Thomas, first appearing in *Conan the Barbarian* Nos. 14 and 15, March and May 1972. Conan ® and © 1972 Conan Properties International LLC. Reprinted by permission of Conan Properties International LLC.

"The World of Elric" map by John Collier and Walter Romanski, © 1976, first published in *Elric of Melniboné*. "Elric in the Young Kingdoms" map by John Collier, © 2009. These corrected versions, previously unpublished, reprinted by permission of John Collier.

Interior artwork and "L'Ère des Jeunes Royaumes" map, both by Philippe Druillet, from *Elric le Necromancien*, Éditions Opta, © 1969. Reprinted by permission of Philippe Druillet.

The Revenge of the Rose, Ace Books, cover artwork © 1991 by Robert J. Gould. Reprinted by permission of Ace Books.

Various Elric artworks by James Cawthorn reprinted by permission of Maureen Bell on behalf of James Cawthorn.

"Dream of a Doomed Lord" © 1978 by James Cawthorn, first published in *Something Else* No. 1, edited by Charles Partington, Spring 1980. Reprinted by permission of Charles Partington.

Cover artwork for *Crucified Toad* No. 4, edited by David Britton, Winter 1974, and a page from *Stormbringer*, graphic adaptation, Savoy Books, © 1976, both by James Cawthorn. Reprinted by permission of David Britton, Savoy Books.

ALSO BY MICHAEL MOORCOCK

Behold the Man
Breakfast in the Ruins
Gloriana
The Metatemporal Detective

CHRONICLES OF THE LAST EMPEROR OF MELNIBONÉ
Elric: The Stealer of Souls
Elric: To Rescue Tanelorn
Elric: The Sleeping Sorceress
Duke Elric
Elric: In the Dream Realms

THE CORNELIUS QUARTET
The Final Program
A Cure for Cancer
The English Assassin
The Condition of Muzak

BETWEEN THE WARS: THE PYAT QUARTET
Byzantium Endures
The Laughter of Carthage
Jerusalem Commands
The Vengeance of Rome

And many more

In Memoriam

Jim Cawthorn
December 21, 1929–December 2, 2008

CONTENTS

FOREWORD

by Tad Williams

Michael Moorcock is my religion.

I'll explain that, I promise. It may take me a few minutes . . .

First off, if you're standing in a store reading this and you don't know Moorcock's work, just buy the book. There. You've done yourself a favor.

If you're one of my readers (I feel presumptuous even mentioning it) and you haven't read any Moorcock, you must. He is one of the field's few living legends and has had a gigantic influence on me (and on most other writers of speculative fiction my age).

If you're new to his work and want to know more about Moorcock's background, go get the first volume of this series, *The Stealer of Souls*, and read Alan Moore's foreword. In fact, get the whole series. That's not what this foreword's about.

And, no, I haven't forgotten that I said I'd explain the religion thing.

See, I sat down to write this foreword and realized that the other writers who had talked about Moorcock in the previous volumes had said pretty much all the general stuff about the man and his work that needed to be said. He's an artist who knocked people's socks off when he was a wunderkind, but he has continued to get better and better every damn year of his life. The scope of his work is probably unmatched in the field—science fiction, fantasy, black humor, surrealism, you name it—and he's had a life full of adventures as well. As editor of *New Worlds* he helped spawn the modern age of science fiction. He's been onstage with Hawkwind. God knows, he probably undertakes secret missions in his spare time to defeat smirking archvillains and save the Earth from destruction. Mike Moorcock just *rules*. That's all there is to it. Discovering his work changed my life as a reader and a writer.

But everyone else has said pretty much the same thing in *their* introductions. So what's left for me? I wondered.

Well, besides all those other things, Michael Moorcock is the prophet of my own personal religion. Yes, now I'm explaining.

First off, you have to understand that I'm one of those folks who grew up in the sixties and seventies, the years in which Moorcock was fizzing up into grand prominence in the fields of SF and fantasy. I read everything you would imagine—Tolkien, Bradbury, Leiber, Howard, Lovecraft and too many others to relate—but Michael Moorcock's books were the first things in the genre that seemed to be truly of my era, even though his fantasy heroes like Elric and Corum lived in time-less fantasy worlds. Something about the melancholy and absurdity of Moorcock's worlds, even during his greenest and most melodramatic beginnings as a writer, struck a note of familiarity that thrilled me. And in his other work, I soon began to discover, the implicit became explicit: the Jerry Cornelius books and *The Dancers at the End of Time* were surreal but nevertheless revealing and accurate mirrors of our shared era, an age when everything fell apart but also when even the ruins themselves seemed to contain the excitement of new possibility.

Years later, long after I'd become a writer myself (and begun to realize to my chagrin that many of my best and most creative ideas were actually fuzzy memories of things I'd read in a well-thumbed Moorcock paperback twenty years earlier), I moved to England. My wife, Deborah, was, for a while, Mr. M.'s British publisher, and because of that I had the great good fortune to meet him and even get to know him. The first social get-together was especially exciting, of course, even when we had a mild argument about Tolkien. (Mike, although admiring *The Lord of the Rings*, seemed to be irritated about the little Englandness of Tolkien's Shire and what Mike felt was the romanti-cization of the peasant-landowner relationship. Or something like that.) But of course mainly I was just thrilled to be talking to him.

During the time I lived in the UK, we spent a few evenings with Mike and his wife, Linda. It was always great, but after a while it wasn't like going backstage to meet the Beatles anymore. It was almost . . . normal.

Then one night Mike called and invited us over for dinner. He and Linda were moving to the United States in a couple of weeks, he reminded us, and he thought we should get together before they left. Of course we said yes.

Comes the appointed night. I was having a crappy day for some reason—small irritations, perhaps a squabble with my publishers, maybe I was just being a jerk for no reason (God knows, it happens). In any case, I was not in a good mood. Deborah came home a little late from work and I was worried about being late. (I don't like being late.) We got a cab and headed across London to the Moorcocks'.

I can still remember that night far better than I remember most of the other important moments of my life. It was raining, not enough to be interesting but too much to ignore, and crosstown traffic was jerky and slow. The taxi windows were striped with an orange sodium glow from the streetlights and I was feeling really tense and grumpy. Deb had sensibly stopped talking to me and was looking out the window. I was probably reviewing some silent list of my grievances against Fate at that moment, when suddenly the sky opened, the trumpets blared, the angels sang!

Well, no. The windshield wipers kept thumping and the sodium light kept strobing in slow motion over the windows (which was frankly a bit migrainous and probably why Deb wasn't talking). But at the moment, the angels should have sung. Because I was having a Revelation.

(I'm not the spiritual type, by the way. This is the only Revelation I've ever had.)

"Look at yourself," a voice told me. I think it was my own voice, and I think it was just in my head, but it seemed really *loud*. "You're in a cab going across London with your beautiful publisher wife. You write books for a living. You get up when you want to and dress the way you want to and take naps at any hour of the day and call it 'plotting.' But even more important, you idiot man, you are on your way to *Michael Moorcock's house!* He called you up—he knows your first name! He invited you to come over just like you were *another human being* and not a slobbering fanboy. He even seems to *like* you.

"HELLO!" the inner voice thundered. "Michael Moorcock called you up and invited you over to dinner. Nobody paid him or put a gun to his head or *anything*. He just called you up and said, 'Come over.'

"So why are you being such a @$%#head?"

And instantly, as if the sky truly had opened up and the top of the cab had popped off and the heavenly sunshine of wisdom had poured down on me, I ceased my @$%#headedness forever (or at least for the rest of the evening).

"Hosanna," I cried, or something like that. "My own fifteen-year-old self would shake his head in awe and tell me that I am the luckiest human being in the world—and he would be right. I must never forget that."

And I never have. And that's why, above all the other reasons (and those reasons are plentiful—among them his writerly skill, his wit, imagination, fiery compassion and gloriously cracked poetic soul), above even the immense influence he's had on my writing . . . that's why Michael Moorcock is my religion.

He changed my life forever. Twice.

Hosanna!

Tad Williams
November 2008

INTRODUCTION

The unexpected death in late 2008 of Jim Cawthorn came as an enormous blow to his friends and admirers. Jim was the first artist to draw Elric and the first to illustrate *The Lord of the Rings* (after Tolkien himself). He was my close friend and collaborator for more than fifty years. I had known him since I was a teenager in the mid-1950s, when I produced a fanzine, *Burroughsania*, originally inspired by the work of Edgar Rice Burroughs.

Jim and I came to the world of fanzines more or less through the same route. We had no contact, originally, with the world of SF fandom and didn't know their publications existed until long after we had been working as amateurs, him as an illustrator and me as a writer. A chance meeting with a fellow fan of imaginative fiction, Don Allen, in his hometown of Gateshead–on–Tyne in northeast England, led Jim to illustrate Don's fanzine *Satellite*. Through *Satellite*, Jim learned of two ERB fanzines which had been running for a while. One was mine and the other was *Erbania*, run by D. Peter Ogden. Jim wrote to us both. Soon our fanzines were transformed as he began to produce a wealth of illustrations, including all my front and back covers and interiors, featuring his versions of most of the great classic fantasy stories of the day (I had soon broadened the contents to include work on Howard, Bradbury and many others). He introduced me to many of the greatest fantasts, including Mervyn Peake, Fritz Leiber and William Hope Hodgson. Within a couple of months, his input had transformed not only *Burroughsania* but the book-collecting and music fanzines I was also producing, including *Book Collectors' News* and *Rambler*. He could do portraits of characters from Leigh Brackett and Poul Anderson, mastheads, thumbnails and gloriously funny cartoons.

No matter how many fanzines I began to turn out (under the grandiose imprint of MJM Publications), Jim found time not only to enhance their appearance but to suggest content. Like Arthur Thomson, another artist who came to improve the look of my fanzines around the same time, he was an absolute master of the art of drawing directly onto the delicate wax stencils from which the fanzines were reproduced on what the Brits call duplicators and the Yanks call mimeographs. This art has gone the way of steel engraving, but those who could do it were craftspeople of the highest order and Jim was recognized by many as the greatest, producing an early sequence of *Lord of the Rings* pictures long before anyone else attempted a similar project. When the Howard fanzine *AMRA*, edited by George Scithers, appeared, reproduced on offset litho, Jim, Roy Krenkel, Frank Frazetta and several others saw their early work appearing there.

At the age of sixteen, I began to contribute to the professional weekly *Tarzan Adventures* and Jim illustrated my features and fiction. A little later, I became editor of the magazine and Jim not only illustrated much of it, he also began writing for it, contributing a sword-and-sorcery series and a comic strip, among others. When I left *Tarzan* and went to work for "the longest-running detective series in history," the Sexton Blake Library at the old Amalgamated Press (now Fleetway publications, publisher of *2000 AD* and many others), Jim produced illustrations for the monthly novels and collaborated with me on a classic locked-room (only it was a locked bathysphere) murder mystery which was published eventually as *Caribbean Crisis*. Originally through those contacts at Fleetway Jim began a long career as a freelancer, writing strips and educational features and illustrating children's books.

While I was still at *Tarzan*, I had begun to discuss with Jim the idea of a new kind of fantasy hero who would be neither noble and decent, like John Carter; barbaric and moody like Conan or Brackett's Eric John Stark; nor a pseudo-juvenile, like Tolkien's hobbits. Influenced by the old gentleman adventurer crooks, like Hornung's Raffles and Skene's Monsieur Zenith, he would not battle against sorcery but embrace it, not shun aristocratic decadence but be part of it. There was a dash of Shakespeare's Richard III in there, too! As we discussed this character, Jim sketched out ideas and passed them back to me. And so Elric and Stormbringer were born. For me, Elric's appearance will always be the one Jim drew in the late 1950s; when I came to write my first story, at the editor's request, for *Science Fantasy*, he was already there, the moody prince of decadent Melniboné. When editor John Carnell asked for more and more stories, Jim even came to my aid then, giving me the outline of "Kings in Darkness." Jim produced covers featuring the albino. He did the covers for my *Kane of Old Mars* books. He produced the first-ever cover for the hardback novel *Stormbringer*. He drew the first Elric graphic novel. He illustrated the DAW editions of the Elric novels, with the Whelan covers, and he illustrated many other DAW titles. He was commissioned to do Elric interiors for my German editions and his work appeared in the first omnibus Elric editions produced in England. Our collaborations lasted as long as our friendship, which remained strong and free from argument.

When, in 1964, I became editor of *New Worlds* magazine, I had to put my first issue together in a very short time. I commissioned a serial from J. G. Ballard, "Equinox," which became *The Crystal World*, and short stories from John Brunner, "The Last Lonely Man" (one of his best); Barry Bayley, "The Star Virus" and others, while asking Jim to do the cover and interiors. I did an editorial on the Beat writer William Burroughs, saying how I thought his absurdist, unrationalized work, with its scientific metaphors, was "a new literature for the Space Age." It was, I still think, a brilliant and influential issue, created from scratch in about two weeks. I was used to working at such speed, having produced weeklies, but the others were not! Jim did the next cover, illustrating my then wife Hilary Bailey's early Hitler-won-WW2 story "The Fall of Frenchy Steiner" while also doing most of the interiors. He would continue to illustrate *New Worlds* throughout my editorship and later ownership, doing wonderful work for *The Dancers at the End of Time* novellas and a magnificent double-page spread for *The Warlord of the Air,* which he would later illustrate for its Ace edition.

Jim lived in a boarding house occupied entirely by *New Worlds* contributors around the corner from Ladbroke Grove in Portland Road. He often produced the illustrations as Disch, Sladek, Bayley, Merril or one of the others wrote the story! He also designed sets for Hawkwind stage shows and painted individual T-shirts for band members. He produced strips and illustrations for *Frendz* and other underground press publications, for SF and fantasy magazines such as *Vision of Tomorrow* and *Vortex*.

I was commissioned in the late 1960s by *The Times of India* to write a serial which the editor hoped would alert Indians to their need to embrace science and technology, to be published in *The Illustrated Weekly of India*. Jim not only illustrated the story extensively but also took over the writing for the second half when overwork caused my temporary exhaustion. When I was asked to produce a script for E. R. Burroughs's novel *The Land That Time Forgot*, Jim became my collaborator, breaking down the scenes as he had done for an earlier planned graphic version. We worked together easily and rapidly. By the 1970s Jim also became artist in residence for Savoy Books (www .savoy.abel.co.uk), under the aegis of David Britton and Michael Butterworth. Not only did he produce the first graphic novel of *Stormbringer*, he did a brilliant version of my Hawkmoon books as *The Jewel in the Skull* and *The Crystal and the Amulet,* while illustrating the book version of *Sojan*, *The Golden Barge* and others.

By 1967 *New Worlds* had become a very different kind of publication from the SF magazine I had taken over. We were the first English-language magazine to feature, for instance, the work of M. C. Escher. We had an ongoing relationship with some of the leading fine artists and poets of the day, some of whom became regular visitors to my apartment in Ladbroke Grove. One of these was Eduardo Paolozzi, whose sculptures and graphics are in most leading museums of modern art around the world, and who had become our Aeronautics Adviser. I remember I had one of Jim's first Elric drawings framed on the wall of my office when Eduardo spotted it and began to enthuse about its line, demanding, as was his way, that I let him have it. Of course, I refused and he then offered to buy it. As I recall I arranged for him to buy something else of Jim's. Today I have work by both men hanging on my walls. Now that Eduardo is dead, I can probably admit that I'm not sure Jim had the same enthusiasm as I did for *Diana as an Engine* or the designs adorning Tottenham Court Road tube station. Jim's heroes were Hal Foster, Milton Caniff, Alex Raymond, Burne Hogarth and the great classic American adventure strip artists. For all that, I continued to run work by fine artists side by side with illustrations by Jim, Mal Dean and some of the outstanding illustrators of the period in the magazine.

Ironically, as well as introducing me to the work of Mervyn Peake, Jim had also made me an enthusiast for many great artists, especially the Pre-Raphaelites and visionaries such as "Mad" John Martin, who painted vast biblical scenes, and Richard Dadd. It's fair to say he had little taste for modernism, but he was no philistine. Indeed, the whole *New Worlds* movement had been to some degree a reaction against what Ballard, Bayley and myself had seen as a descent of modern fiction into a corrupt and generic version of the golden age of modernism as exemplified by Joyce and Eliot, just as the pop artists had rejected abstraction. We had all looked for a revivification of the arts in such popular forms as science fiction and the livelier forms of Victorian expression, in the hope that we could develop a new, viable kind of art which, while not rejecting the best modernism, connected to the sensibilities of a broad audience, and I think we were, at least to a degree, successful. That attempt continues and has become increasingly successful. Jim introduced me not only to fantasts and adventure story writers but to urban noir writers like Chandler and Hammett, humorists like Damon Runyon, surrealist writers and publicists like Maurice Richardson, any number of other absurdists and satirists and as broad a range of the mid-twentieth century's finest writers and artists as anyone could wish to enjoy. Among his favourite books were *Moby-Dick*, *Vanity Fair*, *Great Expectations*, *Huckleberry Finn* and *War and Peace,* but he could also enjoy Nabokov and Pynchon and parody them, too. His own dry wit is evident in much of his writing, especially the many reviews he wrote. Those who would like a taste of his gentle, sardonic, yet highly perceptive criticism should try to find a copy of

Fantasy: The 100 Best Books, which, though credited to us both, is almost wholly Jim's work. It remains, in the view of many, the best handbook of its kind and the best reading list for anyone interested in the history of fantastic literature.

In recent years, Jim confined himself chiefly to private commissions, including a jacket for my own copy of *Stormbringer,* illustrations for other friends' books and so on. His last professional commission was a portrait drawing of some of his favourite characters for Savoy Books, which they have put on their website.

After he returned from London to his native Gateshead, he helped look after his mother, a woman of considerable character whom I liked a great deal and who periodically wondered if I could help him meet a "nice girl" to marry. Jim's standards, as I would tell her, were far too high, perhaps because he knew so many outstanding women of considerable strength of mind. He loved his mother as well as his sister, Maureen, who was very much her mother's daughter. Sadly, he never married. For some years he was in love with a woman who, while being fond of him, did not wish to marry him. This was the tragedy of his life. He had several other relationships but never found another woman with whom he wished to settle down. His love for family and friends was considerable and enduring, and those closest to him often felt they knew his family as well as he did, since he spoke of them constantly. He came from a family of hard, fighting Tyneside men, though he and his father were rather more sensitive than the others and were inclined to use their humour and eloquence to negotiate any trouble. In fact, Jim was one of the gentlest and kindest men I knew. He gave away enormous numbers of drawings and paintings. His close friends and family would get wonderful birthday and Christmas cards, frequently containing humorous drawings and limericks. It's painful to realize we shan't be seeing them anymore.

In the months before he died Jim had become unwell and had not felt like talking on the phone. He explained some of this in terms of the depression he sometimes suffered, but we continued to correspond. One of his last letters was about *The Yiddish Policeman's Union* and *Gen-*

tlemen of the Road by Michael Chabon. He was enthusiastic about these new Elric editions and particularly pleased that his work was being represented in them. He went into hospital for routine tests on November 2, 2008, and died there unexpectedly on December 2. A postmortem diagnosed pancreatic cancer. He leaves his recently widowed sister, Maureen, and a number of nephews, nieces and cousins. Our sympathies go to them. They have lost a particularly fine and talented relative as we have lost a friend. Savoy Books have a tribute on their website and there are plans to produce a memorial volume of his work. It is a matter of particular sadness that he did not live long enough to help put this last Del Rey volume together. We have tried here, in an expansion of our usual archive section, to show some of his best work, which also serves as a tribute to him.

A year or two after the film *The Land That Time Forgot* was released, John Goldstone, one of the producers of *The Final Programme* (the Jerry Cornelius movie done a couple of years before that), suggested that I write a script based on my Eternal Champion series. I agreed, on condition that Jim do the storyboard if and when the project went into production. In those days hardly any company had done a supernatural adventure story of the kind which has since become familiar to movie-goers, so we agreed that it would be best if we eased the audience slowly into the idea. The producers thought we might introduce audiences to the idea of Elric through the device of the Black Sword, Stormbringer, itself. Had this movie been produced, the sword would have been the link between sequels and any Elric movie would have followed from the story provisionally called, in this version, *Stormbringer*. At John Goldstone's request, Jim did a series of wash drawings to accompany the script.

The Revenge of the Rose was the last book Jim illustrated in a commercial edition and later in its omnibus incarnation. This book caused a certain amount of controversy when published because I felt I needed to bring some innovation and new vitality to the series. I needed to feel as ambitious about that book as I had felt in 1961 when I began the series and was one of very few producing this kind of fantasy, establishing the conventions of a budding genre. My work had possessed vitality for the very reason that I was not entirely sure what I was doing, trying out narrative ideas, establishing dynamics, discovering ways of telling this kind of story for the first time. My decision with *The Revenge of the Rose* came as a result of arguments I had made in "Aspects of Fantasy" in *Science Fantasy* magazine, also in the early '60s. I believe that one doesn't serve one's readers by repeating the mixture as before. Whether one is writing popular fiction or literary fiction, one still needs to keep pushing the envelope. I had to continue to find new ways of telling the story, including adding, in this case, elements of comedy and a new kind of character (something I touch upon in the introduction to *The Skrayling Tree*, second in a later Elric trilogy sequence beginning with *The Dreamthief's Daughter*). Some readers were unhappy with me for changing the formula, but others believed the book was the best I had written since *Stormbringer*. I was sorry to disappoint readers, but many have since come to say they liked the book very much, sometimes on rereading it. I had not forgotten that, when I wrote the first Elric stories, some readers were upset that I had broken with the traditions of Howard and Tolkien! Whatever the response, I feel it is my duty to continue producing innovation in all my fiction, whether generic or literary (or both). Yesterday's innovation, as we have seen, becomes tomorrow's convention. However, when I came to write an Elric story for the eightieth-anniversary issue of *Weird Tales*, edited by Ann VanderMeer, I decided to celebrate with an act, if you like, of nostalgia, and thus "Black Petals," harking back to the original stories, was done in a style which might have been found in those early issues when Howard, Lovecraft and Seabury Quinn were first seeing print. My only regret was that Jim was not commissioned to illustrate the story. "Black Petals" will also form the basis of some collaborations I am hoping to write with my friend Fabrice Colin, a young fantasy writer who has already made his mark in France. They will be initially published in French. I spend much of my time in Paris, these days, and have seen many different and outstanding versions of the albino published there. Elric has been successful in France at least as long as he has been published in the United States, and I thought it appropriate to publish a recent piece, talking about French publication. After Jim Cawthorn, Philippe Druillet was the next artist to draw Elric for publication.

One other Elric book Jim didn't illustrate was Ed Kramer's 1994 *Tales of the White Wolf*, a collection of Elric stories by other hands, including Neil Gaiman, Karl Edward Wagner and Colin Greenland. One of the very best of these was by Tad Williams, brilliant author of *Tailchaser's Song* and *Otherland*, in which he introduced a character not unrelated to the late Jimi Hendrix and a story I would love to see reprinted. I enjoyed the story so much that I asked Tad if I could, at some future date, use his character. I still hope to do so. The last time we met was on a long-distance train, on the way, as I recall, to New Orleans, far too many years ago. I'm so pleased he's found time to write a foreword to this last volume. He's one of the best and most influential writers of modern fantasy and a good man, as well as a great cat lover. His foreword augments a volume which closes with the work of my old friend, near neighbour and sometime collaborator, John Picacio, one of the most generous men in the business as well as one of the most talented, who published his own tribute to Jim on his website (http://picacio.blogspot.com) shortly after we learned of the tragedy. While thanking all the people (especially Betsy Mitchell) who helped put these editions together, I'd like to repeat how they would not have been possible if it had not been for general editor John Davey, whose work on the series has been outstanding and whose Reader's Guide is derived from his own excellent longer bibliography of my work, *Michael Moorcock: A Reader's Guide*. He, too, was a friend of Jim Cawthorn's and will be actively engaged in helping organize and take care of Jim's extensive archive. Longtime Cawthorn fan and supporter, the bookseller and writer (and old friend) George Locke has published a tribute to Jim as part of a hard-copy only catalogue listing the items from his personal collection. Fifteen to twenty unpublished Cawthorn drawings were printed. This catalogue is available from Ferret Fantasy, 27 Beechcroft Road, Upper Tooting, London SW17 7BX, England; email address: george_locke@hotmail.com. More of Jim's work can be found in the archive sections of my own website (www.multiverse.org).

Michael Moorcock
Rue St. Maur
Paris
July 2010

ELRIC
SWORDS AND ROSES

THE REVENGE OF THE ROSE

THE REVENGE OF THE ROSE
(1991)

For Christopher Lee—
Arioch awaits thee!

For Johnny and Edgar Winter—
rock on!

For Anthony Skene—
in gratitude.

———

Elric could enjoy the tranquility of Tanelorn only briefly and then must begin his restless journeyings again. This time he headed eastward, into the lands known as the Valederian Directorates, where he had heard of a certain globe said to display the nations of the future. In that globe he hoped to learn something of his own fate, but in seeking it he earned the enmity of that ferocious horde known as the Haghan'iin Host, who captured and tortured him a little before he escaped and joined forces with the nobles of Anakhazhan to do battle with them . . .

—*The Chronicle of the Black Sword*

BOOK ONE

CONCERNING THE FATE
OF EMPIRES

"What? Do you call us decadent, and
* our whole nation, too?*
My friend, you are too stern-hearted
* for these times. These times are new.*
Should you discern in us a selfish introspection;
* a powerless pride:*
In actuality, self-mockery and old age's wisdom
* is all that you descry!"*

—Wheldrake,
Byzantine Conversations

CHAPTER ONE

Of Love, Death, Battle & Exile; The White Wolf Encounters
a Not Entirely Unwelcome Echo of the Past.

FROM THE UNLIKELY peace of Tanelorn, out of Bas'lk and Nish-valni-Oss, from Valederia, ever eastward runs the White Wolf of Melniboné, howling his red and hideous song, to relish the sweetness of a bloodletting . . .

. . . It is over. The albino prince sits bowed upon his horse, as if beneath the weight of his own exaggerated battle-lust; as if ashamed to look upon such profoundly unholy butchery.

Of the mighty Haghan'iin Host not a single soul survived an hour beyond the certain victory they had earlier celebrated. (How could they not win, when Lord Elric's army was a fragment of their own strength?)

Elric feels no further malice towards them, but he knows little pity, either. In their puissant arrogance, their blindness to the wealth of sorcery Elric commanded, they had been unimaginative. They had guffawed at his warnings. They had jeered at their former prisoner for a weakling freak of nature. Such violent, silly creatures deserved only the general grief reserved for all misshaped souls.

Now the White Wolf stretches his lean body, his pale arms. He pushes up his black helm. He rests, panting, in his great painted warsaddle, then takes the murmuring hellblade he carries and sheathes the sated iron into the softness of its velvet scabbard. There is a sound at his back. He turns brooding crimson eyes upon the face of the woman who reins up her horse beside him. Both woman and stallion have the same unruly pride, both seem excited by their unlooked-for victory; both are beautiful.

The albino reaches to take her ungloved hand and kiss it. "We share honours this day, Countess Guyë."

And his smile is a thing to fear and to adore.

"Indeed, Lord Elric!" She draws on her gauntlet and takes her prancing mount in check. "But for the fecundity of thy sorcery and the courage of my soldiery, we'd both be Chaos-meat tonight—and unlucky if still alive!"

He answers with a sigh and an affirmative gesture. She speaks with deep satisfaction.

"The host shall waste no other lands, and its women in their home-trees shall bear no more brutes to bloody the world." Throwing back her heavy cloak, she slings her slender shield behind her. Her long hair catches the evening light, deep vermilion, restless as the ocean as she laughs, while her blue eyes weep; for she had begun the day in the fullest expectation that the best she could hope for was sudden death. "We are deeply in your debt, sir. We are obligated, all of us. You shall be known throughout Anakhazhan as a hero."

Elric's smile is ungrateful. "We came together for mutual needs, madam. I was but settling a small debt with my captors."

"There are other means of settling such debts, sir. We are still obliged."

"I would not take credit," he insists, "for altruism that is no part of my nature." He looks away into the horizon where a purple scar washed with red disguises the falling of the sun.

"I have a different sense of it." She speaks softly, for a hush is coming to the field, and a light breeze tugs at matted hair, bits of bloody fabric, torn skin. There are precious weapons and metals and jewels to be seen, especially where the Haghan'iin nobles had tried to make their escape, but not one of Countess Guyë's sworders, mercenary or free Anakhazhani, will approach the booty. There is a general tendency amongst these weary soldiers to drop back as far as possible from the field. Their captains neither question them on this nor do they try to stop them. "I have the sense, sir, that you serve some Cause or Principle, nonetheless."

He is quick to shake his head, his posture in the saddle one of growing impatience. "I am for no master nor moral persuasion. I am for myself. What your yearning soul, madam, might mistake for loyalty to person or Purpose is merely a firm and, aye, *principled* determination to accept responsibility only for myself and my own actions."

She offers him a quick, girlish look of puzzled disbelief, then turns away with a dawning, woman's grin. "There'll be no rain tonight," she observes, holding a dark, golden hand against the evening. "This mess'll be stinking and spreading fever in hours. We'd best move on, ahead of the flies." She hears the flapping even as he does and they both look back and watch the first gleeful ravens settling on flesh that has melted into one mile-wide mass of bloody meat, limbs and organs scattered at random, to hop upon and peck at half-destroyed faces still screaming for the mercy laughingly denied them as Elric's patron Duke of Hell, Lord Arioch, gave aid to his favourite son.

These were in the times when Elric left his friend Moonglum in Tanelorn and ranged the whole world to find a land which seemed enough like his own that he might wish to settle there, but no such land as Melniboné could be a tenth its rival in any place the new mortals might dwell. And all these lands were mortal now.

He had begun to learn that he had earned a loss which could never be assuaged and in losing the woman he loved, the nation he had betrayed, and the only kind of honour he had known he had also lost part of his own identity, some sense of his own purpose and reason upon the Earth.

Ironically, it was these very losses, these very dilemmas, which made him so unlike his Melnibonéan folk, for his people were cruel and embraced power for its own sake, which was how they had come to give up any softer virtues they might once have possessed, in their need to control not only their physical world but the supernatural world. They would have ruled the multiverse, had they any clear understanding how this might be achieved; but even a Melnibonéan is not a god. There are some would argue they had not produced so much as a demigod. Their glory in earthly power had brought them to decadent ruin, as it brought down all empires who gloried in gold or conquest or those other ambitions which can never be satisfied but must forever be fed.

Yet even now Melniboné might, in her senility, live, had she not been betrayed by her own exiled emperor.

And no matter how often Elric reminds himself that the Bright Empire was foredoomed to her unhappy end, he knows in his bones that it was his fierce need for vengeance, his deep love for Cymoril (his captive cousin); his own needs, in other words, which had brought down the towers of Imrryr and scattered her folk as hated wanderers upon the surface of the world they had once ruled.

It is part of his burden that Melniboné did not fall to a principle but to blind passion . . .

As Elric made to bid farewell to his temporary ally, he was attracted to something in the countess's wicked eye, and he bowed in assent as she asked him to ride with her for a while; and then she suggested he might care to take wine with her in her tent.

"I would talk more of philosophy," she said. "I have longed so for the company of an intellectual equal."

And go with her he did, for that night and for many to come. These would be days he remembered as the days of laughter and green hills broken by lines of gentle cypress and poplar, on the estates of Guyë, in the Western Province of Anakhazhan in the lovely years of her hard-won peace.

Yet when they had both rested and both began to look to satisfy their unsleeping intelligences, it became clear that the countess and Lord Elric had very different needs and so Elric said his goodbyes to the countess and their friends at Guyë and took a good, well-furnished riding horse and two sturdy pack animals and rode on towards Elwher and the Unmapped East where he still hoped to find the peace of an untarnished familiarity.

He longed for the towers, sweet lullabies in stone, which stretched like guarding fingers into Imrryr's blazing skies; he missed the sharp wit and laughing ferocity of his kinfolk, the ready understanding and the casual cruelty that to him had seemed so ordinary in the time before he became a man.

No matter that his spirit had rebelled and made him question the Bright Empire's every assumption of its rights to rule over the demi-brutes, the human creatures, who had spread so thoroughly across the great land masses of the North and West that were called now "the Young Kingdoms" and dared, even with their puny wizardries and unskilled battlers, to challenge the power of the Sorcerer Emperors, of whom he was the last in direct line.

No matter that he had hated so much of his people's arrogance and unseemly pride, their easy resort to every unjust tyranny to maintain their power.

No matter that he had known shame—a new emotion to one of his kind. Still his blood yearned for home and all the things he had loved or, indeed, hated, for he had this in common with the humans amongst whom he now lived and traveled: he would sometimes rather hold close to what was familiar and encumbering than give it up for something new, though it offered freedom from the chains of heritage which bound him and must eventually destroy him.

And with this longing in him growing with his fresh loneliness, Elric took himself in charge and increased his pace and left Guyë far behind, a fading memory, while he pressed on in the general direction of unknown Elwher, his friend's homeland, which he had never seen.

He had come in sight of a range of hills the local people dignified as The Teeth of Shenkh, a provincial demon-god, and was following a caravan track down to a collection of shacks surrounded by a mud-and-timber wall that had been described to him as the great city of Toomoo-Kag-Sanapet-of-the-Invincible-Temple, Capital of Iniquity and Unguessed-At Wealth, when he heard a protesting cry at his back and saw a figure tumbling head over heels down the hill towards him while overhead a previously unseen thundercloud sent silver spears of light crashing to the earth, causing Elric's horses to rear and snort in untypical nervousness. Then the world was washed with red-gold light, as if in a sudden dawn, which turned to bruised blue and dark brown before swirling like an angry current towards the horizon and vanishing to leave a few disturbed clouds behind them in a drizzling and depressingly ordinary sky.

Deciding this event was sufficiently strange to merit more than his usually brief attention, Elric turned towards the small, red-headed individual who was picking himself out of a ditch at the edge of the silver-green cornfield, looking nervously up at the sky and drawing a rather threadbare coat about his little body. The coat would not meet at the front, not because it was too tight for him, but because the pockets, inside and out, were crammed with small volumes. On his legs were a matching pair of trews, grey and shiny, a pair of laced black boots which, as he lifted one knee to inspect a rent, revealed stockings as bright as his hair. His face, adorned by an almost diseased-looking beard, was freckled and pale, from which glared blue eyes as sharp and busy as a bird's, above a pointed beak which gave him the appearance of an enormous finch, enormously serious. He drew himself up at Elric's approach and began to stroll casually down the hill. "D'ye think it will rain, sir? I thought I heard a clap of thunder a moment ago. It set me off my balance." He paused, then cast a look backward up the track. "I thought I had a pot of ale in my hand." He scratched his wild head. "Come to think of it, I was sitting on a bench outside The Green Man. Hold hard, sir, ye're an unlikely cove to be abroad on Putney Common." Whereupon he sat down suddenly on a grassy hummock. "Good lord! Am I transported yet again?" He appeared to recognize Elric. "I think we've met, sir, somewhere. Or were you merely a subject?"

"You have the advantage of me, sir," said Elric, dismounting. He felt drawn to this birdlike man. "I am called Elric of Melniboné and I am a wanderer."

"My name is Wheldrake, sir. Ernest Wheldrake. I have been traveling somewhat reluctantly since I left Albion, first to Victoria's

England, where I made something of a name, before being drawn on to Elizabeth's. I am growing used to sudden departures. What would your business be, Master Elric, if it is not theatrical?"

Elric, finding half what the man said nonsense, shook his head. "I have practised the trade of mercenary sword for some while. And you, sir?"

"I, sir, am a poet!" Master Wheldrake bristled and felt about his pockets for a certain volume, failed to find it, made a movement of the fingers as if to say he needed no affidavits, anyway, and settled his scrawny arms across his chest. "I have been a poet of the Court and of the Gutter, it's alleged. I should still be at Court had it not been for Doctor Dee's attempts to show me our Graecian past. Impossible, I have since learned."

"You do not know how you came here?"

"Only the vaguest notion, sir. Aha! But I have placed you." A snap of the long fingers. "A subject, I recall!"

Elric had lost interest in this vein of enquiry. "I am on my way to yonder metropolis, sir, and if you'd ride one of my pack animals, I'd be honoured to take you there. If you have no money, I'll buy you a room and a meal for the night."

"I would be glad of that, sir. Thanks." And the poet hopped nimbly up onto the furthest horse, settling himself amongst the packs and sacks with which Elric had equipped himself for a journey of indeterminate length. "I had feared it would rain and I am prone, these days, to chills . . ."

Elric continued down the long, winding track towards the churned mud streets and filthy log walls of Toomoo-Kag-Sanapet-of-the-Invincible-Temple while in a high-pitched yet oddly beautiful voice, reminiscent of a trilling bird, Wheldrake uttered some lines which Elric guessed were his own composition. "*With purpose fierce his heart was gripped, and blade gripped tighter, still. And honour struggling within, 'gainst vengeance, cold and cruel. Old Night and a New Age warred in him; all the ancient power, and all the new. Yet he did not stop his slaughtering*. And there is more, sir. He believes that he has conquered himself and his sword. He cries out: 'See, my masters! I force my moral will upon this hellblade and Chaos is no longer served by it! True purpose shall triumph and Justice rule in Harmony with Romance in this most perfect of worlds.' And that, sir, was where my drama ended. Is your own story in any way the same, sir? Perhaps a little?"

"Perhaps a little, sir. I hope you will soon be taken back to whatever demon realm you've escaped from."

"You are offended, sir. In my verse you are a hero! I assure you I had the bones of the tale from a reliable source. A lady. And discretion demands I not reveal her name. Oh, sir! Oh, sir! What a magnificent moment this is for us, when metaphor becomes commonplace reality and the daily round runs into a thing of Fantasy and Myth . . ."

Scarcely hearing the little man's nonsense, Elric continued towards the town.

"Why, sir, what an extraordinary depression in yonder field," said Wheldrake suddenly, interrupting his own verse. "Do you see it, sir? That shape, as if some huge beast presses the corn? Is such a phenomenon common in these parts, sir?"

Elric glanced casually across the corn and was bound to agree that it had, indeed, been forced down across quite a broad area, and not by any obvious human agency. He reined in again, frowning. "I'm a stranger here, also. Perhaps some ceremony takes place, which causes the corn to bend so . . ."

At which there came a sudden snort, which shook the ground under their feet and half-deafened them. It was as if the field itself had discovered a voice.

"Is this odd, to you, sir?" Wheldrake asked, his fingers upon his chin. "It's damned odd to me."

Elric found his hand straying towards the hilt of his runesword. There was a stink in the air which he recognized yet could not at that moment place.

Then there came a kind of crack, a roll like distant thunder, a sigh that filled the air and must have been heard by the whole town below, and then Elric knew suddenly how Wheldrake had entered this realm when he had no real business in it, for here was the creature who had actually created the lightning, bringing Wheldrake in its wake. Here was something supernatural broken through the dimensions to confront him.

The horses began to dance and scream. The mare carrying Wheldrake reared and tried to break from her harness, tangling with the reins of her partner and sending Wheldrake once more tumbling to the ground, while out of the unripe corn, like some sentient manifestation of the Earth herself, all tumbling stones and rich soil and clots of poppies and half the contents of the field, growing taller and taller and shaking itself free of what had buried it, rose an enormous reptile, with slender snout, gleaming greens and reds; razor teeth; saliva hissing as it struck the ground; faint smoky breath streaming from its flaring nostrils, while a long, thick scaly tail lashed behind it, uprooting shrubs and further ruining the crop upon which that metropolitan wealth was based. There came another clap like thunder and a leathery wing stretched upwards then descended with a noise only a little more bearable than the accompanying stink; then the other wing rose; then fell. It was as if the dragon were being forced from some great, earthen womb—forced through the dimensions, through walls which were physical as well as supernatural; it struggled and raged to be free. It lifted its strangely beautiful head and it shrieked again and heaved again; and its slender claws, sharper and longer than any sword, clashed and flickered in the fading light.

Wheldrake, scrambling to his feet, began to run unceremoniously towards the town and Elric could do nothing else but let his pack animals run with him. The albino was left confronting a monster in no doubt on whom it wished to exercise its anger. Already its sinuous body moved with a kind of monumental grace as it turned to glare down at Elric. It snapped suddenly and Elric was crashing to the ground, blood pumping hugely from his horse's torso as the beast's remains collapsed onto the track. The albino rolled and came up quickly, Stormbringer growling and whispering in his hand, the black runes glowing the length of the blade and the black radiance flickering up and down its edges. And now the dragon hesitated, eyeing him almost warily as its jaws chewed for a few moments upon the horse's head and the throat made a single swallowing movement. Elric had no other course. He began running towards his massive adversary! The great eyes tried to follow him as he weaved in and out of the corn, and the jaws dripped, shaking their bloody ichor to sear and kill all it touched. But Elric had been raised among dragons and knew their vulnerability as well as their power. He knew, if he could come in close to the beast, there were points at which he might strike and at least wound it. It would be his only chance of survival.

As the monster's head turned, seeking him, the fangs clashing and the great breaths rushing from its throat and nostrils, Elric dashed under the neck and slashed once at the little spot about halfway up its length, where the scales were always soft, at least in Melnibonéan dragons; yet the dragon seemed to sense his stroke and reared back, claws slicing ground and crop like some monstrous scythe, and Elric was flung down by a great clot of earth, half-buried, so that *he* must now struggle to free himself.

It was at that moment some movement of the beast's head, some motion of the light upon its leathery lids, gave him pause and his heart leapt in sudden hope.

A memory teased at his lips but would not manifest itself as anything concrete. He found himself forming the High Speech of old Melniboné, the word for "bondfriend." He was beginning to speak the ancient words of the dragon-calling, the cadences and tunes to which the beasts might, if they chose, respond.

There was a tune in his head, a way of speaking, and then came a single word again, but this was a sound like a breeze through willows, water through stones; a name.

At which the dragon brought her jaws together with a snap and sought the source of the voice. The iron-sharp wattles on the back of her neck and tail began to flatten and the corners of her mouth no longer boiled with poison.

Still deeply cautious, Elric got slowly to his feet and shook the damp earth from his flesh, Stormbringer as eager as always in his hand, and took a pace backward.

"Lady Scarsnout! I am your kin, I am Little Cat. I am your ward and your guider, Scarsnout lady, me!"

The green-gold muzzle, bearing a long-healed scar down the underside of the jaw, gave out an enquiring hiss.

Elric sheathed his grumbling hellblade and made the complicated and subtle gestures of kinship which he had been taught by his father for the day when he should be supreme Dragon Lord of Imrryr, Dragon Emperor of the World.

The dragon-she's brows drew together in something resembling a frown, the massive lids dropped, half-hiding the huge, cold eyes—the eyes of a beast more ancient than any mortal being; more ancient, perhaps, than the gods . . .

The nostrils, into which Elric could have crawled without much difficulty, quivered and sniffed—a tongue flickered—a great, wet leathery thing, long and slender and forked at the end. Once it almost touched Elric's face, then flickered over his body before the head was drawn back and the eyes stared down in fierce enquiry. For the moment, at least, the monster was calm.

Elric, virtually in a trance by now, as all the old incantations came flooding into his brain, stood swaying before the dragon. Soon her own head swayed, too, following the albino's movements.

And then, all at once, the dragon made a small noise deep in her belly and lowered her head to stretch her neck along the ground, down upon the torn and ruined corn. The eyes followed him as he stepped closer, murmuring the Song of Approach which his father had taught him when he was eleven and first taken to Melniboné's Dragon Caves. Her dragons slept there to this day. A dragon must sleep a hundred years for every day of activity, to regenerate that strange metabolism which could create fiery saliva strong enough to destroy cities.

How this jill-dragon had awakened and how she had come here was a mystery. Sorcery had brought her, without doubt. But had there been any reason for her arrival, or had it been, like Wheldrake's, a mere incidental to some other spell-working?

Elric had no time to debate that question now as he moved in gradual, ritualized steps towards the natural ridge just above the place where the leading part of her wing joined her shoulder. It was where the Dragon Masters of Melniboné had placed their saddles and where, as a youth, he had ridden naked, with only his skill and the good will of the dragon to keep him safe.

It had been many years, and a shattering sequence of events, which had led him to this moment, when all the world was on the change, when he no longer trusted even his memories . . . The dragon almost called now, almost purred, awaiting his next command, as if a mother tolerated the games of her children.

"Scarsnout, sister, Scarsnout kin, your dragon blood is mixed in ours and ours in yours and we are coupled, we are kind; we are one, the dragon rider and the dragon steed; one ambition, mutual need. Dragon sister, dragon matron, dragon honour, dragon pride . . ." The Old Speech rolled, trilled and clicked from his tongue; it came without conscious thought; it came without effort, without hesitation, for blood recalled blood and all else was natural. It was natural to climb upon the dragon's back and utter the ancient, joyful songs of command, the complex Dragon Lays of his remote predecessors which combined their highest arts with their most practical needs. Elric was recollecting what was best and noblest in his own people and in himself, and even as he celebrated this he mourned the self-obsessed creatures they had become, using their power merely to preserve their power and that, he supposed, was true decay . . .

And now the jill's slender neck rises, swaying like a mesmerized cobra, by degrees, and her snout tilts towards the sun, and her long tongue tastes the air and her saliva drips more slowly to devour the ground it touches and a great sigh, like a sigh of contentment, escapes her belly and she moves one hind leg, then the next, swaying and tilting like a storm-tossed ship, with Elric clinging on for his life, his body banged and rolled this way and that, until at last Scarsnout is poised, her claws folding tight as her hind legs rear. Yet still she seems to hesitate. Then she tucks her forelegs into the silk-soft leather of her stomach, and again she tests the air.

Her back legs give a kind of hop. The massive wings crack once, deafeningly. Her tail lashing out to steady her uneven weight, she has risen—she is aloft and mounting—mounting through those miserable clouds into blue perfection, a late afternoon sky, with the clouds below now, like white and gentle hills and valleys where perhaps the harmless dead find peace; and Elric does not care where the dragon flies. He is glad to be flying as he flew as a boy—sharing his joy with his dragon-mate, sharing his senses and his emotions, for this is the true union between Elric's ancestors and their beasts—a union which had always existed and whose origins were explained only in unlikely legends—this was the symbiosis with which, natural and joyful at first, they had learned to defend themselves against would-be conquerors and later, turned conquerors, with which they had overwhelmed all victims. Having become greedy for even more conquests than were offered by the natural world, they sought supernatural conquests also and thus came to make their bond with Chaos, with Duke Arioch himself. And with Chaos to aid them they ruled ten thousand years; their cruelties refined but never abated.

Before then, thinks Elric—before then my people had never thought of war or power. And he knows that it was this respect for all life which must have brought about the original bond between Melni-bonéan and dragon. And, as he lies along the natural pommel, the ridge above his jill's neck, he weeps with the wonder of suddenly recol-lected innocence, of something he believed lost as everything else is lost to him and which makes him believe, if only for this moment, that what he has lost might be, perhaps, restored . . .

Then he is free! Free in the air! Part of that impossible monster whose wings carry her as if she were a wind-dancing kestrel, light as down, through darkening skies, her skin giving off a sweetness like lavender and her head set in an expression which seems in a way to mirror Elric's own, and she turns and dives, she climbs and wheels while Elric clings without any seeming effort to her back and sings the wild old songs of his ancestors who had come as nomads of the worlds to settle here and had, some said, been welcomed by an even older race whom they superseded and with whom the royal line intermarried.

Up speeds Scarsnout, up she flies, and, when the air grows so thin it can no longer support her and Elric shivers in spite of his clothing and his mouth gasps at the atmosphere, down she goes in a mighty, rushing plummet until she brings herself up as if to land upon the cloud, then veers slowly away to where the clouds now break to reveal a moonlit tunnel in the surface and down this Scarsnout plunges while behind her lightning flashes once and a thunder clap seems to seal the tunnel as they descend into an unnatural coldness which makes Elric's whole skin writhe and his bones feel as if they must split and crack within him and yet still the albino does not fear, because the dragon does not fear.

Above them now the clouds have vanished. A blue velvet sky is further softened by a large yellow moon, whose light casts their long shadows upon the rushing meadowlands below, while the horizon shows a glint of the midnight sea and is filled with the emerald points of stars, and only as he begins to recognize the landscape below him does Elric know fear.

The dragon has carried him back to the ruins of his dreams, his past, his love, his ambitions, his hope.

She has brought him back to Melniboné.

She has brought him home.

CHAPTER TWO

*Of Conflicting Loyalties and Unsummoned Ghosts; Of
Bondage and Destiny.*

Now Elric forgot his recent joy and remembered only his pain. He wondered wildly if this was mere coincidence or had the jill-dragon been sent to bring him here? Had his surviving kinfolk struck upon a means of capturing him so as to savour the slowness of his tortured passing? Or did the dragons themselves demand his presence?

Soon the familiar hills gave way to the Plain of Imrryr and Elric saw a city ahead—a ragged outline of burned and mutilated buildings.

Was this the city of his birth, the Dreaming City he and his raiders had murdered?

As they flew closer Elric began to realize that he did not recognize the buildings. At first he thought they had been transformed by fire and siege, but they were not even, he noticed now, of the same materials. And he laughed at himself. He marveled at his secret longings which had made him believe the dragon had brought him to Melniboné.

But then he knew he recognized the hills and woods, the line of the coast beyond the city. He knew that this was once, at least, where Imrryr stood. As Scarsnout sailed to a gentle landing, hopping once to steady herself, Elric looked across half a mile of familiar grassy ridges and knew that he looked not upon Imrryr the Beautiful, the greatest of all cities, but upon a city his people had called H'hui'shan, the City of the Island, in the High Melnibonéan tongue, and this was the city destroyed in one night in the only civil war Melniboné had ever known, when her lords quarreled over whether to compact themselves with Chaos or remain loyal to the Balance. That war had lasted three days and left Melniboné hidden by oily black smoke for a month. When it had risen it had revealed ruins, but all who sought to attack her when she was weak were more than disappointed, for her pact was made and Arioch aided her, demonstrating the fearful variety of his mighty powers (there had been further suicides in Melniboné as her unhonourable victories rose, while others fled through the dimensions into foreign realms). The cruelest remained to relish an ever-tightening grip upon their world-encompassing empire.

At least, that was one of his people's legends, said to be drawn from the Dead Gods' Book.

Elric understood that Scarsnout had brought him to the remote past. But how had the dragon found the means of traveling so easily between the Spheres? And, again he wondered, why had he been transported here?

Hoping Scarsnout might choose some further action, Elric sat upon the monster's back for a while until it became obvious that the dragon had no intention of moving, so with some reluctance he dismounted, murmured the song of "I-would-appreciate-your-continuing-concern-in-this-matter" and, there being nothing else for it, began to stride towards the desolate ruins of his people's earliest glories.

"Oh, H'hui'shan, City of the Island, if only I were here a week earlier, to warn thee of thy bond's consequences. But doubtless it would not suit my patron Arioch to let me thwart him so." And he smiled sardonically at this; smiled at his own aching need to make the past produce a finer present: one in which he did not bear such a burden of guilt.

"Perhaps our entire history is of Arioch's writing!" His bargain with the Duke of Hell was a pact of blood and human souls for aid—whatever the runesword did not feast upon belonged to Duke Arioch (though some old tales would have it that sword and patron demon were one and the same). And Elric rarely disguised his distaste for this tradition, which even he lacked the courage to break. It was immaterial to his patron what he thought so long as he continued to honour their bond. And this Elric understood profoundly.

The turf was still crossed by the trails he had known as a boy. He trod them as surely as he had done when, he recollected, his father—distant upon a charger—called to some servitor to take care with the child but to let him walk. He must grow up to remember every pathway that existed in Melniboné; for in those trails and tracks, those roads and highs, lay the configuration of their history, the geometry of their wisdom, the very key to their most secret understandings.

All these pathways, as well as the pathways to the otherworlds, Elric had memorized, together, where necessary, with their accompanying songs and gestures. He was a master-sorcerer, of a line of master-sorcerers, and he was proud of his calling, though disturbed by the uses to which he, as well as others, had put their powers. He could read a thousand meanings in a certain tree and its branches, but he still failed to understand his own torments of conscience, his moral crises, and that was why he wandered the world.

Dark sorceries and spells, images of horrific consequence, filled his head and threatened sometimes, when he dreamed, to seize control of him and plunge him into eternal madness. Dark memories. Dark cruelties. Elric shuddered as he drew close to the ruins, whose towers of wood and brick had collapsed and yet attained a picturesque and almost welcoming aspect, even in the moonlight.

He clambered over the burned rubble of a wall and entered a street which, at ground level, still bore some resemblance to the thing it had been. He sniffed sooty air and felt the ground still warm beneath his feet. Here and there, towards the centre of the city, a few fires still flickered like old rags in a wind and ash covered everything. Elric felt it clinging to his flesh. He felt it clogging his nostrils and drifting through his clothing—the ash of his distant ancestors, whose blackened corpses filled the houses in mimicry of life's activities, threatening to engulf him. But he walked on, fascinated by this glimpse into his past, at the very turning point in his race's destiny. He found himself wandering through rooms still occupied by the husks of their inhabitants, their pets, their playthings, their tools; through squares where fountains had once splashed, through temples and public buildings where his folk had met to debate and decide the issues of the day, before the emperors had taken all power to themselves and Melniboné had grown to depend upon her slaves, hidden away so that they should not make Imrryr ugly with their presence. He paused in a workshop, some shoe-seller's stall. He grieved for these dead, gone more than ten thousand years since.

The ruins touched something that was tender in him, and he found that he possessed a fresh longing, a longing for a past before Melniboné, out of fear, bargained for that power which conquered the world.

The turrets and gables, the blackened thatch and torn beams, the piles of broken stone and brick, the animal troughs and ordinary domestic implements abandoned outside the houses filled him with a melancholy he found almost sweet and he paused to inspect a cradle or a spinning wheel which showed an aspect of a proud Melnibonéan folk he had never known, but which he felt he understood.

There were tears in his eyes as he roamed those streets, desperately hoping to find just one living soul apart from himself, but he knew the city had stood unpopulated for at least a hundred years after her destruction.

"Oh, that I had destroyed Imrryr so that I might restore H'hui'shan!"

He stood in a square of broken statues and fallen masonry looking up at the enormous moon which now rose directly above his head, sending his shadow to mingle with those of the ruins; and he dragged off his helmet and shook out his long, milk-white hair and turned yearning hands towards the city as if to beg forgiveness, and then he sat down upon a dusty slab carved with the delicacy and imagination of genius and over which blood had flowed, then baked, a coarse glaze; and he buried his crimson eyes in the sleeve of his ashy shirt and his shoulders shook and he groaned his complaint at whatever fate had led him to this ordeal . . .

There came a voice from behind him that seemed to echo from distant catacombs, across aeons of time, as resonant as the Dragon Falls where one of Elric's ancestors had died (in combat, it was said, with himself) and as commanding as the whole of Elric's long and binding royal history. It was a voice he recognized and had hoped, in so many ways, never to hear again.

Once more he wondered if he were mad. The voice was unmistakably that of his dead father, Sadric the Eighty-Sixth, whose company in life he had so rarely shared.

"Ah, Elric, thou weepest I see. Thou art thy mother's son and for that I love her memory, though thou kill'dst the only woman I shall ever truly love and for that I hate thee with an unjust hatred."

"Father?" Elric lowered his arm and turned his bone-white face behind him to where, leaning against a ruined pillar, stood the slender, frail presence of Sadric. Upon his lips was a smile that was terrible in its tranquility.

Elric looked disbelievingly at the face which was exactly as it had been when he had last seen it as his father had lain in funeral state.

"For an unjust hatred there is no release, save the peace of death. And here, as you'll observe, I am denied the peace of death."

"I have dreamed of you, Father, and your disappointment with me. I would that I could have been all you desired in a son . . ."

"There was never a second, Elric, when you could have been that. The act of thy creation was the sealing of her doom. We had been warned of it in every omen but could do nothing to avert that hideous destiny—" and his eyes glared with a hatred only the unrested dead could know.

"How came you here, Father? I had thought you chosen by Chaos, gone to the service of our patron duke, Lord Arioch."

"Arioch could not claim me because of another pact I had made, with Count Mashabak. He is no longer my patron." And a kind of laugh escaped him.

"Your soul was claimed by Mashabak of Chaos?"

"But disputed by Arioch. My soul is hostage to their rivalries—or was. By some sorcery I still command, I betook myself here, to the very beginning of our true history. And here I have some short sanctuary."

"You are hiding, Father, from the Lords of Chaos?"

"I have gained some time while they dispute, for I have here a spell, my last great spell, which will free me to join your mother in the Forest of Souls where she awaits me."

"You have a passport to the Forest of Souls? I'd thought such things a myth." Elric wiped chilly sweat from his forehead.

"I sent thy mother there to remain until I joined her. I gave her the means, our Scroll of Dead-Speaking, and she is safe in that sweet eternity, which many souls seek and which few find. I swore an oath that I would do all I could to be reunited with her."

The shade stepped forward, as if entranced, and reached to touch Elric's face with something like affection. But when the hand fell away there was only torment in the old man's undead eyes.

Elric knew a certain sympathy. "Have you no companions here, Father?"

"Only thou, my son. Thee and I now haunt these ruins together."

An unwholesome frisson: "Am I, too, a prisoner here?" said the albino.

"At my humour, aye, my son. Now that I have touched thee we are bound together, whether thou leavest this place or no, for it is the fate of such as I to be linked always to the first living mortal his hand shall fall upon. We are one, now, Elric—or shall be."

And Elric shuddered at the hatred and the relish in his father's otherwise desolate voice.

"Can I not release you, Father? I have been to R'lin K'ren A'a, where our race began in this realm. I sought our past there. I could speak of it . . ."

"Our past is in our blood. It travels with us. Those degenerates of R'lin K'ren A'a, they were never our true kin. They bred with humans and vanished. It was not they who founded or preserved great Melniboné . . ."

"There are so many stories, Father. So many conflicting legends . . ." Elric was eager to continue the conversation with his father. Few such opportunities had existed while Sadric lived.

"The dead know truth from lies. They are privy to that understanding, at least. And I know the truth of it. We did not stem from R'lin K'ren A'a. Such questings and speculations are unnecessary. We are assured of our origins. Thou wouldst be a fool, my son, to question our histories, to dispute their truth. I had thee taught this."

Elric kept his own counsel.

"My magic called the jill-dragon from her cave. The one I had the strength to summon. But she came and I sent her to thee. This is the only sorcery I have left. It is the first significant sorcery of our race and the purest, the dragon-sorcery. But I could not instruct her. I sent her to thee knowing she would recognize thee or she would kill thee. Both actions would have brought us together, eventually, no doubt." The shade permitted itself a crooked smile.

"You cared no more than that, Father?"

"I could *do* no more than that. I long for thy mother. We were meant to be united for ever. Thou must help me reach her, Elric, and help me swiftly for my own energies and spells weaken—soon Arioch or Mashabak shall claim me. Or destroy me entirely in their struggle!"

"You have no further means of escaping them?" Elric felt his left leg shake uncontrollably for a few seconds before he forced it to obey his will. He realized it had been too long since he had last taken the infusion of herbs and drugs which allowed him the energy of a normal creature.

"In a way. If I remain attached to thee, my son, the object of my unjust hate, then my soul could hide with thine, occupying thy flesh and mine, disguised by blood that is my blood. *They would never sniff me out!*"

Again Elric was seized by a sensation of profound cold, as if death already claimed him; his head was a maelstrom of ungoverned emotions as he sought desperately to take a grip on himself, praying that with the sun's rising his father's ghost would vanish.

"The sun will not rise here, Elric. Not here. Not until the moment of our release or our destruction. That is *why* we are here."

"But does Arioch not object to this? He is my patron, still!" Elric looked for a new madness in his father's face but could find none.

"He is otherwise engaged and could not come to thee now, whether to aid or to punish. His dispute with Count Mashabak absorbs him. That is why thou canst serve me, to perform the task I did not know to perform when alive. Wouldst thou do this thing for me, my son? For a father who always hated thee but did his duty by thee?"

"If I performed this task for you, Father, would I be free of you?"

His father lowered his head in assent.

Elric put a trembling hand upon the pommel of his sword and flung back his head so that the long white hair filled the air like a halo in the moonlight and his uneasy eyes rose to stare into the face of the dead king.

He let out a sigh. In spite of all his horrors, there was some part of him which would be fulfilled if he achieved his father's desire. He wished, however, that he had been permitted the choice. But it was not the Melnibonéan way to permit choice. Even relatives had to be bonded by more than blood.

"Explain my task, Father."

"Thou must find my soul, Elric."

"Your *soul*—?"

"My soul is not with me." The shade itself seemed to make an effort to remain standing. "What animates me now is my will and old sorcery. My soul was hidden so that it might rejoin thy mother, but in avoiding Mashabak's and Arioch's wrath, I lost that which contained it. Find it for me, Elric."

"How shall I recognize it?"

"It resides in a box. No ordinary box, but a box of black rosewood carved all with roses and smelling always of roses. It was your mother's."

"How came you to lose such a valuable box, Father?"

"When Mashabak appeared to claim my soul, then Arioch, I drew up a false soul, which is the spell I taught thee in *Incantations After Death*, to deceive them. This quasi-soul became the object of their feuding for a while and my true soul fled to safety in the box which Diavon Slar, my old body-servant, was to keep safely for me on strictest instructions of secrecy."

"He maintained your secrecy, Father."

"Aye—and fled, believing he had a treasure, believing he could control me through his possession of that box! He fled to Pan Tang with what he understood to be my trapped spirit—some children's tale he had heard—and was disappointed to find no spirit obeyed him at his command. So he planned, instead, to sell his booty to the Theocrat. As it happened, he never reached Pan Tang but was seized by sea-raiders from the Purple Towns. They included the box in their casual booty. My soul was truly lost." And with this came a flicker of a former irony, the faintest of smiles.

"The pirates?"

"Of them, I know only what Diavon Slar told me as I was extracting the vengeance I had warned him I would take. The raiders probably returned to Menii, where they auctioned their booty. My soulbox left our world entirely." Sadric moved suddenly and it was as if an insubstantial shadow shifted in the moonlight. "I can still sense it. I know it traveled between the worlds and went where now only the jill-dragon can follow. That is what has thwarted me. For, until I called thee, I had no means of pursuit. I am bound to this place and now to thee. Thou must fetch back my soulbox, Elric, so that I can rejoin thy mother and rid myself of unjust hate. As thou wilt rid thyself of me."

Trembling with conflicting passions, Elric spoke at last:

"Father, I believe this to be an impossible quest. I cannot but suspect you send me upon it out of hatred alone."

"Hatred, aye, but more besides. *I must rejoin your mother, Elric! I must. I must.*"

Knowing his father's abiding obsession, that convinced Elric of the ghost's veracity.

"Do not fail me, my son."

"And should I succeed? What will happen to us, Father?"

"Bring back my soul and we are both released."

"But if I fail?"

"My soul will leave its prison and enter thee. We shall be united until thy death—I, with my unjust hatred, bonded to the object of my hatred, and thee burdened by all *thou* most hatest in proud Melniboné." He paused, almost to savour this. "That would be my consolation."

"Not mine."

Sadric nodded his corpse's head in silent understanding, and a soft, unlikely laugh escaped his throat. "Indeed!"

"And dost thou have other aid for me in this, Father? Some spell or charm?"

"Only what thou comest by on the way, my son. Bring back the rosewood box and we both can go our own ways. Fail, and our destinies and souls are linked for ever! Thou wilt never be free of me, thy past, or Melniboné! But thou wilt bring the old glories back, eh?"

Elric's drug-enlivened body began to tremble. The flight and this encounter had exhausted him, and there were no souls here on which his sword could feed.

"I am ailing, Father, and must soon return. The drugs that sustain me were lost with my pack animals."

Sadric shrugged. "As for that, thou hast merely to discover a source of souls on which thy blade might feed. There's killing a-plenty ahead. And a little more that I perceive, but yet it does not come clear . . ." He frowned. "Go . . ."

Elric hesitated. Some ordinary impulse wanted him to tell his father that he no longer killed casually to further any whim. Like all Melnibonéans, Sadric had thought nothing of killing the human folk of their empire. To Sadric, the runesword was merely a useful tool, as a stick might be to a cripple. Supernatural schemer though his father was, player of complex games against the gods, he still unquestioningly assumed that one must pledge loyalty to one demon or another in order to survive.

Elric's vision, of universally held power, a place like Tanelorn, owing allegiance neither to Law nor to Chaos but only to itself, was anathema to his father who had made a religion and a philosophy of compromise, as had all his royal race for millennia, so that compromise itself was now raised over all other virtues and become the backbone of their beliefs. Elric wanted, again, to tell his father that there were other ideas, other ways to live, which involved neither excessive violence, nor cruelty, nor sorcery, nor conquest, that he had learned of these ideas not merely from the Young Kingdoms but also from his own folk's histories.

Yet he knew that it would be useless. Sadric was even now devoting all his considerable powers to restoring the past. He knew no other way of life or, indeed, of death.

The albino prince turned away, and it seemed to him at that moment that he had never experienced such grief, even when Cymoril had died on the blade of his runesword, even when Imrryr had blazed and he had known he was doomed to a rootless future, a lonely death.

"I shall seek your rosewood box, Father. But where can I begin?"

"The jill-dragon knows. She'll carry thee to the realm where the box was taken. Beyond that I cannot predict. Prediction grows difficult. All my powers weaken. Mayhap thou must kill to achieve the box. Kill many times." The voice was faint now, dry branches in the wind. "Or worse."

Elric found that he staggered. He was weakening by the moment. "Father, I have no strength."

"*The dragon venom* . . ." But his father was gone, leaving only a sense of his ghostly passing.

Elric forced himself to move. Now every fallen wall seemed an impossible obstacle. He picked his way slowly through the ruins, back over rubble and broken walls, over the little streams and coarse turf terraces of the hills, forcing himself with a will summoned from habit alone to climb the final hill where, outlined against the huge, sinking moon, Scarsnout awaited him, her wings folded, her long muzzle raised as her tongue tasted the wind.

He remembered his father's last words. They in turn made him recollect an old herbal which had spoken of the distillation of dragon venom; how it brought courage to the weak and skill to the strong, how a man might fight for five days and nights and feel no pain. And he remembered how the herbal had said to collect the venom, so before he clambered back upon the dragon he had reached up his helm and caught in hissing steel a small drop of venom which would cool and harden, he knew, into a pastille, a crumb or two of which might be taken cautiously with considerable liquid.

But now he must endure his pain and fight against his weakness as the dragon bears him up into the unwelcoming blackness which lies above the moon; and a single long, slow stroke of silver gashes the dark and a single sharp clap of thunder breaks the terrible silence of the sky, and the jill-dragon raises her head and beats her monstrous wings and roars a sudden challenge to those unlikely elements . . .

. . . While Elric howls the old wild songs of the Dragon Lords, and plunges, in sensuous symbiosis with the great reptile, out of the night and into the blinding glory of a summer afternoon.

CHAPTER THREE

Peculiar Geography of an Unknown Realm; A Meeting of
Travelers. On the Meaning of Freedom.

As if aware of her rider's growing weakness, the dragon flew with long, deliberate strokes of her wings and banked with careful grace through the blue pallor of the sky until they flew over trees so close together, and with foliage so dense, that it seemed at first they crossed dark green clouds until the old forest gave way to grassy hills and fields through which a broad river ran, and again the gentle landscape had a familiarity to it, though this time Elric did not dread it.

Soon a sprawling city lay ahead, built on both banks and making the sky hazy with its smoke. Of stone and brick and wood, of slate and thatch and timber shingles, of a thousand blended stinks and noises, it was full of statues and markets and monuments over which the jill-dragon began slowly to circle while below, in panic and curiosity, the citizens ran to look or dashed for cover, depending upon their natures—but then Scarsnout had flapped her wings and taken them with stately authority back into the upper sky, as if she had investigated the place and found it unsuitable.

The summer day went on. More than once did the great dragon-she seem about to land—on scrubland, village, marsh, lake or elm-glade—but always Scarsnout rejected the place and flew on dissatisfied.

Though he had taken the precaution of tying himself by his long silk scarf to the dragon's spine-horn, Elric was losing strength with every moment. Now, moreover, he had no reason to welcome death. To be reunited with his father through eternity was perhaps the worst of all possible hells. It was only when the dragon flew through rainclouds and Elric was able to capture a little water in his helmet, crumbling into it the merest flake of dried venom and drinking the foul-tasting result off in a single draught, that he knew any hope. But when the liquid filled his every vein with fire whose stink made him loathe the flesh that harboured it and want to tear at offending arteries, muscles, skin, he wondered if he had not merely chosen an especially painful way of ensuring his eternal union with Sadric. With each nerve alight, he yearned for any death, any release from the agony.

But even as the pain filled him, the strength grew until soon it was possible to call on that strength and gradually abolish or ignore the pain until it was gone and he felt a cleaner, sweeter energy fill him, somehow purer than that he received from his runesword.

As the jill-dragon flew through evening skies, Elric felt himself grow whole again. A peculiar euphoria filled him. He sang out the ancient dragon-songs, the rich, silky, wicked songs of his folk who, for all their cruelty, had relished every experience that came their way and this relish for life and sensation came naturally to the albino, despite the weakness of his blood.

Indeed, it seemed to him that his blood was somehow touched by a compensatory quality, a world of almost unrelieved sensuality and vividness, so intense that it sometimes threatened to destroy not only him, but those around him. It was one of the reasons he was prepared to accept his loneliness.

Now it did not matter how far the jill-dragon flew. Her venom sustained him. The symbiosis was near-complete. On without rest beat Scarsnout until, beneath a golden late afternoon sun which made the three-quarters ripened wheat glow and shimmer like burnished copper, where a startled figure in a pointed alabaster cap cried out in delight at the sight of them and a cloud of starlings rose suddenly to trace with their hurried flight some familiar hieroglyph in the delicate blue wash of the sky and leave a sudden silence behind them, Scarsnout extended her great ribbed wings in a sinuously elegant glide towards what seemed at first a road made of basalt or some other rock and then became a mile-wide long-healed scar through the wheatlands, too smooth, unpopulated and vast to be a road, yet with an unguessable purpose. It cut through the crops as if it had been laid that day, heaped on both sides by great unkempt banks on which a few weeds and wildflowers grew and over which hopped, flapped and crawled every kind of carrion vermin. As they dropped lower Elric could smell the vile stuff and almost gagged. His nose confirmed what he saw—piles of refuse, bones, human waste, bits of broken furniture and ruined pots—great continuous banks of detritus stretching on either side of the smoothly polished road from horizon to horizon, with no notion of where or from where it led . . . Elric sang to his jill to take him up and away from all this filth and into the sweet air of the high summer skies, but she ignored him, wheeling first to the north, then to the south, until she was swooping down the very middle of that great, smooth scar, which had something of the brownish-pink of sunned flesh, and she had landed, almost without any sensation, in the centre of it.

Now Scarsnout folded back her wings and settled her clawed feet upon the ground, clearly indicating that she intended to carry Elric no further. With some reluctance he climbed off her back, unraveling the ruined scarf and wrapping it around his waist, as if it would secure him from any dangers hereabouts, and sang the farewell chant of thanking and kinship and, as he called the last lines, the great jill-dragon lifted up her beautiful, reptilian head and joined, with sonorous gravity, in the final cadences. Her voice might have been the voice of Time itself.

Then her jaws snapped shut, her eyes turned once upon him, half-lidded, almost in affection, and, once her tongue had tasted the evening air, she had widened her wings, hopped twice, shaking the surface so that Elric thought it must crack, and was at last a-sky, mounting into the atmosphere again, her graceful body curling and twisting as her wings carried her up to the eastern horizon, the setting sun casting her long, terrible shadow across the fields, and then, near the horizon, a single flash of silver suggested to Elric that his jill-dragon had returned to her own dimension. He raised his helm in farewell, as grateful for her venom as her patience.

All Elric wished to do was to get free of this unnatural causeway. Though it gleamed like polished marble, he could see now that it was nothing more than beaten mud; earth piled on earth until it had almost the consistency of solid rock. Perhaps the whole thing was built of garbage? For some reason, this thought disturbed him and he began to walk rapidly towards the southern edge. Wiping sweat from his forehead, he wondered again what purpose the place had. Flies now surrounded him and buzzards regarded him as a possible contender for their sweetmeats. He coughed again at the stink but knew he must climb the stuff to get to the wholesome air of the wheatfields.

"Safe passage to your home-cave, sweet Lady Scarsnout," he murmured as he moved. "I owe you both life and death, it seems. But I bear you no ill will."

His scarf wrapped around his nose and mouth, the albino began to climb the yielding filth, disturbing bones and vermin with every movement and making slow progress, while around him birds and winged rats hissed and chittered at him. Again he wondered what kind of creature could have created such a path, if path it were. It could not, he felt sure, be the work of any human agency and this made him all the more anxious to return to the known qualities of the wheatfield.

He had reached the rim and was clambering along it to find a firmer foothold down. Scattering rotted matter and angry rodents as he went, he wondered what kind of culture brought its waste to line a track created by some supernatural being. Then he thought he saw something larger shift below, near where the wheat grew, but the light was bad and he put it down to his imagination. Was the refuse some kind of holy offering? Did this realm's people worship a god who patrolled from one habitation to another in the form of a gigantic snake?

There was another movement below him, as he slid down a few feet and came to rest on an old cistern, and he saw a soft felt hat rise above a pile of rags and an avian face stare up at him in astonished amusement. "Good heavens, sir. This cannot be coincidence! But what purpose has Fate for pairing we two, do you think?" It was Wheldrake, stumbling up from the wheatfield. "What lies behind you, sir, that's duller than this? More corn? Why, sir, this seems a world of corn!"

"Of corn and garbage and a somewhat idiosyncratic pathway of baffling purpose which slices through all, from east to west. It has a sinister air to it."

"So you go the other way, sir?"

"To avoid whichever unpleasant creation of Chaos has chosen to slither this route and take its choice of these offerings. My horses, I suppose, were not carried through the dimensions with you?"

"Not to my knowledge, sir. I'd guessed you eaten, by now. But the reptile was one of those with a sentimental weakness for heroes, I take it?"

"Something of the sort." Elric smiled, grateful in an odd way for the red-headed poet's ironies. They were preferable to his most recent conversation with his father. As he slid down some powdery and decomposing substance alive with maggots, he embraced the little man who almost chirped with pleasure at their reunion. "My dear sir!"

Whereupon, arm in arm they went, back to the bottom and the sweetening wheat, back in the direction of a river Elric had seen from his dragon steed. There had been a town upon that river which, he guessed, might be reached in less than a day. He spoke of this to Wheldrake, adding that they were sadly short of provisions or the means of obtaining any, unless they chewed the unripe wheat.

"I regret my poaching days in Northumberland are long behind me, sir. But as a lad I was apt enough with snare and a gun. It might be, since your scarf is rather badly the worse for wear, that you would not mind if I unraveled it a little more. It's just possible I might remember my old skills."

With an amiable shrug, Elric handed the birdlike poet his scarf and watched as the little fingers worked swiftly, unraveling and reknotting until he had a length of thin cord. "With evening drawing close, sir, I'd best get to work at once."

By now they were some distance from the wall of garbage and could smell only the rich, restful scents of the summer fields. Elric took his ease amongst the wheatstalks while Wheldrake went to work and within a short space of time, having cleared a wide area and dug a pit, they were able to enjoy a young rabbit while they speculated at such a strange world which grew such vast fields and yet seemed to have so few farmsteads or villages. Staring at the rabbit's carcass turning on a spit (also of Wheldrake's devising) Elric said that, for all his sorcerous education, he was not the familiar traveler through the realms that Wheldrake seemed to be.

"Not by choice, sir, I assure you. I blame a certain Doctor Dee, whom I consulted on the Greeks. It was to do with metre, sir. A metric question. I needed, I thought, to *hear* the language of Plato. Well, the story's long and not especially novel to those of us who travel, willy-nilly, through the multiverse, but I spent some while on one particular plane, shifting a little, I must admit, through time (but not the other dimensions) until I had come to rest, I was sure, in Putney."

"Would you return there, Master Wheldrake?"

"Indeed I would, sir. I'm growing a little long in the tooth for extra-dimensional adventuring, and I tend to form firm attachments, so it is rather hard on me, you know, to miss so many friends."

"Well, sir. I hope you will find them again."

"And you, sir. Good luck with whatever it is you hope to discover. Though I suspect you are the kind who's forever searching for the numinous."

"Perhaps," said Elric soberly, chewing upon a tender leg, "but I think the numinosity of what I presently seek would surprise you greatly . . ."

Wheldrake was about to ask more when he changed his mind and stared instead, with abiding pride, at his spit and his catch. Elric's own cares were considerably lightened by his relish for the little man's company and quirks of character.

And now Master Wheldrake has found his sought-for volume and has a handy candle to light at the fire so that he might read aloud to the last Prince of Melniboné an account of some demigod of his own dimension and his challenge of a kingship, when there comes a sound of a horse walking slowly through the wheat—a horse which hesitates with every few steps as if controlled by a clever master. So Elric shouts out—

"Greetings, horseman. Would you share our meat?"

There's a pause, then the answering voice is muffled, distant, yet courteous:

"I'd share your heat, sir, for a while. It's mighty cold just now, to me."

The horse continues towards them at the same pace, still pausing from time to time, still cautious, until at last they see its shadow against the firelight and a rider dismounts, walking softly towards them, a silhouette of alarming symmetry, a big man clad from head to foot in armour that flashes silver, gold, sometimes blue-grey. On his helm is a plume of dark yellow and his breastplate is etched with the yellow-and-black Arms of Chaos, the arms of a soulbonded servant of the Lords of Unlikelihood, which are eight arrows radiating from a central hub, representing the variety and multiplicity of Chaos. Behind him his perfect war-stallion was furnished with a hood and surcoat of radiant black-and-silver silk, a high saddle of ornamental ivory and ebony, and silver harness bound with gold.

Elric got to his feet, ready for confrontation but chiefly puzzled by the stranger's appearance. The newcomer wore a helm apparently without a visor, but all of a piece from neck to crown. Only the eye-slits relieved the smoothness of the coruscating steel, which seemed to contain living matter just below its polished surface: matter that flowed and stirred and threatened. Through those slits peered a pair of eyes displaying an angry pain which Elric understood. He was unable to identify a feeling of close affinity with the man as he came up to the fire and stretched gauntleted hands towards the flames. The firelight caught the metal and again suggested that something living was contained in it, trapped in it—some enormous energy, so powerful it could be observed *through* the steel. And yet the fingers stretched and curled like any fleshly finger warmed back to circulation, and the stranger's sigh was one of simple comfort.

"Will you take a little rabbit, sir?" Wheldrake gestured towards the roasting coney.

"Thank you, no, sir."

"Will you unburden yourself of your helm and sit with us? You're in no danger."

"I believe you, sir. But I am unable to remove this helm at present and have not, I'll be frank, fed upon commonplace sustenance for some while."

At this Wheldrake raised a ruddy eyebrow. "Does Chaos send her servants to become cannibals, these days, sir?"

"She's had servants a-plenty who have been that," said the armoured man, turning his back now to the fire's heat, "but I am not of their number. I have not eaten flesh, fruit or vegetable, sir, for nigh on two thousand years. Or it could be more. I ceased attempting such a reckoning long ago. There are realms that are always Night and realms sweltering in perpetual Day and others where night and day fly by with a speed not of our usual perception."

"Some sort of vow, is it, sir?" says Wheldrake tentatively. "Some holy purpose?"

"A quest, aye, but for something simpler, sir, than you would believe."

"What are you seeking, sir? A particular lost bride?"

"You are perceptive, sir."

"Merely well-read, sir. But that is not all, eh?"

"I seek nothing less than death, sir. It is to that unhappy doom that the Balance did consign me when I betrayed her those numberless millennia since. It is also my doom to fight against those who serve the Balance, though I love the Balance with a ferocity, sir, that has never dissipated. It was ordained—though I have no reason to trust the oracle in question—that I should find peace at the hand of a servant of the Balance—one who was as I once was."

"And what were you once?" enquired Wheldrake, who had followed this last a little more swiftly than the albino.

"I was once a Prince of the Balance, a Servant and Confidant of that Unordinary Intelligence that tolerates, celebrates and loves all life throughout the multiverse and yet which both Law and Chaos would overthrow if they could. Discontented with multiplicity and massive adjustment in the multiverse, guessing something of a great conjunction which must come throughout the Key Planes and set the realities for countless aeons—realities where the Balance might no longer exist, I gave in to experiment. The notion was too strong for me. Curiosity and folly, self-importance and pride led me to convince myself that in doing what I attempted to do, I served the interests of the Balance. And for my failure, or my success, I would have paid an equal price. The price I now pay."

"That is not the whole of your story, sir." Wheldrake was enthralled. "You will not bore me, I know, if you wish to embroider it with more detail."

"I cannot, sir. I speak as I do because that is all I am allowed to unburden of my tale. The rest is for me alone to know until such time I shall be released and then it can be told."

"Released by death, sir? It would create some difficulties regarding the telling, I'd guess."

"The Balance doubtless will decide such things," said the stranger, without much humour.

"Is general death all you look for, sir? Or has death a name?" Elric spoke softly, with some sympathy.

"I am seeking three sisters. They came this way, I think, a few days since. Would you have seen three sisters? Riding together?"

"I regret, sir, that we are but recently transported to this realm, through no desire of our own, and thus are newly here without maps or directions." Elric shrugged. "I had hoped you would know a little of the place."

"It is in what they call the Nine Millionth Ring, the maguses here. It exists within what they have formalized as the Realms of Central Significance, and it is true there is an unusual quality to the plane which I have yet to identify. It is not a true Centre, for that is the Realm of the Balance, but it is what I would call a quasi-centre. You'll forgive the jargon, sir, I hope, of the philosopher. I was for some generations an alchemist in Prague."

"Prague!" cries Wheldrake with a caw of delighted recognition. "Those bells and towers, sir. And do you know Mirenburg, perhaps? Even more beautiful!"

"The memories are no doubt pleasant enough," says the armoured man, "since I do not recall them. I would take it that you, too, are upon a quest here?"

"Not I, sir," says Wheldrake, "unless it be for Putney Common and my lost half-pint."

"I am seeking something, aye," agreed Elric cautiously. He had hoped to learn a little of the geography rather than the mystical and astrological placing of this world. "I am Elric of Melniboné."

His name does not seem of any great significance to the armoured man. "And I am Gaynor, once a Prince of the Universal, now called the Damned. Perhaps we have met? Without these names or even faces? In some other incarnation?"

"It is not my misfortune to recall any other lives," says Elric softly, at last disturbed by Gaynor's enquiries. "I understand you only a little, sir. I am a mercenary soldier en route to a new location with a view to finding myself a fresh patron. To the supernatural, I am almost a stranger."

And he was grateful that Wheldrake's eyebrows were rising at that moment from behind Gaynor. Why he should decide upon such subterfuge he did not understand, only that, for all his being drawn to Gaynor, for all their mutual patronage under Chaos, he feared something in him. Gaynor had no reason to wish him harm and Elric guessed that Gaynor did not waste anything of himself in meaningless challenges or killings, yet still Elric grew more close-lipped, as if he, too, were fated by the Balance never to speak of his own story, and at length they settled down to sleep, three strange figures in what appeared to be an infinity of wheat.

Early the next morning, Gaynor resumed his saddle. "I was glad of the company, gentlemen. If you travel yonder, you'll find a pretty settlement. The people there are traders and welcome strangers. They treat us, indeed, with unusual respect. I go on my way. I have been informed that my sisters journeyed towards a place called the Gypsy Nation. Know you anything of that?"

"I regret, sir," said Wheldrake, wiping his hands upon an enormous red cotton handkerchief, "we are virgins in this world. Innocent as babes. We are wholly at a disadvantage, having but recently arrived in this realm and having no notion of its people or its gods. Perhaps, if I might be somewhat forward, I would suggest that you are yourself of divine or semi-divine origin?"

The answering laugh seemed to find an internal echo, as if the prince's helm disguised the entrance to some infinite chasm. It was far away, yet oddly intimate. "I told you, Master Wheldrake. I was a Prince of the Balance. But not now. Now, I assure you, sir, there is nothing divine about Gaynor the Damned."

Murmuring that he still did not understand the significance of the prince's title, Wheldrake subsided. "If we could help, sir, we would—"

"Who are these women you seek?" Elric asked.

"Three sisters, similar in looks and upon a quest or errand of some singular urgency to themselves. They are searching, I gather, for a lost countryman or perhaps even a brother and had asked hereabouts for the Gypsy Nation. When the people heard they sought the Nation they put them on their way but refused all further intercourse. My only advice to you would be to avoid the subject completely, unless it is raised by them! I have a suspicion, moreover, that once you encounter this band of nomads, you have precious little chance of leaving their ranks unscathed."

"I am grateful for your advice, Prince Gaynor," said Elric. "And did you learn who grows so much wheat, and why?"

"Fixed tenants they are called, and when I asked the same question I was told with a somewhat humourless laugh that it was to feed the locusts. I have heard of stranger practices. There is some tension with the gypsies, I gather. They will not speak much of any of this but become unsettled. The realm's called by them Salish-Kwoonn, which, you'll recall, is the name of the city in the Ivory Book. An odd irony, that. I was amused." And he turned his horse away from them as if he escaped wholly into the abstract, his natural environment, and rode slowly towards that distant depression, those hills of refuse, whose presence was already marked on the horizon by crows and kites, by masses of flies swarming like black smoke.

"A scholar," said Wheldrake, "if a little on the cryptic side. You understand him better than do I, Prince Elric. But I wish he had traveled our way. What do you make of the fellow?"

Elric paused, choosing his words, fiddling with the buckle of his belt. Then he said: "I am afraid of him. I fear him as I have never feared a human creature, mortal or immortal. His doom is terrible, indeed, for he has known the Sanctuary of the Balance, and that is what I yearn for. To have had it—and lost it . . ."

"Come, now, sir. You must exaggerate. Odd, he was, to be sure. But affable, I thought. Given his circumstances."

Elric shuddered, glad to see Prince Gaynor gone. "Yet I fear him as I fear nothing else."

"As you fear yourself, maybe, sir?" And then Wheldrake looked with regret upon the face of his new friend. "I beg you, sir, I did not wish to seem forward."

"You are too intelligent for me, Master Wheldrake. Your poet's eye is perhaps sharper than I would like."

"Random instinct, sir, I assure you. I understand nothing and say everything. That's *my* doom, sir! Not as grand as some, no doubt, but it gets me in and out of trouble in roughly equal proportions."

And with that Master Wheldrake assures himself of a dead fire, breaks down his spit and buries it with regret, keeps hold of his snare, which he tucks in his pocket with a volume which has lost its binding to reveal some vulgar marbling, throws his frock-coat over his shoulder and plunges through the wheat in Elric's wake. "Did I recite my verse epic, sir, concerning the love and death of Sir Tancred and Lady Mary? In the form of the Northumberland ballad, which was the first poetry I ever heard. The family estates were remote, but I was not lonely there."

His voice chirruping and trilling the cadences of a primitive dirge, the red-combed scrivener skipped and scampered to keep up with the tall albino.

Four hours later, they reached the broad, slow-flowing river and could see, rising on picturesque cliffs above the water, the town Elric sought. Meanwhile Wheldrake declaimed the ballad's last resounding couplets and seemed as relieved as Elric that his composition was concluded.

The town appeared to have been carved by fanciful master masons from the glinting limestone of the cliffs and was reached by a fairly narrow track, evidently of artificial construction in places, which wound above the rocks and white water some distance below, rising gradually before it blended with the town's chief street to wind again between tall, many-storeyed dwellings and warehouses, fanciful public buildings and statuary, topiary and elaborate flower-gardens to become lost among a maze of other thoroughfares and alleys which lay below an ancient castle, itself covered in vines and flowering creepers, dominating both the town and the thirteen-arched bridge which spanned the river at its narrowest point and crossed to a smaller settlement beyond where, evidently, the wealthy citizens had built their pale villas.

The town had an air of contented prosperity and Elric became optimistic as he saw it lacked any real walls and clearly had not needed to defend itself against aggressors for many years. Now a few local people, in bright, much-embroidered clothing, very different in style from Elric's or, indeed, Wheldrake's, greeted them cheerfully and openly, like men and women who know considerable security and are used to strangers.

"If they welcomed Gaynor, Prince Elric," said Wheldrake, "then I would guess we would not seem especially alien to them! This place has a Frenchified air to it, reminding me of certain settlements along the Loire, though it lacks the characteristic cathedral. Is there any clue, do you perceive, to their form of religion?"

"Perhaps they have none," said Elric. "I have heard of such races." But clearly Wheldrake disbelieved him.

"Even the French have religion!"

The road took them past the first houses, perched on rocks and terraces above them and all displaying the richest flower-gardens Elric remembered. A scent came off them, mingling with the faint smells of paint and cooking, and both travelers found themselves relaxing, smiling at those who hailed them, until Elric stopped for a moment and enquired of a young woman in a white and red smock the name of the town.

"Why, this is Agnesh-Val, sir. And across the river is Agnesh-Nal. How came you here, gentlemen? Was your boat wrecked at the Forli rapid? You should go to the Distressed Travelers House in Fivegroat Lane, just below Salt Pie Alley. They'll feed you there, at least. Do you carry the medal of the Insurer's Guild?"

"I regret not, madam."

"Sadly, then, you will be entitled only to our hospitality."

"Which would seem more than generous, lady," said Wheldrake, offering her a rather inappropriate wink before skipping to catch up with his friend.

Eventually, through the twists and turns of the old, cobbled streets, they reached the Distressed Travelers House, a gabled building of considerable antiquity which leaned at all angles, as if too drunk to stand without the support of the houses on either side of it, and whose beams and walls bulged and warped in ways Elric would have thought impossible for natural matter not touched by Chaos.

Within the doorway of this establishment, seeming entirely of a piece with it, both in terms of posture and of age, leaned and sprawled, his limbs at every angle, his head this way, his hat that, a tooth jutting one direction, his pipe another, a creature of such profound thinness and gauntness and melancholy that Elric was moved, obscurely, to apologize and enquire if he had come to the right place.

"It's the place that you face, sir, by Our Watcher's Grace, my lord. Come for charity, have you? For charity and some smart advice?"

"Hospitality, sir, is what we were offered!" There was an edge to Wheldrake's outraged chirrup. "Not, sir, charity!" He resembled an angered grouse, his face almost as red as his hair.

"I care not what fancy words dress the action, my good lords," and the creature rose, folding and collapsing and extending itself in such a way as to bring itself upright, "I call it *charity*!" Tiny diamond-lights glittered from cavernous sockets and ill-fitting teeth clacked in flaccid lips. "I care not what dangers you have faced, what calamities have befallen you, what hideous losses you have sustained, what rich men you were, what poor men you have become. Had you not considered these risks, you would not have come this far and ventured across the Divide! Thus you have yourselves alone to blame for your misfortunes."

"We were told we might find food at this house," said Elric evenly. "Not ill-tempered crowfrighters and discourtesy."

"Hypocrites that they are, they lied. The House is closed for redecoration. It is being converted to a restaurant. With luck, it should soon turn a profit."

"Well, sir, we have put such narrow notions of accountability behind us in my world," said Wheldrake. "However, I apologize for disturbing you. We have been misinformed, as you say."

Elric, unused to such behaviour and still a Melnibonéan noble, found that he had gripped his sword-hilt without his realizing it. "Old man," he said, "I am discommoded by your insolence . . ." Then Wheldrake's warning hand fell upon the albino's arm and he collected himself.

"The old man lies! He lies! He lies!" From behind them, up the hill, a large key ready in his hand, bustled a stocky fellow of fifty or so, his grey hair bristling from beneath a velvet cap, his beard half-tangled, his robes and suitings all awry, as if he had dressed in a hurry from some half-remembered bed. "He lies, good sirs. He lies. (Be off with you, Reth'chat, to plague some other institution!) The man is a relic, gentlemen, from an age most of us have only read about. He would have us judged by our wealth and our martial glory rather than our good will and tranquility of spirit. Good morrow, good morrow. You've come to dine, I hope."

"Cold and tasteless is the bread of charity," grumbled the Relic, scuttling down the street towards a group of playing children and failing to scatter them with his stick-insect arms. "Accountability and self-sufficiency! They will destroy the family. We shall all perish. We shall serve at the marching boards, mark my words!"

And with that he turned the corner into Old Museum Gate and

disappeared with a final display of miraculous angularity into an arcade of shops.

The genial middle-aged man waved his key before inserting it in the ancient door. "He is an advertizement for himself only. You'll find such blowhards in every town. I take it that our gypsy friends exacted a 'tax' from you. What would you have been bringing us?"

"Gold, mostly," said Elric, understanding at last the manners and ready lies of a mercenary and a thief, "and precious jewels."

"You were brave to make the attempt. Did they find you this side of the Divide?"

"It would seem so."

"And stripped you of everything. You are lucky to have your clothing and weapons. And 'tis as well they did not catch you crossing the Divide."

"We waited a season before we were sure of our chance." This from Wheldrake, entering the spirit of it, as if in a childish game, a knowing grin upon his broad lips.

"Aye. Others have waited longer." The door opened silently and they entered a passage lit by glowing yellow lamps, its walls as twisted inside as they were without; its staircases rising in unlikely places and going where none could guess, its passages and chambers appearing suddenly and always of peculiar shapes and angles, sometimes brilliant with candles, sometimes gloomy and musty, as their host led them on, deeper and deeper into the house until they came at last to a large, cheerful hall in the centre of which was a great oaken table, lined with benches—enough space for two score of hungry travelers. There was, however, only one other guest, already helping herself to the rich stew steaming in a pot over the hearth. She was dressed in simple clothes of russet and green, a slender sword on her hip, a dagger to balance it, a muscular, full-hipped figure, broad shoulders and a face of brooding beauty beneath a mass of red-gold hair. She nodded to them as she swung her legs back over the bench and began to eat, clearly showing she did not wish to talk.

Their host dropped his voice. "I understand your fellow traveler to have experienced exceptional inconvenience to her person and her ambitions just recently. She has expressed some wish not to engage in conversation today. You will find all you need here, gentlemen. There is a servant about somewhere who will see to any particular needs, and I will return in a couple of hours to see what other aid we can supply. We do not discourage failed venturers in Agnesh-Val or we should never trade! It is our policy to help the failed ones just as we profit from the successful ones. This appears both fair and sane to us."

"And so it is, sir," said Wheldrake with approval. "You are of the Liberal persuasion, evidently. One hears so much Toryism as one travels throughout the rea—that is, the world."

"We believe in enlightened self-interest, sir, as I think do all civilized peoples. It is in the interest of the community and that larger community beyond to ensure that all are courteously and properly enabled to make what they wish of themselves. Will you eat, sir? Will you eat?"

Elric was aware of the woman's moody eyes regarding them as they spoke together and remarked to himself that he had not seen a face more lovely and more determined since Cymoril had lived. Her wide blue eyes were steady and unselfconscious as she chewed slowly, her thoughts unreadable. And then, suddenly, she smiled once before she gave her full attention to her food, leaving Elric with more of a mystery than before.

Having helped their deep plates to the stew, which gave off a delicious smell, they found themselves places at the table and ate for a while in silence until at last the woman spoke. There was unexpected warm humour in her voice and a certain heartiness which Elric found attractive. "What lie brought you this free meal, boys?"

"A misunderstanding, lady, rather than a lie," said Wheldrake diplomatically, licking his spoon and wondering whether to take a second trip to the cauldron.

"You are no more traders than am I," she said.

"That was the chief misunderstanding. Apparently they can imagine no other kind of traveler here."

"Apparently so. And you are recently here in this realm. By the river, no doubt."

"I do not understand the means," said Elric, still cautious.

"But you both seek the three sisters, of course."

"It seems that everyone does that," Elric told her, letting her believe whatever she wished. "I am Elric of Melniboné and this is my friend Master Wheldrake, the poet."

"Of Master Wheldrake I have heard." There was perhaps some admiration in the lady's voice. "But you, sir, I fear are unknown to me. I am called the Rose and my sword is called Swift Thorn while my dagger is called Little Thorn." She spoke with pride and defiance and it was clear that she uttered some kind of warning, though what she feared from them Elric could not guess. "I travel the time streams in search of my revenge." And she smiled down at her empty bowl, as if in self-mocking embarrassment at a shameful admission.

"And what do the three sisters mean to you, madam?" asked Wheldrake, his little voice now a charming trill.

"They mean everything. They have the means of leading me to the resolution of all I have lived for, since I swore my oath. They offer me the chance of satisfaction, Master Wheldrake. You are, are you not, that same Wheldrake who wrote *The Orientalist's Dream*?"

"Well, madam—" in some dismay—"I was but newly arrived in a new age. I needed to begin my reputation afresh. And the Orient was all the rage just then. However, as a mature work—"

"It is exceptionally sentimental, Master Wheldrake. But it helped me through a bad hour or two. And I still enjoy it for what it is. After that comes *The Song of Iananthe*, which is of course your finest."

"But Heavens, madam, I have not yet written the work! It is sketched, that's all, in Putney."

"It is excellent, sir. I'll say no more of it."

"I'm obliged for that, madam. And—" he recovered himself— "also for your praise. I, too, have some affection for my Oriental period. Did you read, perhaps, the novel which was just lately published— *Manfred; Or, the Gentleman Hoorii?*"

"Not part of your canon when I last was settled anywhere, sir."

And while the pair of them talked of poetry, Elric found himself leaning his head upon his arms and dozing until suddenly he heard Wheldrake say:

"And how do these gypsies go about unpunished? Is there no authority to keep them in check?"

"I know only that they are a nation of travelers," said the Rose quietly, "perhaps a large nomad horde of some description. They call themselves the Free Travelers or the People of the Road and there is no doubt that they are powerful enough for the local folk to fear. I have some suggestion that the sisters rode to join the Gypsy Nation. So I would join it, too."

And Elric remembered the wide causeway of beaten mud and wondered if that had any connection with the Gypsy Nation. Yet they would not league themselves, surely, with the supernatural? He became increasingly curious.

"We are all three at a disadvantage," said the Rose, "since we allowed our hosts to assume we were victims of the gypsies. This means we cannot pursue any direct enquiries but must understand elliptically what we can. Unless we were to admit our deception."

"I have a feeling this would make us somewhat more unpopular. These people are proud of their treatment of traders. But of non-traders, we have not learned. Perhaps their fate is less pleasant." Elric sighed. "It matters not to me. But if you would have company, lady, we'll join forces to seek these sisters."

"Aye, for the moment I see no harm in such an alliance." She spoke sagely. "Have you heard anything of them?"

"As much as have you," said Elric, truthfully. Within him now a voice was speaking. He tried to quiet it but it would not be silent. It was his father's voice. *The sisters. Find them. They have the box. They have the box.* The voice was fading now. Was it false? Was he deceived? He had no other course to follow, he decided, so he might as well follow this one and hope, ultimately, it might lead him to the rosewood box and his father's stolen soul. Besides, there was something he enjoyed in this woman's company that he felt he might never find again, an easy, measured understanding which made him, in spite of his careful resolve, wish to tell her all the secrets of his life, all the hopes and fears and aspirations he had known, all the losses; not to burden her, but to offer her something she might wish to share. For they had other qualities in common, he could tell.

He felt, in short, that he had found a sister. And he knew that she, too, felt something of the same kinship, though he were Melnibonéan and she were not. And he wondered at all of this, for he had experienced kinship of a thoroughly different kind with Gaynor—yet kinship, nonetheless.

When the Rose had retired, saying she had not slept for some thirty-six hours, Wheldrake was full of enthusiasm for her. "She's as womanly a woman, sir, as I've ever seen. What a magnificent woman. A Juno in the flesh! A Diana!"

"I know nothing of your local divinities," said Elric gently, but he agreed with Wheldrake that they had met an exceptional individual that day. He had begun to speculate on this peculiar linking of fathers and sons, quasi-brothers and quasi-sisters. He wondered if he did not sense the presence of the Balance in this—or perhaps, more likely, the influence of the Lords of Chaos or of Law, for it had become obvious of late that the Dukes of Entropy and the Princes of Constancy were about to engage in a conflict of more than ordinary ferocity. Which went further to explaining the urgency that was in the air—the urgency his father had attempted to express, though dead and without his soul. Was there, in this slow-woven pattern that seemed to form about him, some reflection of a greater, cosmic configuration? And, for a second, he had a glimmering of the vastness of the multiverse, its complexity and variousness, its realities and its still-to-be-realized dreams; possibilities without end—wonders and horrors, beauty and ugliness—limitless and indefinable, full of the ultimate in everything.

And when the grey-haired man came back, a little better dressed, a little neater in his toilet, Elric asked him why they did not fear direct attack from the so-called Gypsy Nation.

"Oh, they have their own rules about such things, I understand. There is a status quo, you know. Not that it makes your circumstances any more fortunate . . ."

"You parley with them?"

"In a sense, sir. We have treaties and so forth. It is not Agnesh-Val we fear for, but those who would come to trade with us . . ." And again he made apologetic pantomime. "The gypsies have their ways, you know. Strange to us, and I would not serve them directly, I think, but we must see the positive as well as the negative side of their power."

"And they have their freedom, I suppose," said Wheldrake. "It is the great theme of *The Romany Rye*."

"Perhaps, sir." But their host seemed a trifle doubtful. "I am not aware of what you speak—a play?"

"An account, sir, of the joys of the open road."

"Ah, then it would be of gypsy origin. We do not buy their books, I fear. Now, gentlemen, I do not know if you would take advantage of what we offer distressed travelers by way of credit and cost-price equipment. If you have no money, we will take kind. Perhaps to be sure one of *those* books, if you like, Master Wheldrake, for a horse."

"A book for a horse, sir! Well, sir!"

"Two horses? I regret I have no notion of the market value. Book-reading is not a great habit among us. Perhaps we should feel ashamed, but we prefer the passive pleasures of the evening arena."

"As well as the horses, perhaps a few days' provisions?" suggested Elric.

"If that seems fair to you, sir."

"My books," pronounced Wheldrake through gritted teeth, his nose seeming more pointed than ever, "are my—my *self*, sir. They are my identity. I am their protector. Besides, though through the oddity of some telepathy we all enjoy, we can *understand* language, we cannot *read* it. Did you know that, sir? The ability does not extend to that. Logical, in one sense, I suppose. No, sir, I will not part with a page!"

But when Elric had pointed out that Wheldrake had already explained that one of the volumes was in a language even he did not know and suggested that their lives might depend upon acquiring horses and throwing in with the Rose, who already had her horse, Wheldrake at last consented to part with the *Omar Khayyam* he had hoped one day to read.

So Elric, Wheldrake and the Rose all three rode back down the white road beside the river, back to where they had joined the trail on the previous day, but now they remained on the path, letting it carry them slowly and sinuously southward, following the lazy flow of the river. And Wheldrake sang his *Song of 'Rabia* to an entranced Rose, while Elric rode some distance ahead, wondering if he had entered a dream and fearing he would never find his father's soul.

They had reached a part of the river road Elric did not remember passing over and he was remarking to himself that this had been close to where the dragon had headed due south, away from the water's winding course, when his sensitive ears caught a distant noise he could not identify. He mentioned it to the others but neither could hear it. Only after another half-hour had passed did the Rose cup her hand to her ear and frown. "A kind of rushing. A sort of roar."

"I hear it now," said Wheldrake, rather obviously piqued that he, the poet, should be the least well-tuned. "I did not know you meant that rushing, roaring kind of noise. I had understood it to be a feature of the water." And then he had the grace to blush, shrug and take an interest in something at the end of his beaklike nose.

It was another two hours before they saw that the water was now gushing and leaping with enormous force, through rocks which even the most skilled navigator could not have negotiated, and sending up such a whistling and shouting and yelling it might have been a live thing, voicing its furious discontent. The roadway was slippery with spray and they could scarcely make themselves heard above the noise, could scarcely see more than a few paces in front of them, could smell only the angry water. And then the road had dropped away from the river and entered a hollow which made the noise suddenly distant.

The rocks around them still ran with water sprayed from above, but the near-silence was almost physically welcome to them and they breathed deep sighs of pleasure. Then Wheldrake rode a little ahead and came back to report that the road curved off, along what appeared to be a cliff. Perhaps they had reached the ocean.

They had left the hollow and were on the open road again where coarse grass stretched to an horizon which still roared, still sent up clouds of spray, like a silver wall. Now the road led them to the edge of a cliff and a chasm so deep the bottom was lost in blackness. It was into this abyss that water poured with such relentless celebration and when Elric looked up he gasped. Only at that moment had he seen the causeway overhead—a causeway that curved from the eastern cliff of a great bay to the western cliff—the same causeway, he was sure, that he had seen earlier. Yet this could not be made of beaten mud. The mighty curving span was woven of boughs and bones and strands of metal supporting a surface that seemed to be made of thousands of animal hides fixed one on top of another by layers of foul-smelling bone-glue— utterly primitive in one way, thought Elric, but otherwise a sturdy and sophisticated piece of engineering. His own people had once possessed similar ingenuity, before magic began to absorb them. He was admiring the extraordinary structure as they rode beside it, when Wheldrake spoke up.

"It's no wonder, friend Elric, nobody chooses to consider the river route below what is, I'm sure, the thing they call the Divide."

And Elric was forced to smile at this irony. "Does that strange causeway lead, do you think, to the Gypsy Nation?"

"*Leads to death, disorder and dismay; leads to the craven Earl of Cray,*" intoned Wheldrake, the association sparking, as it did so often, snatches of self-quotation. "*Now Ulric takes the Urgent Brand and hand in hand they trembling stand, to bring the justice of the day, the terrible justice of the day, to evil Gwandyth, Earl of Cray.*"

Even the admiring Rose did not applaud, nor think his verse appropriate to this somewhat astonishing moment, with the roaring river to one side, the cliffs and the chasm to another; above that a great causeway of primitive construction stretching for more than a mile from cliff to cliff, high over the water's spray—and some distance off the wide waters of a lake, blue-green and dreamy in the sun. Elric yearned for the peace it offered. Yet he guessed the peace might also be illusory.

"Look, gentlemen," says the Rose, letting her horse break into a bit of a canter, "there's a settlement ahead. Can it be an inn, by any happy chance?"

"It would seem an appropriate place for one, madam. They have a similar establishment at Land's End, in my last situation..." says Wheldrake, cheering.

The sky was overclouded now, dark and brooding, and the sun shone only upon the far-off lake, while from the chasm beside them came unpleasant booming noises, sounds like wailing human voices, savage and greedy. And all three joked nervously about this change in the landscape's mood and said how much they missed the easy boredom of the river and the wheat and would gladly return to it.

The unpainted, ramshackle collection of buildings—a two-storey house with crooked gables surrounded by about a dozen half-ruined outhouses—did, indeed, sport a sign—a crow's carcass nailed to a board. Presumably the indecipherable lettering gave a name to the place.

"'The Putrefied Crow' is good enough for me," says Wheldrake, seemingly in more need of this hostelry than the other two. "A place for pirate meetings and sinister executions. What think you?"

"I'm bound to agree." The Rose nods her pale red curls. "I would not choose to visit it, if there were any choice at all, but you'll note there's none. Let's see, at least, what information we can gain."

In the shadow of that causeway, on the edge of that abyss, the three unlikely companions gave their horses somewhat reluctantly up to an ostler of dirty, though genial, appearance, and stepped inside "the Putrefied Crow," to look with surprise upon the six burly men and women who were already enjoying such hospitality as the place offered.

"Greetings to you, gentlemen. My lady." One of them doffed a hat so trimmed in feathers, ribbons, jewels and other finery its outline was completely lost. All these folk were festooned in lace, velvet, satin, in the most vivid array, with caps and hats and helmets of every fanciful style, their dark curls oiled to mingle with the blue-black beards of the men or fall upon the olive shoulders of the women. All were armed to the teeth and clearly ready to address any argument with steel. "Have you traveled far?"

"Far enough for a day," said Elric, stripping off his gloves and cloak and taking them up to the fire. "And you, my friends. Do you come far?"

"Why," says one of the women, "we are the Companions of the Endless Way. We are travelers, always. Pledged to it. We follow the road. We are the free auxiliaries of the Gypsy Nation. Pure-bred Romans of the Southern Desert, with ancestors who traveled the world before there were nations of any sort!"

"Then I'm delighted to meet you, madam!" Wheldrake shook his hat into the fire, causing it to hiss and spit. "For it's the Gypsy Nation we seek."

"The Gypsy Nation requires no seeking," said the tallest man, in red and white velvet. "The gypsies will always come to you. All you must do is wait. Put a sign upon your door and wait. The season is near-ended. Soon begin the seasons of our passing. Then you shall see the crossing of the Treaty Bridge, by which we keep to our old trail, though the land has long since fallen away."

"The bridge is yours? And the road?" Wheldrake was puzzled. "Can gypsies own such things and still be gypsies?"

"I smell walkerspew!" One of the women rose, a threatening fist upon her dagger's hilt. "I smell the droppings of a professor-bird. There's nonsense in the air and the place for nonsense isn't here."

It was Elric who broke that specific tension, by moving easily between the two. "We are come to parley and perhaps to trade," he said, for he could think of no other excuse they might accept.

"Trade?" This caused a general grinning and muttering amongst the gypsies. "Well, gentlemen, everyone's welcome in the Gypsy Nation. Everyone who has the taste for wandering."

"You'll take us there?"

Again they seemed to find this amusing and Elric guessed few residents of this plane volunteered to travel with the gypsies.

It was clear to Elric that the Rose was deeply suspicious of this cut-throat half-dozen and not at all sure she wished to go with them, yet again she was determined to find the three sisters and would risk any danger to follow them.

"There are friends of ours gone ahead," said Wheldrake, ever the quickest wit in such situations. "Three young ladies, all very alike? Would you have made their acquaintance?"

"We are Romans of the Southern Desert and do not as a rule make small-talk with the *diddicoyim*."

"Ha!" exclaims Wheldrake. "Gypsy snobs! The multiverse reveals nothing but repetitions! And we continue to be surprised by them . . ."

"This is no time for social observation, Master Wheldrake," says the Rose severely.

"Madam, it is always time for that. Or what are we else, but beasts?" He's offended. He winks at the tall gypsy and raises his tiny voice in song. "*I'd rather go with the Gypsy Wild; And bear a Gypsy's nut-brown child!*" He hums the air. "Are you familiar with the ballad, good friends?"

And he charms them enough to make them ease their bodies more comfortably upon their benches and tell patronizing jokes about a variety of non-gypsy peoples, including, of course, Wheldrake's own, while Elric's strange appearance soon gets him nicknamed "the Ermine." which he accepts with the equanimity with which he accepts all other names presented by those who find him unnatural and disturbing. He bides his time with a patience that has become almost physical, as if it is a shell he can strap around himself, to make himself wait. He knows he has but to draw Stormbringer for a minute and six gypsies would lie, drained of life and soul, upon the stained boards of the inn; but also, perhaps that the Rose would die, or Wheldrake, for Stormbringer is not always satisfied merely with the lives of enemies. And because he is an adept, and no other person here, at the roaring edge of the world, has any inkling of his power, he smiles a little to himself. And if the gypsies take it for a placatory grin and tell him he's thin enough to wipe out a whole warren-full of rabbits, then he cares not. He is Elric of Melniboné, prince of ruins, last of his line, and he seeks the receptacle of his dead father's soul. He is a Melnibonéan and he draws upon this atavistic pride for all the strength it can give him, remembering the almost sensuous joy that came with the assumption of his superiority over all other creatures, natural and supernatural, and it armours him, though it brings back, too sharply, the pain in memory.

Meanwhile Wheldrake is teaching four of the gypsies a song with a noisy and vulgar chorus. The Rose engages the landlord in a discussion of the menu. He offers them rabbit couscous. It is all he has. She accepts it on their behalf, they eat as much of the food as they can bear, then retire to a mephitic loft where they sleep as best they can while a variety of bugs and small vermin search across their bodies for some worthwhile morsel, and find little. Elric's blood is never lusted after by insects.

Next morning, before the others wake, Elric creeps down to the kitchen and finds the water-tub, crumbling a little dragon's venom into a tankard, and muffling his own shrieks as the stuff punishes each corpuscle, each cell and atom of his being, and then his strength and arrogance return. He can almost feel the wings beating on his body, bearing him up into the skies where his dragon brothers wait for him. A dragon-song comes to his lips but he stifles that, too. He wishes to learn, not to draw attention to himself. It is the only way he can discover the whereabouts of his father's soul.

The other two find their traveling companion in jovial humour when they come down, already grinning at a joke concerning a famished ferret and a rabbit—the gypsies have a wealth of such bucolic reference, a constant source of amusement to them.

Elric's attempts at similar banter leave them puzzled, but when Wheldrake joins in with a string of stories concerning sheep and jackboots, the ice is thoroughly broken. By the time they ride towards the west cliff and the causeway, the gypsies have decided they are acceptable enough companions and assure them that they will be more than welcome in the Gypsy Nation.

"*Hark, hark, the dogs do bark,*" warbles Wheldrake, still with his mug of breakfast porter in his hand as he leans upon his saddle and admires the grandeur of it all. "To tell you the truth of the matter,

Prince Elric, I was growing a little bored with Putney. Though there was some talk of moving to Barnes."

"They are unsavoury places, then?" says Elric, happy to make ordinary conversation as they ride. "Full of sour magic and so forth?"

"Worse," says Wheldrake, "they are *South of the River*. I believe now I was writing too much. There is little else to do in Putney. Crisis is the true source of creativity, I think. And one thing, sir, that Putney promises is that you shall be free from Crisis."

Listening politely, as one does when a friend discusses the more abstruse or sticky points of their particular creed, Elric let the poet's words act as a lullaby to his still-tortured senses. It was clear that the venom's effect did not lessen with increasing use. But now, he knew, if their gypsy guides proved treacherous he would be able to kill them without much effort. He was a little contemptuous of local opinion. These ruffians might have terrorized the farmers of these parts, but they were clearly no match for trained fighters. And he knew he could rely on the Rose in any engagement, though Wheldrake would be next to useless. There was an air of awkwardness about him which made it clear that his use of a sword was more likely to confuse than threaten any opponent.

From time to time he shared glances with his friends, but it was clear neither had any idea of an alternative. Since the ones they sought had searched for the Gypsy Nation there could be no reason for not at least discovering what exactly the Gypsy Nation was.

Elric watched as the Rose, to release some of her anxiety no doubt, suddenly let her horse have free rein and went galloping along the narrow track beside the chasm while stones and tufts of clay and turf went tumbling down into the darkness and the roar of the unseen river. Then, one by one, the gypsies followed, galloping their horses with daredevil skill in the Rose's wake, yelling and hallooing, jumping up in their saddles, leaping and diving, as if all this were completely natural to them, and now Elric laughed joyously to see *their* joy, and Wheldrake clapped and hooted like a boy at the circus. And then they had come to the great wall of garbage, higher than anything Elric had seen earlier, where more gypsies waited at a passage they had made through the waste and they greeted their fellows with all manner of heartiness, while Elric, Wheldrake and the Rose were subjected to the same off-hand contempt with which they treated all non-gypsies.

"They wish to join our free-roaming band," said the tall man in red and white. "As I told them, we never reject a recruit." And he guffawed as he accepted a somewhat overripe peach from one of the other gypsies' bags. "There's precious little to forage as usual. It's always thus at the end of the season, and at the beginning." He cocked his head suddenly. "But the season comes. Soon. We shall go to meet it."

Elric himself thought he felt the ground shivering slightly and heard something like a distant piping, a far-off drum, a drone. Was their god slithering along his causeway from one lair to the next? Were he and his companions to be sacrifices for that god? Was that what the gypsies found amusing?

"Which season?" asked the Rose, almost urgently, her long fingers combing at her curls.

"The Season of our Passing. Indeed, the *Seasons* of our Passing," said a woman spitting plum stones to the ashy filth of the ground. Then she had mounted her horse and was leading them through the passage, out onto the fleshy hardness of the great causeway, which trembled and shook as if from a distant earthquake and now, in the far distance, from the east, Elric looked down the mile-wide road and he saw movement, heard more noise, and he realized something was coming towards them even as they approached.

"Great Scott!" cried Wheldrake, lifting his hat in a gesture of amazement. "What can it be?"

It was a kind of darkness, a flickering of heavy shadows, of the occasional spark of light, of a constant and increasing shaking, which made the banks of garbage bounce and scatter and the carrion creatures rise in squawking flurries of flesh and feather. And it was still many miles off.

To the gypsies the phenomenon was so familiar they paid it not the slightest attention, but Elric, the Rose and Wheldrake could not keep their eyes away.

Now the rocking increased, a steady motion doubtless created partly by the free span of the road over the bay, until it was gentle but relentless, as if a giant's hand rocked them all in some bizarre cradle, and the shadow on the horizon grew larger and larger, filling the causeway from bank to bank.

"We are the free people. We follow the road and call no man our master!" sang out one of the women.

"Hear! Hear!" chirrups Wheldrake. "Hey-ho, for the open road!" But his voice falters a little as they draw nearer and see what now approaches, the first of many.

It is like a ship, but it is not a ship. It is a great wooden platform, as wide across as a good-sized village, with monstrous wheels on gigantic axles carrying it slowly forward. Around the bottom edge of the platform is a kind of leather curtain; around the top edge is built a stockade, and beyond that are the roofs and spires of a town, all moving on the platform, with slow, steady momentum, with dwellings for an entire tribe of settled folk.

It is only one of hundreds.

Behind that first comes another platform, with its own village, its own skyline, flying its own flags. Behind that is another. The causeway is crowded with these platforms, rumbling and creaking and, at turtle pace, ploughing steadily on, packing the refuse into the ground, making still smoother the smoothness of their road.

"My God!" whispers Wheldrake. "It is a nightmare by Brueghel! It is Blake's vision of Apocalypse!"

"It's an unnerving sight, right enough." The Rose tucks the tongue of her belt into its loop another notch and frowns. "A nomad nation, to be sure!"

"You are, it seems, pretty self-sufficient," says Wheldrake to one of the gypsies, who assents with proud gravity. "How many of those townships travel this way?"

The gypsy shakes his head and shrugs. He is not sure. "Some two thousand," he says, "but not all move as swiftly as these. There are cities of the Second Season following these, and cities of the Third Season following those."

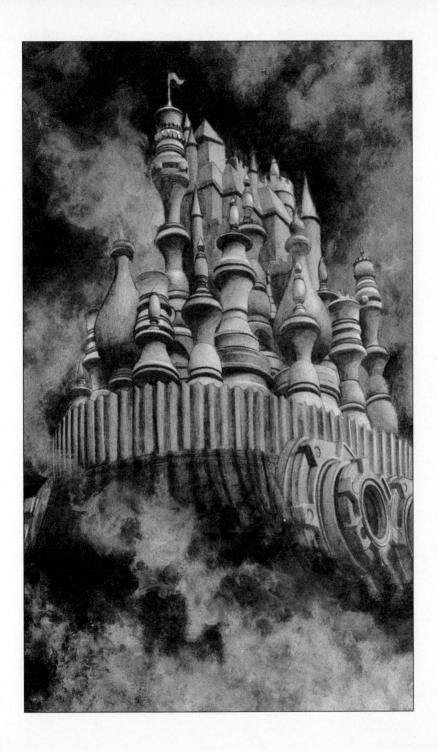

"And the Fourth Season?"

"You know we have no fourth season. That we leave for you." The gypsy laughs as if at a simpleton. "Otherwise we should have no wheat."

Elric listens to the babble and the hullabaloo of the massive platforms, sees people climbing upon the walls, leaning over, shouting to one another. He smells all the stenches of any ordinary town, hears every ordinary sound, and he marvels at the things, all made of wood and iron rivets and bits bound together with brass or copper or steel, of wood so ancient it resembles rock, of wheels so huge they would crush a man as a dog-cart casually crushes an ant. He sees the washing fluttering on lines, makes out signs announcing various crafts and trades. Soon the traveling platforms are so close they dwarf him and he must look up to see the gleam of the greased axles, the old, metal-shod wheels, each spoke of which is almost as tall as one of Imrryr's towers, the smell, the deep smell of life in all its variety. And high above his head now geese shriek, dogs put their front paws upon the ramparts and bark and snarl for the pure pleasure of barking and snarling, while children peer down at them and try to spit on the heads of the strangers, shouting catcalls and infant witticisms to those below, to be cuffed by parents who in turn remark on the oddness of the strangers and do not seem over-enthusiastic that their ranks have grown. On both sides of them now the wheels creak by and from the sides are flung the pails of slops and ordure which form both banks, while here and there, walking behind the platforms, come men, women and children armed with brooms with which they whisk the refuse up onto the heaps, disturbing the irritated carrion eaters, creating clouds of dust and flies, or sometimes pausing to squabble and scrabble over a choice piece of detritus.

"Raggle-taggle, indeed," says Master Wheldrake, putting his huge red handkerchief to his face and coughing mightily. "Pray tell me, sir—where does this great road go?"

"Go, man?" The gypsy shakes his head in disbelief. "Why nowhere and everywhere. This is our road. The road of the Free Travelers. It follows itself, little poet! It winds around the world!"

CHAPTER FOUR

On Joining the Gypsies. Some Unusual Definitions
Concerning the Nature of Liberty.

And now, as Elric and his companions wandered in amazement amongst the advancing wheels, they saw that behind this first rank of moving villages came a vast mass of people; men, women and children of all ages, of all classes and in all conditions, talking and arguing and playing games as they went, some walking with an air of unconcerned familiarity in the wake of those pounding rims; others unaccountably miserable, hats in hands, weeping; their dogs and other domestic animals with them, like people on a pilgrimage. The mounted gypsies had disappeared by now, to join their own kind, and had no interest at all in the three they had found.

Wheldrake leaned down from his horse and addressed a genial matron, of the type which often took a fancy to him. His hat was swept from his red comb, his little bantam's eyes sparkled. "Forgive me for this interruption, madam. We are newcomers to your nation and thought perhaps we should seek out your authorities . . ."

"There are no authorities, little rooster, in the Gypsy Nation." She laughed at this absurdity. "We are all free here. We have a council, but it does not meet until the next season. If you would join us, as it seems you have already done, then you must find a village which will accept you. Failing that, you must walk." She pointed behind her without interrupting her stride. "Back there is best. The forward villages tend to be full of purebloods and they are never very welcoming. But someone there will be glad to take you in."

"We're obliged to you, ma'am."

"Many welcome the horseman," she said, as if quoting an old adage. "There is none more free than the gypsy rider."

On through this great march, which spanned the road from bank to squalid bank, rode Elric, Wheldrake and the Rose, sometimes greeting those who walked, sometimes being greeted in turn. There was in many parts a festive quality to the throng. There were snatches of song from here and there, a sudden merry barrel-organ reel, the sound of a fiddle. And elsewhere, in rhythm with their stride, people joined in a popular chant.

> "We have sworn the Gypsy Oath,
>   To uphold the Gypsy Law,
>   Death to all who disobey!
>   Death to all who disobey!"

Of which Wheldrake was disapproving on a number of moral, ethical, aesthetic and metrical counts. "I'm all for primitivism, friend Elric, but primitivism of the finer type. This is mere xenophobia. Scarcely a national epic . . ."

—But which the Rose found charming.

While Elric, lifting his head as a dragon might, to scent the wind, caught sight of a boy running at unseemly speed from beneath the wheels of one of the gigantic platforms and over to the banks of refuse (now being freshened by every settlement that rolled slowly by). The boy was trying to scramble up armed with pieces of board on hands and feet which were meant to aid his progress but actually only hampered him.

He was wild with terror now and screaming, but the chanting crowd marched by as if he did not exist. The boy tried to climb back to the road but the boards trapped him further. Again his cry was piteous over the confident chanting of the marching gypsies. Then, from somewhere, a black-fletched arrow flew, taking him in the throat to silence him. Blood ran from between his writhing lips. The boy was dying. Not a soul did more than flick a glance in his direction.

The Rose was forcing her horse through the people, shouting at them for their lack of concern, trying to reach the boy whose dying movements were burying him deeper in the filth. As Elric, Wheldrake and the Rose arrived it was clear that he was dead. Elric reached towards the corpse—and another black-fletched arrow came from above to bury itself squarely in the child's heart.

Elric looked back, enraged, and only Wheldrake and the Rose

together stopped him from drawing his sword and seeking the source of the arrow.

"Foul cowardice! Foul cowardice!"

"Perhaps he committed a fouler crime," cautioned the Rose. She took hold of Elric's hand, leaning from her saddle to do so. "Be patient, albino. We are here to learn what these people can tell us, not challenge their customs."

Elric accepted her wisdom. He had witnessed far crueler actions amongst his own people and knew well enough how an outrageous deed of torture could seem like simple justice to some. So he controlled himself, but looked with even more wariness upon the crowd as the Rose led them on towards the next rank of moving villages, creaking with infinite slowness, no faster than an old man's pace, along the flesh-coloured highway, their long leather skirts brushing the ground as they advanced like so many massive dowagers out for an evening stroll.

"What sorcery powers those settlements," murmured the Rose as they moved, at last, through the stragglers, "and how can we get aboard one? These people won't chat. There is something they fear . . ."

"Clearly, madam." Elric looked back to where the boy had died, his sprawled corpse still visible upon the piled garbage.

"A free society such as this must pay no taxes, therefore can pay no-one to police it—therefore the family and the blood-feud become the chief instruments of justice and the law," said Wheldrake, still very distressed. "They are the only recourse. I would guess the boy paid for some relative's misdemeanour, if not his own. '*Blood for blood! groaned the Desert King, And an eye, I swear, for an eye. 'Ere this day's sun sets on Omdurman, the Nazarene must die!*' Not mine! Not mine!" he said hastily, "but a great favourite amongst the residents of Putney. M.C. O'Crook, the popular pantomime artist, wrote it I was told . . ."

Believing the little poet merely babbled to comfort himself, Elric and the Rose paid him little attention, and now the Rose was hailing the nearest gigantic platform which approached, its skirts scraping and hissing, and from which, through a gap in the leather curtains, there strolled a man in bright green velvet with purple trimmings, a gold ring through his earlobe, more gold about his wrists and throat, a gold chain about his waist. His dark eyes looked them over, then he shook his head curtly and returned through the curtain. Wheldrake made to follow him, but hesitated. "For what, I wonder, are we being auditioned?"

"Let's discover that by trial," said the Rose, pushing her hair back from her face and flexing a strong hand as she rode towards the next slow-moving mass, to find a head poked out at her and a red-capped woman glancing at them without much curiosity before turning back in. Another and another followed. A fellow in a painted leather jerkin and a brass helmet was more interested in their horses than themselves, but eventually jerked his thumb to dismiss them, making Elric murmur that he would have no more to do with these barbarians but would find some other path and fulfill his quest that way.

The next village sent out a well-to-do old gypsy in a headscarf and embroidered waistcoat, his black velvet breeches tucked into white stockings. "We need the horses," he said, "but you seem like intellectuals to me. The last thing this village requires are trouble-makers of that sort. So I'll bid thee fare-thee-well."

"We are valued neither for our looks nor our brains," said Wheldrake with a grin, "and only a little, it seems, for our horses."

"Persevere, Master Wheldrake," the Rose was grim, "for we must find our sisters and it's my guess a village that will admit them will also have something in common with a village that will welcome us."

It was poor logic, reflected the albino, but logic, at least, of a sort, and he had nothing better to offer.

Five more villages inspected them and five more times they were rejected until, out of a village that seemed smaller and perhaps a little better-kept than most of the others, sauntered a tall man whose somewhat gaunt appearance was tempered by a pair of amused blue eyes, his attention to costume suggesting a pleasure in life belied by his features. "Good evening to you, gentlefolk," he said, his voice musical and a little affected, "I am Amarine Goodool. You have something interesting about you. Are you artists, by any chance? Or perhaps story-tellers? Or you have, possibly, some affecting story of your own? As you see, we grow a trifle bored in Trollon."

"I am Wheldrake, the poet." The little coxcomb stepped forward without reference to his companions. "And I have written verse for kings, queens and commoners. I have published verse, moreover, in more than one century and have pursued the vocation of poet in more than one incarnation. I have a facility with metre, sir, which all envy— peers and my betters, sir, as a matter of fact. And I also have a certain gift for spontaneous versification, of sorts. *In Trollon, elegant and slow, dwelled Amarine Goodool, famed for his costume and his wit. To friends so valuable was he, they even saved his—*"

"And I am called the Rose and travel upon a quest for vengeance. My journey has taken me through more than one realm."

"Aha!" said Amarine Goodool. "You have followed the megaflow! You have broken down the walls between the realms! You have crossed the invisible barriers of the multiverse! And you, sir? You, my pale friend? What skills have you?"

"At home, in my own quiet town, I had some reputation as a conjuror and philosopher," said Elric meekly.

"Well, well, sir, but you would not be with this company if you had not something to offer. Your philosophy, perhaps, is of an unusual sort?"

"Fairly conventional, sir, I would say."

"Nonetheless, sir. Nonetheless. You have a horse. Please enter. And be welcome to Trollon. I think it very likely you will find yourselves amongst fellow spirits here. We are all a little odd in Trollon!" And he raised his head in a friendly bray.

Now he led them through the skirts of the village, into a musky darkness lit by dim lamps so that first it was possible to perceive only the vaguest of shapes. It was as if they had entered a vast stable, with row upon row of stalls disappearing into the distance. Elric smelled horses and human sweat and as they passed up a central aisle he could look down the rows and see the glistening backs of men, women and adolescents, leaning hard against poles reaching to their chests and pushing the huge edifice forward, inch by inch. Elsewhere horses were harnessed in ranks, also, trudging on heavy hoofs as they hauled at the thick ropes attached to the roof beams.

"Leave your horses with the lad," said Amarine Goodool, indicating a ragged youth who held out his hand for a small coin and grinned with pleasure at the value of what he received. "You'll be given receipts and so on. You'll be at ease for at least a couple of seasons to be sure. Or, if you are otherwise successful, for ever. Like myself. Of course," he lowered his tone as he swung up a wooden stairway, "there are other responsibilities one must accept."

The long staircase led them, spiral by spiral, to the surface until they clambered out into a nondescript narrow sidestreet from whose open windows people looked idly down without breaking their conversation. It was a picture of such ordinariness that it contrasted all the more with the scenes below.

"Are those people down there slaves, sir?" Wheldrake had to know.

"Slaves! By no means! They are free gypsy souls, like myself. Free to wander the great highway that spans the world, to breathe the air of liberty. They merely take their turn at the marching boards, as most of us must for some time in their lives. They perform a civic duty, sir."

"And should they not wish to perform such duty?" asked Elric quietly.

"Ah, well, sir, I can see that you are indeed a philosopher. Things so abstruse are beyond me, I fear, sir. But there are people in Trollon who would be only too pleased to debate such abstractions." He patted Elric amiably upon the shoulder. "Indeed, I can think of more than one friend of mine who will gladly welcome you."

"A prosperous place, this Trollon." The Rose looked through the gaps in the buildings to where similar villages moved at a similar pace.

"Well, we like to preserve certain standards, madam. I will arrange for your receipts."

"I do not think we plan to trade our horses here," said Elric. "We need to travel on as soon as possible."

"And travel you shall, sir. Travel, after all, is in our blood. But we must put your horses to work. Or, sir," he uttered a little snigger, "we shall not be traveling far at all, eh?"

Again a glance from the Rose stilled Elric's retort. But he was growing increasingly impatient as he thought of his dead father and the threat which hung over them both.

"We are only too happy to accept your hospitality," said the Rose diplomatically. "Are we the only people to join Trollon in recent days?"

"Did you have friends come ahead of you, lady?"

"Three sisters, perhaps?" suggested Wheldrake.

"Three sisters?" He shook his head. "I should have known if I had seen them, sir. But I will send enquiry of our neighbouring villages. Meanwhile, if you are hungry, I shall be only too happy to loan you a few credits. We have some wonderful restaurants in Trollon."

It was clear that there was little poverty in Trollon. The paint was fresh and the glass sparkling, while the streets were neat and clean as anything Elric had ever seen.

"It seems all the squalor and hardship is kept out of sight below," whispered Wheldrake. "I shall be glad to leave this place, Prince Elric."

"We might find ourselves in difficulties when we decide to end our stay." The Rose was careful not to be overheard. "Do they plan to make slaves of us, like those poor wretches down there?"

"I would guess they have no immediate intention of sending us to their marching boards," said Elric, "but I have no doubt they want us for our muscles and our horses as much as for our company. I do not intend to remain long in this place if I cannot quickly discover some clue to what I seek. I have little time." His old arrogance was returning. His old impatience.

He tried to quell them, as signs of the disease which had led to his present dilemma. He hated his own blood, his sorcery, his reliance upon his runesword, or other extraordinary means of sustenance. And when Amarine Goodool brought them into the village square (complete with shops and public buildings and houses of evident age) to meet a committee of welcome, Elric was less than warm, though he knew that lies, hypocrisy and deception were the order of the moment. His attempt to smile did not bring any answering gaiety.

"Gweetings, gweetings," cried an apparition in green, with a little pointed beard and a hat threatening to engulf his entire head and half his body. "On behalf of the Twollon weins-men and -morts, may we vawda yoah eeks with joy. Or, in the common speech, you must considah us all, now, your bwothahs and sistahs. My name is Filigwip Nant and I wun the theatwicals . . ." Whereupon he proceeded to introduce a miscellaneous group of people with odd-sounding names, peculiar accents and unnatural complexions whose appearance seemed to fill Wheldrake with horrified recognition. "It could be the Putney Fine Arts Society," he murmured, "or worse, the Surbiton Poetasters—I have been a reluctant guest of them both, and many more. Ilkley, as I recall, was the worst . . ." and he lapsed into his own gloomy contemplations as, with a smile no more convincing than the albino's, he suffered the roll-call of parochial fame, until he opened his little beak to a sky still filled with cloud and spray and began a kind of protective declamation which had him surrounded at once by green, black and purple velvet, by rustling brocade and romantic lace, by the scent of a hundred garden flowers and herbs, by the gypsy literati. And borne away.

The Rose and Elric also had their share of temporary acolytes. This was clearly a village of some wealth, which yearned for novelty.

"We're very cosmopolitan, you know, in Trollon. Like most of the 'diddicoyim' (ha, ha) villages, we are now almost wholly made up from outsiders. I, myself, am an outsider. From another realm, you know. From Heeshigrowinaaz, actually. Are you familiar—?" A middle-aged woman with an elaborate wig and considerable paint linked her bangled arm in Elric's. "I'm Parapha Foz. My husband's Barraban Foz, of course. Isn't it boring?"

"I have the feeling," said the Rose in an undertone as she went by with her own burden of enthusiasts, "that this is to be the greatest ordeal of them all . . ."

But it seemed to Elric that she was also amused, especially by his own expression.

And he bowed, with graceful irony, to the inevitable.

There followed a number of initiating rituals with which Elric was unfamiliar, but which Wheldrake dreaded as being all too familiar, and the Rose accepted, as if she, too, had once known such experiences better.

There were meals and speeches and performances, tours of the oldest and quaintest parts of the village, small lectures on its history and its architecture and how wonderfully it had been restored until Elric, brooding always on his father's stolen soul, wished that they would turn into something with which he could more easily contend—like the hopping, slittering, drooling monsters of Chaos or some unreasonable demigod. He had rarely wished so longingly to draw his sword and let it silence this mélange of prejudice, semi-ignorance, snobbery and received opinion, of loud, superior voices so thoroughly reassured by all they met and read that they believed themselves confidently, unvulnerably, totally in control of reality . . .

And all the while Elric thought of the poor souls below, pressing their bodies against the marching boards and sending this village, in concert with all the other free gypsy villages, in its relentless progress, inch by inch, around the world.

Unused to gaining the information he required by any means less direct than torture, Elric left it to the Rose to glean whatever she could and eventually, when they were alone together, Wheldrake having been taken as a trophy to sport at some dinner, she relaxed into a mood of satisfaction. They had been given adjoining rooms in what they were assured was the best inn of its sort in any of the second-rank villages. Tomorrow, they were told, they would be shown what apartments were available to them.

"We have survived this first day well, I think," she said, sitting on a chest to remove her doeskin boots. "We have proven interesting enough to them so that we still have our lives, relative liberty and, most important now, I think, our swords . . ."

"You mistrust them thoroughly, then?" The albino looked curiously at the Rose as she shook out her pale red-gold hair and peeled off her brown jerkin to reveal a blouse of dark yellow. "I have never encountered such folk before."

"Save that they are drawn from every part of the multiverse, they are very much of a type I left behind me long ago and like poor Wheldrake hoped never to encounter again. The sisters reached the Gypsy Nation less than a week before we did. The woman who told me this had it from a woman she knows in the next village. The sisters, however, were accepted by a village of the forward rank."

"And we can find them there?" Elric knew so much relief he only then realized how desperate he had become.

"Not so easily. We have no invitation to visit the village. There are forms to be observed before we can receive such an invitation. However, I also learned that Gaynor, of whom you spoke, is here, though he disappeared almost immediately and no-one has any notion of his whereabouts."

"He has not left the Nation?"

"I gather that is not easily done, even by the likes of Gaynor." There was suddenly an extra bitterness to her voice.

"It is forbidden?"

"Nothing," she echoed sardonically, "is forbidden in the Gypsy Nation. Unless," she added, "it is change of any kind!"

"Then why was the boy killed?"

"They tell me they know nothing about it. They told me they thought I was probably mistaken. They said they felt it was morbid to study the garbage heaps and think one saw things lurking in them. In short, as far as they are concerned, no boy was killed."

"He was trying to escape, however. We both saw that. From what, my lady?"

"They will not say, Prince Elric. There are subjects forbidden by good manners, it seems. As in many societies, I suppose, where the very fundamentals of their existence are the subject of the deepest taboos. What is this terror of reality, I wonder, which plagues the human spirit?"

"I am not, at present, looking for the answers to such questions, madam," said Elric, finding even the Rose's speculations irritating after so much babble. "My own view is that we should leave Trollon and head back to the village which accepted the three sisters. Did they know the name?"

"Duntrollin. Odd that they should accept the sisters at all. They are some kind of warrior-order, I understand, pledged to the defense of the road and its travelers. The Gypsy Nation is comprised of thousands of such mobile cantons, each with its peculiar contribution to the whole. A dream of democratic perfection, one might suppose."

"Were it not for the marching boards," said Elric, disturbed, even now, to know that as he prepared himself for rest, the great platform on which all this existed was being pushed gradually forward by emaciated men, women and children.

He slept badly that night, though he was not plagued by his usual nightmares. And for that small mercy he was grateful.

Breakfasting in a common hall, still hygienically free of any sign of a real commoner, served by young women in peasant frocks who found their work amusing rather than arduous, like children in a play, the three friends again shared what little they had discovered.

"They never stop moving," said Wheldrake. "The very thought is hideous to them. They believe their entire society will be destroyed if once they bring this vast caravan to a halt. So their *hoi polloi*, whatever their circumstances, push, with or without the help of horses, the villages on. And it is debtors and vagabonds and defaulters and creators of minor grievances who make up the throng walking on the road. These are, as it were, middle-class offenders of no great consequence. The fear of all is that they should join those at the marching boards and therefore lose their status and most chances of regaining it again. Their morals and their laws are based upon the rock, as it were, of perpetual motion. The boy wanted to stop walking, I gather, and there is only one rule where that is concerned—Move or Die. And Move Forward Always. I've lived in Gloriana's age, and Victoria's, and Elizabeth's, yet never have I encountered quite such fascinating and original hypocrisies."

"Are there no exceptions? Must everyone constantly move?" asked the Rose.

"There are no exceptions." Wheldrake helped himself to a dish of mixed meats and cheeses. "I must say that their standard of cuisine is excellent. One becomes so grateful for such things. If you were ever, for instance, in Ripon and had a positive dislike of the pie, you would starve." He poured himself a little light beer. "So we have our sisters. We believe Gaynor could be with them. We now need an invitation to

Duntrollin, I take it. Which reminds me, why have they not asked you to give up your weapons? None here appears to sport a blade."

"I think they might be our next means of earning a season or two away from the boards," said Elric, who had also considered this. "They have no need to demand them. They will, they believe, possess them soon—for rent, or food or whatever it is they know people always prefer to liberty . . ." And he chewed moodily on his bread and stared into the middle-distance, lost in some unhappy memory.

> "Thus by deep injustice is that Unjust State upheld;
> Thus by gags of deedless piety old Albion's voice is
> still'd."
> .

intoned the little poet, rather mournful himself. "Is there no luxury that is not the creation of someone else's misery?" he wondered. "Was there ever a world where all were equal?"

"Oh, indeed," said the Rose with some alacrity. "Indeed, there was. My own!" And then she hesitated, thought better of her outburst, and fell silent over her porridge, leaving the others at something of a loss for conversation.

"Why, I wonder, are we discouraged from leaving this paradise?" said Elric at last. "How does the Gypsy Nation justify its strictures?"

"By one of a thousand similar arguments, friend Elric, I'm sure. Something circular, no doubt. And singularly apt, all in all. One is never short of metaphors as one travels the multiverse."

"I suppose not, Master Wheldrake. But perhaps that circular argument is the only means by which any of us rationalizes their existence?"

"Indeed, sir. Quite likely."

And now the Rose was joining in with *sotto voce* reminders to Wheldrake that they were not here as Detectives of the Abstract but were searching with some urgency for the three sisters, who carried with them certain objects of power—or, at least, a key to the discovery of those objects. Wheldrake, knowing his own weakness for such tempting trains of thought, apologized. But before they could resume the subject of leaving Trollon and somehow gaining access to Duntrollin the outer doors of the room swung inwards to reveal a magnificent figure, all ballooning silks and lace, a mighty wig staggering on his head and his exquisite face painted with all the subtlety of a Jharkorian concubine.

"Forgive my interrupting your breakfast. My name is Vailadez Rench, at your service. I am here, dear friends, to offer you a choice of accommodation, so that you may begin to fit in with our community as quickly as possible. I gather you have the means of taking quarters of the better type?"

Having no choice for the moment, unless they were to arouse the Trollonian's suspicions, they followed meekly in Vailadez Rench's wake as the tall exquisite led them through the tidy and rather over-polished lanes of his picturesque little town. And still, inch by inch, the Gypsy Nation rolled on along the road it had beaten for centuries, creating a momentum that must be maintained above all other considerations. And forever returning to the identical point of arrival and departure.

They were shown a house upon the edge of the platform, looking out over the walls towards the distant walkers and the other snail-crawling settlements. They were shown apartments in quaint old gabled houses or converted from warehouses or stores, and eventually they were led by Vailadez Rench, whose sole conversation revolved, like some tight-wrought fugue, about the subject of Property, its desirability and its value, to a little house with a patch of garden outside it, the walls covered in climbing tea-roses and brilliant nunshabit, all glowing purples and golds, the windows glittering and framed by lace, and smelling sweet and fresh as spring from the herb-beds and the flowers; the Rose clapped her hands and for a moment it was clear she was tempted by the house, with its crooked roof and time-black gables. Something within her longed for such ordinary beauty and comfort. And Elric saw her expression change and she looked away. "It's pretty, this house," she said. "Perhaps it could be shared by all of us?"

"Oh, yes. It has a family, you see. Quite large. But they had their tragedies, you know, and must leave." Vailadez Rench sighed, then grinned and wagged a finger at her. "You've chosen the most expensive, yet! You have taste, dear lady."

Wheldrake, who had taken a gloomy dislike of this Paladin of Property, made some graceless remark which was ignored by everyone, for all their different reasons. He reached his nose towards a luscious paeony bush. "Is their scent here?"

Vailadez Rench rapped upon a door he could not open. "They were given their documents. They should be gone. There was some kind of disaster . . . Well, we must be merciful, I suppose, and thank the stars we are not ourselves sliding towards the board-hold and the eternal tramp."

The door was opened with a snap—wide—and there stood before them a disheveled, round-eyed, red-faced fellow, almost as tall as Elric, with a quill in one hand and an inkpot in the other. "Dear sir! Dear sir! Bear with me, I beg you. I am at this very moment addressing a letter to a relative. There is no question of my credit. You know yourself what delays exist, these days, between the villages." He scratched his untidy, corn-coloured hair with the nib of his pen, causing dark green ink to run down his forehead and give him something of the appearance of a demented savage prepared for war. While his alert blue eyes went from face to face, his lips appealed. "I have such clients! Bills are not paid, you know, by dead people. Or by disappointed people. I am a clairvoyant. It is my vocation. My dear mother is a clairvoyant, and my brothers and sisters and, greatest of all, my noble son, Koropith. My Uncle Grett was famous across the Nation and beyond. Still more famous were we all before our fall."

"Your fall, sir?" asked Wheldrake, very curious and taking to the man at once. "Your debts?"

"Debt, sir, has pursued us across the multiverse. That is a constant, sir. It is *our* constant, at least. I speak of our fall from the king's favour, in the land my family had made its own and hoped to settle. Salgarafad, it was called, in a rim-sphere long forgotten by the Old Gardener, and why should it be otherwise? But death is not our fault, sir. It is not. We are friends to Death, but not His servants. And the king swore we had brought the plague by predicting it. And so we were forced to flee. Politics, in my view, had much to do with the matter. But we are not permitted to the counsels of the steersmen, let alone the Lords of the

Higher Worlds, whom we serve, sir, in our own way, my family and myself."

This speech concluded, he drew breath, put one inky fist upon his right hip, the second, still holding the bottle, he rested across his chest. "The credits are," he insisted, "in the post."

"Then you can be found easily enough, dear sir, and reinstated here. Perhaps another house? But I would remind you, your credits were based upon certain services performed by your sister and your uncle on behalf of the community. And they are no longer resident here."

"You put them to the boards!" cried the threatened resident. "You gave them up to the marching boards. Admit it!"

"I am not privy to such matters. This property, sir, is required. Here are the new renters . . ."

"No," says the Rose, "not so. I will not be the cause of this man and his family losing their home!"

"Sentiment! Silly sentiment!" Vailadez Rench roared with laughter that held in it every kind of insult, every heartless mockery. "My dear madam, this family has rented property it cannot afford. You *can* afford it. That is a simple, natural rule, sir. That is a fact of the world, sir." (These last addressed to the offending debtor.) "Let us through, sir. Let us through. We uphold our time-honoured Right to View!" With which he pushed past the unfortunate letter-writer and drew the puzzled trio behind him into a dark passageway from which stairs led. From the landing peered bright button-eyes which might have belonged to a weasel, while from the stairs another pair of eyes regarded them with smouldering rage. They entered a large, untidy room, full of threadbare furnishings and old documents, where, in a wheeled chair made of ivory and boarwood, a tiny figure sat hunched. Again only the eyes seemed alive—black, penetrating eyes of no apparent intelligence. "Mother, they invade!" cried the besieged householder. "Oh, sir, you are cruel, to practise such fierce rectitude upon a frail old woman! How can she walk, sir? How can she move?"

"She must be pushed, Master Fallogard! She will roll as we all roll. Forward, always forward. To a finer future, Master Fallogard. We work for that, you know." Vailadez Rench stooped to peer at the old woman. "Thus do we maintain the integrity of our great Nation."

"I had read somewhere," said Master Wheldrake quietly, stepping a little further into the room and inspecting it as if he truly intended to make it his home, "that a society dedicated solely to the preservation of her past, soon has only her past to sell. Why not stop the village, Master Rench, so that the old lady shall not have to move?"

"You enjoy these obscenities, I suppose, sir, in your own realm? They are not appreciated here." Vailadez Rench looked down his long nose—a stork offering a parakeet only disdain. "The platforms must *always* move. The Nation must *always* move. There can be no *pause* to the gypsy's way. And any who would *block* our way are our *enemies*! Any not invited to set foot on our road but who tread it in defiance of our laws—they are our *deadly* enemies, for they represent the many who would block our way and attempt to bring to a halt the Gypsy Nation, which has traveled, for more than a thousand times, the circumference of the world, over land and sea, along the road of their own making. The Free Road of the Free Gypsy People!"

"I, too, was taught schoolboy litanies to explain the follies of my own country," said Wheldrake, turning away. "I have no quarrel with such wounded, needy souls as yourself, who must chant a creed as some kind of primitive charm against the unknown. It seems to me, as I travel the multiverse, that reliance upon such insistencies is what all mortals have in common. Million upon million of different tribes, each with its own fiercely defended truth."

"Bravo, sir!" cries Fallogard Phatt with a wave of his generous quill (and ink goes flying over mother, books and papers), "but do not elaborate on such sentiments, I warn you! They are mine. They are my whole family's, yet they are forbidden here, as in so many worlds. Do not speak so frankly, sir, lest you'd follow my uncle and my sister to the boards and the Long Stroll to Oblivion."

"Heretic! You have no right to such fine Property!" Vailadez Rench's lugubrious features twist with dismay, his delicate paint glowing from the heat of his own offended blood, as if some exotic fruit of Eden had bloomed and given voice simultaneously. "Evictors must be summoned and that will not be pleasant for Fallogard Phatt and the Family Phatt!"

"What remains of it," grumbles Phatt, suddenly downhearted, as if he had always anticipated his defeat. "I have a dozen futures. Which to pick?" And he closes his eyes and screws up his face as if he, too, has sipped a dragon's diluted venom, and he lets out a great keening noise, the cry of a wronged soul, the despairing voice of a creature which sees Justice suddenly as a Chimera and all displays of it a mere Charade. "A dozen futures, but still no fairness for the common folk! Where does this Tanelorn, this paradise, exist?"

And Elric, who is the only one Phatt is ever likely to meet who could supply him with anything but a metaphysical answer, remains silent, for in Tanelorn he took a vow as all do who receive her protection and her peace. Only true seekers after peace shall find Tanelorn, for Tanelorn is a secret carried by every mortal. And Tanelorn exists wherever mortals gather in mutual determination to serve the common good, creating as many paradises as there are human souls . . .

"I was told," he said, "that it exists within oneself."

At which Fallogard Phatt laid down his pen and ink, picked up a sack in which he had already, it appeared, packed his necessities, and began with downcast eyes to wheel his old mother from the room, calling out for the other members of his family as he did so.

Vailadez Rench watched them trail off with their bundles and their keepsakes and sniffed with considerable satisfaction as he looked around the house. "A lick of paint will soon brighten this property," he assured them, "and we will, of course, have all this clutter sent for salvage and put to efficient use. We are well rid, I'm sure you will agree, of the Family Phatt and that disgusting valetudinarian!"

By now Elric's self-control was growing weak and had it not been for the Rose's steady eyes upon him, for Wheldrake's grim and furious silence, he would have spoken his mind. As it was, the Rose approved the house, agreed the lease and accepted the keys from the fastidious fingers of that Sultan of Sophistry, dismissed him swiftly and then led them in hurried pursuit of the exiled debtors, sighting them as they made their way slowly towards the nearest downside stairway.

Elric saw her catch up with Fallogard Phatt, place a comforting hand upon the shoulder of an adolescent girl, whisper a word in the ear of the mother, give a friendly tug to the hair of the boy, and bring them, bewildered, back with her. "They are to live with us—or at least upon our credit. That cannot, surely, be against even the Gypsy Nation's peculiar sense of security."

Elric regarded the threadbare group with some dismay, having no wish to burden himself with a family, especially one which seemed to him so feckless. He glanced at the girl, dark and petulant in her blossoming beauty, her expression one of almost permanent contempt for everything she looked upon, while the boy, aged about ten, had the black eyes he had noted on the stairs: the weasel's alert and eager eyes, and a narrow, pointed face to add to the effect, his long, blond hair slicked hard against his skull, his small-fingered hands twitching and eager, the nose questing, as if he already scented vermin. And when he grinned, in grateful understanding of the Rose's charity, he revealed sharp little teeth, white against the moist redness of his lips. "You shall see an end to your quest, lady," he said. "Blood and sap shall blend again—lest Chaos decide to challenge this prognosis. There is a road between the worlds that leads to a better place than the one on which we travel. You must take the Infinite Path, lady, and look at the end of it for the resolution to your troubles."

Instead of responding with puzzlement or fear to his strange words, the Rose smiled and bent to kiss him. "Clairvoyant, all of you?" she asked.

"It is the chief business of the Family Phatt," said Fallogard Phatt with some dignity. "It has always been our privilege to read the cards, see through the crystal's mist and know the future such as it ever can be foretold with any certainty. Which is why, of course, we were not unhappy when we found we must join the Gypsy Nation. But, we discovered, these folk have no true clairvoyance, merely a collection of tricks and illusions with which to impress or control others. Once their people had the richest powers of all. They dissipated, little by little, on their pointless march around the world. They gave them up for security you see. And now we, too, have no use for our powers..." He sighed and scratched rapidly at himself in several places, adjusting buttons and loops and ties as he did so, as if he only just realized his disheveled condition. "What are we to do? Should we become walkers, we shall inevitably be doomed to end our days at the marching boards."

"We would join forces with you," Elric heard the Rose say, and he looked at her in surprise. "We have the power to help you against the jurisdiction of the Gypsy Nation. And you have the power to help us find what we seek here. There are three sisters we must discover. Perhaps they have another with them now, an armoured man whose face is never revealed."

"It is my mother you must ask in that respect," said Fallogard Phatt absently, as he considered her words. "And my niece. Charion has all her grandmother's skills, I think, though she must learn more wisdom yet . . ."

The girl glared at him, but she seemed flattered.

"It is my boy Koropith Phatt, who is the greatest of all Phatts," said his father, laying a proud and perhaps proprietorial hand upon the infant, whose little black eyes regarded his father with amused affection and a certain knowing sympathy. "There has never *been* a Phatt as full of the gift as Koropith. He is *brimming* with psychic advantages!"

"Then he and we must come to our arrangements quickly," said the Rose. "For the time is here when we must seek a means of charting a specific course between the worlds. If we can free you, can you lead us where we must go?"

"I have that ability, at least," said Fallogard Phatt, "and will gladly aid you however I can. But the boy has found pathways through the realms I had not even heard rumoured. And the girl can seek out an individual through all the layers of the multiverse. She is a bloodhound, that child. She is a terrier. She is a spaniel . . ."

Interrupting this effusion of canine comparisons, Master Wheldrake found a book in one of his inner pockets and drew it forth with a flourish. "Here's what I remembered having! Here it is!"

They looked at him in polite expectation as he pulled his newly received credits from his waistcoat and pushed them into the hands of the baffled boy. "Here, young Master Koropith, go with your cousin to the market! I'll give you a list. Tonight I intend to make us all a meal substantial enough to help us through our coming adventure!"

He brandished the scarlet book. "Between Mrs. Beeton and myself I think I can provide us with a supper the like of which you'll not have tasted in a twelvemonth!"

CHAPTER FIVE

Conversations with Clairvoyants Concerning the Nature of the Multiverse &c. Dramatic Methods of Escape.

The elaborate and exquisite feast over, and soothed by a recitation of some excellent sonnets, even Elric was able to divert his attention, for a little while, away from the persistent memory of his dead father waiting for him in that dead city.

"We have lived by our wits, the Phatts, for generations." Fallogard Phatt was in his cups. Even his old mother put wine to her wizened lips and occasionally giggled. His son and niece were either in bed or hidden in the stairwell's shadows. Wheldrake refilled Mother Phatt's bumper while the Rose sat back in her chair, the only one determined to keep her mind upon the crucial issues of their circumstances. She drank no wine, but seemed content to let the others relax as they wished. Next to her around the table, Elric sipped the dark blue-black stuff and wished that it could have some effect upon him, reflecting sardonically to himself that after a draught of dragon's venom most drinks had something of an insipid quality . . .

"There are only a few adepts," Fallogard Phatt was saying, "who have ever explored even a fraction of the multiverse, but the Phatts, I must say, are as experienced as any. Mother here, for instance, has the routes of at least two thousand different pathways between some five thousand realms. Her instincts are occasionally a little dulled, these days, but our niece is learning well. She has the same talent."

"So you sought this plane deliberately?" said the Rose suddenly, as if his remarks coincided with her own thoughts.

This produced a wild peal of laughter in Fallogard Phatt, threatening to burst his thoroughly buttoned waistcoat while his hair sprang up around his head and his face grew red. "No, madam, that's the joke of it. Few here *ever* came because they had heard of the Gypsy Nation and wished to join it. But the Nation has set up its own peculiar field—a kind of psychic gravity—which draws many here who would otherwise be in limbo. It acts—in a psychic, but also in an oddly material way, too—as a kind of false-limbo, a world of lost souls, indeed."

"Lost souls?" Elric now grew alert. "Lost souls, Master Phatt?"

"And bodies, too, of course. For the most part." Fallogard Phatt made a drunken movement with his hand then paused, as if he heard something, then peered with sudden intelligence into the albino's crimson eyes. "Aye, sir," he said in a quieter tone, "lost souls, indeed!" And Elric felt for a few seconds the sense of some benign presence within him, sympathetic and perhaps even protective. The sensation was quickly gone and Phatt was holding forth to Wheldrake on some jolly abstraction which seemed to excite them both, but the Rose was, if anything, more thoughtful as she glanced from Phatt to Elric and, frequently, at the busy head of little Mother Phatt, who sat with her two hands clutching her wine-cup, nodding and smiling and scarcely following, or caring to follow, the general drift, yet seemingly content and alert in her own mysterious way.

"I find it difficult to imagine, sir," Wheldrake was saying. "It is a trifle frightening, too, moreover, to contemplate such vastness. So many worlds, so many tribes, and each with a different understanding of the nature of reality! Billions of them, sir. Billions and billions—an infinity of possibilities and alternatives! And Law and Chaos fight to control all that?"

"The war is at present unadmitted," said Phatt. "Instead there are skirmishes here and there, battles for a world or two, or at best a realm. But a great conjunction is coming and it is then that the Lords of the Higher Worlds wish to establish their rule throughout the Spheres.

Each Sphere contains a universe and there are thought to be at least a million of them. This is no ordinary cosmic event!"

"They fight to control infinity!" Wheldrake was impressed.

"The multiverse is not infinite in the strictest sense..." began Phatt, to be interrupted by his mother, suddenly shrill with irritability.

"Infinity? Loose talk! Infinity? The multiverse is *finite*. It has limits and dimensions which only a god may occasionally perceive—but they *are* limits and dimensions! Otherwise there would be no point in it!"

"In what, Mother?" Even Fallogard was surprised. "In what?"

"In the Family Phatt, of course. It is our firm belief that we shall one day—" And she left her son to recite the bulk of what was evidently the family creed...

"—learn the plan of the entire multiverse and travel at will from Sphere to Sphere, from realm to realm, from world to world, travel through the great clouds of shifting, multicoloured stars, the tumbling planets in all their millions, through galaxies that swarm like gnats in a summer garden, and rivers of light—glory beyond glory—pathways of moonbeams between the roaming stars.

"Why, sir, have you ever sometimes stood alone and seen visions? That moment, you recall, when you pause and are granted a glimpse of near-eternity, the multiverse? You might glance at a cloud or a burning log, you might notice a certain fold in a blanket, or the angle at which a blade of grass stands—it does not matter. You know what you have seen and it brings that larger vision. Yesterday, for instance—?" And he cocked an enquiring eye at the poet before receiving his new friend's approval to continue.

"—for instance, I look up at about noon. Silver light pours like water down the massed clouds, themselves vast floating asymmetric sea-beasts so large they are host to whole nations of other species, including, surely, Man? As if they entirely surfaced from their element, ready to plunge again into depths as mysterious to those below as oceans are to those above them." His face glowed a richer red with all this bright recollection, his eyes appeared to focus again upon those clouds, upon those monumental natural barges, like raised wrecks, alarmingly complete after millennia, alien beyond imagining, beyond any impulse of ordinary mortals to follow, which one's very soul yearned to forget, those obscenely ancient beast-ships grown insubstantial in their sudden element, this brilliancy of sun and sky, and gradually their outlines dim, turn grey and fade one into another until only the sun and the sky remain, witnesses of their unmourned passing. "Have they grown invisible or are they gone for ever, even from our blood's strange memory, that tiny speck of ancestral matter that informs our race's united soul? Would that be to say they never existed and never could exist? Many things existed before our ancestors ever lifted one webbed foot upon a steamy shore . . ."

And Elric smiled at this, for his race's memory went back before mankind's, at least in his own realm. His folk, older and unhuman settlers, pursued or banished or otherwise escaping through the realms, had been victims of a mighty catastrophe, perhaps of their own creation.

Memory follows memory, memory defeats memory; some things are banished only into the realms of our rich imaginings—but this does not mean that they do not or cannot or will not exist—they exist! They exist!

The last Melnibonéan thinks of his people's history and legends, and he tells his human friends some of what he knows and one day a human scribe will write these remembered words which will become in turn the foundation for whole cycles of myths, whole volumes of legend and superstition, so that a grain of a grain of prehuman memory is carried over to us, blood to blood, life to life. And the cycles turn and spin and intersect at unpredictable points in an eternity of possibilities, paradoxes and conjunctions, and one tale feeds another and one anecdote provides others with entire epics. Thus we influence past, present and future and all their possibilities. Thus are we all responsible for one another, through all the myriad dimensions of time and space that make up the multiverse . . .

"Human love," says Fallogard Phatt, turning his eyes from his vision, "it is finally our only real weapon against entropy . . ."

"Without Chaos and Law in balance," says Wheldrake, reaching for some cheese and wondering, idly, which terrorized region along the road provided that particular tribute, "we rob ourselves of the greatest possible number of choices. That is the singular paradox of this conflict between the Higher Worlds. Let one become dominant and half of what we have is lost. I cannot but sometimes feel that our fate is in the hands of creatures hardly more intelligent than a stoat!"

"Intelligence and power were never the same thing," murmurs the Rose, departing from her own train of thought for a moment. "Frequently a lust for power is nothing more than an impulse of the stupidly baffled who cannot understand why they have been treated so badly by Dame Fortune. Who can blame those brutes, sometimes? They are outraged by random Nature. Perhaps these gods feel the same? Perhaps they make us endure such awful trials because they know we are actually superior to them? Perhaps they have become senile and forget the point of their old truces?"

"You speak truth in one area, madam," said Elric. "Nature distributes power with about the same lack of discrimination as she distributes intelligence or beauty or wealth, indeed!"

"Which is why mankind," says Wheldrake, revealing a little of his own background, "has a duty to correct such mistakes of justice that Nature makes. That is why we must provide for those whom random Nature creates poor, or sick or otherwise distressed. If we do not do this, I think, then we are not fulfilling our own natural function. I speak," he said hastily, "as an agnostic. I am a thorough-going Radical, make no mistake. Yet it does seem to me that Paracelsus had it when he suggested . . ."

Whereupon the Rose, growing skillful at such things, halted his ascent into the realms of abstraction by enquiring loudly of Mother Phatt if she required more cheese.

"Cheese enough tonight," said the old woman mysteriously, but her smile was friendly. "Always moving. Always moving. Heel and toe, the walkers go. Heel and toe, heel and toe. All walking, my dear, in the hope of escaping their damnation. Unchanging; generation upon generation; injustice upon injustice; and sustained by further injustice. Heel and toe, the walkers go. Always moving. Always moving . . ." And she subsided almost gratefully into staring silence.

"Ah, such an infamous society, sir," says her son, with a sage nod, an approving wave of a biscuit. "Infamous. It is a lie, sir. A mighty deception, this 'free nation' that always seems to proceed, yet never changes! Is that not true decadence, sir?"

"Shall it be Engeland's fate, I wonder," mused Wheldrake of some lost home. "Is it the fate of all unjust empires? Oh, I fear I see the future of my country!"

"Certainly it became the only future of my own," said Elric with a grin that revealed much more than it attempted to hide. "And that is why Melniboné collapsed like a worm-eaten husk, almost at a touch . . ."

"Now," says the Rose, "down to business." And she sketches a plan to move at night between the wheels and find Duntrollin, there to skulk amongst the marching boards until such time as they could gain the stairs—from there Fallogard Phatt would be their bloodhound, his clairvoyance focused to find the three sisters. "But we must discuss the details," she says, "there could be practicalities, Master Phatt, that I have overlooked."

"A few, ma'am, to be sure." Politely, he listed them. The flaps to the marching boards would be guarded. The warrior inhabitants of Duntrollin would almost certainly be prepared for such an attempt as theirs. He had never seen the sisters and therefore his gift would be unreliable. What was more, even when they had reached the sisters there was no certainty they would be welcomed by them. And then, how were they to leave the Gypsy Nation? The barriers of garbage were almost impossible to cross and the guardians always detected would-be escapers. Besides, it was useless for the Family Phatt to consider such things since they were trapped by that peculiar form of psychic gravity which brought so many poor souls to this road, to dwell upon it, or under it, for ever. "We are all of us trapped here by more than a few black-fletched arrows and a refuse heap," he said. "The Gypsy Nation controls this world, my friends. It has gained a strange, dark power. It has struck bargains. It has harnessed something of Chaos to its own uses. That, I believe, is why they dare not stop. Everything depends on maintaining their momentum."

"Then we must stop the Nation moving," said the Rose simply.

"Nothing can do that, madam." Fallogard Phatt shook a sad and despairing head. "It exists to move. It moves to exist. That is why the road is never changed, but rebuilt, even when land has fallen away, as in the bay we shall soon be crossing. They *cannot* change the road. I put it to them, when we first arrived. They told me it was too expensive, that the community could not afford it. But the fact is they can no more break their orbit than can a planet change her course around the sun. And if we tried to escape it would be like a pebble attempting to escape gravity. We were told that our main concern here should be to stay in the villages but never *below* the villages!"

"This is a mere prison," says Wheldrake, still picking at the cheeses, "not a nation. It is a foul disturbance in the order of things. It is dead and maintained by death. Unjust and maintained by injustice. Cruel and sustained by cruelty. And yet, as we have seen, the folk of Trollon congratulate themselves upon their urbanity, their humanity, their kindness and their graceful manners: while the dead stagger under their feet, supporting them in all their self-deceiving folly! Producing this parody of progress!"

Mother Phatt's old head turned to regard Wheldrake. She chuckled at him, not mockingly but with affection. "My brother told them as much, and continued to tell them as much. But he died on the marching boards, nonetheless. I was with him. I felt him die."

"Ah!" said Wheldrake, as if he shared that death also. "This is an evil parody of freedom and justice! It is a lie of profound dishonesty! For while *one* soul in this world suffers what hundreds of thousands, perhaps millions, now suffer, they are culpable."

"They are fine fellows all, in Trollon," said Fallogard Phatt ironically. "They are persons of good will and charity. They pride themselves on their wisdom and their equity . . ."

"No," says Wheldrake with an angry shake of his flaming comb, "they may accept that they are *lucky*, but cannot believe themselves either wise or good! For in the end such folk agree to any device which keeps them in privilege and ease, and so maintain their rulers, electing them with every show of democratic and republican zeal. It is the way of it, sir. And they do not ever address the injustice of it, sir. This makes them hypocrites through and through. If I had my way, sir, I would bring this whole miserable charade of progress to a halt!"

"Stop the progress of the Gypsy Nation!" Fallogard Phatt laughed with considerable glee, adding with pretended gravity, "Be careful, my dear sir. Here you are amongst friends—but in other circles such sentiments are the sheerest heresy! Be silent, sir. For your own sake!"

"Be silent! That is the perpetual admonition of Tyranny. Tyranny bellows 'Be silent!' even to the screams of its victims, the pathetic moans and groanings and supplications of its trampled millions. We are one, sir—or we are fragmented carrion which worms permit the false appearance of Life—corpses that twitch and tremble with their weight of maggots—the rotten carcass politic of an ideal freedom. The Free Gypsy Nation is an enormous falsehood! Movement, sir, is not Freedom!" Wheldrake drew furious breath.

From the corner of his eye, Elric saw the Rose get up from her chair and leave the room. He guessed that she had grown bored with the debate.

"The Wheel of Time groans and turns a million cogs which turn a million cogs again and so on, through infinity—or near infinity," said Phatt with a glance at his mother, who had closed her eyes again. "All mortals are its prisoners and its stewards. That is the inescapable truth."

"One may mirror the truth or seek to assuage it," said Elric. "Sometimes one can even try to change it . . ."

Wheldrake took a sudden pull on his bumper. "I was not raised to a world, sir, where truth was malleable and reality a question of what you made it. It is hard for me to hear such notions. Indeed, sir, I will admit to you that it alarms me. Not that I fail to appreciate the wonder of it, sir, or the optimism which you are, in your own way, expressing. It is just that I was born to trust and celebrate certain senses and accept that a great unchanging beauty was the order of the universe, a set of natural laws which, as it were, coincided in subtle ways with a mighty machine—intricate and complex but ultimately rational. This Nature, sir, was what I celebrated and worshipped, as others might celebrate and worship a Deity. What you suggest, sir, seems to me retrogressive. These, surely, are closer to the discredited notions of alchemy?"

And so the discussion continued until they all grew weary with the sound of their own voices and were not reluctant to seek their beds.

As Elric climbed the stairs, his lamp throwing enormous shadows on the limewashed walls, he wondered at the Rose's sudden departure from the table and hoped that something had not offended her. Normally he would have cared little about such things, but he had a respect for the woman which went beyond mere appreciation of her intelligence and beauty. There was also an air of tranquility about her which reminded him, in an odd way, of his time in Tanelorn. It was hard to believe that a woman of such evident integrity and wisdom was bent upon the resolution of a crude blood-feud.

In the narrow room he had chosen for himself, little more than a cupboard with a cot in it, he prepared himself for sleep. The Family Phatt had readily made them comfortable while involving themselves in only the minimum disruption, and had agreed to use their psychic powers in the service of the Rose's quest. Meanwhile, the albino would rest. He was weary and he was yearning deeply now for a world he could never know again. A world that he himself had destroyed.

Now the albino sleeps and his lean, pale body turns this way and that; a groan escapes the large, sensitive lips and once, even, the crimson eyes open wide and stare with terror into the darkness.

"Elric," says a voice, full of old rage and grief so great it has actually become a fixed aspect of the timbre, "my son. Hast thou found my soul? It is hard for me here. It is cold. It is lonely. Soon, whether I wish it or no, I must join thee. I must enter thy body and be forever part of thee . . ."

And Elric wakes with a scream that seems to fill the void in which he floats and his scream continues in his ears, finding an echo in another scream, until both are screaming in unison and he looks for his father's face, but it is not his father who screams . . .

It is an old woman—wise and tactful, full of extraordinary knowl-edge—who screams as if demented, as if in the grip of the most horrible tor-ture, screams out "NO!"—screams "STOP!"—screams "THEY FALL—OH, DEAR ASTARTE, THEY FALL!"

Mother Phatt is screaming. Mother Phatt has a vision of such unbear-able intensity her screaming cannot relieve the pain she experiences. And she becomes silent.

As the world is silent, save for the slow rumbling of the monstrous wheels, the steady, faraway sound of marching feet, never stopping, march-ing around the world . . .

"STOP!" cries the albino prince, but does not know what he com-mands. He has had just the merest glimpse of Mother Phatt's vision . . .

Now there are ordinary sounds outside his door. He hears Fallogard Phatt calling to his mother, hears Charion Phatt sobbing and realizes there is uproar close to hand . . .

With his lamp relit and in his borrowed linen, Elric goes out upon the landing and sees through the open door Mother Phatt, bolt upright in her bed, her old lips flecked with foam, her eyes staring ahead of her, frightened and sightless. "They fall!" she moans. "Oh, how they fall. It should not come to this. Poor souls! Poor souls!"

Charion Phatt holds her grandmother in her arms and rocks her a little, as if she seeks to comfort a child wakened in a nightmare. *"No, Granny, no! No, Granny, no!"* Yet it is evident from her own expression that she, too, has seen something utterly terrifying. And her uncle, beside himself—sweating, red, flustered, pleading, holding his own poor tangled head as if to shield it from bombardment, cries: "It is not! It cannot! Oh, and she has stolen the boy!"

"No, no," says Charion, shaking her head. "He went willingly. That was why you did not sense any danger. He did not believe there was any!"

"She plans this?" moans Fallogard Phatt in outraged disbelief. "She plans such *death*?"

"Bring him back," says Mother Phatt harshly, her eyes still blind to the world around her. "Get her back quickly. Find her and you shall save him."

"They went to Duntrollin to seek the sisters," Charion says. "They found them, but there was another . . . A battle? I cannot read in such confusion. Oh, Uncle Fallogard, they must be stopped." She grimaces in agony, clutching at her face. "Uncle! Such psychic disruptions!"

And Fallogard Phatt, too, is shaking with the pain of the experience while Elric, joined by Wheldrake, tries urgently to discover what it is they fear so much. "It is a wind howling through the multiverse," says Phatt. "A black wind howling through the multiverse! Oh, this is the work of Chaos. Who would have guessed it?"

"No," says Mother Phatt. "She does not serve Chaos, neither does she call on Chaos! Yet . . ."

"Stop them!" cries Charion.

And Fallogard Phatt raises long fingers in helpless despair. "It is too late. We are already witnessing the destruction!"

"Not yet," says Mother Phatt. "Not yet. There could be time . . . But it is so strong . . ."

Elric no longer bothered with thought. The Rose was in danger. Hurriedly the albino returned to his room and dressed, buckling on his blade. Wheldrake was with him as they left the house and ran through the wooden streets of Trollon, taking wrong directions in the unfamiliar darkness, until they found a stairway down to the marching boards and Elric, to whom caution was only ever a half-learned lesson, had drawn Stormbringer from its scabbard so that the black blade glowed with a formidable darkness and the runes writhed and twisted along its length, and suddenly was killing anyone with a weapon who sought to stop him.

Wheldrake, seeing the faces of the slain, shuddered and hardly knew whether to stay close to the albino or put a safe distance between them while Fallogard Phatt and what remained of the Family Phatt were themselves attempting to follow, carrying the old woman in her chair.

Elric knew only that the Rose was in certain danger. At last his patience had deserted him and it was almost with relief that he let the hellsword take its toll of blood and souls, while he felt a huge, thrilling vitality fill him and he cried out the impossible names of unlikely gods! He cut at the harnesses that held the horses, he struck at the chains which pegged the marchers to their boards, and then he had mounted a great black warhorse which whinnied with the sheer pleasure of its release and, with Elric clinging to its mane, reared, striking at the air with its massive hoofs, then galloped towards the opening.

From somewhere now could be heard a new sound—human voices yelling with mindless panic—and Mother Phatt sobbed still louder. "It is too late! It is too late!" Wheldrake took hold of one of the horses but it shook itself free and avoided him. He abandoned any further attempt to find himself a mount and instead ran in pursuit of the albino. Reaching the bottom of the staircase, Fallogard Phatt took hold of his mother's wheelchair while the old woman still opened her mouth in a wail of grieving terror. His niece covered her ears, running beside the chair.

Out into the night now—Elric a raging shadow ahead of them and the massive wheels of the ever-moving villages grinding inexorably forward—into a cold wind carrying rain—the wild night lit by the guttering fires and lamps of the walkers as they marched, of the distant villages of the first rank. There was a certain spring to the road now, which suggested they were approaching the bridge that spanned the bay.

Wheldrake heard snatches of song. He did not break his stride but forced himself to lengthen it, breathing expertly as he had once been taught. He heard laughter, casual conversation, and he wondered for a moment if this were merely a dream, with all the lack of consequence he associated with dreams. But there were other voices ahead—oaths and yells as Elric forced his horse between the walkers, hampered by so many bodies but refusing to use the runesword against this unarmed mass.

And behind him Mother Phatt grew quieter while her granddaughter's sobs grew louder.

Somehow Wheldrake and the Phatts were able to keep pace with Elric, even getting closer to him as he pushed on through the crowd and Mother Phatt cried "Stop! You must stop!" And all the folk of the Free Gypsy Nation who heard this obscenity upon an old woman's tongue drew away fastidiously, disgusted.

More confusion followed. Wheldrake began to wonder if they had not acted thoughtlessly, in response to a senile woman's nightmare. No wheel had stopped turning, no foot had ceased walking; everything was as it should be on the great road around the world. By the time they had made their way through the main mass and were able to move freely, Elric had slowed the horse to a canter, surprised not to be followed by the rest of Trollon's guard. Wheldrake, however, was prudent and waited until the albino had sheathed the great runesword before approaching him. "What did you see, Elric?"

"Only that the Rose was in danger. Perhaps something else. We must find Duntrollin swiftly. She was foolish to do what she did. I had thought her wiser than that. It was she, after all, who counseled us to caution!"

The wind blew harder and the flags of the Gypsy Nation cracked and snapped in the force of it.

"It will be dawn, soon," said Wheldrake. He turned to look back at the Family Phatt: three faces bearing the same stamp, of a fear so all-consuming it made them almost entirely blind to their surroundings. Imploring, wailing, shouting warnings, sobbing and shrieking, Mother Phatt led them in a hymn of unspeakable despair and pain. From which the free walkers discreetly removed themselves, casting the occasional disapproving glance.

Calmly onward moves the Gypsy Nation, wheels turning with steady slowness, propelled by her marching millions, making her perpetual progress around the world . . .

Yet there is something *wrong*—something profoundly alarming ahead—something which Mother Phatt can already see, which Charion can already hear and which Fallogard Phatt yearns with all his soul to avert!

It is only as the dawn comes up behind them, soaring pinks, blues and faint golds, washing the road ahead with pale, watery light, that

Elric understands why Mother Phatt screams and Charion holds her hands over her ears, and why Fallogard Phatt's face is a tormented mask!

The light races forward over the great span of the causeway, revealing the lumbering settlements, the tramping thousands, the smoke and the dimming lamps, the ordinary domestic details of the day—but ahead—ahead is what the clairvoyants have foreseen . . .

The mile-wide span across the bay, that astonishing creation of an obsessively nomadic people, has been cut as if by a gigantic sword—sheared in a single blow!

Now the two halves rise and fall slowly with the shock of this catastrophe. That massive bridge of human bones and animal skins, of every kind of compacted ordure, trembles like a cut branch, lifting and dropping almost imperceptibly, with steady beats, while on the landside the boiling waters release all their fury and the white spray makes rainbows high overhead.

One by one, with appalling deliberation, the villages of the Gypsy Nation crawl to the edge and plunge into the abyss.

To stop is obscene. They do not know how to stop. They can only die.

Elric, too, is screaming now, as he forces his horse forward. But he screams, he knows, at the apparent inevitability of human folly, of people who can destroy themselves to honour a principle and a habit that has long since ceased to have any practical function. They are dying because they would rather follow habit than alter their course.

As the villages crawl to the broken edge of the causeway and drop into oblivion, Elric thinks of Melniboné and his own race's refusals in the face of change. And he weeps for the Gypsy Nation, for Melniboné, and for himself.

They will not stop.

They cannot stop.

There is confusion. There is consternation. There is growing panic in the villages. But still they will not stop.

Through the falling mist rides Elric now, crying out for them to turn back. He rides almost to the edge of the causeway and his horse stamps and snorts in terror. The Gypsy Nation is dropping not into the distant ocean but into a great blossoming mass of reds and yellows, whose sides open like exotic petals and whose hot centre pulses as it swallows village after village. And it is then that Elric knows this is Chaos work!

He turns the black stallion away from the edge and gallops back through that doomed press to where Mother Phatt in her chair shrieks: "No! No! The Rose! Where is the Rose?"

Elric dismounts and seizes Fallogard Phatt by his lean, trembling shoulders. "Where is she? Do you know? Which village is Duntrollin?" But Fallogard Phatt shakes his head, his mouth moving dumbly, until at last all he can do is repeat her name. "The Rose!"

"She should not have done this," cries Charion. "It is wrong to do this!"

Even Elric could not condone what was happening, careless as he often was of human life, and he longed to call upon Chaos to bring a halt to the dreadful destruction. But Chaos had been summoned to perform this deed and he knew he would not be heeded. He had not believed the Rose capable of raising such formidable allies; he could scarcely accept that she would willingly permit such horror as thousands upon thousands of living creatures plunged into the abyss, their cries of terror now unified in the air, while overhead the white spray spumed and the rainbows glittered.

Then he had turned, hearing a familiar voice, and it was young Koropith Phatt, running towards them, his clothes in shreds and blood pouring from a score of minor cuts.

"Oh, what has she done!" cried Wheldrake. "The woman is a monster!"

But Koropith was panting, pointing backwards to where, as bloody and ragged as himself, her hair slick with sweat, her sword Swift Thorn in her right hand, her dagger Little Thorn in her left, staggered the Rose, with tears like diamonds upon her haggard face.

Wheldrake addressed her first. He, too, was crying. "Why did you do this? Nothing can justify such murder!"

She looked at him in exhausted puzzlement before his words made sense to her. Then she turned her back on him, sheathing her weapons. "You wrong me, sir. This is Chaos work. It could only be Chaos work. Prince Gaynor has an ally. He wreaks great sorcery. Greater than I could have guessed. It seems he does not care who or what or how many he kills in his desperate search for death . . ."

"Gaynor did this?" Wheldrake reached out to take her arm, but she resisted him. "Where is he now?"

"Where he believes I will not follow," she said. "But follow I must." There was an air of weary determination about the woman and Elric saw that Koropith Phatt, far from blaming her for his ordeal, had placed his hand in hers and was comforting her.

"We shall find him again, lady," said the child. He began to lead her back the way they had come.

But Fallogard Phatt intercepted them. "Is Duntrollin destroyed?"

The Rose shrugged. "No doubt."

"And the sisters?" Wheldrake wished to know. "Did Gaynor find them?"

"He found them. As did we—thanks to Koropith and his clairvoyance. But Gaynor—Gaynor had possession of them in some way. We fought. He had already summoned aid from Chaos. He had doubtless planned everything in detail. He had waited until the Nation was approaching the bridge . . ."

"He has escaped? To where?" Elric already guessed some of the answer and she confirmed what he suspected.

She made a motion with her thumb towards the edge. "Down there," she said.

"He found his death then, after all." Wheldrake frowned. "But he wished to have as much company as possible, it seems, on his journey to oblivion."

"Who can say where he journeys?" The Rose had turned and was going slowly back towards the edge where now a village perched, half-toppled, her inhabitants wailing and scrambling, yet making no real attempt to escape. Then the whole thing had gone, tumbling down into that flaring manifestation of Chaos, to be swallowed, to be engulfed. "I would guess that only he knows that."

Leading his horse, Elric followed her. Her hand was still in Koropith's. Elric heard the boy say: "They are still there, lady. All of them. I can find them, lady. I can follow. Come." The boy was leading her now, leading her to the very lip of the broken causeway, to stand staring into the abyss.

"We shall find a way for you, lady," Fallogard Phatt promised, in sudden fear. "You cannot—"

But he was too late, for without warning both the woman and the boy had flung themselves into space, out over the pulsing, glowing maw that seemed so hungry, so eager for the souls which fell by their hundreds and thousands down. Down into the very stuff of Chaos!

Mother Phatt screamed again. It was one long, agonized scream that no longer mourned the general destruction. This time she voiced a thoroughly personal grief.

Elric ran to the edge, saw the two figures falling, dwindling, to be swiftly absorbed by the foul beauty of that voracious fundament.

Impressed by a courage, a desperation which seemed to him even greater than his own, he stepped backwards, speechless with astonishment—

—and was too late to anticipate Fallogard Phatt's single bellow of agonized outrage as the man pushed his mother to the lip of the broken causeway, hesitated for only a split second, then, with his niece clinging to his coat-tails, plunged after his disappearing child. Three more figures spun down through those pulsing, hungry colours, into the flames of Chaos.

Sickened, confused and attempting to control a fear he had never known before, Elric drew Stormbringer from its scabbard.

Wheldrake came to stand beside him. "She is gone, Elric. They are all gone. There is nothing you can fight here."

Elric nodded slowly in agreement. He stretched the blade before

him then brought it up flat against his heaving chest, placing his other hand near the tip of the great broadsword on which runes flickered and glowed. "I have no choice," he said. "I would endure any danger rather than earn the fate my father has promised me . . ."

And with that he had screamed the name of his own patron Duke of Demons and had hurled his howling battle-blade, and his body with it, out over the Chaos pit, a wild, unlikely song upon his bloodless lips . . .

The last thing Wheldrake saw of his friend were crimson eyes glaring with a kind of terrible tranquility as the Sorcerer Emperor was pulled remorselessly down into the flaming hub of that hellish abyss . . .

BOOK TWO

ESBERN SNARE;
THE NORTHERN WEREWOLF

*Of the Troll of the Church they sing the rune
By the Northern Sea in the harvest moon;
And the fishers of Zealand hear him still
Scolding his wife in Ulshoi hill.*

*And seaward over its groves of birch
Still looks the tower of Kallundborg church,
Where, first at its altar, a wedded pair,
Stood Helva of Nesvek and Esbern Snare!*

—Wheldrake,
Norwegian Songs

CHAPTER ONE

*Consequences of Ill-Considered Dealings with the
Supernatural; Something of the Discomforts of Unholy Compacts.*

ELRIC FELL THROUGH centuries of anguish, millennia of mortal misery and folly; he roared his defiance as he fell, his sword like a beacon and a challenge in his grip, down towards the luscious heart of Chaos while everywhere around him was confusion and cacophony, swift images of faces, cities, whole worlds, transmogrified and insane, warping and reshaping; for in unchecked Chaos everything was in perpetual change.

He was alone.

Very suddenly everything was still. His feet touched stable ground, though it was little more than a slab of rock floating in the flaming light of the quasi-infinite—universe upon universe blending one into the other, each ripple a different colour in a different spectrum, each facet a separate reality. It was as if he stood at the centre of a crystal of unimaginable complexity and his eyes, refusing the sights they were offered, somehow became blind to everything but the intense, shifting light, whose colours he could not identify, whose odours were full of hints of the familiar, whose voices offered every terror, every consolation and yet were not mortal. Which set the albino prince to sobbing, conquered and helpless as his strength drained from him, and his sword grew heavy in his hand, an ordinary piece of iron, and a soft, humorous song sounded from somewhere beyond the fires, becoming words:

"Thou hast such courage, sweetest of my slaves! Impetuous Champion of the Ever-Changing, where is thy father's soul?"

"I know not, Lord Arioch." Elric felt his own soul freeze on the very point of extermination, the imminent obliteration of everything he had ever been or would be—less than a memory. And Arioch knew he did not lie. He took away the chill. And Elric was soothed again . . .

He had never before experienced such a sense of impatience in his patron Lord of Hell. What emergency alarmed the gods?, he wondered.

"Mortal morsel, thou art my darling and my dear one, pretty little sweetmeat . . ."

Elric, familiar with the cadences of his patron's moods, was both fascinated and afraid. Much that was in him wished for the approval of his patron at all costs. Much wished only to give itself up forever to the mercies of Duke Arioch, whatever they might be, to suffer whatever agonies his lord decided, such was the power of that godling's presence, embracing him and coaxing him and praising him and blessed always with the absolute power of life or death over his eternal soul. Yet still, in the most profoundly secret part of his mind Elric kept a resolution to himself, that one day he would rid his world of gods entirely—should his life not be snuffed away the next second (such was his patron's present mood). Here, in his own true element, Arioch had his full power and any pact he had ever made with a mortal was meaningless; this was his own Dukedom and here he required no allies, honoured no bargains and demanded instant compliance of all his slaves, mortal and supernatural, on pain of instant extinction.

"Speak, sweetmeat. What brought thee to my domain?"

"Mere chance, I think, Lord Arioch. I fell . . ."

"Ah, fell!" The word held considerable meaning, considerable understanding. "You *fell*."

"Into an abyss which only a Lord of the Higher Worlds could sink between the realms."

"Yes. You fell. IT WAS MASHABAK!"

Elric knew mindless relief that the rage was directed away from him. And he, too, understood what had occurred—that Gaynor the Damned had served Arioch's arch rival, Count Mashabak of Chaos . . .

"You had servants in the Gypsy Nation, lord?"

"It was mine, that near-limbo. A useful device that many sought to control. And because he could not possess it for himself, Mashabak destroyed it . . ."

"Upon a whim, lord?"

"Oh, he served some creature's petty ends, I believe . . ."

"It was Gaynor, lord."

"Ah, Gaynor. He has become a politician, eh?"

Elric grew aware of his patron's brooding silence. After what might have been a year, the Duke of Hell murmured, with better humour, "Very well, sweetmeat, go upon thy way. But recollect that thou art mine and thy father's soul is mine. Both are mine. Both must be delivered up to me, for that is our ancient compact."

"Go where, patron?"

"Why, to Ulshinir, of course, where the three sisters have escaped their captor. And could be returning home."

"To Ulshinir, my lord?"

"Fear not, thou shalt travel like a gentleman. I shall send thy slave after thee." The Lord of the Higher Worlds had his attention upon other affairs now. It was not in the nature of a Duke of Chaos to dwell too long upon one matter, unless it was of monumental importance.

The fires went out.

Elric still stood upon that spur of rock, but now it was attached to a substantial hill, from which he could look down into a rugged valley, full of sparse grass and limestone crags across which a thin powder of snow blew. The air was cold and sharp and good to his senses and, though he was cold, he brushed vigorously at his naked arms and face as if to rid them of the grime of hell. At his feet something murmured. He looked down to see the runesword where he had dropped it during his audience with Arioch. He wondered at the power of his patron, that even Stormbringer felt compelled to acknowledge. He raised the blade almost lovingly, cradling it like a child. "We have need of each other still, thee and I."

The blade was sheathed, the terrain inspected again, and he thought he saw a thread of smoke rising over the next hill. From there he might begin his search for Ulshinir.

He thanked chance that he had drawn on his boots before rushing in pursuit of the Rose, for he needed them now, against the jagged stones and treacherous turf down which he made his way. The cold was resisted with the expediency of dragon venom, again painfully absorbed, and in less than an hour he was striding down a narrow path to a stone cottage, thatched with peat and straw, which gave off the smell of earth, warmth and a wholesome fecundity, and was the first of several such dwellings, all as comfortably settled into the landscape as if they had grown naturally from it.

In answer to Elric's polite knock upon the gnarled oak door, a fair-skinned young woman opened it and smiled at him uncertainly, eyeing his appearance with a curiosity she attempted to disguise. She blushed as she pointed along the road to Ulshinir and told him it was less than three hours' easy walking from there, to the sea.

Gentle hills and shallow dales, a white limestone road through the mellow greens, coppers and purples of the grasses and heathers; Elric was glad to be walking. He wished to clear his head, to consider Arioch's demands, to wonder how Gaynor had come to lose the mysterious three sisters. And he wondered what he must find in Ulshinir.

And he wondered if the Rose still lived.

Indeed, he thought with some surprise, he cared if the Rose still lived. He was curious, he assured himself, to hear more of her story.

Ulshinir was a harbour town of steep-roofed houses and narrow spires, all with a scattering of early snow. The smell of woodsmoke, drifting through the autumnal air, somehow consoled him a little.

Within his belt he still had tucked a few gold coins which Moonglum had long ago insisted he carry and he hoped that gold was acceptable currency in Ulshinir. The town certainly seemed of familiar appearance, very much like any town of the Northern Young Kingdoms, and he guessed this plane was close to his own part of the Sphere, at least, and possibly the realm. And this, too, gave him a little comfort. The few citizens he encountered upon the cobbled streets found his appearance strange, but they were friendly enough and were happy to point the way to the inn. The inn was spare, in the manner of such places in his own world, but warm and clean. He was glad of the nutty, full-bodied ale they brought him, of the broth and the pie. He paid for his bed in advance and, while his landlady was counting out considerable change in silver, he asked if she had heard of other visitors to the town—three sisters, in fact.

"Dark haired, pale beauties, with such wonderful eyes—not unlike your own in shape, sir, though theirs were of such a dense blue as to be almost black. And exquisite clothes and traps! There's not a woman in Ulshinir who did not turn out to get a glimpse of them. They took ship yesterday and their destination is the subject of considerable dispute amongst us, as you can imagine." She smiled tolerantly at her own weakness. "Legend says they're people from beyond our Heavy Sea. Were you a friend, perhaps? Or a relative?"

"They have a small thing that belonged to my father, that's all," said Elric casually. "They inadvertently took it with them. I doubt they know they have it! They had a boat, you say?"

"From the harbour yonder." She pointed through the window to the grey water enclosed by two long quays, each terminated by a tall lighthouse. There were only fishing boats moored there now. "The *Onna Peerthon*, she was. She calls here regularly with a cargo of haberdashery and needle-goods, usually, from Shamfird. Captain Gnarreh normally refuses passengers, but the sisters offered him a price, we heard, that he would have been a fool to refuse. But as to their destination . . ."

"Captain Gnarreh will return?"

"Next year, almost certainly."

"And what lies beyond your shores, lady?"

She shook her head and laughed as if she had never heard such a joke before. "First the island reefs and then the Heavy Sea. Should anything exist on the other side of the Heavy Sea—should it have a far side, indeed—then we have no knowledge of it. You are very ignorant, sir, if I may say so."

"You might say so, madam, and I apologize to you. I have been lately under some little enchantment and my mind is clouded."

"Then you should rest, sir, not be journeying towards the very edge of the world!"

"Which island might they have wished to visit?"

"Any one of a score, sir, would be my guess. If you like, I can find you an old map we have."

Gratefully Elric accepted her offer and took the map up to his room, poring over it in the hope that perhaps some instinct would direct his attention to the appropriate island. After half-an-hour of this, he was no wiser and was about to prepare for bed when he heard a sound below, a raised voice, that he thought he recognized.

It was with lifting heart that Elric, who had thought he would never see the man again, ran to the top of the stairs and looked down into the inn's main hall where a small red-headed poet, in frock-coat and trousers, waistcoat and cravat which looked as if they had come rather too close to a fire, declaimed some ode he hoped would buy him a bed—or at least a bowl of soup—for the night. *"Gold was the colour Gwyneth gave to Gwinefyr. And coral for cheeks, eyes blue as the sea. And bearing so perfect, so gracious, so fine. And lips red as Burgundy grapes, lush on the vine. These were the gifts she gave unto her tragic Queen. Her Queen of Caprice, by Tragedy Redeem'd.* Great Scott, sir! I thought you gone to perdition a year or more ago! It's good to see you, sir. You can help me with your Memoriam. I had so few particulars. I am afraid you will not like it. If I remember, it is not your preferred style. It tends, I will admit, to the Heroic. And the *ballade* form is considered merely quaint by many." He began to search his pockets for his manuscript. "It has gone, I fear, the way of the *triolet*. Or, indeed, the *rondel*—*'Lord Elric left his homeland weeping, For his dear young bride whom he loved of yore. We see him stand by the open door. While the sweet tears down her cheeks are creeping.'*—an attempt, dear friend, I must admit, to catch the popular taste. Such trifles have great general appeal and your subject, sir, I felt might attract public fancy. I had hoped to immortalize you, while at the same time—Aha! No, that is upon a Hugnit I met last week—

and you will say that the *rondel* is inappropriate to epic form—but one has to *dress up* one's epics, these days—sweeten them in some way. And a few innocuous cadences do a great deal to achieve that end. I have no money, you see, sir . . ."

And the poor little fellow looked suddenly wan. He sat himself down upon a bench, his shoulders slumped, even his shock of red hair limp upon his avian head, his fingers screwing up miscellaneous pieces of paper in some unconscious pantomime of self-disgust.

"Why, then, I must commission a work from you," said Elric descending. He put a sympathetic hand upon his friend's shoulder. "After all, did you not tell me once that patronage of the artist was the only valuable vocation to which a prince might aspire?"

At which Wheldrake grinned, cheered by this confirmation of a friendship he believed gone for ever. "It has not been easy for me, sir, just lately, I must admit." There was a wealth of recent horror in the poet's eyes and Elric did not tax him on it. He knew himself that all Wheldrake wished to do at present was rid his mind of the memories. The poet had a momentary recollection and smoothed out the last piece of paper he had crumpled. "Yes, the *Ballade Memoriam*, I recall—I suppose it is a somewhat limited form. But for parody, sir—unexcelled! *A warrior rode death's lonely road, No lonelier road rode he . . .*" Again this brief revival of his old spark failed to ignite, as it were, the flashpan of his soul. "I am rather wanting, sir, I think, of food and drink. This is the first human settlement I have seen in several months."

And then Elric had the pleasure of ordering food and ale for his friend and watching him come slowly back to something like his old self. "Say what you will, sir, no poet ever did his best work starving, though he may have starved himself whilst doing the work, that I'll grant. They are different things, however." And he sat back from the bench, adjusting his bony bottom upon the boards, and belched discreetly before letting out a great sigh, as if only now could he afford to allow himself to believe that his fortunes had changed. "I am mighty glad to see you, Prince Elric. And glad, too, of your aristocratic conscience. I hope, however, you'll allow me to discuss the technicalities of the commission in the morning. As I remember, sir, you have only a passing interest in the profession of versification—questions of metre, rhyme—Licence, Poetic Combination, Mixed Metre—Orthometry in general—do not concern you."

"I'll take your advice on all of that, my friend." Elric wondered at his affection for the little man, his admiration for that strange, clever mind so thoroughly lost to its proper context that it must be for ever grasping at the only constancies it had, those of the poetic craft. "And there is no haste. I would be glad of your company on a voyage I expect to be undertaking. As soon as a likely ship is free. Failing that, I might be forced to employ a little sorcery . . ."

"As a last resort, sir, I beg you. I've rather had my fill of wizardry and wild romance for the moment." Master Wheldrake took a conclusive pull upon his ale-pot. "But I seem to recall such stuff is as familiar to you, Prince Elric, as the Peckham Omnibus is to me, and I would rather link my fortune with one like yourself, who has at least some understanding of Chaos and her whimsical eruptions. So I shall be glad to accept both commission and companionship. I am mighty glad to see you again, sir." And with that he fell upon his own arm, snoring.

Then the albino prince took the little poet up and carried him, as if he were a child, to his room before returning to his own bed and his contemplation of the map—the islands of the great reef and, beyond it, darkness, an impossible ocean, unnavigable and unnatural, the Heavy Sea. Reconciled to hiring some fishing boat to visit the islands one by one, he fell into a deep sleep and was awakened by a scratching at his door and the bellow of some maid informing him that it was past the one thousand and fifteenth hour (their largest division of yearly time in Ulshinir) and there would be no breakfast for him if he did not rise at once.

He did not care for breakfast, but he was anxious to confer with Wheldrake on the subject of the three sisters and was somewhat surprised, once he had prepared himself for the day, to discover the poet declaiming on the very subject—or so it seemed . . .

"Lord Soulis is a keen wizard,
 A wizard mickle of lear:
Who cometh in bond of Lord Soulis,
 Thereof he hath little cheer.

"He hath three braw castles to his hand,
 That wizard mickle of age;
The first of Estness, the last of Westness,
 The middle of Hermitage.

"He has three fair mays into his hand,
 The least is good to see;
The first is Annet, the second is Janet,
 The third is Marjorie.

"The firsten o' them has a gowden crown,
 The neist has a gowden ring;
The third has sma'gowd her about,
 She has a sweeter thing.

"The firsten o' them has a rose her on,
 The neist has a marigold;
The third of them has a better flower,
 The best that springeth ower wold."

The inn's female servant, the landlady and her daughter, listened enraptured to Wheldrake's sing-song rendering. But it was the words that captured Elric's imagination . . .

"Good morning, Master Wheldrake. Is that a dialect of your own land?"

"It is, sir." Wheldrake kissed the hands of the ladies and strutted with all his old vigour across the room to greet his friend. "A border ballad, I believe, or something made very like one . . ."

"You did not write it?"

"I cannot answer you honestly, Prince Elric." Wheldrake sat down on the bench opposite the albino and watched him sip a dish of stewed herbs. "Have some honey in that." He pushed the pot forward. "It makes it palatable. There are some things I do not know if I wrote, if I heard, if I copied from another poet—though I doubt there's any can match Wheldrake's command of the poetic arts (I do not claim genius—but mere craft)—for I am prolific, you see. It is my nature, and perhaps my doom. Had I died after my first volume or two I should even now reside in Westminster Abbey."

Not wishing a lengthy and impossible-to-follow explanation on the nature of this particular Valhalla, Elric, as had become his habit, merely let the unfamiliar words roll by.

"But this Lord Soulis. Who is he?"

"A mere invention, for all I know, sir. I was reminded of the ballad by the three ladies here, but, of course, perhaps our three elusive sisters struck a memory, too. Certainly, if I remember further verses I'll speak up. But I believe it no more than a coincidence, Prince Elric. The multiverse is full of specific numbers of power and so on, and three is particularly popular with poets since three names are always excellent means of ringing changes on something long—which, of course, is the nature of narrative verse. Again, this slides from favour wherever I go. The artist is beyond fashion, but his purse, sir, is not. That's an odd ship, isn't it, sir, come into the harbour overnight?"

Elric had seen no ship. He put down his bowl and let Wheldrake lead him to the window where the landlady and her daughter still leaned, staring at a craft whose hull gleamed black and yellow and whose prow bore the marks of Chaos, while from her mast there flew a red-and-black flag centred with a sign in some unlikely alphabet. On her forecastle, weighting the ship oddly so that she was stern-light in the water and showing too much of her rudder, was a tall, square object swathed in black canvas and filling almost the whole deck. Occasionally the thing moved in a sudden convulsion and then was still again. There was no clue to what the canvas hid. But, as Elric watched, a figure strolled from the cabin under the forward deck, stood for a second on the polished planks and seemed to look directly at him. Elric could scarcely return the gaze, since the helmet had no eyes he could make out. It was Gaynor the Damned and the standard he flew was, Elric now recollected, that of Count Mashabak. They were fully rivals, it seemed, serving warring patrons.

Gaynor returned to his cabin and next a plank was lowered from the moored galley and laid onto the mole. The ship's hands moved with lithe speed, almost like monkeys, to secure the gangplank as there stepped onto it a lad of no more than fifteen, clad in all the vivid, pretty finery of a pirate lord, a cutlass in one side of his sash, a sabre in the other, to stride up towards the town with the confident swagger of a conqueror.

It was only as the figure drew close to the inn that Elric recognized who it was—and he wondered again at the turning Spheres of the multiverse, marveled at the extraordinary combinations of events and worlds, both in and out of the dimensions of time, that were possible within the undiscoverable parameters of the quasi-infinite.

While, at the same moment something within him warned him that what he saw might be an illusion or worse: it could be someone whom illusion had consumed, who had given themselves up wholly to Chaos and was nothing more than Gaynor's marionette.

Yet, by her walk and the way she had of looking about her, alert and cheerful as she seemed, Elric could hardly believe she was unwillingly in Gaynor's service.

He left the window and went to greet her as the door was opened by Ernest Wheldrake, whose bright blue eyes went wide as he piped, with joyful surprise:

"Why, Charion Phatt, disguised as a boy! I am in love! You have grown up!"

CHAPTER TWO

In Which Old Acquaintanceships Are Resumed
and New Agreements Reached.

Charion Phatt had reached womanhood since their last meeting and there was something about her which suggested her air of confidence was founded on faith in herself, rather than any artificial bravado. She was only a little surprised to see Wheldrake and even as she grinned a greeting at him her eyes searched inside the inn and found Elric.

"I bring an invitation from the ship's master for you—for you gentlemen—to join him this evening," she murmured.

"How long have you been in Prince Gaynor's service, Mistress Phatt?" asked Elric, with proper care to keep his tone neutral.

"Long enough, Prince Elric—more or less since I last saw you— that dawn on the gypsy bridge . . ."

"And your family?"

She smoothed chestnut hair against the lace and silk of her shirt. Her lids for a second hid her eyes. "They, sir? Why, I'm in alliance with Prince Gaynor on account of them. We are seeking them and have been seeking them since that great destruction."

And briefly she explained how Gaynor had found her imprisoned as a witch in a distant realm and had told her that he, too, sought her uncle and grandmother, since they alone, he believed, could tread with any certainty the pathways between the dimensions and lead him to the three sisters.

"You are certain they survived?" asked Wheldrake gently.

"Uncle and Grandmama, at least," she said, "of those I'm certain. And I think little Koropith is further off—or veiled from me, perhaps. I'd guess something of him continues to exist—somewhere . . ." Then she took her leave of them and walked on into the town to buy, she said, a few luxuries.

"I am truly, truly in love," Wheldrake confided to his friend, who refrained from suggesting that there was a certain unsuitability in their ages. Wheldrake was approaching fifty, he would guess, and the young woman was not much more than eighteen.

"Such differences as exist between us mean nothing when two hearts beat in harmony," said Wheldrake rapturously, and it was not certain if he quoted himself or some admired peer.

Elric fell silent, ignoring his friend's effusions, and wondering at the ways of the multiverse, this environment which, as a sorcerer, he had until then only understood in terms of symbols.

He considers the symbol of the Balance, of that equilibrium which once all philosophers strove to achieve, until, by expediency or by threats to their lives and souls, they began to strike bargains, some with Law but mostly with Chaos, which is an element closer to the natures of most sorcerers. And so they ensured that they could never reach the goal for which they had been trained: For which some of them had been born: For which a few of them were fated. These last were the ones who understood the great perversion which had taken place, who understood all that they had given up.

Gaynor, ex-Prince of the Universal, understood better than any other, for he had known perfection and lost it.

It is at this moment, as he closes the door to an ordinary inn, that Elric realizes his terror has turned to something else, a kind of determination. A kind of cold insanity. He gambles not only upon his own soul's fate, not only upon his father's—but far more. Rather than continue to be baffled by events, controlled by them, he makes up his mind to enter the game between the gods, and play it to the full, play it for himself and his mortal friends, the remaining creatures that he loves—for Tanelorn. This is no more than a promise he makes within himself, as yet scarcely coherent—but it will become the foundation of his future actions, this refusal to accept the Tyranny of Fate, to let his destiny be moved by every whim of some half-bestial divinity, whose only right over him is due to the superior power he wields. It is a reality his father accepted, even as he played the game, subtly and carefully, with his life and soul as the main stake—it is a reality, however, that Elric is beginning to refuse . . .

There is in him, too, another kind of coldness, the coldness of anger at any creature that can casually have so many of its fellows slain. It is an anger not only directed at Gaynor, but at himself. Perhaps that is why he fears Gaynor so much, because they are almost the same creature. If some philosophies were to be believed, they could indeed be aspects of a single creature. Deep memories stir in him but are unwelcome. He drives them down to where they lurk again, like the beasts of some impossible deep, terrifying all that encounter them, but themselves terrified by the light . . .

That other part of Elric, the part that is all Melnibonéan, chides him for a fool, wasting time with useless niceties of conscience and suggests that an alliance with Gaynor might give them, together, the power he desires to challenge—and perhaps even vanquish.

Or, even a temporary truce between the two would gain him, perhaps, his immediate needs—though what then? What would take place when Arioch demanded everything he had enjoined Elric to find? Could a Duke of Hell be tricked, even defeated, banished from a certain plane, by a mortal?

Elric realizes that these are the ideas which brought his father to his present dilemma and, with a sardonic smile, he settles back behind his bench to enjoy his interrupted breakfast.

He will decide nothing until this evening, when he dines aboard Gaynor's ship.

Wheldrake looks once more after the departing beauty, takes parchment from one pocket, pen from another, a traveling inkwell from his top left waistcoat pocket, and begins first a sestina, *next a* roundelay, *then a* villanelle, *until settling again upon the* sestina . . .

> *This was the measure of my soul's delight;*
> *It had no power of joy to fly by day,*
> *Nor part in the large lordship of the light;*
> *But in a secret moon-beholden way*
> *Had all its will of dreams and pleasant night,*
> *And all the love and life that sleepers may.*

Whereupon the Prince of Ruins slips away, back to his maps and his particular problems, as Wheldrake pauses, sighs, and makes a stab this time at a sonnet . . .

"Or I had thought, perhaps, after all, an Ode. Along the lines, perhaps, of something I wrote in Putney.

> "Golden eastern waters rocked the cradle where she
>   slept
> Songless, crowned with bays to be of sovereign song,
> Breathed upon with balm and calm of bounteous seas
>   that kept
> Secret all the blessing of her birthright, strong,
> Soft, severe, and sweet as dawn when first it laughed
>   and leapt
> Forth of heaven, and clove the clouds that wrought it
>   wrong!

"Good evening, Prince Gaynor. I trust you have an explanation for your destruction of a nation? Your sophistries should, at least, be entertaining." The little poet looked up at the mysterious helm, his knuckles upon his hips, his beak flaring with disdain, unmoved by fear of Gaynor's power, nor of any social stricture to hold his tongue on the subject of his host's genocide as he stepped aboard the ship.

Elric, for his part, said little, keeping a distance between himself and the others, which he had once been taught to do as a matter of course, as a Melnibonéan princeling. This coolness was new to Wheldrake but would have been very familiar to Moonglum, were he here and not, perhaps, still in Tanelorn. Elric adopted the manner when circumstances led him once more towards a kind of cynicism, that cynicism oddly tinged with other qualities, harder to judge or to define. The long-fingered bone-white hand hung upon the pommel of the massive runesword and the head was set at a certain angle, as if further withdrawn, while the brooding crimson eyes held a humour which, on occasions, even the Lords of the Higher Worlds had considered dangerous. Yet he bowed. He made a movement with his free hand. He looked steadily into the eyes behind the helm, the eyes that smoked and glittered and writhed with the fires of hell.

"Good evening, Prince Gaynor." There was at once a softness and a steely sharpness to Elric's voice which reminded Wheldrake of a cat's claws sheathed in downy fur.

The ex-Prince of the Balance cocked his head a little to one side, perhaps in irony, and spoke with that musical voice which had served Chaos as a lure for so many centuries. "I am glad to see you, Master Wheldrake. I have only recently learned we should experience the privilege of your company. Though I was told by mutual friends that you, Elric, could be found in Ulshinir." He shrugged away the question. "We have, whatever you may call it, some kind of fresh luck forming, it seems. Or are we mere ingredients? Eggs in some mad god's omelette? My chef is excellent, by the way. Or so I'm told."

Then here came Mistress Charion Phatt, in black and white velvet and lace, her youthful beauty shining like a jewel from its box.

Half-swooning, Master Wheldrake made his elaborate courtesies, which she received with amused good will and drew him to her as they strolled towards the forward cabin where the looming shadow of that peculiar cargo rocked and shifted on the roof above and which Prince Gaynor and Charion Phatt both ignored as if they heard or saw nothing out of place.

Then came the dining. Elric, who frequently cared nothing for the refinements of appetite, found the food as delicious as Gaynor had promised. The damned prince told a tale of a voyage to Aramandy and the Mallow Country there to find Xermenif Blüche, the Master Chef of Volofar. And they might have been dining again amongst the wealthy intelligentsia of Trollon, heedless of any unusual circumstances—of warring gods, of stolen souls and lost clairvoyants and so on—and commenting on the delicacy of the mousse.

Prince Gaynor, in a carved black chair at the head of his table, which was swathed with a dark scarlet cloth, turned an enigmatic helm towards Elric and said that he had always preserved certain standards, even when in battle or in command of semi-brutes, as one so frequently was, these days. One had after all, he added in some amusement, to control what one could, especially since one's fate grew so unmalleable as the Conjunction approached.

Elric had heard little of this and he moved impatiently in his seat, pushing away the plates and cutlery. "Will you tell us, Prince Gaynor, why you make us your guests here?"

"If you will tell me, Elric, why you fear me!" said Gaynor in a sudden whisper, the cold of limbo slicing into Elric's soul.

But Elric held his psychic ground, conscious of Gaynor's testing him.

"I fear you because you are prepared to go to any ends to achieve your own death. And since life has no value to you, you are to be feared as all such animals are feared. For you desire power only for that most selfish of all ends, and therefore you know no boundaries in the seeking and the gaining of it. That is why I fear you, Gaynor the Damned. And that is why you *are* damned."

The faceless creature flung back its steel-shod head, the colours behind the metal quivering and flaring, and laughed at this. "I fear *you*, Elric, because you are damned yet continue to behave as if you were not . . ."

"I have made no bargains such as yours, prince."

"Your whole race has made a bargain! And now it is paying the price—somewhere, not far from here, in a realm you will call home, the last of your people are being marshaled to march in the armies of Chaos. The time for that last great fight is not yet. But we are preparing for it. Would you survive it, Elric? Or would you be blasted to non-existence, not even your memory remaining—less enduring, say, than one of Master Wheldrake's verses—"

"I say, sir! You have already proved yourself an unmitigated villain! Pray, remember at least that you are a gentleman!" Then Wheldrake's eye returned to his beloved.

"Can you bear the prospect of everlasting death, Elric? You, who love life as much as I hate it. We could both have our deepest desire . . ."

"I think you fear me, Prince Gaynor, because I refuse that final compromise," said Elric. "I fear you because you belong wholly to Chaos. But you fear me because I do not."

A querulous noise issued from within the helm, almost like the snuffling of some cosmic pig. Then in came three sailors with a tambourine, a pipe and a musical sword, to play some mournful shanty, and who were swiftly dismissed by Gaynor, to the relief of all.

"Very well, sir," said Gaynor, all his equilibrium recovered, it seemed. "Then can I put a modest suggestion to you?"

"If you wish to join forces to seek the three sisters, I will consider your proposals," said Elric. "Otherwise I see little left to discuss between us."

"But that is just what I would discuss, Elric. We all desire something different, I suspect, of those sisters, and the reason why so much upheaval flings us this way and that through the multiverse is because there are several interests and several Lords of the Higher Worlds involved. You accept that, gentlemen?" Now he included Wheldrake. Charion Phatt sat back in her chair, evidently already privy to her ally's plan.

They nodded their agreement.

"In some ways we are all at odds," Gaynor continued, "but in others we have no battle between us. And I see you agree. Well, then, so let us search for the sisters, as well as the Family Phatt—or what remains of it—together. At least until such time as our interests are no longer the same."

And thus did Elric of Melniboné and Master Ernest Wheldrake accept the logic of the damned prince's compromise and agreed to sail with him when his ship left harbour the next morning, as soon as they had selected another sailor or two from the braver or more desperate seadogs of Ulshinir.

"But," said Elric, as they made to return ashore, while a scuffling and shifting went on, together with the occasional light pounding, overhead, "you have not yet discussed your destination, Prince Gaynor. Do we trust you in that or will you tell us the name of the island the three sisters have reached?"

"Island?" Gaynor's helm grew dark, almost in puzzlement, and blues and blacks swirled across its smooth, sometimes opaque, surface. "Island, sir? We do not go to any island."

"Then where are the three sisters?"

"Where *we* journey, sir, though they are lost to any immediate meeting between us, I fear."

"And where," said Wheldrake with a certain justified impatience, "do *we* journey, sir?"

Again the helm tilted a little as if in amusement and the musical voice sounded the words with considerable relish:

"Why, sir, I thought you'd guessed. Tomorrow we set sail into the Heavy Sea."

Chapter Three

Unusual Methods of Sea Travel; Disappointments of Piracy.
A Hellblade Misplaced.

It was not until Ulshinir was well below the horizon and the reefs still invisible ahead that Gaynor the Damned gave the order to "let some light on the poor toad" and the sailors obeyed with perhaps a touch of reluctance, drawing off and rolling up the black canvas to reveal the iron bars of a large cage from which, blinking, appeared two enormous green-lidded eyes set in a gnarled reptilian head whose nostrils flared and whose long scarlet mouth opened to reveal a pink, flickering tongue, while the extraordinarily dense weight of scaly flesh was supported on

massive webbed feet, limbs as thick as elm-trunks, the whole thing shuddering and rippling with the effort of its breathing.

The eyes, like dark, semi-precious stones, sought Gaynor and fixed on him where he stood below, looking up at the cage. The red, spongy lips opened and closed and deep, groaning sounds issued from the monster. It was only after a moment of listening that Elric realized the reptile was speaking.

"*I am discontented, master. I am hungry.*"

"Soon you will be allowed to feed, my pretty one. Very soon." Gaynor chuckled as he climbed the companionway and gripped the bars of the cage with his gauntleted hands and peered at the gigantic toad which was five times his size and weight, at least.

Wheldrake had no wish, himself, to get closer. He hung back as Charion Phatt, laughing at his hesitation, went to the toad which responded to her cluckings and cooings with more grumblings and shufflings.

"It's a self-pitying creature," said Elric, staring at the thing with a certain sympathy. "Where did you find it? Is it a gift of Count Mashabak's, something even Chaos will not suffer?"

"Khorghakh is a native of a nearby realm, Prince Elric." Gaynor was amused. "He will help us to cross the Heavy Sea."

"And what lies beyond?" Elric asked, watching as Charion Phatt took her sword and scratched the toad's belly, making him grunt with a certain pleasure and seem to relax a little, though he still insisted he was hungry.

"Khorghakh is a denizen of the Heavy Sea?"

"Not exactly," said Gaynor, "a denizen. But he is familiar with that singular ocean, or so I have been reassured. After three years of seeking him I acquired Khorghakh from some adventurers we encountered. They were coasting the islands looking for Ulshinir . . ."

"Looking for you," said Charion. "I knew you were here. It was only later that I sensed the presence of the three sisters. I had thought they were following you. Yet you sensed them, also. I did not know you were clairvoyant."

"I am not," said Elric. "At least, not in the way you imply. I had no choice in my destination. For you, as I can see, some years have passed. For me, very little has occurred since the moment I followed you all into the Chaos pit. Wheldrake has had at least a year of wandering. It suggests that even if we should find the three sisters or, indeed, your family, they could be children or wizened oldsters by the time we reach them."

"I like not this randomness at all," says Wheldrake. "Chaos was never to my taste, though my critics did not believe that. I was raised to accept that there were certain universal laws obeyed by all. To discover that this hyper-reality has only a few fundamental rules which, on occasions, may also be changed, is disturbing to me."

"It disturbed my uncle, also," said Charion. "It was why he elected to lead a life of quiet domesticity. Of course, he was not allowed that choice, after all. He lost my mother, his brother and his wife to the machinations of Chaos. For my part, I have accepted the inevitable. I am aware that I live in the multiverse which, though it follows certain courses and measures, though, as I have been told, it obeys a great and inviolable logic, is so vast, so variable, so varied, that it appears to be ruled by Chance alone. So I will accept that my life is subject not to the consistency offered by Law but the uncertainty promised by Chaos."

"A pessimistic view, sweet lady." Wheldrake restrained his own feelings on the matter. "Is it not better to live as if there were some abiding logic to our existence?"

"Make no mistake, Master Wheldrake." She touched him with a certain affection. "I have accepted the abiding logic—and it is the logic of power and conquest . . ."

"So decided my own ancestors," said Elric quietly. "They perceived a multiverse that was all but random, and they conceived a philosophy to formalize what they saw. Since their world was controlled by the random whims of the Lords of the Higher Worlds, they argued, then the only way of ensuring their survival was to gain as much power as they could—power at least as great as that of certain minor deities. Power enough, at least, to make Chaos bargain with them, rather than threaten and destroy. But what did that power gain them in the end? Less, I suspect, than your uncle gained by his decision . . ."

"My uncle had no sense," said Charion, bringing an end to the conversation. She turned her attention back to the toad, who had settled again and, while she scratched its vast back with her blade, stared moodily towards the horizon where dark ridges had begun to appear, the first sight of the reefs separating, according to the folk of Ulshinir, the inhabitable world from the uninhabitable.

They could hear surf now, could see it spuming against the volcanic rocks so that they gleamed with an unwelcoming blackness.

"*I am discontented, mistress. I am hungry.*" The toad turned its eyes upon Charion, and Wheldrake understood that he had a rival. He enjoyed the peculiar experience of being amused, jealous and profoundly terrified all at the same time.

Elric, too, had witnessed the toad's expression when it looked at Charion and he frowned. Some instinct informed him but was not, as yet, a conscious thought. He was content to wait until the instinct had matured, found words, had confirmation and become an idea. Meanwhile he smiled at Wheldrake's discomfort. "Fear not, friend Wheldrake! If you lack that fellow's beauty and perhaps even his specific charm, you almost certainly have the superior wit."

"Oh, indeed, sir," said Wheldrake, mocking himself a little, "and I know that wit usually counts for nothing in the game of love! There is no verse form invented that could easily carry such a tale—of a poet whose rival is a reptile! The heartache of it! The uncertainty! The folly!"

And he paused suddenly, eyeing the monstrous toad as it returned his attention, glaring at him as if it had understood every word.

Then it opened its lips and spoke slowly.

"*Thou shalt not have mine egg . . .*"

"Exactly, sir. Exactly what I was remarking to my friend here." With a bow so theatrical and elaborate even Elric was unsure what, at certain times, the poet was performing, Wheldrake went off for a while to concern himself with some business in the stern.

From the crow's nest came the cry of the lookout and this brought Gaynor round from where he had been staring apparently out to sea, almost as if he slept, or as if his soul had left his body. "What? Ah, yes. The navigator. Fetch up the navigator!"

And now, up from the starboard lower deck, comes a grey man—a man whose skin has been tanned by rain and wind but never by the sun, a man whose eyes are hurt by the light, yet grateful for it, also. He rubs at wrists which, by the chafing on them, have lately been tied. He sniffs at the salty wind and he grins to himself, in memory.

"Navigator. Here's your means of earning your freedom," says Gaynor, signaling him up towards the prow which rises and falls with graceful speed as the wind takes the sail and the rocky shores of a dozen islands lie ahead—black, wicked teeth in mouths of roaring foam.

"Or killing us all and taking everyone to hell with me," says the navigator carelessly. He is a man of about forty-five, his light beard grey-brown as his shaggy hair and with grey-green eyes so piercing and strange that it is clear he has learned to keep them hooded, for now he squints as if against strong sun, though the sun lies behind him, and, with lithe movements of a man glad to be active again, he springs to the foredeck, squeezes around the toad's cage as though he encounters such beasts every day, and joins Gaynor in the prow. "You'd better haul in that sail as soon as you can," says the navigator, raising his voice above the gaining wind, "or turn about completely and take another approach. A couple of minutes and nothing will save us from those rocks!"

Gaynor turned shouting to his crew and Elric admired the skill with which the sailors went to their work, turning the ship just enough so that the sail hung limp on the mast, then hauling it in before the wind could find it again. The navigator shouted out encouragement, sending the men to their oars, for this was the only way to navigate the reefs at the edge of the world.

Slowly now the black-and-yellow ship moved through the tugging currents of the reef—a few inches this way, a few that, sometimes touching a rock so lightly there was the barest whisper of friction, sometimes seeming to squeeze between pillars of basalt and obsidian, while the wind yelled and the surf crashed and the whole world seemed once more to be given up to Chaos. It was noon before they had negotiated the first line of reefs and lay at anchor in the calm waters between themselves and the second line. Now the navigator gave instructions for the crew to eat well and to rest. They would not attempt the next line until the following day.

Next day they plunged again into cacophony and wave-tossed con-

THE REVENGE OF THE ROSE   125

fusion as the navigator called out first one direction and then another, sometimes running back along the ship to take the wheel, sometimes clambering to the crow's nest to remind himself of what lay ahead, for it was clear he had navigated these reefs more than once.

Another river of clear, blue ocean running over pale sand; another patch of calm water—and the navigator made them rest another day.

Twelve days it took them to reach the farthest reef and look with unpleasant emotions upon the black surf pouring like oily smoke onto the massive natural barrier created by the last line of islands, onto beaches of smooth, fused obsidian. The Heavy Sea moved with extreme precision, the waves rising and falling with agonizing slowness, and the deep sounds it made hinted at this sea having a voice largely inaudible to the human ear, for a peculiar silence existed over its dark, slow waters.

"It is like a sea of cold, liquefied lead," said Wheldrake. "It offends all natural laws!" At which remark of his own he shrugged, as if to say "What does not?" "How can any ship sail across that? The surface tension is rather more adequate than is needed, I would guess . . ."

The navigator lifted his head from where he had been resting it on the rail. "It can be crossed," he said. "It has been crossed. It is a sea that flows between the worlds, but there are folk for whom that ocean is as familiar as the one we have just left behind is to us. Mortal ingenuity can usually find a means of traveling through or over anything."

"But is it not a dangerous sea?" asked Wheldrake, looking upon it with considerable distaste.

"Oh, yes," agreed the navigator. "It is very dangerous." He spoke carelessly. "Although it could be argued, I suppose, that anything which becomes familiar is less dangerous . . ."

"Or more," said Elric with some feeling. He took one last look at the Heavy Sea and went below, to the cabin he shared with Wheldrake. That night he remained in his quarters, brooding on matters impossible to discuss with any other creature, while Wheldrake joined the navigator and the crew in celebration of their successful crossing of the reefs and in the hope of gaining a little more courage for the voyage that remained. But if Wheldrake had planned to learn more of the navigator, save that Gaynor had taken him aboard only a couple of days before they came to Ulshinir, he was disappointed. Nor did he see anything else of Charion, his beloved, that night. Something stopped him from returning to the cabin—some sense of discretion—and he stayed, instead, upon the deck for a while, listening to the sluggish breakers splashing against the sea-smoothed obsidian and he thought of the Egyptian Book of the Dead and the stories of the Boat of Souls, of Charon, Boatman to the Gods, for to him this truly seemed like some netherworld ocean—perhaps the waters which lapped the very shores of limbo.

And now Wheldrake found himself beside the cage where the monster slept, its eyes tight shut as it snored and snuffled and smacked its loose, spongy lips, and at that moment the poet felt a certain sympathy for the creature, who was as surely trapped into compromise with Gaynor as almost everyone else aboard the ship. He leaned his arm on the rail of black, carved wood and watched as the moon emerged from behind a cloud and its light fell upon the scales, the leathery folds of flesh, the almost translucent webbing between the enormous fingers, and marveled at such ugliness, enraptured of such beauty. Whereupon he thought of himself, thought of a phrase, a certain cadence, felt about his pockets for his ink, his quill and his parchment and set to work in the moonlight to find romantic comparisons between Wheldrake the Poet and Khorghakh the Toad which was, he felt with a certain degree of self-satisfaction, all the more difficult if one attempted, for instance, some version of trochaic dimeter . . .

> Of this schism
> Occultism,
> Lately risen,
> (Euphemism)
> Calls for heroism rare.

Which occupied him so successfully that it was not until dawn that he placed his pining head upon his pillow and fell into the sweetest dreams of love he had ever known . . .

Dawn found all but Wheldrake on deck, faces upturned towards a lowering sky from which fell a languorous rain. It had grown warmer overnight and the humidity was very high. Elric tugged at his clothes and wished that he were naked. He felt as if he walked through tepid mead. The navigator was up on the foredeck with the toad; they seemed to be in conference. Then the grey man straightened and came back to where Elric, Gaynor and Charion stood together under a rough awning upon which the rain drops thumped with deliberate rhythm. He brushed his own woolen sleeve. "It's like mercury, this stuff. You should try to swallow some. It won't harm you, but it's almost impossible—you have to chew it. Now, Prince Gaynor the Damned, you struck a bargain with me and I have fulfilled the first part. Whereupon you said you would return to me what was mine. Before, you agreed, we advance into the Heavy Sea."

The grey-green gaze was steady upon that shifting helm. They were eyes that feared almost nothing.

"True," says Gaynor, "such a bargain was made—" and he seems to hesitate, as if weighing the odds of breaking his oath, then deciding he would gain more by honouring it—"and I shall keep it, naturally. One moment." He leaves the quarter-deck to go below and re-emerge with a small bundle—perhaps a wrapped greatcoat—which he puts into the navigator's hands. For a second those strange eyes flare and the mouth grins oddly, then the grey man is impassive again. Carrying the bundle he returns to take a further word or two with the toad. Then it's "Get a man to the lookout" and "Oarsmen to their positions" and "Keep that sail down—'tis a slow wind that will fill her, but 'tis worth the attempt" and the navigator is moving about the black-and-yellow ship—a man of the wild sea, a man of well-garnered wisdom and natural intellect, everything that a ship's commander should be—encouraging, shouting, whistling, joking with all—even the great old toad that grumbled his way from the cage as Charion released him, to creep bit by bit to the prow, and lie along the creaking bowsprit, forcing the ship still further down into the sea—down now through a narrow channel (pointed out by the navigator hanging in the rigging above the toad's green head) where white water meets black, where airy foam meets leaden droplets, suspended in the thick air. The prow of the ship—sharp and honed like a razor in the manner of the *bakrasim* of the Vilmirian Peninsula—sliced into that sluggish mass, driven by the toad's weight, guided now by the toad's bellows translated by the navigator to the steersman, and they are entering the Heavy Sea, going into darkness, going into the place where the sky itself seems like a kind of skin off which all sounds echo and the fading echoes are themselves returned until it seems the voices of tormented mortals in all their billions are sounding in their agonized ears and it is impossible to hear anything but that. They are tempted to signal to Prince Gaynor, standing himself at the helm now, to turn the ship about, for they must all die of the noise.

But Gaynor the Damned would not heed them. His terrible helm is lifted against the elements, his armoured body challenges the multiverse, defiant of the natural or the supernatural, or any other form which might threaten him! For he is never alarmed by death.

The toad croaks and gestures, the navigator signs with his hands, and Gaynor turns the wheel a little this way, a little that, fine as a needlewoman at her stretcher, while Elric holds his hands against his ears, seeks for something to stuff into them, to stop the pain which must surely burst his brain. Up on deck, ghastly, comes Wheldrake—

—and then the sound is over. A silence encloses the ship.

"You, too," says Wheldrake in some relief. "I thought it was last night's wine. Or possibly the poetry . . ."

He stares in dismay at the slow-moving darkness all around them, looks up at the bruised sky from which the leisurely rain still falls, and returns without further remark to his cabin for a moment.

The ship still moves, the Heavy Sea still heaves, and through this liquid maze the craft of Chaos cleaves. The toad groans out his orders, the navigator shouts; and Gaynor on his quarter-deck turns the wheel a fraction south. The toad's webbed hand makes urgent signs, the wheel is turned again, and onward into laggard seas drive Gaynor and his men. And on every single face of them, save Elric and his friend, is a wild, dark glee, and a sniffing at the sea for the smell of purest fear. They sniffed for fear like hounds for blood; they sniffed on that sluggish air; they sniffed for danger and scent of death and they tasted the wind like bread. And the toad groans out his orders and his mouth is wet with greed, and the toad's breath wheezes in the toad's dark maw, for soon he must come to feed.

"Master, I must feed!"

The strange water rolls like mercury over the ship's decks as she plunges on, sometimes threatening, it seems, to become stuck in a glutinous wave. And at last the ship will not move at all. The toad takes ropes from the prow and, its wide feet spread upon the water, long enough to break the surface tension before treading on again at what is clearly a natural gait, hauls the whole ship behind it. Behind him, momentarily, in the heavy water are the toad's footprints and then the tension is broken by the prow until at last the toad is swimming again, gasping with something akin to pleasure as the great droplets roll over his scales. There is a noise from it; a noise of joy: a noise that finds distant echo somewhere above, suggesting that they are in fact within a vast cave, or perhaps some more organic manifestation of Chaos. Then the booming song of the toad dies away and the creature comes paddling back to the ship, to crawl slowly aboard, tipping down the prow again, and resume its position along the bowsprit while the navigator climbs back overhead and once more Gaynor takes up the wheel.

Elric, fascinated by these events, watches the drops of water roll from the toad's glistening body and fall back into the sea. Above, in the rolling darkness, come sudden flashes of dusky scarlet and deep blue, as if whatever sun burns on them is not like any they have seen before. Now even the air is so thick that they must gulp at it like stranded fish and one man falls to the deck in a fit, but Gaynor does not lift a gauntleted hand from the wheel nor make any movement of his head to suggest that they must stop. And not one, now, asks him to stop. Elric realizes they are like-minded nihilists who have suffered too much already to fear any pain that might lie ahead. Certainly they do not fear a clean death. Unlike Gaynor, these men are not questing for death with his desperation. These are men who would kill themselves if they did not believe that living was just a little more interesting than dying. Elric recognized in them something of what he frequently felt—a terrible, deep boredom with all the reminders one met of human venality and folly—yet there was also in him another feeling, a memory of his people before they founded Melniboné, when they were gentler and lived with the existing realities rather than attempt to force their own; a memory of justice and perfection. He went to the rail and looked out over the slow-heaving waters of the Heavy Sea and he wondered where, in all that sluggish darkness, were the three sisters to be found. And did they still have the box of black rosewood? And did that box still contain his father's soul?

Wheldrake appeared, with Charion Phatt, chanting some rhyme of almost mesmeric simplicity and then blushing suddenly and stopping.

"It would be useful, something like that," said Mistress Phatt, "for the rowers. They need a steady sort of rhythm. I have no intention, I assure you, Master Wheldrake, of marrying that toad. I have no intention of marrying at all. I believe you have heard my views on the perils of domesticity."

"Hopeless love!" wailed Wheldrake, with what was almost relish. He cast a scrap of paper over the side. It fell flat upon the water, undulating with it as if given a spark of life of its own.

"Whatever pleases you, sir." She winked at Elric cheerfully.

"You seem in excellent spirits," said the albino, "for one who is embarked upon such a voyage as this."

"I can sense the sisters," she said. "I told Prince Gaynor. I sensed them an hour ago. And I can sense them now. They have returned to this plane. And if they are here, then soon my uncle and my grandmother, and perhaps my cousin, will find them, too."

"You think the sisters will reunite you with your family? That's the only reason you seek them?"

"I believe that if they live it is inevitable that we shall meet, most probably through the sisters."

"But the Rose and the boy are dead."

"I said I did not know where they were, not that they were dead . . ." It was clear she feared the worst but was refusing to admit it.

Elric did not pursue the subject. He knew what it was like to live with grief.

And on sailed the Chaos ship, into the slow silence of the Heavy Sea, with the croaking of the great toad and the voice of the navigator the only sounds to cut through the swampy air.

That night they dropped anchor and all but Gaynor retired. The damned prince strode the deck with a steady pace, almost in rhythm with the languid waves, and occasionally Elric, who could not sleep but had no wish to join Gaynor on deck, heard the creature cry out as if startled. "Who's there?"

Elric wondered what kind of denizens occupied the Heavy Sea. Were there others, like the toad but of a more malevolent disposition?

At Gaynor's third cry, he got to his feet, pulling on some clothes, his scabbarded sword in his hand. Wheldrake, too, was disturbed, but merely raised himself up in his bunk and murmured a question.

Out into the salty miasma went Elric, seeking the source of Gaynor's shout. Then he saw, looming over the port rail, the bulk of what could only be some kind of ship. A tall, wooden construction—a kind of castellated tower from which were already swinging half-a-dozen figures, all of them armed with long, savage pikes and flenchers—brutal weapons, but effective in this kind of fighting.

But not, reflected Elric with a certain humour, as effective as a black runesword.

And with that he dragged the hellblade from its scabbard and ran on bare feet along the deck to greet the first of the pirates as they dropped aboard the ship.

Above them, on the foredeck, the navigator appeared for a moment, glaring upward and moving with an odd series of leaps back into the rigging. "Dramian Toad-hunters!" he cried to Elric. "They're after our guide! We are dead without it!"

Then the navigator had disappeared again and the first of the hunters stabbed at Elric with the jagged points of his pike—

—and died almost without realizing it, wriggling like a speared fish as his soul was sucked into the blade . . .

Stormbringer seemed to purr with pleasure. The sword's song grew louder, greedier as one by one the hunters went down.

Elric, used to supernatural foes, stood amongst the growing pile of corpses like a farmer scything hay on a pleasant summer's day and it was left to Charion and the crew to finish off the few who now tried desperately to get back to their ship . . .

. . . But Elric was ahead of them, clambering up one of their own lines as a hunter desperately tried to saw at it with his pike. Elric reached the hunter before the rope was sheared and he drove the sword deep through the man's breastbone, watching him writhe. The hunter tried to keep his hold on the rope, then grasped the blade itself with both hands, as the sword relished its gradual feasting on the rich marrow of his soul. He tried to push himself off the sword, to cast himself into the dark water that now showed between the two ships, and on an impulse Elric released his grip on Stormbringer and watched with a sense of profound calm as sword and victim went plunging downwards. Weaponless, he continued his climb up the rope, swinging over the crenelations to discover that the bulky forward tower belonged to a vessel of singular slimness. It was a ship designed to race upon the surface of this peculiar ocean. Elric could see large outriggers, like the limbs of some huge water-insect, curving into the darkness.

And then, from a hatch in the deck, came more of the hunters, all armed with flenchers and grinning with the prospect of their butchery. Elric cursed himself for a fool and backed away from them, his eyes searching for some means of escape.

The hunters had the look of men who intended to enjoy their work. The first made an experimental swing with his flencher. The broad, curved blade whistled in the sultry air.

They were almost upon Elric when the albino heard a deep growling from somewhere over his head and thought the toad had climbed the tower undetected. But what he saw instead was a great snarling dog, silvery in the darkness, springing for the throat of the nearest hunter and tearing at it until it was nothing more than bloody meat, glaring up with a triumphant flaring of its nostrils as the other hunters fled. Elric did not care at that moment where his rescuer had come from. He merely thanked the animal and glanced down onto the deck to see how his companions fared. He saw Charion finishing off an adversary and lifting her lovely head in a high, ululating note.

The few hunters who still lived ran for the sides in blind panic; for now, over the starboard rail, its lips smacking and its eyes gleaming, breathing with wheezing slowness, crawled the toad they had sought to capture for themselves. The dog had vanished.

Khorghakh hesitated once he was aboard, his bulk enveloping parts of the rail and the hatches, and he cocked his head enquiringly.

From somewhere on the Chaos ship Elric heard Gaynor's voice crying out, exultant and full of an unusual excitement.

"Now, toad! Now, my darling, now you can feed!"

Later, when what was left of the hunters and their ship was burning in the darkness of the Heavy Sea and Khorghakh in his cage was snoring with monstrous hands upon a swollen belly, and Charion sat cross-legged beside him, as if comforted by the beast's enormous power, Elric walked slowly along the deck searching for his sword.

He had not for a moment believed that he had rid himself of the blade when he let it go with its victim. In the past whenever he had tried to abandon Stormbringer it had always returned to him. Now he regretted his folly. He was likely to need his sword. In trepidation, wondering if the blade had been stolen by some supernatural agency, he continued to search.

He searched again, in the shadows of the ship. He knew the blade refused to be separated from him. He had fully expected it to return. Yet the scabbard was gone, too, which suggested theft. He looked, also, for the dog which had appeared to help him and which had gone again so suddenly. Who, aboard, had owned such a dog? Or had it belonged to the hunters and, like the toad, taken vengeance on its oppressors?

As he passed the cabin under the foredeck, he heard a familiar sound. It came from Gaynor's berth—a low, peculiar moaning. He was astonished and further alarmed at the power commanded by the Prince of the Damned. No mortal could have taken up that naked sword and not been harmed, especially when it had so recently drawn enormous psychic force into itself!

Softly Elric moved to Gaynor's door. Now there was only silence on the other side.

The door was not locked. Gaynor was careless of any mortal attempt on his life or his person.

Elric paused for a second before flinging open the door, to reveal a sudden eruption of yelling light, a screeching and a hissing, and then Gaynor stood before him, adjusting his helm with one metal-shod hand, holding the runesword in the other. The runes along the blade juddered and whispered, as if the sword itself understood that the impossible had occurred. Yet Elric noticed that Gaynor trembled and that he had to put his other hand upon the runesword's hilt, to hold it steady, though his stance remained apparently casual.

Elric stretched his open palm towards the blade.

"Even you, Prince of the Damned, could not wield my runesword with impunity. Do you not understand that the blade and I are one? Do you not know that we are brothers, that sword and I? And that we have other kin who may be summoned to our aid when we require it? Know you nothing of that battle-blade's qualities, prince?"

"Only what I have heard of in legends." Gaynor sighed within his helm. "I would test it for myself. Will you lend me your sword, Prince Elric?"

"I could more easily lend you a limb." The albino gestured again for the return of his sword.

Prince Gaynor was reluctant. He studied the runes, he tested the balance. And then he returned the blade to both steel hands. "I do not fear your sword will kill me, Elric."

"I doubt it has the power to kill you, Gaynor. Is that what you desire of it? It might take your soul. It might transmogrify you. I doubt, however, if it will grant you your desire."

Before he gave it up, Gaynor laid one metal-clad finger upon the blade. "Is that the power of the anti-balance, I wonder?"

"I have not heard of such a power," said Elric. He slid the scabbard back onto his belt.

"They say it is a power even more ambitious than the Lords of the Higher Worlds. More dangerous, more cruel, more effective than anything known to the multiverse. They say the power of the anti-balance has the means of changing the whole nature of the multiverse in a single stroke."

"I know only that Fate has forged us together, that blade and I," said Elric. "Our destinies are the same." He glanced around Gaynor's sparely furnished cabin. "I have little interest in the broadly cosmic, Prince Gaynor. I have desires rather less exaggerated than most I have met of late. I seek only to find the answers to certain questions I have asked myself. I would gladly be free of all Lords of the Higher Worlds and their machinations. Even of the Balance itself."

Gaynor turned away from him. "You are an interesting creature, Elric of Melniboné. Ill-suited to serve Chaos, it would seem."

"Ill-suited for most things, sir," said Elric. "To serve Chaos is merely a family tradition with us."

Gaynor's helm came round again to stare broodingly at the albino. "You believe it is possible to banish Law and Chaos entirely—to banish them from the multiverse?"

"Of that I am not so sure. But I have heard of places where neither Law nor Chaos have jurisdiction." Elric was too cautious to mention Tanelorn. "I have heard of worlds where the Balance rules unchallenged, also . . ."

"I, too, have known such places. I dwelled in one . . ." There came a frightful chuckling from within the shifting steel helm and then a pause as the Prince of the Damned moved slowly to the far side of his cabin and appeared to be staring through the porthole.

His final words were uttered with such chilling ferocity that Elric, completely unprepared for them, felt he had been struck physically, to his vitals, by iron of such infinite coldness it reached to his soul . . .

"Oh, Elric, I hate thee with such jealous hate! I hate thee for thine insistent relish of life! For what I once was and what I might have become, I hate thee! For what thou aspireth to, I hate thee most of all . . ."

As he bent to close the door, the albino looked back at the figure of Gaynor and it seemed to him that the armour which enclosed the damned prince had long since ceased to protect him from any of the things he truly feared. Now the armour had become nothing more than a prison.

"And for my part, Gaynor the Damned," he said with gentle subtlety, "I pity thee with all my soul."

Chapter Four

Land at last! A Certain Conflict of Interests. Concerning the Anatomy of Lycanthropy.

"In my own world, sir, sad to say, human prejudice is matched only by human folly. Not a soul *claims* to be prejudiced, of course, as there are few who would describe themselves as fools . . ." Ernest Wheldrake addressed the grey navigator as they sat at breakfast on deck the next morning beneath a leaden sky upon the Heavy Sea and watched black waves rise and fall with what seemed unnatural slowness.

Elric, chewing on a piece of barely palatable salt beef, remarked that this seemed a quality of a good deal of society, throughout the multiverse.

The navigator turned his sharp green-grey eyes upon the albino and there was a certain restrained humour in his face when he spoke. "I have known whole Spheres where reason and gentleness, respect for self and for others, have existed together with vigorous intellectual and artistic pursuits—and where the supernatural world was merely a metaphor . . ."

At which Wheldrake smiled. "Even in my England, sir, such perfection was rarely found."

"I did not say perfection was common," murmured the grey man, and he curled his lithe old body off the bench and stood to peer into the green-black sky and stretch his long limbs and lick his thin lips and sniff at the wind and turn towards the prow and the toad, whose sleepy bellows had sounded like rage to the waking passengers. "There is a comet up there!" He pointed one tapering finger. "It means a prince has died." He listened for a moment until, mysteriously satisfied, he loped on about his duties.

"Where I once lived," came the sepulchral melody of Gaynor the Damned as he climbed up from his cabin, "they said that when a comet died a *poet* died." He clapped a shimmering gauntlet upon Wheldrake's resisting shoulder. "Do they say that, where you are from, Master Wheldrake?"

"You are in ungentle spirits I see, this morning, sir," Wheldrake spoke gently, his cool anger overwhelming his fear. "Perhaps you have your toad's indigestion?"

Gaynor withdrew his hand and acknowledged the little man's admonishment. "Well, well, sir. Some princes are more eager for death than others. And poets, for life, we know. Lady Charion." A bow that set his whole helm to flowing with angry fire. "Prince Elric. Aha! And Master Snare—" for back from his post ran the grey navigator.

"I sought you earlier, Prince Gaynor. We had an agreement between us."

"There is no hope for you," said Gaynor the Damned, making a movement forward, perhaps of sympathy. "She is dead. She died when the church collapsed. You must seek your bride in limbo now, Esbern Snare."

"You promised you would tell me—"

"I promised I would tell thee the truth. And the truth is what I have told thee. She is dead. Her soul awaits thee."

The grey navigator bowed his shaggy head. "You know I cannot join her! I have forfeited my right to life after death! And in return, O, Heaven help me! I have joined with the Undead . . ." With that sudden statement of feeling, Esbern Snare rushed back to the forecastle and ran up into the rigging, to stare blindly into the seething horizon.

Whereupon Gaynor the Damned made a sound like a sigh, deep within his helm, and Elric understood how he had been rescued on the ship and why there was a fellow-feeling evident between the navigator and the deathless prince.

But Wheldrake was gasping with a kind of joy and clapping his hand upon the breakfast table, making the stewed herbs slop, unmourned, from cup to cloth. "By Heaven, sir, that's Esbjorn Snorre, is it not? Now I have the trick of your pronunciation—and his, I note. I make no claims. We are, after all, rather grateful for that singular telepathy which provides us with the means, so frequently, of our survival in some highly inclement social weather—we should not begrudge benign Mother Nature a few regional accents—by way of a little light-hearted relief to her in her ever-vigilant concern for our continuing existence. Astonishing sir, when you think of it."

"You have heard of the navigator?" Lady Charion caught, as it were, at the coat-tails of his conversation's substance.

"I have heard of Esbern Snare. But the ending of his tale was a happy one. He tricked a troll into building a church for him and his bride to be married in. The troll's wife gave away the troll's name and so released Esbern Snare from his bargain. The troll's wife can still be heard wailing, they say, under Ulshoi hill. I wrote a kind of ballad about it in my *Norwegian Songs*. Pillaged, of course, by Whittier, but we'll say no more of that. No doubt he needed the money. Still, plagiarism's only dishonourable if the coin you earn with it is worth less than the coin you stole."

Again, Charion clutched bravely for the original substance:

"He married happily, you say? But you heard what Gaynor told him?"

"This is a sequel, it seems, to the original tale. I only know of the successful trickster. Any subsequent tragedy had been forgotten by the folklore of my day. Sometimes, you know, it occurs to me that I am in a dream in which all those heroes and heroines, villains and villainesses of my verses have come to life to haunt me, to befriend me, to make me one of themselves. A man, after all, could rarely hope to find such varied company in Putney . . ."

"So you do not know why Esbern Snare is aboard this ship, Master Wheldrake?"

"No better than you, my lady."

"And you, Prince Elric?" She attracted the albino's wandering attention. "Do you know this story?"

Elric shook his head.

"I only know," he said, "that he is a shape-changer and, that most cursed of souls, a person of rare goodness and sanity. Imagine such torment as is his!"

Even Wheldrake bowed his head, as if in respect. For there are few more terrible fates than that of the immortal separated, by force of the most profound natural logic, from those immortal souls it cherishes in life. It can know only the pain of death but never the ecstasy of everlasting life. Its pleasures and rewards are short-lived; its torment, eternal.

And this made Elric think of his father, lingering in that timeless destruction of Imrryr's ancestor; himself separated from his one abiding love by his willingness to bargain with his patron demon—even betray him—for a little more unearned power on Earth.

The albino found himself brooding upon the nature of all unholy bargains, of his own dependency upon the hellsword Stormbringer, of his willingness to summon supernatural aid without thought of any spiritual consequences to himself and, perhaps most significantly, of his *unwillingness* to find a way to cure himself of the occult's seductive attraction; for there was a part of his strange brain that was curious to follow its own fate; to learn whatever disastrous conclusion lay in store for it—it needed to know the end of the saga: the value, perhaps, of its torment.

Elric found that he had walked up the deck to the forecastle, past the reverberant toad, to put his back against the bowsprit's copper-shod knuckle and stare up at the navigator as he hung, still motionless, in the rigging.

"Where do you journey, Esbern Snare?" he asked.

The grey man cocked his head, as if hearing a distant but familiar whistle. Then his pale green-grey eyes stared down into the albino's crimson orbs and a great gust of air escaped him, and a tear appeared upon his cheek.

"Nowhere, now," said Esbern Snare. "Nowhere, now, sir."

"Would you continue in Gaynor's service?" Elric asked. "Even when land is sighted?"

"Until I choose to do otherwise, sir. As you shall yourself observe. There is land ahead, no more than a mile before us."

"You can see it?" Elric asked in surprise, attempting to peer into the swirling vapours of the Heavy Sea.

"No, sir," said Esbern Snare. "But I can smell it."

And land it soon was. Land rising up from the slow, awful waters of the Heavy Sea; land like a wakened monster, an angry shadow, all sharp ridges and jagged points; cliffs of black marble; beaches of carbon, and black breakers which poured like the smoke of hell upon that squealing shore . . .

Land so inhospitable the voyagers who looked at it now were all pretty much of the same accord, that the Heavy Sea was less daunting; and it was Wheldrake who suggested they sail on until they found a more accessible island.

But Gaynor shook his flickering helm and lifted up his glowing fist and put his steel palm upon the slender shoulders of Charion Phatt. "You told me, child, that the other Phatts are here. Have they found the sisters?"

The young woman shook her head slowly. Her face was grave and her eyes seemed to look into some different reality. "They have not found the sisters."

"Yet they—and the sisters—are here?"

"Beyond this—aye—in there . . ." Her mouth grew a little slack now as she lifted her head and pointed towards the massive cliffs dashed by that black foam. "Aye—there—and there, they go—yet— oh, Uncle! I see why! The sisters ride on. But Uncle? Where is grandma? The sisters go towards the East. It is in their nature to bear always eastward, now. They are going home."

"Good," says Gaynor with deep satisfaction. "We must find a place to land."

And Wheldrake confided to Elric that he had the feeling Gaynor was prepared to wreck them all now, in order to make landfall and continue his pursuit.

And yet the ship was beached at last upon that black, salty shingle up which the gougy tide lazily rolled and as lazily retreated.

"It is like," said Wheldrake in distaste as, the skirts of his frock-coat wrapped around his narrow chest, he stepped gingerly through the shallows, "a form of molasses. What causes this, Master Snare?"

His bundle under his arm, Esbern Snare lifted his long legs through the liquid. "Nothing," he said, "save a minor distortion in the fabric of time. Such places are not uncommon in this particular Sphere. In my own they were rare. I came across a small one—a matter of a few feet—near the North Pole. That would have been around the turn of your century, Master Wheldrake, I think."

"Which one, sir? I am a native of several. I am, as it were, timeless. Perhaps I have been granted my own particular ironic doom, ha, ha!"

Now Esbern Snare loped ahead, up the beach to where a great crack had opened in the wall of marble and through the jagged open-ing poured a shaft of watery golden light. "I think we have our path-way to the cliff-top," he said.

His bundle between his teeth, he was already climbing—his long limbs perfect for the route he chose from jutting crag to jutting crag— a great, grey spider scuttling up the rock, finding first one ledge and then another, until he had marked a path for the others, an easy means of climbing from the beach to the surface of the cliff. They mounted this, one at a time, with Elric bringing up the rear. On Gaynor's orders the sailors were already letting down their sail and moving the ship back into the water while from the forecastle came the wailing and groanings of a recently awakened toad who only now realized that its beloved was departing, perhaps for ever.

Soon they all stood upon the cliff and tried to look back at the ocean, but already billowing black cloud buried the Heavy Sea from view, and all they could hear was the sinister tide scraping on the beaches, increasingly faint—as if the entire scene retreated downwards, away from them—or as if the cliff rose up.

Elric turned. They were above the cloud-line now and the air was easier to breathe. Stretching away from them was a flat plain of gleaming rock—an immense vista of marble in which, here and there, gleamed little lights, as if there were creatures so densely constituted that they lived in the marble as we might live in oxygen, and were occupied, domestically, below.

Esbern Snare voiced his own provincial fears. "This has the look of troll country," he said. "Have I traveled so far to endure the hospitality of Trollheim? What an irony that would be."

Gaynor silenced him. "If we were all left to stand about bemoaning the particulars of our special dooms, gentlemen, we should be here for ever. Given that at least two of our company are immortal, this could prove singularly boring. I would beg of you, Esbern Snare, neither to keen nor to make any other vocal reminder of your soul's agony."

And the grey navigator frowned, perhaps a little surprised by an accusation which might have been better applied, he guessed, to the accuser himself. But Gaynor made no such acknowledgment. Of that socially misliked company he seemed the only one unwilling to extend to others the tolerance he longed for, the tolerance exemplified by the sublime justice of the Cosmic Balance which he had forsaken. Increasingly, it seemed, he grew both frightened and impatient, perhaps because he had secrets from them—a prior knowledge of this land and its inhabitants? He fell silent now and spoke no more to them until at last the uncompromising hardness of the marble gave way to earth and then to grass and the land began to slope downwards towards a surprisingly lovely valley through which a stream meandered and whose hills were clad with all kinds of thickly growing winter trees. Yet there was no sign of habitation and the air grew steadily colder as they descended the trackless slopes towards the valley floor until they were glad of the extra garments they had brought in their packs.

Only Esbern Snare refused to put his bundled apparel about his shoulders. Instead he hugged the parcel tighter to his chest, as if threatened. And again Elric felt a frisson of understanding for the grey man who only today had lost the last of his hope.

They camped that night in a pine-spinney, with a big fire roaring against the bitter cold and a moon appearing, almost unexpectedly overhead in the clear winter sky, huge and silver and casting deep shadows amongst the trees—shadows which were calm contrast to the leaping, unsettled shadows made by the great fire.

Soon the fire had grown so hot, fed by a lucky find of dead wood, that Elric, Charion and Wheldrake were forced to move a little further away, lest they be scorched in their sleep. Only Esbern Snare and Gaynor the Damned were left in the blaze of firelight, the grey, sad man, and the supernatural prince in his unstable armour—two doomed immortals attempting to warm their souls against the chill of eternal night; creatures who would have chosen the flames of hell rather than endure their present suffering, who longed for another reality, such as once they had both known, where pain was banished, and men and women were rarely tempted to give up the peace of their souls in return for the gaudy treasures, the greedy pleasures of the occult.

"What a beautiful thing," said Charion, almost in echo of these thoughts, "is a butterfly's wing. The bounty of nature bestow'd on a rose. Do you know that one, Master Wheldrake?"

The poet admitted that it was not in his repertoire. He considered the metre. He wondered if it were the best choice for the sentiment.

"I think I am ready for sleep now," she said, a hint of regret in her tone.

"Sleep is a preferred theme in my own work," he agreed. "Daniel's sonnet on the subject is excellent. At least, academically speaking. Do you know it?"

"Care-charmer Sleep, son of the sable Night,
    Brother to Death, in silent darkness born,
Relieve my languish, and restore the light;
    With dark forgetting of my care return,
    And let the day be time enough to mourn
    The shipwreck of my ill-adventured youth."

He quoted on, while a thin, cold breeze ran amongst the trees and soon his snores had gently and unostentatiously joined the rest . . .

Dawn had brought some snow. While most of the party shivered against it and cursed their bad luck, Esbern Snare opened his mouth and drew in the smell of it, licked his lips at the taste of it; a spring in his gait as he performed his tasks in the making of the morning meal. But already there was conflict as Gaynor cried: "Do you not recall a bargain made between us, my lady? A bargain which you yourself proposed!"

"A bargain which is now ended, sir. You have had your several uses of me. I become my own woman again. I brought you here and you shall seek your sisters here, but with no help from me!"

"Our interests are the same! It is folly to separate." Prince Gaynor's hand was upon the pommel of his broadsword as if he would threaten her had his pride permitted it. He had thought his native power was enough to persuade her and this was evident in every thwarted movement of his body, his frustrated tones. "Your family will find the sisters. They are bound to. We are upon the same quest!"

"No," said Charion. "For whatever reason—and I cannot detect one—the sisters go that way, but my uncle goes yonder—and to my uncle, sir, I must follow!"

"You agreed we should seek the sisters together."

"That was until I knew my uncle and grandma were in danger. I go to them. I go, sir, unquestionably, to them!"

And with that she was off through the trees, bidding farewell to no-one, dashing the snow from the branches she bent in her progress, her breath steaming and her wiry body gathering speed, as if she had no more time to lose.

Wheldrake was picking up his books and his miscellaneous possessions shouting out for her to pause. He would go with her! She needed a man, he said, upon her adventure. His own farewells were rapid and half-ended as he fled upon his beloved's trail leaving a cold and sudden silence behind him as, over the ashes of the guttering fire, the three doomed men regarded one another in uncertain camaraderie.

"Will you seek the sisters with me, Elric?" Gaynor asked at last. His voice was calmer now, almost chastened.

"The sisters have what I require, so I must find them in order to ask them for it," said Elric.

"And you, Esbern Snare?" Gaynor asked. "Are you with us, still?"

"I have no interest in your elusive sisters," said Esbern Snare, "unless they have the key to my release."

"They carry two keys, it seems," said Elric, putting a friendly hand on the grey man's shoulder, "so perhaps they have a third for you."

"Very well," said Esbern Snare. "I will join you tomorrow. Do you go towards the East?"

"Always east, we've learned, for our sisters," said Gaynor.

So the three of them—tall figures, lean as winter weasels—began their journey eastward, up the steep slopes of the valley, through frozen foothills, to a range of ancient mountains, whose rotting granite threatened to collapse with every foot they set upon it, while the snow came thicker now and they must break ice to get their water, save at noon, when the thin sun warmed the world enough to make it run; wide ribbons of silver racing through the glittering white shards.

Gaynor continued to brood in silence while Esbern Snare, loping ahead much of the time, grew increasingly alert as if he had found his native element. And all the while his bundle never left him, whether he slept or ate, so that one day, as they made cautious progress above a deep gorge which had filled with snow to make a sort of glacier, below which a fierce torrent could be heard rushing through caverns and tunnels it had carved through the ice, Elric asked him why he valued the thing so greatly. Was it some keepsake, perhaps?

They had paused for breath upon the narrow path, their feet hardly as long as the track was wide, but Gaynor had marched tirelessly on, apparently oblivious of the depth and steepness of the gorge.

"It is a treasure in a sense, sir!" Esbern Snare uttered a humourless laugh. "For I must value it as I value nothing else. As I value, if you like, my very life. My soul, I fear, has modest worth now, or I would name that, also."

"So it is precious to you, indeed," said Elric. He talked chiefly to rid himself of the grief he felt for losing Wheldrake's company, as if part of him—that part which relished life and human love—was forbidden to him, banished. He felt as frozen as the glacier below, with a torrent bursting within him, unable to find expression in the ways he most valued—the ordinary ways of loving the world and the friends it offered. Perhaps he lacked the refinements of language required to adapt and modify his sentiments and yet he understood, better than anyone, how language itself was the perfect and perhaps the only honourable way of earning his right to respect among those denizens of the natural world whom he, in turn, respected. Yet still it was through action, rather than words, that he tried to accomplish his unvoiced ambitions. Thoughtless action, blind romance, had led him to destroy everything he cherished and he had sought understanding in taking only the action suggested by others, by following the trade of other impoverished Melnibonéan nobles, of mercenary—and a mercenary of exceptional accomplishments and gifts. Even now his quest was not of his own devising. In his heart of hearts he knew he must soon begin to look for some more positive means of achieving what he had hoped to achieve with the sack of the Dreaming City and the destruction of the Bright Empire of Melniboné. Thus far he had looked chiefly at the past. But there were no answers there. Only examples which scarcely suited his present condition.

There was a long silence as the two men stood together on the narrow ridge, staring across the gorge at the far banks, at the lifeless landscape, where not a bird or a rabbit could be seen, as if time, already slowing in the Heavy Sea, had come almost to a stop, and the crashing of the water underneath the ice seemed to fade away to leave only the steady sound of their breathing.

"I loved her," said the grey man suddenly, his breast convulsing, almost as if struck by something heavy. Another pause, as if he drowned, and then his manner was steady again. "Her name was Helva of Nesvek, daughter of the Lord of Nesvek, and the finest and most womanly of mortals, in all her wit and art, her grace and her charity; there was none saintlier, nor more natural (in natural matters), than my Helva. Well, I was of good family but not wealthy in the way that Lord Nesvek was wealthy and it had been pronounced by the great lord himself that his daughter's hand should go to the man worthiest of God. I understood that in Lord Nesvek's judgment God was inclined to bless those worthiest of Him with worldly riches and this, to Nesvek's lord, was the true and proper order of things. So I knew I could not win my Helva's hand, though she had already chosen me. I conceived the notion of seeking supernatural aid and, in short, made a bargain with a troll, by which the troll should build me a fine cathedral church—the finest in the Northlands—whereupon, when the building was completed, I was to have discovered the name of the architect or forfeit my eyes and heart to him. Well, by happy chance, I overheard the troll's wife singing to her infant child, telling him that he should not cry, for soon Fine, his father, would be home with a human's eyes and heart for him to feast upon.

"Thus did I achieve my end and Lord Nesvek found it impossible, of course, to refuse a suitor who could build such a magnificent monument to God, and at monumental cost, quite evidently.

"Meanwhile, of course, the poor troll-wife, the source of my salvation, was beaten regularly by her infuriated spouse and I began the building of our estate, about a mile from Kallundborg, where I had built the church and would be able to see the spire from my new house's tower. The building went well, even without trollish labour, and soon the hall was raised, with good outhouses and cottages for the servants, on prime land, thanks to my Helva's dowry. Thus were we all accommodated, it seemed. Until the coming of the wolf to our land that next winter, when we settled to enjoy the long nights with merriment and stories and all manner of festivity, as well as the hard work of winter stock-caring. Made harder, now, because of our wolf. A huge beast, twice the weight and bulk of a tall man, the wolf had killed dogs, cattle, sheep and a child in its search for food. Few bones had been found, and those gnawed through for the marrow, as if the wolf fed cubs as well as itself. Which we found strange for dead of winter, though it has been known for wolves to bear more than one litter in a year, especially after a mild previous winter and an early spring. Then the wolf killed the pregnant wife of my steward and carried off what remains we did not find in the shallow hole it had rested in while it devoured the flesh it needed to continue its rapid escape from us. For, of course, we pursued it.

"One by one the other men gave up, for a variety of reasons which the steward and I accepted with good grace, and then there were only the two of us following the wolf's trail into a deep, wooded ravine, until one night the wolf leapt over the fires we had built, believing ourselves safe, and took my steward—killing him before he dragged him off through the fires as if they did not exist.

"I will admit, Prince Elric, that I was near-frozen with terror! Though I had shot arrows at the beast and cut at it with my sword, I had not harmed it. The wounds I made healed immediately. I knew then—and only then, sir—that I was dealing with no natural animal."

For a little while Esbern Snare inched his way along the path, to keep circulation and in the hope of reaching a better thoroughfare before nightfall. When next they took breath, he concluded his story.

"I continued to track the beast, though I believe it thought itself free of pursuit—perhaps deliberately killing my steward, not because it was hungry, but because it wished to be rid of our company. Indeed, I found most of his remains a day later and was surprised to discover that what I assumed to be some human traveler had helped itself to the dead man's effects, though the clothes, of course, were too bloody and torn to be of use.

"I grew so angry and greedy for revenge that I could no longer sleep. Unrested and yet untired now, I kept up a steady pursuit until one night, under a three-quarter moon, I came upon a human camp. It was a woman who camped there. I watched her through the trees, too cautious to announce myself, yet ready to defend her if the wolf attacked. Now, to my concern, I saw that she had two small children with her, a boy and a girl, both clad in a mixture of animal hides and a miscellany of other garments, who were eating soup from a pot she had built over her fire. The woman looked weary and I assumed she was fleeing from some brutish husband, or that her village had been destroyed by raiders—for we were now on the borderland between the Northern people and the Easterners, those cruel nomads who are without Christian religion nor any pagan honesty. Yet something in me still kept me back. I realized at length that I was using her as a lure—as bait for the wolf. Well, the wolf did not come, and as I watched I took note of everything within that camp, until I saw the great wolfskin which hung upon the tree under which she slept with her children, and I took it for some kind of charm, some way in which the wolf could be resisted. So I watched another day and another night, following the woman up towards the far mountains, where the savage Eastern nomads roamed, and I thought to warn her of her danger, yet it was becoming gradually clear to me that she was not the one who was in danger. Her movements were sure, and she cared for her children with the air of someone who had long lived a wild life beyond the very outposts of civilization. I admired her. She was a good-looking woman and the way she moved made me forget my marriage oath. Perhaps, too, I watched her for that reason. I began to feel a sense of power in this observation, this secret knowledge of her. I know now that I did, indeed, possess a kind of power which only those of her like might possess and those were the only creatures whose presence she could not detect. Had another been with me, she would have known at once.

"It was on the night of the full moon that I saw her take out the folded wolfskin and drape it around her shoulders, saw her drop to all fours and in a bewildering instant stand, growling faintly at the children to stay close to the fire, looking out into the night, an enormous wolf. Yet still she did not see me, did not scent me. I was invisible to her supernatural senses. She moved off towards the mountains and was back at noon that next day with a kill, some nomad boy, probably a herder, and two lambs, which she had dragged, using the boy's body as a kind of sledge. The human remains she left for herself, but assumed her woman form once she had brought the lambs into camp. These she prepared for her children. Later that evening, as they ate the rich-smelling stew she had cooked, she returned to her human kill and devoured a good deal of him, almost certainly in wolf shape. I was too cautious to get closer to her.

"By now, of course, I understood that the woman was a werewolf. A werewolf of special ferocity, since she had two human cubs to feed. These little creatures were innocent children and had no lycanthropic taint. My guess was that she had taken to this life from desperation, in order that her children should not starve. Yet this had meant other children would starve and more would die, merely to sustain her brood, so my sympathy was limited. As soon as she slept that night, glutted with food, I gathered the courage to sneak into the camp, tear the wolfskin from the tree and make my way back into the forest.

"She awakened almost immediately, but now that I possessed the skin, with which she transformed herself into an invincible beast, I knew I was safe. From the shadows I spoke to her. 'Madam, I have the frightful thing you have used to kill my friends and their families. It will be burned outside the church of Kallundborg when I return! I would not kill a mother before her own children, so while you are with them you are safe from my vengeance. I bid thee farewell.'

"At which the poor creature began to wail and scream—quite

unlike the self-possessed mother who had cared for her young in the wild. But I would not listen to her. I knew she must be punished. What I did not know then, of course, was how cruel her punishment would be. 'Do you understand how I must survive if you take away my skin?' she asked. 'Aye, madam, I do,' said I. 'But you must suffer those consequences now. There is meat enough for several days in your pot—and a little meat left outside your camp, which I do not think you are too squeamish to use. So farewell again, madam. This evil thing will be burning soon upon a Christian pyre.'

"'You must have pity,' she said, 'for you are of my blood. Few can change as I can change—as you can change. Only you could steal that skin. I knew that I should fear you more. Yet I spared you, for I recognized my kindred. Would you not, sir, show loyalty to our common blood and spare my children their unthinkable fate?'

"But I listened no more and I left. As I went away she set up a terrible wailing and howling—a screaming and begging—a bestial, horrible whining—as she called out for her only means of any dignity, any vestige of humanity. That is the final irony of the Undead—that they cling to such shreds of human pride—cling to the memory of the very thing they have bartered in order to become what they have become! Surely the worst fate, I thought, that a werewolf could know. But there are worse fates than that, sir—or at least refinements on them. I left that wolf-woman howling and slavering—already a maddened wretch. It was almost impossible to imagine such agony as she already expressed, let alone imagine the pain to come.

"Oh, well, sir, the story's the usual miserable tale of folly and expediency you know so well. Trapped by the winter of the Eastern wastes, I resorted to using the skin myself. By the time I returned to Kallundborg I was wedded to it more powerfully than I was wedded to my sweetheart and my wife, Helva of Nesvek. I sought religious help and found only horror at my tale. Thus I left to wander the world, seeking some salvation, some means of returning to the past I had known, of being reunited with my darling. More unearthly adventures befell me, sir, from Sphere to Sphere, and then I learned that the troll itself sought vengeance and tricked some cleric, some visiting bishop, into a bargain that brought down the whole cathedral while the larger part of the population, my wife among them, prayed for my lost soul . . .

"That is what Gaynor promised to tell me—the fate of my wife. And that is why I weep now, sir, so long after the event."

Elric could find no words of reply and none of consolation for this good man cursed to rely for his only existence upon that horrible skin, forced to perform the most inhuman acts of evil savagery or go forever into nothingness, never to be united with his lost love, even in death.

Perhaps it was not therefore surprising that Elric fingered the pommel of his hellsword and thought deeply upon his own relationship with the blade and saw in poor Esbern Snare a fate more terrible than his own.

The next time he extended a generous hand to the grey man as he stumbled through the twilight, there was a peculiar sense of kinship in the gesture. Slowly, the two whose stories were so different, and whose fates were so similar, continued their progress along that narrow ridge of rock above the sinister whisper of water as it cut its way through the snows of the ravine.

CHAPTER FIVE

Detecting Certain Hints of the Higher Worlds;
A Convention of the Patrons and the Patronized;
Sacrifice of the Sane and Good.

Prince Gaynor the Damned paused upon the rocky slopes of the last mountain and peered across a waste of scrub grass towards a far distant range. "This land seems all mountains," he said. "Perhaps, however, that is the rim of the far shore? The sisters must be close. We could scarcely miss them on this barren plain."

They had eaten the last of their food and still had seen no signs of animals on earth or in the sky.

"It's as if it never had inhabitants," said Esbern Snare. "As if life has been exiled from this plain completely."

"I've seen such sights before," Elric told him. "They make me uncomfortable—for it can be a sign that Law has conquered everything or that Chaos rules, as yet unmanifested . . ."

They agreed that they had all shared such experiences, but now Gaynor grew even more impatient, exhorting them to make better speed towards the mountains, "lest the sisters take ship from the farther shore," but Esbern Snare, sustained neither by whatever hellish force fed Gaynor nor by the dragon venom which Elric used, grew hungry and began to fall back, fingering the bundle he carried, and sometimes Elric thought he heard him slavering and growling to himself and when he turned once to enquire, he looked into eyes of purest suffering.

When they broke camp next morning, Esbern Snare, the Northern Werewolf, was gone, succumbing to the temptation which had already destroyed any hope that was ever in him. Twice, Elric thought he heard a mournful howling which was echoed by the mountains and so impossible to trace. Then, once more, there was nothing but silence.

For a day and a night, Elric and Gaynor exchanged not one word but marched in a kind of dogged trance towards the mountains. With the following dawn, however, they found that the plain was rising slightly, in a gentle hill, beyond which they thought they could detect the faintest sounds of a settlement, perhaps even a large town.

Gaynor, in good spirits, clapped Elric upon the back and said, almost jauntily, "Soon, friend Elric, we shall both have what we seek!"

And Elric said nothing, wondering what Gaynor would do if, by some strange chance, they both sought the same thing—or, at least, the same container. And this made him think of the Rose again and he mourned the loss of her.

"Perhaps we should determine the exact nature of our quest," he said, "lest we are unprepared when we eventually meet the sisters."

Gaynor shrugged. He turned his helm towards Elric and his eyes seemed less troubled than they had been of late. "We do not seek the same thing, Elric of Melniboné, of that you can be assured."

"I seek a rosewood box," said Elric bluntly.

"And I seek a flower," said Gaynor carelessly, "that has bloomed since time began."

They were close to the brow of the hill now and had almost reached it when the earth was suddenly shaken by an enormous booming which threatened to throw them off their balance. Again came the great reverberant noise. Seemingly some vast gong was being struck, and struck again, until Elric was covering his ears, while Gaynor had fallen to one knee, as if pressed to the ground by a gigantic hand.

Ten times in all the great gong sounded, but its reverberations continued, almost endlessly, to shake the crags of the surrounding mountains.

Able to move forward again, Elric and Gaynor reached the top of the hill to stare upwards at the enormous construction which, both could have sworn, had not been there even a moment before. Yet here it was in all its solid and complicated detail, a network of wooden gantries and monstrous cogs, all creaking and groaning and turning with slow precision, while metal whirled and flashed within—copper and bronze and silver wires and levers and balances, forming impossible patterns, peculiar diffractions—revealing the thousands of human figures toiling upon this vast framework, turning the handles, walking the treadmills, carrying the sand or the pails of water up and down the walkways, balancing between pegs which were carefully placed to maintain some delicate internal equilibrium, and the whole thing shuddering as if it must fall at any moment and send every naked man, woman and child who worked perpetually upon it to their immediate destruction. At the very top of this tower was a large globe which Elric thought at first must be of crystal but then he realized it consisted entirely of the strongest ectoplasmic membrane he had ever seen—and he guessed at once what the membrane imprisoned, for there was scarcely a sorcerer on Earth who had not sought its secret . . .

Gaynor, too, understood what the membrane contained and it was clear he feared what must soon be revealed as that vast, unearthly skeleton-clock measured off the moments and a humorous voice spoke casually from nowhere.

"See, my little treasures, how Arioch brings time to a timeless world? Merely one of the small benefits of Chaos. It is my homage to the Cosmic Balance."

And his laughter was hideous in its easy cruelty.

The immense clock clicked and clattered, whirred and grunted, and the structure trembled, shivering with every movement, while from within the globular membrane at the very top, which turned and shook with the passing of each second, an angry eye occasionally appeared, while a fanged mouth raged in supernatural silence and claws, fiercer than any dragon's, flashed and scratched and tore, but never with effect, for the entity was trapped within the most powerful prison known in, below or beyond the Higher Worlds. The only entity Elric knew which required such bonds to hold it was a Lord of the Higher Worlds!

Now Gaynor, realizing the same thing at the same time, took steps backwards and looked about him, as if he might find some sudden refuge, but there was none and Arioch laughed the louder at his dismay. "Aye, little Gaynor, your silly strategies have gained you nothing. When will you all learn that you have neither the resources nor, indeed, the character required to gamble against the gods, even such petty gods as myself and Count Mashabak here?" The laughter was richer now.

This was what Gaynor had feared. His master, the only creature capable of protecting him against Arioch, had lost whatever engagement had taken place between them. And this meant, too, that Sadric's attempt to cheat his patrons of their tribute might also have failed.

Yet Gaynor had lost too much already, faced too much horror, contemplated too many repellent fates, caused and observed too much suffering, to show any distress of his own. He drew himself up, his hands folded before him, and lowered his helmeted head in the slightest of acknowledgments. "Then I must call thee master now, Lord Arioch," he said.

"Aye. Always thy true master. Always the master concerned for his slaves. I take a great interest in the activities of my little humans, for in so many ways their ambitions and dreams mirror those of the gods. Arioch was ever the Duke of Hell most mortals turn to when they have need of Chaos's ministrations. And I love thee. But I love the folk of Melniboné most, and of these I love Sadric and Elric most of all."

And Gaynor waited, his helm still slightly bowed, as if expecting some doom of singular and exquisite savagery.

"See how I protect my slaves," Arioch continued, still invisible, his voice moving from one part of the valley to the next, yet always intimate, always amused. "The clock sustains their lives. Should any one of them, old or young, for a moment fail in their specific function, the whole structure will collapse. Thus do my creatures learn the true nature of interdependence. One peg in the wrong socket, one pail of water in the wrong sluice, one false step upon a treadmill, one hesitant hand upon a lever, and all are destroyed. To continue to live, they must work the clock, and each creature is responsible for the lives of all the rest. While my friend Count Mashabak up there would not, of course, be greatly harmed, there would be a certain pleasure for me in watching his little prison rolling about at random amongst the ruins. Do you see your ex-master, Gaynor? What was it he told you to seek?"

"A flower, master. A flower that has lived for thousands of years, since it was first plucked."

"I wonder why Mashabak would not tell me that himself. I am pleased with thee, Gaynor. Wouldst thou serve me?"

"As thou wishest, master."

"Sweet slave, I love thee again! Sweet, sweet, obedient slave! Oh, how I love thee!"

"And I love thee, master," came Gaynor's bitter response—a voice that had known millennia of defeat and frustrated longing. "I am thy slave."

"My slave! My lovely slave! Wouldst thou not remove thine helm and reveal thy face to me?"

"I cannot, master. There is nothing to reveal."

"As thou art nothing, Gaynor, save for the life I permit in thee. Save for the forces of the pit which empower thee. Save for the all-consuming greed which informs thee. Wouldst thou have me destroy thee, Gaynor?"

"If it pleases thee, master."

"I think you should work for a while upon the clock. Would you serve me there, Gaynor? Or would you continue your quest?"

"As it pleases thee, Lord Arioch."

Elric, sickened by this, found himself full of a peculiar self-loathing. Was it his fate, also, to serve Chaos as thoroughly as Gaynor served it—without even the remains of self-respect or will? Was this the final price one paid for all bargains with Chaos? And yet he knew his own doom was not the same, that he was still cursed with a degree of free will. Or was that merely an illusion with which Arioch softened the truth? He shuddered.

"And Elric, would you work upon the clock?"

"I would destroy thee first, Lord Arioch," said the albino coolly, his hand upon the hilt of his hellsword. "My compacts with thee are of blood and ancient inheritance. I made no special bargain of my soul. 'Tis others' souls, my lord, I dedicate to thee."

He sensed within himself now some strength which even the Duke of Hell could not annihilate—some small part of his soul which remained his own. Yet, also, he saw a future where that tiny fragment of integrity could dissipate and leave him as empty of hope and self-respect as Gaynor the Damned . . .

His glance at the ex-Prince of the Universal held no contempt—only a certain understanding and affinity with the wretched creature Gaynor had become. He was but a step away from that ultimate indignity.

There came a kind of thin screech from the ectoplasmic prison and Count Mashabak seemed to take some small pleasure in his rival's discomfort.

"Thou art my slave, Elric, make no mistake," purred the Chaos Lord. "And will ever remain so, as all your ancestors were mine . . ."

"Save one before me," Elric said firmly. "The bargain was broken by another, Lord Arioch. I have inherited no such thing. I told thee, my lord—when thou aidest me, I giveth thee the immortal plundering to thyself—souls like these, who worketh thine clock. These, great Duke of Hell, I do not begrudge thee, neither am I sparing in the numbers I allot thee. Without my summoning, as thou knowest, it is all but impossible for any Lord of the Higher Worlds to get to *my* world and upon that world I am the most powerful of all mortal sorcerers. Only I have the native powers to call to thee across the dimensions of the multiverse and provide a psychic path which thou canst follow. That thou knowest. That is why I live. That is why thou aideth me. I am the key which one day Chaos hopes to turn and open wide all the doors throughout the unconquered multiverse. That is my greatest power. And, Lord Arioch, it is mine to use as I desire, to bargain with as I choose and with whom I choose. It is my strength and my shield against all supernatural fierceness and threatening demands. I accept thee as my patron, Noble Demon, but not as my master."

"These are just silly words, little Elric. Wisps of dandelion on the summer breeze. Yet here you are, through no decision of your own. And here I am, by determined effort, exactly where I wish to be. Which freedom seems the best to you, my poorly pigmented pet?"

"If you are saying, Lord Arioch, would I rather be myself or thyself, I must still say that I would be myself; for perpetual Chaos must be as tedious as perpetual Law, or any other constant. A kind of death. I believe I still have more to relish of the multiverse than hast thou, Sir Demon. I still live. I am still of the living."

And from within the helm of Prince Gaynor the Damned came a great groan of anguish, for he, like Esbern Snare, was neither of the living nor the dead.

Then, sitting astride the ectoplasmic ball in which Count Mashabak squatted and glared, there appeared the naked, golden image of a handsome youth, a dream of fair Arcadia, whose goodness was sweeter than honey, whose beauty was richer than cream, and whose wicked eyes, delirious with cruelty, flashed the appalling lie for everything unholy and perverse that it was.

It giggled.

Arioch giggled. Then grinned. Then made water over the bulging membrane, as his helpless rival, engorged with the psychic energies of a hundred suns, raged and shouted from within, as helpless as a weasel in a snare.

"Mad Jack Porker ran the cripple down again; seized him by the brain,

they said; didn't stop till he was dead ... Greedy Porker, Greedy Porker, hung him by his humpo-storker ... Sit still, my dear count, while I take my comforts, sir, I pray you. You are an ill-mannered demon, sir. I always said so ... Hee, hee, hee ... Do you smell cheese, sir? Would you have a piece of ice about you, Jim? Hee, hee, hee ..."

"As I believe I observed earlier," said the albino prince to the still-cowed Gaynor, "the most powerful of beings are not necessarily the most intelligent, nor, indeed, sane, nor well-mannered. The more one knows of the gods, the more one learns this fundamental lesson ..." He turned his back upon Arioch and his clock, trusting that his patron demon did not decide, upon a whim, to extinguish him. He knew that while he protected that tiny spark of self-respect within him, nothing could destroy him in spirit. It was his own thing; what some would have called his immortal soul.

Yet with every movement and every word he trembled and weakened, wanting to cry out that he was no more than Arioch's creature, to do his master's every bidding and be rewarded by his master's every bounty: and, even so, be struck down, as he might be struck now, on a chance change of his master's mood.

For this was the other thing that Elric knew; that to compromise with Tyranny is always to be destroyed by it. The sanest and most logical choice lay always in resistance. This knowledge gave Elric his strength—his profound anger at injustice and inequality—his belief, now that he had visited Tanelorn, that it was possible to live in harmony with mortals of all persuasions and remain vital and engaged with the world. These things he would neither sell nor offer for sale and, in refusing to give himself up wholly to Chaos, it meant he bore his weight of crimes upon his own conscience and must live, night and day, with the knowledge of what and whom he had killed or ruined. This, he guessed, was a weight that Gaynor had been unable to bear. For his part, he would rather bear the weight of his own guilt than the weight that Gaynor had chosen.

He turned again to look up at that obscene clock, Arioch's cruel joke upon his slaves, upon his conquered rival, and every atom of his deficient blood cried out against such casual injustice, such delight in the terror and misery of others, such contempt for everything that lived within the multiverse, including itself; such cosmic cynicism!

"Have you brought me thy father's soul, Elric? Where is that which I told thee to find, my sweet?"

"I seek it still, Lord Arioch." Elric knew that Arioch had not yet established his rule across this whole realm and that his hold upon his new territory must still be tenuous. This meant that Arioch had nothing like the power he possessed in his own domain, where only the most crazed sorcerer would ever consider venturing. "And when I find it, I shall give it up to my father. Then, I would say, the rest is between yourself and him."

"You are a brave little stoat, my darling, now that you are no longer in my kingdom. But this one shall soon be mine. All of it. Do not anger me, darling pale one. *Soon the time will come when thou shalt serve mine every command!*"

"Possibly, great Lord of Hell, but meanwhile that time is not here. I make no further bargains. And I believe that thou wouldst as readily keep our old bargain as have none at all."

A growl of rage escaped Lord Arioch as he pummeled at the ectoplasmic prison with his fists, while Count Mashabak screamed with insane laughter from within. The Duke of Hell looked down upon the labouring thousands, each one of whom maintained, only by the most accurate and mechanical rhythms, the lives of its fellows, and he smirked, threatening with a pointed, golden finger to poke at one of the little figures and so bring the whole complicated structure to collapse.

Then he looked up at where Gaynor the Damned stood, unmoving, as he had been for some time. "Find me that flower and I will make you a Knight of Chaos, immortal nobility, ruling in our name a thousand kingdoms!"

"I will find the flower, great duke," said Gaynor.

"We shall make an example of thee, Elric," said Arioch. "Even now. By conquering thee, I shall establish Chaos fully upon this plane." And one golden hand stretched suddenly, longer and longer, larger and larger, towards Elric's face. But the albino had drawn his runesword with all the rapid skill of years and the great battle-blade roared out a challenge and a threat to all the myriad denizens of the Lower, Middle and Higher Worlds, to come to it, to cast themselves upon it, to feed it and its master, for this thing was not an owned thing at all, but had become, if it had not always been, an independent force whose sole loyalty was to its own existence, yet was as dependent upon Elric's wielding it as Elric was dependent upon its energy for his own survival. This unholy symbiosis, more profoundly mysterious than the wisest philosophers could fathom, was what made Elric the chosen child of Fate and it was what had, in the end, robbed him of his happiness.

"This must not be!" Arioch pulled back in thwarted anger. "Force must not fight force! Not yet. Not yet."

"There is more than Law and Chaos at work in the multiverse, my lord," said Elric calmly, the sword still held before him, "and more than one of these is thine enemy. Do not anger me too much."

"Ah, most dangerous and courageous of my souls, thou art truly fitted to be my chosen mortal above all the others, ruling in my name, with my power. Whole worlds would be thine, Elric—whole Spheres to mould to thy every whim. All pleasure can be thine. All experience. And unendingly. Without price or consequence. Eternal pleasure, Elric!"

"I have made myself clear, already, Lord Duke, on the subject of perpetuality. It could be that one day in the future I shall determine that my fate lies wholly with thee. But until that time . . ."

"I shall attack thy memory. That I *can* do!"

"Only in some ways, Lord Arioch. Never in dreams. In my dreams, I recall everything. But with this pell-mell twirling from plane to plane and Sphere to Sphere, the worlds of memory and dreams become confused with the worlds of reality and immediacy. Aye, you can attack my mind, my lord. But not my soul's memory."

Which set insane Count Mashabak to cackling again. "*Gaynor!*" His wild eyes caught sight of his former servant. "*Free me from this and thy reward will be tenfold what I promised.*"

"Death," said Gaynor suddenly. "Death, death, death is all I'm greedy for. And that you all deny me!"

"Because we value thee, dear one . . ." said the honey-sweet boy, lifting its head and chittering, like a startled wren. "I am Chaos. I am everything. I am the Lord of the Non-Linear, Captain of the *Random Particle* and Entropy's greatest celebrant! I am the wind from nowhere and I am the drowner of worlds; I am the Prince of Infinite Possibility! What glorious changes shall bloom upon the face of the multiverse, what unlikely and perverse marriages shall be sanctified by hell's priesthood, and what wonders and pleasures there will be, Elric! Nothing predictable. The only true justice in the multiverse—where all, even the gods, are subject to random birth and random annihilation! To banish Resolution and have instead eternal Revolution. A multiverse in permanent, gorgeous Crisis!"

"I fear I have spent too long with the gentler folk of the Young Kingdoms," said Elric softly, "to be much tempted by thy promises, my lord. Nor can I say I am much feared of thy threats. Prince Gaynor and myself are upon a quest. If we are to be of service to one another, sir, then I propose you let us continue upon that quest."

At which Arioch shifted his beautiful rump upon the yielding globe and said pettishly, "The damned one can go on his way. As for thee, recalcitrant servant, I cannot punish thee directly, but I can hamper thy quest until this more trustworthy servant achieves his end—whereupon I shall promise him far more than Mashabak promised him. I shall promise him a true death."

There came a sob from within Gaynor's peculiar helm and he fell to his knees, perhaps in gratitude.

Now Arioch raised a golden hammer in either fist and his youthful features were ablaze with glee as he brought first one hammer and then another down upon the yielding surface of the ectoplasmic womb, and with each blow came an unlikely booming, like that of a great gong, while within the prison Count Mashabak clapped scaly claws to his asymmetrical ears and howled in fearsome silence, as if whole universes were in anguish.

"It is the Time," cried Arioch. "It is the Time!"

Down falls Elric, screaming, with his hands, too, upon his ears.

And Gaynor goes down, crawling and shrieking in a voice so high-pitched it sounds above the booming of the hammers.

And then there is a low whistling and Elric feels his substance being sucked away, bit by bit, from this plane to another. And he tries to fight against that force which only a Duke of Hell would use, since it damages whole histories and peoples with the violence of the dimensional rupturing, but he is helpless and his runesword will not help him. Stormbringer seems glad to leave that lifeless plane; it needs to feed on living souls and Arioch had offered it not a morsel from his store.

Yet, even as he watches the monstrous clock shimmer and grow misty to his sight, even as Gaynor's mysterious armour becomes faintly outlined against a fainter landscape, the albino sees a huge grey shape loping towards him, the red tongue lolling, the grey-green eyes glaring, the white fangs clashing in its ferocious head, and he knows that it is the hungered werewolf, become so maddened by its lack of food that it is ready to risk even Stormbringer's edge!

But then it has turned, sniffing, its savage mouth grinning and the hot saliva showering from its jaws, the ears laid first forward, then laid back, and it seems to curve in mid-air, a single fluid motion, and direct its great body straight upwards to where Lord Arioch giggles, then squeals in genuine surprise as Esbern Snare buries his fangs in the throat of one he recognizes as his true tormentor.

So startled was Arioch, and so sparing now of his remaining powers upon this plane, that he could neither change his shape nor did he wish to flee—for by fleeing he would leave his captured rival, who might then be freed, and that he could not bear. So he struggled upon the swaying clock while the damned souls below worked frantically to correct every unpredictable motion of the thing, and the last Elric saw of Esbern Snare was his wolf body burning with a fierce, red-gold light as if he gave up, with selfless joy, his last few embers of life.

Then Elric saw the ectoplasmic sphere topple and fall towards the earth, with Arioch and Esbern Snare still locked together in conflict, and something flared and a darkness poured in upon him and swal-

lowed him up and carried him relentlessly through the broken walls of a thousand dimensions, every one of which lifted a separate voice in protest; every one of which exploded with a different angry colour. He was propelled through the multiverse with almost the last remaining energy Arioch had been able to summon upon that plane.

That was what Esbern Snare had known and that was why he had awaited this opportunity to help his companions.

For Esbern Snare was, indeed, a man of rare goodness and sanity. He had lived too long in thrall to an evil power. He had seen all that he valued destroyed because of it. So, though he could not reclaim his immortal soul, he could ensure himself at least an immortal memorial, some action to ensure that his name, and the name of the love he could never find again, would be forever linked in the tales told amongst the realms, in all the various futures which lay ahead.

Thus did Esbern Snare the Northern Werewolf redeem his honour, if not his soul.

A ROSE REDEEMED; A ROSE REVIVED

Three swift swords for the sisters three;
The first shall be of ivory;
The second sword's forged of rarest gold;
The third shall be cut from a granite fold.

The first sword's name is 'Just Old Man';
And the second is called 'The Urgent Brand';
While the third thirsty sword of that glamour'd
three
Is the hungry blade named 'Liberty'.

—Wheldrake,
Border Ballads

CHAPTER ONE

Of Weapons Possessed of Will; A Family Reunion;
Old Friends Found; A Quest Resumed.

NOW ELRIC FOUGHT to resist the force of Arioch's rage; stretching out his left hand as if to grasp at the fabric of time and space and slow his rush through the dimensions; clinging to his runesword while it howled and gibbered in his right hand, itself insane with mysterious supernatural anger at the Lord of Hell who had expended the last of his temporal energy on this plane in one final act of petty, and passing, vengeance. For Arioch had proved himself as whimsical as any other denizen of Chaos, willing to destroy all hoped-for futures in order to satisfy a momentary irritation. Which was why Chaos could be trusted no better than Law (which was inclined to permit similar actions, but in the name of principles whose purpose and point were frequently long-forgotten, creating as much mortal misery in the name of Intellect as Chaos wrought in the name of Sensibility).

Such thoughts were available to the albino, as he was flung through the radiantly pierced barriers of the multiverse—*for almost an eternity*—because, when eternity eludes the consciousness, then soon all which that consciousness knows is the singular agony of an expectation never *quite* fulfilled. Eternity is the end to time; the end to the suffering of anticipation; it is the beginning of life, of life unbounded! And thus Elric sought to embrace the beauty and the psychic grace of that perfect promised multiverse, perpetually in a state of transformation, between Life and Death, between Law and Chaos—accepting all, loving all, protecting all— that state of forever-changing societies, natural intelligences, benign supernature, evolving realities, forever relishing their own and others' differences, all in harmonious anarchy—that natural state, the wise ones knew, of each and every creature in each and every world, and which some imagined as a single omniscient entity, as the perfect Sum of Entirety.

Human love, thought the albino, as universe upon universe engulfed and expelled him, is our only constancy, the only quality with which we may conquer the inescapable logic of Entropy. And at that the sword trembled in his hand and seemed to be trying to twist free, almost as if it were disgusted by such sentimental altruism. But Elric clung to the blade as his only reality, his only security in this wildness of ruptured time and space, where the meaning of colour became profound and the meaning of sound unfathomable.

Again it wrenched at his grasp so that he must hold tighter to the quillons as the hellsword began to take its own determined course through the dimensions. It was at this point that Elric grew to respect the extraordinary power which dwelled within the black blade, of a power which seemed born of Chaos yet which had loyalty neither to Chaos nor to Law—yet neither did it serve the Balance—of a power so thoroughly a thing of itself that it required few outward manifestations and yet which might be the profound opposite of everything Elric valued and fought to create—as if some warring force were symbolized by this ironic bond between yearning idealist and cynical solipsist, a force, perhaps, which might be discovered in most thinking creatures, and which found over-dramatic resolution in the symbiosis between Stormbringer and the Last Lord of Melniboné . . .

Now the albino flew behind the runesword as it carved a path for itself—almost as if it drove back against Arioch's power, refusing the consequences not from any emotion Elric could understand, but to prove some principle as thoroughly upheld as any perhaps less mysterious principles of Law, almost as if it sought to correct some obscene malformation in the fabric of the cosmos, some event which it refused to permit . . .

Now Elric was caught up in a kind of intradimensional hurricane, in which a thousand reverses occurred within his brain at once and he became a thousand other creatures for an instant, and, where he lived through more than ten other lives; a fate only minimally different from the one that was familiar to him and so vast did the multiverse become, so unthinkable, that he began to go mad as he attempted to make sense of just a fraction of what laid siege to his sanity and he begged the sword to rest, to pause in its complex flight, to spare him.

But he knew that the sword considered him secondary to its chief concern, which was to re-establish itself at the point it felt was *right* for it in the multiverse . . . Perhaps it was an impulse no more conscious than instinct . . .

Elric's senses multiplied and became changed.

There was a sweet, calm sound of roses while his father's music flooded his arteries with bewildered sadness . . . with excruciating anxiety . . . as if to let him know that the time was almost over when Sadric had any choice but to seek out his son's soul and join it with his own . . .

At which the howling runesword gave up a bellow of resistance, as if this, too, attacked its own ambitions and the logic of its own unreasoning determination to survive without compromise with any other entity in the multiverse—even, ultimately, Elric who must be extinguished, as soon as he had fulfilled his final destiny, which at present was known to no-one, even the runesword, which did not live in any past, present or future understood by creatures of the Lower, Middle or Higher Worlds; yet it wove a pattern of its own, calling upon vaster energies than any Elric had witnessed, than any it had ever been required to utilize in giving aid to him in return for the souls not apportioned to Arioch . . .

"Elric!"

"Father, I fear I have lost thy soul . . . !"

"My soul shall never be lost to thee, my son . . ."

A bright and sudden gleam of hard, pink-gold light, like a weapon against his eyes, and a smack of freezing air against his flesh, and a rhythmic sound, so familiar, so wonderful to him, that he felt the hot tears fall once, then twice, upon his chilled cheeks . . .

> *"So Gaynor rode to The Ship That Was,*
> *And made of it his own,*
> *And three sisters rare he did ensnare,*
> *To insure the Chaos Throne.*
>
> *The first of these sisters was The Unfolded Flower,*
> *The second was Duty's Bud,*
> *While the third-born they christened Secret Thorn*
> *And her bower was built of blood."*

And, sobbing, Elric fell into the welcoming arms of that great-hearted, if dwarfish, poet, Master Ernest Wheldrake. "My dear, good, sir! My good, old friend! Greetings to thee, Prince Elric. Does something pursue thee?" And he pointed back up through the deep snow-banks terracing the valley wall, where a fresh-ploughed furrow ran, as if Elric had slid from the top of the cliff to the bottom.

"I am glad to see thee, Master Wheldrake." He brushed caked snow from his clothing, wondering, not for the first time, if he had dreamed his journey through the multiverse or if the dragon venom, perhaps, possessed more than restorative qualities. He glanced across the fresh-trod snow of a small clearing in the winter birchwood and saw Stormbringer leaning, almost casually, against a tree, and for a pure, clear moment, he knew absolute hatred of the blade, that part of himself he could no longer exist without or (as some small voice continued to tell him) that part, perhaps, that he wished to keep alive, since only in the rage of supernatural battle did he ever know any true relief from the burden of his conscience.

With deliberate slowness he strolled to the tree, picked up the blade and sheathed it as a man might sheath any ordinary weapon, his attention still upon his friend's disheveled features. "How came you here, Master Wheldrake? Is it a plane familiar to you?"

"Familiar enough, Prince Elric. And to yourself, I should think. We have not left the realm where flows the Heavy Sea."

And now Elric realized exactly what the Black Sword had done, dragging them both back to the very world from which Arioch had sought to banish them. And this suggested that the hellblade had motives of its own for ensuring his remaining here. He said none of this to Wheldrake but listened while his friend explained how Charion Phatt was at last reunited with her Uncle Fallogard and her grandmother.

"But Koropith remains lost to us at present," the poet concluded. "Fallogard, however, has a close sense of his son's presence. So we are hopeful, dear prince, that soon all surviving Phatts shall know again the pleasures of family security." He lowered his voice to a kind of conspiratorial squeak. "There is some talk of marriage between myself and my beloved Charion."

And, before he could burst into verse, the snowy branches of a forest path parted and here came the confident Charion, carrying the handles of a litter on which Mother Phatt sat, smiling and nodding, like a queen in a procession, the other end borne by her tall, untidy son who flashed a smile of jolly recognition towards the albino, as one might greet a familiar face at a local tavern. Only Charion seemed a little disturbed to discover the newcomer. "I sensed your destruction a year ago," she said quietly, after she had lowered her grandmother's litter to the ground. "I sensed you blasted out of any recognizable form of existence. How could you have survived that? Are you Gaynor or some shape-changer in Elric's guise?"

"I assure you, Mistress Phatt," said Elric, also disturbed, "I am only the one you know. For some reason, Fate does not want me annihilated as yet. It seems, indeed, that I am surviving annihilation rather successfully."

It was this last little irony that seemed to convince her and she relaxed. But it was clear every psychic sense in her was probing his being for signs of imposture. "You are indeed a remarkable creature, Elric of Melniboné," said Charion Phatt as she turned away to attend to her grandmother.

"I am glad you found us, sir. We ourselves have some rather excellent intimations concerning my missing son," called out Fallogard Phatt cheerfully, oblivious of his niece's suspicions. "So, gradually, we become, as it were, concrete again. You already know, I believe, my niece's intended?"

At which Charion Phatt blushed girlishly, to her own furious embarrassment, yet the eye she cast upon the little coxcomb was not unlike that which a certain toad had once cast upon her: for there is never anything but apparent paradox in the choices made by lovers.

And Mother Phatt opened her merry red mouth in which a few fangs still glittered and cried: "Ding dong, for the six sad drabs! Ding dong for the dilly-o!" As if, in senility, she had become possessed by a mad parrot. Yet she waved an approving hand upon her granddaughter's choice and her wink at Elric was full of knowing wit and, when he returned it, he was sure she smiled. "Dark days for the lily-white boy; bright days for the darkling joy! Feast of evil, feast of good, feasting fine the Chaos brood. Feast the devil, feast the Son; dark days for the shining one. For the flowers of the forest are blooming at night, and the ships of the ocean are sailing on land. Ding dong for the lily-white lad, ding dong for the good and the bad; sail through the wild-wood, sow grain on the sea; Chaos has come to the Land of the Three."

But when they taxed her on the meaning, if any, of her rhymes, she merely chuckled and called for her tea. "Mother Phatt is a greedy old woman," she confided to Elric. "But she's done her bit in the past, vicar, I think you'll agree. Mother Phatt sat under a tree; bore five strong sons to Eternity."

"Koropith, then, is not far from here?" Elric spoke to Fallogard Phatt. "You can sense him, you said, sir."

"Too much Chaos, you see," exclaimed the tall clairvoyant with a vigorous nod. "Hard to part it—hard to look through. Hard to call. Hard to hear an answer. Fuzzy, sir. The cosmos is always fuzzy when Chaos goes to work. This world is threatened, sir, you see. The first invaders have long since gained their foothold. Yet something holds them back, it seems."

Elric thought again of the runesword, yet had the notion that his blade was neither helping nor resisting the complicated flow of events; it had merely fought to return to the plane on which it must be at a certain time, during a certain movement of the multiverse. Some other power fought Chaos here, of that he was sure. And he wondered about the three sisters and their part in this. That they possessed certain trea-sures, which both he and Gaynor coveted, was almost all he knew—save for Wheldrake's ballad, which was mostly the poet's own invention and therefore of little use as an objective oracle. Did the sis-ters exist at all? Were they wholly the creation of the Bard of Putney? Was everyone pursuing a chimera—the invention of a highly romantic and over-coloured imagination?

> "In the third grey month on the third grey day,
>   Three sistren rode to Radinglay,
>   Seeking three treasures they had lost,
>   To the laughing lord of The Ship That Was."

"Well, sir," says Elric, helping with the fire they are building, for they had planned to make camp here, even before his sudden arrival, "do those old rhymes of yours give you any clue to the whereabouts of the sisters?"

"I must admit, sir, that I have modified the verses a little, to allow for the new things I have learned, so I am an unreliable source of truth, sir, save in its most fundamental sense. Like a majority of poets, sir. Speaking of Gaynor, we have intimations of him, but none of Master Snare. We were wondering what had become of him."

"He sacrificed himself," said Elric bluntly. "I think he saved me, also, from Arioch's full fury. To the best of my knowledge Arioch was driven from this plane by him—and he died in that act of banishing the Lord of Hell."

"You have lost your ally, then?"

"I have lost an ally, Master Wheldrake, as much as I have lost an enemy. I also appear to have lost a year in this realm. However, I do not mourn the loss of my patron Duke of Entropy . . ."

"Yet Chaos still threatens," said Fallogard Phatt. "This plane stinks of it. Hovering, as it were, before it devours the entire world!"

"Is it ourselves that Chaos desires?" Charion Phatt wished to know. Her uncle shook his head. "Not us, child. It is not *greedy* for us. We are merely, at present, an irritant to it, I think. No longer useful. But it would be rid of us." He closed his heavily lidded eyes. "It grows angry, I know. There is Gaynor now . . . See—smell—taste him—Gaynor—feel his presence—see him riding . . . gone, gone . . . There he is—riding—I think he seeks the sisters still. And is close to discovering them! Gaynor serves it and himself. A subtle power. They desire to possess it. Without it they can never fully conquer this plane. The sisters—at last—I can sense the sisters. They seek another. Gaynor? Chaos? What is this? An alliance? They seek—not Gaynor, I think . . . Ah! The Chaos stuff, it is too strong . . . Mist again. Uncertain mist . . ." He lifted his head and gasped at the cold twilight air as if he had been close to drowning in that psychic sea on which he was, often, the only voyager . . .

"Gaynor rode to the eastern mountains," said Elric. "Are the sisters still there?"

"No," said Fallogard Phatt, frowning. "They have long since left the Mynce and yet—time—Gaynor has gained time—he has been aided in this—is there a trap? What? What? I cannot see him!"

"We must break camp early," said Charion with all her usual practicality, "and try to reach the sisters before Gaynor. Yet our first duty is to family. Koropith is here."

"On this plane?" Elric asked.

"Or one that presently intersects this realm." She broke off a piece of candied leather and offered it to the albino who shook his head, having no love for the sweetmeats of her world where, Wheldrake swore, the taste in food was even worse than in his own. "I wonder," she added, "if anyone but me has any notion of Gaynor's positive will to evil?" And when she looked into the fire, her eyes were hidden from them all.

The snow came softly in the morning, covering the scars they had made behind them, covering the paths ahead, and the world was bitter with cold and silence as they trudged on through the forest, following the line of the cliff-top above and guessing, from thin sunlight, the direction in which they walked—yet they moved without hesitation, doggedly onward, following a psychic scent through this world where they appeared to be the only living creatures. They paused briefly to rest, to tend to Mother Phatt's needs, to boil her warming drinks of the herbs she herself had told them to pick and which were chiefly what they now lived on, together with the sweet jerky Charion carried. Then they were up again and marching where the snow was shallow and Mother Phatt inspected the moss and the bark they brought her and she told them that the realm had been in the grip of winter for more than a year and that this was Chaos work without doubt, and she murmured of old Ice Giants and the Cold Folk and the legends of her mother's people, who had been of the race, she claimed, that came before Man, that had ruled Cornwall before it was named by human tongues. There had been one, then, she said, that was also a prince, and that prince was of the old race, while the woman he married was of the new. The children of that union were her mother's ancestors. "It is why we have so great a gift of the Second Sight," she said to Elric intimately, patting his shoulder as he knelt beside her during one of their brief rests. She spoke to him as she might a favourite grandchild. "And they were not unlike you in appearance, save for the pigment, those folk."

"They were of Melniboné?"

"No, no, no! The word is meaningless. These were the great Vadhagh people who came before the Mabden. So, we are related, perhaps, you and I, Prince Elric?" Her intelligence was undisguised for a moment and complemented her humour. And Elric, looking into that face, thought that he looked into the face of Time itself.

"Are we," she asked him, "both of that Heroic blood?"

"It seems likely, madam," said Elric gently, scarcely aware of what she spoke, but glad to help her ease the burden she carried and which in some ways she appeared to resent.

"And born to bear a greater share of the world's grief, I fear," she said.

At which she began to cackle again, and to sing. "Dingly-dongly-bongly! Old Pim's a-dabbling-o! Ring the rich and lively boy to bleed his heart for May to bloom!" Whereupon she began to beat a kind of savage dirge with her spoon and plate. "Up from the blood and into the brain jumps that memory of pain!"

"O, Ma! O, Loins of my Creation! When Chaos mists so much, your recollection of ancient savageries does further encloud my sight!" Fallogard Phatt spoke with nervous grace and entreating hands.

"They'll gnaw and pick at poor old Ma's few remaining bits of brain." The ancient matron drew upon her store of pathos to charm her son, but he was adamant.

"Ma, we're almost onto Koropith and the going looks to get hard from now on. We must save our energies, Ma! We must hold our tongues and stop the scattering of random charms and jingles or you'll leave a witch-trail behind us to march an army up. Which is never prudent, Ma."

"Prudence never pickled no rats," said Ma Phatt with a reminiscent chuckle, but she obeyed her son. She accepted his logic.

Elric had begun to notice that the air grew warmer and the ice was melting in the trees, while snow fell heavily to mushy ground and was quickly absorbed. By that afternoon, under an intense sun, they had crossed a line of grotesquely armoured beast-men tortured into even stranger shapes and enshrouded in ice which was burning hot to the touch but through which the travelers saw eyes moving, lips straining to speak, limbs frozen in attitudes of perpetual agony. A small Chaos army, Fallogard Phatt had agreed with Elric, defeated by some unknown sorcery, perhaps an effort of Law? Now they rode across a desert through which ran what was almost certainly an artificial watercourse and from which they could drink.

The desert ended by the next day and they saw ahead of them the immense foliage of a dark, lush forest, whose trees bore leaves as long as a man, with trunks as slender and sinewy as human bodies, whose gorgeous foliage was deep scarlets and deep yellows, dusty browns and clouded blues, while mingling with these rich, threatening colours were strands of pale pink and veins of purple or grey, as if the forest was fed by blood.

"It is there, I think, we shall find our missing prodigal!" announced Fallogard Phatt heartily, though even his mother looked doubtfully at that menacing tangle of massive blooms and sinuous branches. There seemed to be no hint of a pathway through it.

But Fallogard Phatt, now at the head of the litter, trotted forward, causing his shorter niece to take quicker steps to maintain the balance and momentum of their progress, until she cried out for her uncle to stop as he plunged forward into the sticky, almost reptilian forest.

Glad to be in the shade, Elric leaned against a yielding trunk. It was as if he sank into soft flesh. He straightened his back and shifted his weight to his feet. "This is without doubt Chaos work," he said. "I am familiar with these creations, half-animal, half-vegetable, which are usually the first growths Chaos achieves on any world. They are essentially the detritus of unskilled sorceries and no self-respecting emperor of Melniboné would have wasted time on such stuff. But Chaos, as you no doubt have already learned, has very little taste— whereas Law, of course, has rather too much."

They found the forest easier going than they had imagined, for the fleshy branches parted easily and only occasionally did a pod cling sensually to an arm or part of a face, while a glossy green tentacle embraced the body like the arms of a lover. Yet the things were not greatly animated by Chaos-energy and Fallogard Phatt's progress was scarcely ever blocked for long.

Until, without warning, the jungle was no longer organic.

It became crystalline.

Pale light of a thousand shades fell through the prisms of the forest roof, flashed and skipped from branch to crystal leaf, flooded down trunks and across canopies—and still Fallogard Phatt continued his relentless advance through the jungle, for the crystals yielded as easily as had the branches.

"And this is Law's work, surely?" said Charion Phatt to Elric. "This sterile beauty?"

"I would admit—" said Elric studying the way the light fell in multicoloured slabs one upon the other until the forest floor ran with flooding light, like rubies and emeralds and dark amethysts, until they were knee-deep in it, wading on through this wealth of pigment which was also reflected in their skins so that Elric himself was at last one with his friends, for all looked in wondering pleasure at their swirling motley flesh which seemed to glint and dance with the crystals all around them. Then they had reached and entered a mighty cavern of cool, silver radiance—where distant water lapped gentle banks and they knew an intense peace, such as Elric had only known before in Tanelorn.

And it was here that Fallogard Phatt stopped and signed for his niece to lower the litter to the sweet-smelling moss of the cavern floor. "We have entered a zone where neither Law nor Chaos rules—where the Rule of the Balance is undertaken, perhaps. Here we shall find Koropith. Here we shall seek the three sisters."

Then, from somewhere above them, where the cavern roof caught the light of a setting sun and reflected it down to them, they heard a thin, angry shout and a voice calling from a distant gallery:

"Hurry, you idiots! Come up! Come up! Gaynor is here! He has captured the sisters!"

CHAPTER TWO

A Rose Rejoined; Further Familial Joy;
Gaynor's Rape Thwarted and the Sisters Found at Last—
Still Another Strange Turn of Fate's Wheel.

"Koropith, my heartsease! Oh, my beauty! Oh, my fruit!" Fallogard
Phatt peered up through the shafts of intersecting light, through the
galleries of green foliage and dark rock, through the richly scented
blooms, and stretched slender fingers out for his son.

"Quick, Pa! All of you! Up here! We must not let him succeed!"
The boy's voice was clear as a mountain spring. His tone was desperate.

Elric had found steps cut into the cave wall, winding up towards
the roof. Without further thought he began to climb these, followed by
Fallogard and Charion Phatt who left Wheldrake to protect Mother
Phatt.

Through the cool tranquility of that tall cave they climbed and Fallogard Phatt, panting, observed that the place was like a natural cathedral, "as if God had placed it here as an example to us" (by disposition
and background he was a monotheist) and had it not been for his son's
urgent cries from above he would have paused to observe the beauty
and the wonder of it.

"There he is! There's two of 'em, now!" cries Wheldrake crypti-
cally from below. "You're almost there! Carefully, my delicacy! Look
out for her, Pa!"

Charion needed help from no-one. Sure-footed, her sword already
in her hand, she followed quickly behind Elric and would have passed
him had there been room on the narrow steps.

They came to a gallery whose wall was made of a kind of hedge,
growing thickly from the side of the cliff and clearly designed to protect anyone who used the path. Elric wondered at the artistry of the
people who had lived here and if any of them had survived the coming
of Chaos to their world. If so, where were they?

The gallery widened and became the entrance to a large tunnel.
And there stood Koropith Phatt, gasping with the burning

immediacy of his predicament yet weeping to see his father and cousin again. "Quick, Pa! Gaynor will destroy her if we do not hurry! There is some chance he will destroy them all—destroy everyone!"

And he was dashing ahead of them, pausing to make sure they followed, dashing on again, calling. He had gained height and seemed to have lost weight; was turning into a skinny youth, as angular and gangling as his father. Dashing through galleries of green light, through peaceful chambers, through suites of rooms which looked out over the vastness of the cave itself, from windows set cunningly near the roof, and none of them occupied, all of them with a faint air of desolation. Dashing up curving stairways and gracefully sinuous corridors, through a city that was a palace or a palace that was large as a city, where a gentle people had lived in civilized harmony—

—and then comes the sounding of a pair in psychic, supernatural and physical combat—an explosion of orange light, a collapsing of a certain kind of darkness, the swirl of unnatural colours, followed by sounds, as if of a deep, irregular heartbeat—

—and Elric leads the others into a hall that, in its artfulness and delicate architectural intelligence, rivals the great cave below—almost an homage to it . . .

—and lying upon a floor of pale blue marble shot through with veins of the most subtle silver is the body of a young woman in brown and green, a great shock of pink-gold hair identifying her at once. There is a sword near her unmoving right hand, a dagger still in her left.

"Ah! No!" cries Koropith Phatt in anguish. "She cannot be dead!"

Elric, sheathing Stormbringer, knelt beside her, feeling for a pulse and finding one, faint, steady, in her cool throat just at the moment she opened her lovely hazel eyes and frowned at him. "Gaynor?" she murmured.

"Gone, it seems," said Elric. "And the sisters with him, I think."

"No! I was sure I had protected them!" The Rose made a weak movement of her arms, tried to rise and failed. Koropith Phatt hovered at Elric's shoulder, murmuring and crooning with helpless concern. She gave him a reassuring smile. "I am unharmed," she said. "Merely exhausted . . ." She drew two quick breaths. "Gaynor has a Lord of

Chaos to help him in this, I think. It took all the spells I bought in Oio to resist him. I have little left."

"I did not understand you to be a sorceress as well as a swordswoman," Elric said, helping her to sit.

"Our magic is of a natural order," she said, "but not all of us chose to practise it. Chaos has fewer weapons against it, which proved an advantage to me, though I had hoped to imprison him and learn more from him."

"He is in Count Mashabak's employ still, I think," said Elric.

"That much, sir, I know," said the Rose softly and with a significance only clear to herself.

Soon they had her seated on a cushioned settle, her skin pale pink in the gentle light of the blue hall, her hair folding about her delicate skull like petals.

It was some while, after Koropith had returned with Wheldrake and Mother Phatt, through tunnels easier to climb than the outer steps, before the Rose was ready to tell them what had occurred after she had reached this cave ("slithering through the dimensions like sneak-thieves"). She had found the sisters hidden, having failed in a quest of their own, which had taken them so far afield. Not for the first time she had offered them her aid, and they had been glad to accept it, but some rupturing of the cosmic fabric had been detected by Gaynor, whose own stronghold lay not fifty miles from here, and he had arrived with a small army to seize the sisters and their treasure. He had not expected to be resisted, especially by the singular magic commanded by the Rose, which was of a nature too subtle for Chaos easily to understand.

"My magic draws neither from Law nor from Chaos," she said, "but from the natural world. Sometimes it takes a century for one of our spells to stifle the roots of some spectacular tyranny, but when it is dead, it is thoroughly dead. It was our vocation to seek out tyranny and destroy it. So successful were we that we began to anger certain Lords of the Higher Worlds, who ruled through such people."

"You are the Daughters of the Garden," said Wheldrake, breaking in and then stopping apologetically. "There is an old Persian tale which speaks of you, I think. Or perhaps it is from Baghdad. The Daughters of Justice was another name . . . But you were Martyred . . . Forgive me, madam. There was a tale . . .

> "Came cruel Count Malcolm to that land,
>> With fire and steel in either hand,
> And a curse which fouled his breath;
>> I seek the Flowers of Bannon Brae;
> I bring them pain and death.

"Good heavens, madam, sometimes I feel I am trapped in some vast, unending epic of my own invention!"

"You recall the old ballad's ending, Master Wheldrake?"

"There are one or two," said Wheldrake diplomatically.

"You recall a certain ending, however, do you not?"

"I recall it, madam," said Wheldrake in dawning horror. "Oh, madam! No!"

"Aye," said the Rose. And she spoke slowly, with great, weary strength . . .

> "Each brand that burn'd in Bannon Brae,
>> Was a soul in cruel torment.
> Count Malcolm who cut the bright flowers down,
>> Left but one to sing Lament.

"I," said the Rose, "was the only flower not, eventually, cut down by him whom the ballad calls 'Count Malcolm'. The one whom Gaynor had preceded, with his lies to us concerning his own heroic struggles against the forces of the Dark." And she paused, as if she stilled a tear. "That was how we were caught unawares of the invasion. We trusted Gaynor. Indeed, I spoke for him! He is economical in his methods, I learned. He deceives us all with the same few tales. Our valley was a wasteland within hours. You can imagine the upheavals, for we were unprepared for Chaos, which could only enter our realm through mortal agency. Through Gaynor's agency. And that of the unwitting fools he deceived . . ."

"Oh, madam!" says Wheldrake again. At which she reaches out a friendly hand to comfort him. But he would comfort her. "The only flower..."

"Save one," she said, "but she resorted to desperate sorcery and died an unholy death..."

"The sisters are not your kinswomen, then?" murmured Fallogard Phatt. "I had assumed..."

"Sisters in spirit, perhaps, though they are not of my vocation. They seek to resist a common enemy, which is why I have aided them until now. For they, among others, possess the key to my own particular goal."

"But where has Gaynor taken them?" Charion Phatt wished to know. "His stronghold is only fifty miles from here, you say?"

"And it is surrounded by a Chaos army awaiting only his order to march against us. But I do not know yet if he has the sisters."

"He took them, surely?" Charion Phatt said.

But the Rose shook her head. Gradually, she was restoring herself and was now able to walk unaided. "I had to hide them from him. There was so little time. I could not hide their treasures with them. But I do not know if I acted swiftly enough."

It was evident she did not want to be asked further questions about that incident, so they asked her and Koropith what had happened on the Gypsy causeway. She told them how she had found Gaynor and the sisters at the very moment Mashabak was about to cut the bridge. He had been summoned, of course, by Gaynor. "I sought to stop Mashabak and save as many lives as I could. But in so doing I allowed Gaynor to escape—though not with the sisters, who had managed to free themselves from him. I had tried to warn the gypsies and when that failed I went in search of Gaynor—or Mashabak. We have come close, Koropith and I, to finding them at different times, but now we know they have returned here, as have the sisters. Chaos gathers strength. This realm is almost theirs, save for the resistance provided by ourselves, and the sisters."

"I have little stomach for a journey to a Court of Chaos, madam," said Wheldrake slowly, "but if I can be of any assistance to you in this matter, please feel free to make use of me however you wish." He offered her a grave little bow.

And Charion, at her intended's side, donated her own sword and wits in the Rose's service.

All of which was accepted graciously but with lifted hand. "We do not yet know what we must do," she said and then she raised herself to her feet, the velvet robe falling in folds upon the marble couch, and, lifting her marvelous head, pursed her lips in a whistle.

There came the sound of padded feet upon those marble floors and a hot panting, as if the Rose had summoned the Hounds of Hell to aid them; then into the hall bounded three huge dogs—great wolf-hounds with lolling red tongues and fangs of pre-human heritage—a white hound, a blue-grey hound and a pale golden hound, ready, it seemed, to do battle with any enemy, pursue any prey. And they grouped at the Rose's side and looked up into her face as if ready to obey her slightest order.

But then one of the dogs glanced to one side and saw Elric. Immediately it became agitated, growling softly and attracting the attention of the other two hounds, until Elric began to wonder if these were not some close relatives of Esbern Snare who did not approve of the were-wolf's act of sacrifice on Elric's behalf.

Next they were up and moving towards the albino while the Rose cried out in surprise; cried for them to return to heel.

But they would not.

Elric did not fear the great hounds as they approached him. Indeed, there was something about them which reassured him. But he was deeply puzzled.

Now they came closer, prowling around him, sniffing, quizzing, with the soft growls forever being exchanged between them until at last they seemed satisfied and returned, passively, to the Rose's side.

The Rose was mystified. "I was about to explain," she said, "why we must wait before we take further action. These hounds are the three sisters. I put a glamour on them to protect them from Gaynor's sorcery, as well as to give them a means of defending themselves, for they are spent, you see, of magic and all ingenuity. They have failed in their quest."

"What was that quest?" asked Elric softly, stepping from behind the others and looking with a new curiosity at the dogs, who returned his gaze with a kind of abstracted longing.

"It was for thee," said the golden hound as she rose from all fours and in a single flowing motion became a woman clad in silk the colour that her fur had been, and her face was of that long, refined sort which Elric recognized at once as belonging to his own people. Grey-blue fur turned to grey-blue silk, white to white, until all three sisters were standing there before him, tiny figures, yet unmistakably of Melni-bonéan stock. "It was for thee, Elric of Melniboné, that we sought," they said again.

They had black hair framing their exquisite features like helmets, large slanting violet eyes, fair skin like the palest brass, their lips were perfect bows—

—and they had spoken to him alone. They had used the old High Speech of Melniboné which even Wheldrake found hard to under-stand.

Confronted by this unexpected turn of events, Elric had taken an unwitting step backward. Then he steadied himself, bowed briefly and discovered himself, in spite of all he'd ever sworn, making the old blood greeting of the Bright Empire's ruling families. "I am bonded to thee and thine interests . . ."

". . . and we to thine, Elric of Melniboné," said the golden woman. "I am the Princess Tayaratuka and these are my sisters, also of the Caste, Princess Mishiguya and Princess Shanug'a. Prince Elric, we have hunted thee through millennia and across a thousand Spheres!"

"I have hunted thee only a few hundred years and perhaps five hundred Spheres," said Elric modestly, "but it seems I am the tail that chases the weasel . . ."

"When Mad Jack Porker staked his leg!" cried Ma Phatt from where she enjoyed the luxury of a fresh couch and luxurious linen. "We have been chasing one another in circles, then? See! I knew there was a pattern to it! Somewhere, there is always a pattern to it. Dongle-my-dingle, the lad's lost his jingle. It's the famous race, you know. Porker's Trial by Accident. His last dash was pure heroism. Everyone said so. Ladies and gentlemen, they are nailing our feet to the ground. That is not fair play!" And she relapsed into some comic dialogue with herself in which she relived her girlhood on the boards. "Buffalo Bill and the Wandering Jew! It was our grand finale. The last touch."

To which the three sisters listened with perfect patience before continuing . . .

"We sought thee to ask of thee a boon," said Princess Tayaratuka, "and to offer thee in exchange for that boon a gift."

"I am bound to thee as if I were thine own hands," said Elric automatically.

"And we to thee," replied the sisters, equally familiar with the ritual.

Then Princess Tayaratuka dropped to one knee, raising her hands to place them on his arms and bring him down to her so that he, too, was kneeling as she kneeled. "My lord, good power to thee," she said, and offered her forehead for his kiss. This ritual was performed until all had spoken and been kissed in turn.

"How may I help thee, sisters," said Elric when they had next kissed the triple kiss of kinship. All his old Melnibonéan blood stirred in him and he grew chill with a longing for his homeland and the speech and customs of his own unhuman folk. These women were his peers; already a deep understanding existed between them, stronger than blood, stronger than love, yet in no way encumbering or demanding. Elric knew in his bones that their command of sorcery might well have been the match of his own, before they exhausted all their strength in their search for him. He had known and loved many powerful women, including his lost betrothed Cymoril, and Myshella, the Dark Lady of Kaneloon, the sorceress he had but lately served, but, save for the Rose, the three princesses were the most striking of all the living women he had yet encountered, since he had left Imrryr as the pyre for his beloved's corpse.

"I am flattered that you should have sought me, your majesties," he said, relaxing for good manners' sake into the common tongue. "How may I be of service to you?"

"We would borrow your sword, Elric," said Princess Shanug'a.

"Borrow it you shall, madam. And myself to wield it for you." He spoke gallantly, as honour bade him do, but he still feared the threat of his father's ghost hovering somewhere not too far off, ready to flee at the first threat of extinction and pour his soul into Elric's being, to blend for ever . . . And had not Gaynor coveted the Black Sword?

"You do not ask why we would borrow the blade," said Princess Mishiguya, seating herself beside the Rose and helping herself to the small fruits which had been placed on the arm of the couch. "You would not bargain with us?"

"I would expect you to help me as I help you," said Elric in a matter-of-fact tone, "but I have sworn the blood-oath, as have you. It is done. We are the same. Our interests are the same."

"Yet you have a deep fear in you, Elric," said Charion Phatt suddenly. "You have not told these women what you fear if you allow yourself to aid them!" She spoke out as a child might, for justice, without understanding why the albino did not wish to betray his own anxieties.

"And they have not told me of what *they* fear if I agree to aid them," said Elric quietly to the young woman. "We are riding the stallions of terror, every one of us at present, Mistress Phatt, and the best we can hope to do is to keep some kind of grip upon the reins."

Charion Phatt accepted this and subsided, though she glanced furiously at Wheldrake, as if she wished him to speak on her behalf. But the poet remained a diplomat, unsure of the game he witnessed or of the stakes, but willing to go wherever his almost-betrothed determined.

"Where would you have me bear this blade?" Elric asked again.

Princess Tayaratuka glanced at her sisters before getting their unspoken assent to continue. "We do not need you to bear the blade," she said gently. "We spoke quite literally. We wish to borrow your runesword, Prince Elric. I will explain."

And she told a tale of a world where all lived in harmony with nature. This world had possessed few cities in the usual sense and its settlements were built to conform with the contours of the hills and valleys, the mountains and the streams, to blend with the forest but not to encroach upon it, so that anyone visiting their plane would have seen virtually no signs of habitation upon the continent where they lived. But Chaos came, led by Gaynor the Damned, who sought their hospitality and betrayed it, as he had betrayed so many other souls through the centuries, summoning in his patron lord who had immediately put the marks of Chaos upon their land.

"Few of our habitations were ever visible to potential enemies from other continents, so well-protected were we by the Heavy Sea, which encircles us. So dense were our forests and wide and winding our rivers that no-one cared to risk their lives on seeking after any legends which might have crept to other parts of the world. It is true we lived in paradise. But it was a paradise achieved at the expense of no other creature, including those of the wild, with whom we lived. Yet within a day or two all that had gone and we were left with a few barricaded outposts like this one, where our sorcery was used to maintain our world as it had been before Chaos came."

"And Chaos has laid siege here for a long while, madam?" asked Fallogard Phatt sympathetically, and raised his eyebrows at her answer.

"For something over a thousand years there has been a sort of stalemate. Most of our people left this world to found new settlements in other planes, but some of us felt duty-bound to stay and fight Chaos. We are the last of those. While we sought Elric, many of our kinfolk were killed in forays with Chaos attempting to attack the main stronghold."

"But what achieved the amnesty?" Elric asked.

"A feud between two Dukes of Hell took up their attention, especially after Arioch, employing some complicated strategy which involved Mashabak's cutting of the gypsy bridge and various other machinations and manipulations of the multiverse, was able to capture Mashabak in the territory he considered his own—our realm. Without demonic aid, Gaynor had to hope that the sisters would lead him back here. However, all that is altered. Some event occurred recently which ended the truce, such as it was. Mashabak has returned here and must soon send all his forces against us. Whoever broke that cosmic stalemate robbed us of whatever time we thought we had left . . ."

And Elric said nothing, remembering Esbern Snare and his leap at the Duke of Hell; remembering the courage of the Northern Werewolf as he had sought to save his friend—and had unwittingly broken the balance of power which had allowed the sisters some respite in their own palace.

Gaynor, insanely determined, abandoned by Mashabak, battled his own way through the dimensions, sworn to reclaim his conquests not in Mashabak's name, but his own! He challenged Chaos as he had once challenged the Balance! To him, no master was tolerable! The ex-Prince of the Universal had been lost, forced to spend years of subjective time searching for a way back to this realm. He had employed every strategy, every trick—furious that his cosmic ally had, apparently, deserted him, but determined to establish his rule here! Eventually he decided that he would follow the sisters, since they must eventually return to their own realm. Originally Mashabak had sent him on a quest—to follow the escaping sisters through the dimensions and bring back the living rose. But when Mashabak no longer aided him, the rose had become secondary to Gaynor. He desired Elric's sword rather more urgently.

Now he had returned, and demonstrated that the palace was no longer proof against him. He had entered and threatened the sisters at sword-point, demanding their now-legendary Three Treasures which they had carried back with them to return to the one who had loaned them. Gaynor's plan was to force the sisters out of the palace and into the cavern, at the eastern entrance of which his Chaos pack waited, unable themselves to enter that unlikely place.

With Koropith Phatt's skills stretched to snapping, and almost overwhelmed by a desperate urgency as the young Phatt sensed the sisters' danger, the Rose at last broke through into this realm—barely in time to place a protective glamour on the sisters and challenge Gaynor, whom she drove back into the palace by her sword-play and her witchcraft. But he, in turn, had found a source of sorcery and had eventually left her for dead, escaping back to his stronghold as Elric and the others arrived.

"We were prepared for nothing but death," said Princess Shanug'a, "until this moment. I wonder what has brought us together now? And *why* should it bring us together at this moment? Do you have a hint of that, Master Phatt? Are we all moved by the hand of some manipulative Destiny?"

"It can only be the Balance," said Fallogard Phatt with nodding certainty.

But Elric said nothing. He knew that Stormbringer did not serve the Balance, and, were it not for the runesword, he would not now be here—ready to help the sisters. But did the sword know what they required of it?

Then, suddenly, Elric was struck by a terrifying thought. What if he had already served the sword's purpose so that Stormbringer no longer had use of the symbiosis on which the albino had come to rely? While this notion filled him with panic, he also loathed himself for his dependency upon the blade. He unhooked its scabbard from his belt and, volunteering what he had earlier refused Gaynor, offered it to the sisters.

"Here is the sword you sought, my kinswomen." He offered it without question, either in expression or gesture, without hesitation or any sign of reluctance. Honour required nothing else.

Princess Tayaratuka stepped forward and, bowing, received the sword in both her little hands. Her muscles flexed with the blade's weight, but she did not flinch. She was considerably stronger than she appeared to be.

"We have our Rune," she said. "We have always had it. Since our people first came here and made this world their own. Even when the dragons left, we were not afraid, for we had our Rune. The Rune of Final Resort, it was called by some. But we had no sword. For the Rune of Final Resort must be spoken in conjunction with a ritual and a certain object. First it is required that the Black Sword be present: then he who wields the Sword must join us in the rune-calling. Then we must know the names of certain entities which must be summoned. All these things must come together at the same time. This is the pattern we must make, to mirror that which already exists and so create a duality which, in turn, releases the raw life-force of the multiverse. And only then, if we are accurate in our delicate weaving, will we revive the allies we seek against Chaos—the power to drive Mashabak and Gaynor and all their minions from our realm! If we are successful in this, Prince Elric, we are prepared to offer you one of three reclaimed treasures . . ." She glanced towards the Rose, but Wheldrake was quoting excitedly—

> "The first of these treasures of Radinglay,
>   Was a rosewood box with roses 'graved,
>   While the second was that maiden's dower,
>   A fresh-pick'd summer rose in flower.
>   The third of these treasures were briar rings three,
>   To make fast the Kind of the Cold Country."

"Exactly," said Princess Mishiguya with something of a lifted eyebrow, as if she had scarcely expected her tale to be the subject of a minstrel's repertoire.

"He has," said Charion Phatt by way of apology for her near-betrothed, "something of a memory for verse . . ."

"Especially," said Wheldrake, bridling at what he interpreted as snobbery, "my own! Disapprove, if you like. I'm adrift in my own rhymes and rhythms." And he mumbled another stanza or two to himself.

Princess Mishiguya was gracious. The Rose also came to the poet's defense. "Without Master Wheldrake's cadences and remembered names we should even now be separated," she said. "His talents have proved of subtle usefulness to us all."

"Should we succeed," said Elric, replying, "I would accept your promise of a gift. For, I must admit, my own fate is somewhat bound up with one of those Objects of Power you have carried so long . . ."

"Not knowing which of the three you would accept. We did not even know you to be our kin—though it should have occurred to us. Sadly, of course, we no longer have those borrowed gifts in our possession . . ."

"The gifts are not redeemed!" said the Rose in sudden agitation. "We hid them from Gaynor . . ."

"You were able to protect us," said Princess Tayaratuka, "but not your treasures. Gaynor raped them from their hiding place before he fled back to *The Ship That Was*. Those Objects of Power, lady, are already in the hands of Chaos. I thought you understood that."

The Rose sat slowly down upon a bench. Something like a groan escaped her. She waved them on. "Which makes your ritual all the more important to us . . ."

And Elric, following behind the women as they bore his sword into the depths of the palace where the ritual must take place, knew that both his own and his father's soul must now be truly doomed.

CHAPTER THREE

*Rituals of Blood; Rituals of Iron. Three Sisters of
the Sword. Six Swords Against Chaos.*

Through cloisters of pink-and-red mosaic, down avenues of flowering bushes lit by glowing, refracted sunshine from hidden skylights, past galleries of paintings and sculpture, the four moved steadily. "This has a hint of Melniboné and yet is not Melniboné," said Elric thoughtfully.

Princess Tayaratuka was almost offended. "There is nothing of your Melniboné here, I hope. We have no strain in us of that warlike line. We are of those Vadhagh who fled the Mabden when Chaos aided them . . ."

"We of Melniboné determined we should flee no more," said Elric quietly. He had no quarrel with his ancestors' determined learning of the arts of battle lest they be scattered again. It was what such easy logic led to that he feared.

"I intended no criticism," said the princess. "We prefer, if necessary, to wander, rather than imitate the ways of those who would destroy us . . ."

"But now," said Princess Shanug'a, "we must do battle with Chaos, to defend what is ours."

"I did not say that we would not fight," her sister said firmly, "I said that we would not resort to the building of empires. These are two distinct things."

"I understand you, my lady," said the albino, "and I accept that difference. I have no liking for my people's penchant for empire-building."

"Well, my lord, there are many other ways to achieve security," said Princess Mishiguya a little mysteriously, even sharply, as they continued their way through the lovely apartments and galleries of this most civilized of settlements.

Princess Tayaratuka still carried the great sword, though with a certain effort. Even when Elric offered to take the weight for a while she refused, as if this were her duty.

Now a corridor widened into another triangular cloister which surrounded a cool rose garden open to the dark blue sky above. At the centre of the garden was a fountain. The base of the fountain was carved with all manner of odd and grotesque creatures, somewhat out of keeping with the general style, and the plinth rose up in a three-sided column to where it widened into a large bowl around which were carved the sinuous shapes of dragons and maidens engaged in some cryptic dance. Silvery water still sprayed from the fountain and Elric felt that it was a kind of blasphemy to bring the Black Sword to a place of such peace.

"This is the Garden of the Rune," said the Princess Mishiguya. "It lies at the very centre of our realm, our land; at the centre of this palace. This was the first garden built by the Vadhagh when they came here." She took a deep breath of the ancient rosy scent. She held it as if it might be her last.

Princess Tayaratuka set the scabbarded runesword upon a bench and went to put her hands in the cool water, pouring it over her head almost as if she sought a blessing. Princess Shanug'a walked to the far end of the first of the three galleries and returned almost immediately bearing a cylinder of pale gold set with rubies which she handed now to Princess Mishiguya who drew from the cylinder another tube, of finely carved ivory bound with gold, and this tube she handed to Princess Tayaratuka who, in turn, drew from that a rod of engraved grey stone whose dark blue runes twisted and writhed as if alive and were like those same runes Stormbringer bore. Elric had seen such things on only one other object, the sword Mournblade, which his cousin had sought to bear against him, the sister sword to Storm-bringer. Dimly, he recalled other tales of runic objects, but he had studied little in such areas. Did they have qualities in common?

Princess Tayaratuka was holding up the stone cylinder now, wondering at the shifting runes as if she had never seen them alive before, and her lips moved as she read them, forming words she had been taught in a time before she had learned to read any ordinary alphabet. This was her inheritance, this Rune of Power . . .

"Only three virgins born of the same mother and the same father at the same time may know the Ritual of the Rune," said Shanug'a in a whisper. "But the Rune cannot be completed until we have seen the Black Sword's runes and read those aloud in the Garden of the Rune. All these things must happen at once. Then, if we have spoken the Rune correctly, and if the magic has not faded in the centuries since it was distilled then perhaps we shall regain those things with which our ancestors brought us to this realm."

Princess Mishiguya went to the bench where the hellsword rested, almost passively, and she picked it up and took it to the fountain where her sister, Shanug'a, waited, the water flowing over her and seeming to merge with the silken gown she wore, and Shanug'a took the sword's grip in both her little hands and pulled deliberately so that bit by bit the blade emerged from the scabbard, the angry scarlet runes glowing already along the black metal, and a song escaped the sword that was unlike anything Elric had heard before. In all other hands, even perhaps Gaynor's, the unscabbarded hellsword would have resisted, turned upon the one who sought to hold it and almost certainly killed them. Important sorcery was needed to hold the Black Sword even for a short while. Yet now it sang a song so strange and so sweet, high and unhappy, full of longing and unfulfilled hungers, that Elric was momentarily terrified. He had never suspected such qualities in the sword.

Even as Stormbringer continued its strange, unlikely song, Princess Shanug'a raised it high in the air and brought the tip down into the centre of the oddly carved bowl so that suddenly the fountain ceased to gush and at once there was a silence in the rose garden.

A stillness came to the sky above, as if the dark-blue light froze; a stillness in the garden, as if every flower and bud waited; a stillness in that triangular cloister, as if the very stones held themselves in readiness for some momentous event.

Even the three sisters seemed frozen in the attitudes of their ritual.

Awed by the scene, Elric felt he intruded and it occurred to him to withdraw, as if he were not required here, but Princess Tayaratuka was turning to him, smiling—offering him the runestone as it writhed and glowed in her palm.

"It is for you to read," she said. "Only you, of all the creatures in the multiverse, have this power. That is why we sought you so eagerly. You must read our Rune—as we read the Black Sword's. Thus shall we begin the weaving of this powerful magic. This is what we have been trained to do, almost since birth. You must believe us and trust us, Prince Elric."

"I have sworn the blood-bond," said Elric simply. He would do whatever they required of him, even if it meant his death, the enslavement of his immortal soul, the prospect of a hellish eternity. He would trust them without question.

The monstrous battle-blade stood upright in the bowl, the song still escaping it, the runes still flickering up and down its radiant black metal. It was almost as if it were about to speak, to transform itself into another shape, possibly its true shape. And Elric felt a chill in his soul and it seemed for a second that he looked into his future, to some predetermined doom for which this was a kind of rehearsal. Then he disciplined his mind and contemplated the task at hand.

One sister now stood on each side of the column, looking up at the sword. Their voices began to chant in unison, until it was no longer possible to distinguish their cadences from the sword's . . .

. . . Then Elric found that he was lifting up the runestone in his two hands stretched before him and his lips began to form wordless, beautiful sounds . . .

They had sought him for his sword; but they had sought him also for this unique gift. Only Elric of Melniboné, of all living mortals, had the power and the skills to read such potent symbols, to voice them as they must be voiced, matching each part of a note to each nuance of the rune. This rune, the sisters knew by heart, but the rune that blazed upon the Black Sword they themselves had to read. Thus they combined all their resources, all their talents, into the reading of a double rune, the mightiest of all Runes of Power.

The runesong rose in volume and became increasingly complicated—

—for now the four adepts were rune-weaving—folding their spells in and out of time, moving their voices beyond the audible range, making the air crease and shiver into thousands of strands which they wove and threaded—

—weaving the runes into a thing of impossible strength, making the very atmosphere bubble and dance, while all around now the shrubs and flowers swayed, as if adding their own rhythms and cadences to the runesong.

Everything was alive with a thousand different qualities, blending and separating, changing and transforming. Colours ran through the air like rivers. Eruptions of nameless forces came and went around them, while the bowl and the sword and the runestone seemed to become the only constancies in that double triangle.

Elric now understood how this was a place of enormously concentrated psychic energy. From this source, he guessed, they had drawn the power with which they had so far resisted Chaos—enough at least to protect a few settlements like these. But with the power of the Black Sword combined, the Garden of the Rune was becoming something infinitely mightier than anything it could have become on its own.

. . . to shatter the Sword of Alchemy and make the One power Three . . .

Elric realized he was hearing a story woven in amongst the runes, almost an incidental to the ritual they performed. It was a story of how these people were led by a dragon through the dimensions—a dragon which had dwelled once within a sword. Such legends were common to his folk and doubtless referred to some long-forgotten part of their wandering history. At last they had come to this land, which was uninhabited by human folk. So they made it their own, building to follow the existing contours of the earth, its forests and rivers. But first they had built the Garden of the Rune. For through their considerable sorcery they had changed and hidden the power which, they believed, was the result of their salvation and any future salvation for their descendants.

The runesong went on. The story continued. Into the fountain were built what the song called 'the tools of last resort'. The princesses' ancestors passed the runestone down from mother to daughter since they believed no man capable of carrying the secret.

Only against Chaos could these tools of last resort be used, and only then when all else had failed them. They could only be used in combination with another great Object of Power. The borrowed Objects of Power which the sisters had held, and with which they had intended to bargain for Elric's help, ignorant of how close a kinsman he was, were not strong enough for the work.

Gaynor had stolen those Objects, knowing that Chaos feared them and desired them. One such Object had already been stolen from the Rose and returned to her possession by a surprising and circuitous means. The others she had guarded better. But none had been powerful enough to use in the Ritual of the Garden.

Yet while the three sisters sought Elric and the Black Sword, others, like Elric, had sought what the sisters carried. Now the circle was completed. Now every proper element in the psychic model was in place, giving the four of them the astral means to range free, to let their minds and souls roam beyond the dimensions, beyond the Spheres, even beyond the multiverse; to re-enter it with a fresh knowledge, a deeper understanding of that complex geometry whose secrets were the basis for all sorcery; whose forms were the basis for all poetry and all song; whose language was the basis of all thought and whose shapes were the basis for all aesthetics, for all beauty; all ugliness ... Into this the four plunged, weaving with their runesongs fresh and original psychic patterns which had the effect of healing wounds and ruptures in the walls of time and space, while at the same time creating an enormous force with which to reanimate three other ancient Objects of Power.

More urgent and more complex were the runes now as they sang with their bodies and swam with their minds through near-infinities of screaming rainbows; sailing through their own bodies and out again into worlds and worlds of desolation, millennia of unchecked joy and a hint of that seductive ordinariness where so much of the human heart must always lie but which it so rarely celebrates . . .

So those old unhuman folk wove their spell, making manifest the promise of the runes, controlling the potency of un-moral magic which knew no loyalty save to itself.

The spell grew upon its own volition now, as it was meant to do, twisting and curling and creeping like the supple boughs of the yew-hedge which clung together to create so much modest strength, and then they began to fashion what they had woven, forming it and re-forming it over and over again between them, twisting it and turning it, throwing it one to the other, touching it and tasting it and sniffing it and stroking it, until the force they now balanced between them, which hovered over the Black Sword itself, was of the perfect supernatural shape and almost ready for release . . .

Yet still the songs must be sung, to hold the force, to channel it; to bridle it and saddle it; to charge it with a moral will, to force it to make a *choice*—for this *stuff*, this prime matter, was constitutionally incapable of choice, of moral direction or persuasion. And so *must* be forced . . .

Forced by a concentration of psychic energy, of disciplined will and moral strength which resisted all attack upon it, either from without or within, and which refused to be deflected from its purpose by an argument, example or threat . . .

Forced by four creatures so similar that they were almost one flesh and, at this moment, essentially one mind . . .

Forced downwards through the Black Sword which was not itself the receptacle of that power but merely the final and much-needed conductor . . .

Forced through the living stone, into the slab of rock from which the bowl, column and plinth had been carved, thousands of years before . . .

To transform it—to alter it entirely from any kind of material remotely akin to stone—a living form of energy so immense it was impossible, even for the adepts themselves, to imagine the fullness of its power, or how such power could possibly be contained.

Now this energy, coruscating, swirling, dancing, celebrating its own incredible being, joined in the song of the sisters, the albino and the runesword, until they formed a choir which could be heard throughout the multiverse, in every Sphere, upon every part of every planet; echoing forever throughout the multitude of planes and dimensions of the quasi-infinite. To be heard always, now, somewhere, while the multiverse existed. It was a song of promise, of responsibility and of celebration. A promise of harmony; the triumph of love; a celebration of the multiverse in balance. It was through an exquisite metaphysical harmony that they controlled this force and made it obey them, releasing it once more . . .

. . . Releasing it into three great Objects of Power which, as the fountain faded away, were revealed, grouped around the Black Sword standing in the centre of the small pool . . .

. . . Three swords, the weight and length of Stormbringer, but otherwise very different in appearance:

The first sword was made of ivory, with an ivory blade that looked oddly sharp and an ivory hilt and an ivory grip, bound about with bands of gold which seemed to have grown into the ivory.

The second sword was made of gold, yet was as sharp as its companion, and it was bound with ebony.

The third sword was of blue-grey granite furnished in silver.

These were the swords the Rune had hidden so well and which were now infused with a power to match that of Stormbringer itself . . .

Princess Tayaratuka, all in flowing gold, reached a golden hand towards the golden sword and took it to her breast with a deep sigh . . .

Her sister Mishiguya, in grey-blue silks, stretched out her own hand to the granite sword, seized it and gasped, grinning with the ecstasy and triumph of their success . . .

. . . and Princess Shanug'a, very grave in white robes, took down the ivory sword and kissed it. "Now," she said, turning to the others, "we are ready to do battle with a Lord of Chaos."

Elric, still weak from the rune-weaving, staggered to take hold of his own sword. Out of some sense of respect, or some unremembered ritual, he replaced it with the runestone, from which he had read the beginning of that great Casting . . .

Elric, my son—hast thou my soulbox? Did the sisters give it thee?

His father's voice. Some intimation of what he would know for always should he fail. And it seemed that he had certainly failed . . .

Elric, the time is almost here. My sorcery cannot hold me much longer . . . I must come to thee, my son . . . I must come to the one I hate most in the entire multiverse . . . To live with him for ever . . .

"I have not found your soulbox, Father," he murmured and then looked up to see the sisters watching him curiously when, all of a sudden, into the cloister came a breathless Koropith Phatt.

"Oh, thank heaven! I thought you all destroyed! There was a—a kind of storm. But you are here! They did not attack from within as we had feared."

"Gaynor?" said Elric, rescabbarding the oddly quiescent runeblade. "Has he returned?"

"Not Gaynor—at least, I think not—but a Chaos army—coming against us. Oh, prince, dear princesses, we are upon the point of our extinguishment!"

Which had them running as fast as they could go in the wake of the youth as he took them up to join the others in a room formed from a ledge of rock and disguised by foliage; this formed a natural balcony from which they could look out over the surrounding countryside and see the crystalline trees shattering and smashing as a great river of armoured semi-humanity pressed towards their retreat.

An army of bestial men and manlike beasts, some with natural carapaces, like gigantic beetles, all armed with pikes and morningstars and maces and broadswords and meat-cleavers of every description, some riding one upon the other, some dragging snoring companions, some in mysterious congress, some pausing to throw dice or settle a quarrel before being beaten back into line by their officers, whose helms sported the yellow blazon of eight-arrowed Chaos.

Snorting and wheezing, whiffling and sneezing; grunting and squealing and yelping; bellowing like bulls in a slaughterhouse, the Chaos army advanced: a single appetite.

The Rose turned frightened eyes to greet her friends. "There is nothing we have can withstand that army," she said. "It is retreat again, then . . . ?"

"No," said Princess Tayaratuka. "This time we do not need to retreat." She was leaning on a sword almost as tall as herself but which she carried with considerable panache, as if she and the blade had always been one.

Her sisters, too, bore their swords as casually, and with fresh confidence.

"These swords are powerful enough to challenge Chaos?" Wheldrake was the first to voice the question. "Good heavens, your majesties! See how the old rhyme does poor justice to the true value of the epic! It is what I always tell them when they accuse me of being over-imaginative! I cannot *begin* to describe what is really out there! What I *actually* see!" He virtually crowed with excitement. "What, indeed, the world around them is *really* like! Are we to do battle with Chaos at last?"

"You must stay here with Mother Phatt," said Charion. "It is your duty, my dear."

"You must stay, too, dear child!" cried Fallogard Phatt in great dismay. "You are not a warrior! You are a clairvoyant!"

"I am both now, Uncle," she said firmly. "I have no special blade to aid me, but I have my special wit, which gives me considerable advantage of most opponents. I learned much, Uncle, in the service of Gaynor the Damned! Let me go with you, ladies, I beg."

"Aye," said Princess Mishiguya, "you are well-fitted to battle Chaos. You may go with us."

"And I would go with you, also," said the Rose. "My magic is exhausted, but I have fought Chaos many times and survived, as you know. Let me bear my Swift Thorn and my Little Thorn into battle beside you. For if we are to die at this time, I would rather die fulfilling my vocation."

"Then so be it," said Princess Shanug'a and looked enquiringly towards her kinsman. "Five swords against Chaos—or six?"

Elric was still staring at that horrific army which looked as if everything obscene and evil and brutish and greedy in the human race had been given features. He turned back with a shrug. "Six, of course. But they will require our every resource to defeat them. I suspect that we do not see all that Chaos sends against us. Yet I, too, have not made use of everything . . ."

He raised his gauntleted hand to his lips, brooding on a matter which had just entered his mind.

Then he said: "The others must stay here, to make their escape if need be. I charge you, Master Wheldrake, with the well-being of Mother Phatt and Koropith Phatt, as well as Fallogard . . ."

"Really, sir. I am capable . . ." said that untidy idealist.

"I have every respect for your capabilities, sir," said Elric, "but you are not experienced in these matters. You must be ready to flee, since you have no means of defending yourself or your people. Your psychic gifts might help you find a means of escape before Chaos discovers you. Believe me, Master Phatt, if it seems we are about to be defeated you must flee this realm! Use whatever powers you still possess to find a means of escape—and take the others with you."

"I will not leave while Charion is here," said Wheldrake firmly.

"You must, for everyone's sake," Charion said. "Uncle Fallogard will have need of you."

But it was fairly clear from Wheldrake's manner that he had made up his own mind on the matter.

"The horses are ready for us in the stables below," said Princess Tayaratuka. "Six horses of copper and silver, as the weaving demands."

Wheldrake watched his friends leave. Something he disliked in himself was grateful that he did not have to go with them and face such disgusting foes; something else yearned to go with them, yearned to be part of their epic fight, rather than its mere recorder . . .

A little later, as he leaned upon the balcony and watched the slow, sickening advance of that evil, brutified pack, crushing all it encountered and taking only absent-minded pleasure in the destruction it caused, the poet saw six figures leave the shadows of the cliff and ride on chestnut, silver-maned horses without hesitating into the clashing crystals of the forest. Elric, the three sisters, Charion Phatt and the Rose—side by side they cantered—straight-backed in their saddles— to do battle with that manifestation of perverse evil and greedy cruelty—to fight for their very future: for their history; for the merest memory of their ever having existed somewhere in the vast multiverse . . .

At this sight, Wheldrake laid down his expectant pen and, instead of concocting some glorious Romance from the action of those six brave riders, he offered up an impassioned prayer in respect of the lives and the souls of his cherished friends.

Pride in his companions, together with his fears for their wellbeing, had struck the little man speechless.

Now he watched as the Rose broke away from her fellows and rode a little way ahead until she was only a few yards from the first swaying howdahs of the massive war-beasts, part-mammal, partreptile, which Chaos habitually used in its attacks. Already the stupid heads, lips and nostrils glistening with ichor which hung like dirty ropes from their orifices and left a trail of slime for the others to follow, were turning to sniff some alien scent, some body not yet touched and warped by the limitless, cruel and casual creativity of Chaos.

Then, from the leading howdah, all hung with human skins and other savageries, poked out a head to peer down at the Rose as she advanced upon the throng.

The helmet was immediately recognized by Wheldrake.

It belonged to Gaynor, ex-Prince of the Universal.

The death-seeker had come personally to savour the final agonies of these most irritating of his enemies.

CHAPTER FOUR

The Fight in the Crystalline Wood: Chaos Regenerated.
The Tangled Woman. To The Ship That Was.

"Prince Gaynor," said the Rose, "you and your warriors have invaded this land." She spoke with angry formality. "And we now order you to leave. We are here to banish Chaos from this realm."

Gaynor said coolly: "Sweet Rose, you have been driven mad by your knowledge of our power. You should not resist us further, lady. We ourselves are here to establish Gaynor's rule once and for all upon your realm. We offer you the mercy of immediate death."

"That mercy is a lie!" said Charion Phatt from where she sat on her silver-maned horse beside the others. "All that you say is a lie. And what is not a lie is mere vainglory!"

Gaynor's mysterious helm turned slowly to regard the young woman and a deep, assured chuckle escaped the Prince of the Damned. "You have a naïve courage, child, but it is by no means sufficient to offer resistance to the power Chaos commands. Which *I* command."

There was a fresh note in Gaynor's voice, a new kind of confidence, and Elric wondered, with some unease, how the Prince of the Damned had come by it. Gaynor seemed to believe his position was, if anything, stronger. Did more Chaos Lords group behind him? Was this to be the beginning of the great battle between Law and Chaos which so many oracles had predicted in recent centuries?

As he watched the Rose raise herself in her saddle and draw her sword Swift Thorn, Elric marveled at the woman's self-control; for she faced the creature that had betrayed her and caused the agonized deaths of all her people. She faced him and did not reveal in any way her contempt and hatred of him. Yet twice he had bested her in a struggle without beating her and this he must know. Perhaps that was the reason for his new-found braggadocio? Perhaps he sought to deceive them into believing he had more power than was apparent?

Now the Rose was riding back to rejoin her friends crying: "Know this, Gaynor the Damned, whatever is the worst thing you fear, *that* shall be your fate after this day! This I promise you!"

Gaynor's answering laughter had little humour, merely threat. "There is no punishment I fear, madam. Do you not know that yet? Since I am not permitted the luxury of death, then I shall find it for myself—and make millions seek it with me! Each death I cause, lady, consoles me for an instant. You die in my place. All of you shall die in my place. For me." His tone became a lover's and his words caressed her retreating back like the foul coaxing hand of Vice personified. "For *me*, lady."

When she took her place again with the others, the Rose looked steadily into Gaynor's helm, which squirmed with the flames and smoke of his own myriad torments, and she said: "None of us shall die, Prince Gaynor. Least of all, on your behalf!"

"My surrogates!" called Gaynor, laughing again. "My sacrifices! Go to find death! Go! You do not realize I am your benefactor!"

But already the six of them, Elric and the Rose slightly ahead of their companions, were cantering through the shimmering, jangling forest, their swords drawn, their chestnut, silver-maned horses, bred in a distant age only for war and brought here by the sisters from some more barbaric realm, lifting their hoofs in sprightly anticipation of battle, their heavy harness clattering in unison with the broken branches of the crystal trees, their great heads nodding in impatience, their nostrils flaring as they anticipated the stink of blood, snorting and gnashing their teeth, rolling their eyes and glorying in the anticipation of the coming fight, for this was what they had been bred to do; becoming only fully alive when in the thick of violent destruction.

Elric, glad to feel such a fine war-stallion under him, understood how these horses looked forward to the ecstatic oblivion of battle. He, too, knew that singular joy, when every sense was alert and at its sharpest, when life never seemed sweeter or death more fearsome— and yet he knew what a false lure it was to lose himself in such mind- less struggle. He wondered, not for the first time, if he was fated always to seek such struggles out, as if he, like the horses, had been bred for one special task? Hating it, he swiftly gave himself up to the thrilling delight of his battle-lust, and soon, as the first of Chaos's creatures came against him, he knew nothing but that lust . . .

Wheldrake, watching from the bower far above, saw the six riders converge upon the forces of Chaos and it seemed that they must be immediately swallowed. The very size of the Chaos beasts, the weight and grotesque power of the Chaos army, was more than enough, surely, to crush them in an instant?

Now a great shaft of scintillating light illuminated the riders as they merged with the colossal war-beasts who rumbled relentlessly on through the coruscating forest. Wheldrake saw six points flickering in that generality of lumbering limbs and widening jaws—one was a dark radiance he recognized as Stormbringer's—two were of ordinary, metallic glint—one more was a creamy white light, another the grey hard gleam of granite, and the last was the warm glow of ancient gold. Half-blinded by the crystal's shattered brightness, Wheldrake lost sight of the swords again and, when he could see clearly once more, he was astonished!

Four half-reptilian monsters lay in agony upon the radiant crystals, their howdahs crushed as they rolled and bellowed.

Wheldrake saw Gaynor's agitated figure, all angry, living metal, running back into the heart of his army, seeking a fresh mount. There was a sword in his gauntleted fist now—a sword that forked black and yellow—a sword whose blade seemed to twist in and out of the dimensions even as the Damned One wielded it . . .

And Wheldrake guessed that the three sisters were not the only adepts who had sung a great rune or cast some other potent spell, for the sword in Gaynor's hand was unlike any he had borne before.

Yet elsewhere, still, the Chaos creatures fell before a kind of thin ribbon of glittering light which carved into their ranks as surely as a scythe through wheat . . .

Hand raised against his eyes to see through the blinding crystalline multicoloured rays that mirrored in some terrible way the beauty of the multiverse, Elric swung his great black blade this way and that, feeling only the faintest of resistance as, with thirsty ease, Stormbringer feasted upon the lives and souls of the warped half-beasts who had once been men and women before they pledged their miserable lives to Chaos . . .

There was no satisfaction at this killing, even though there was joy in the act of battle. Each fighter at Elric's side knew that, but for chance and a certain firmness of purpose, they, too, might be part of this army of damned souls . . . for Chaos was not the master most readily chosen by the majority of mortals . . .

Yet kill them they must—or be killed. Or see whole realms perish as Chaos gathered momentum, drawing upon the power of the conquered worlds to accomplish further conquests . . .

With the grace of dancers, with the precision of surgeons, with the sorrowing eyes of unwilling slaughterers, the three sisters joined in battle with those who had already destroyed most of their kinfolk.

Charion Phatt, dismounted from a horse she found too unresponsive, darted here and there with her sword, cutting swiftly at a Chaos creature's vitals and slipping in to cut again, using her psychic gifts to anticipate attack from any quarter and never being present when the attack came. Like the sisters', her movements were efficient and she took no pleasure in the destruction . . .

. . . Only the Rose shared some of Elric's joy, for she, like him, had been trained to battle—even if her enemies were somewhat different— and Swift Thorn struck with expert skill at exposed organs and vulnerable places on the malformed half-men, using subtlety and speed as her chief defense—guiding her chestnut-and-silver warhorse into the densest parts of the Chaos pack's ranks and slicing so accurately at a chosen target that she brought one monster tumbling down upon another, a churning of heavy paws and legs which killed more of their own kind even as they, themselves, perished.

The wild exultant battle-song of his ancestors came to Elric's lips as he followed the Rose into the heart of the enemy and the sword fed him the energy it did not take itself until his eyes glowed almost as hotly as Gaynor's, so that it seemed he, too, was filled to bursting with the fires of hell . . .

Now Wheldrake began to gasp as he saw that the six thin needles of radiance still flickered amongst all that slaughter—and already more than half the apparently invincible Chaos army was destroyed, a mass of torn and crushed flesh, of grotesque limbs and even more grotesque heads lifted in the final torments of unholy death . . .

. . . while clambering through this carnage, pushing aside imploring claws and pleading faces, plunging his steel heels into screaming mouths or agonized eyes, using for leverage any limb or organ or foothold in bone or flesh he could find, his flaring Chaos-blazoned armour all spotted with the blood and offal of his ruined army, came Gaynor the Damned, the black-and-yellow sword forking and fluttering in his hand like some living flag, and now there were names on his lips—names which became curses—names which became the synonyms for everything he hated, feared and most longingly desired . . .

. . . but this was a hatred expressed through random, disruptive violence and destruction; a fear which found its swiftest form in raging aggression; a desire so intense and so eternally frustrated that this had become the thing in himself Gaynor hated worst of all and hated in every creature he encountered . . .

. . . and it was upon Elric of Melniboné, who might have been his alter ego, some cosmic opposite, who had chosen the hardest of roads to follow rather than the easiest, that Gaynor the Damned concentrated the greatest volume of his enraged hatred. For Elric might yet become what Gaynor the Damned had been and which he could never be again . . .

. . . so thoroughly saturated with the air of Chaos was Gaynor that at this moment he was little more than a half-beast himself. He growled and he shrieked as he crawled over the corpses of his slain warriors, he made hideous, wordless noises, he slobbered as if he already tasted Elric's deficient blood . . .

"Elric! Elric of Melniboné! Now I shall send thee to do eternal service with thy banished master! Elric! Arioch awaits thee. I offer up to him in friendly reconciliation the soul of his recalcitrant servitor . . ."

But Elric did not hear his enemy. His own ears were full of ancient battle-songs, his concentration was upon his immediate opponents as, one by one, he cut them down and took their souls for himself.

These souls he did not dedicate to Arioch, for Arioch had proved himself too fickle a patron and, as was clear, had no power in this realm. Whatever was left of Esbern Snare had carried Arioch back through the dimensions to his own domain, where he must recoup his strength and make fresh plots in his eternal rivalry with his fellow lords.

Elsewhere Charion Phatt and the Rose continued their delicate butchery, while Stormbringer's sister swords rose and fell and made their own sweet, eerie music, as subtle and as dangerous as the three sisters who wielded them. Elric had never known such mortal peers. The knowledge that they were nearby filled him with a kind of pride and made his battle-joy the greater as he continued his sorcerous slaughter while, dimly now, through all that din of outraged militancy, he thought he heard his own name being called.

Two Chaos warriors, with spiked armour half-hiding skin like barnacles, struck at him together but were too slow for Elric and his hellblade—their heads flew like buckets at a sideshow and one spiked an eye in a second pair who came against him, confusing them both so that they slew each other, but meanwhile Elric galloped beside a wading half-reptile as it clambered over the ruined flesh towards the Rose and with two quick strokes had severed secret tendons and brought the Chaos beast crashing upon the bodies of its fallen fellows, roaring out its impotent anger, its stupefied astonishment at this discovery of its own mortality . . .

Yet more insistent now was that faint, familiar sound . . .

"*Elric! Elric! Chaos awaits thee, Elric!*" A high, keening sound; a vengeful wind.

"*Elric! Soon we shall see an end to all thine optimism!*"

Up a mound of Chaos carrion rode Elric on his war-trained steed, to take stock of their battle . . .

Wheldrake on his balcony saw Elric's horse climb that rise in the carpet of the conquered, saw the Black Sword raised in the albino's black-gauntleted right hand, saw the left hand lifted against the blazoning rays which still sprang from every direction, wherever the crystal trees were broken. That dazzling intermixture of colour and light gave still more distance to the scene and Wheldrake, seeing what Elric did not yet see, offered up another prayer . . .

. . . Gaynor, carving his way through a pile of already rotting corpses, his armour now almost wholly encrusted with the remains of his warriors, plunged forward, still snarling Elric's name, still obsessed with nothing but vengeance . . .

"*Elric!*"

A thin sound, like the warning cry of a faraway bird, and Elric recognized the voice as Charion Phatt's.

"*Elric! He is close to you. I can sense him. He has more power than we suspected. You must destroy him somehow . . . Or he will destroy us all!*"

"ELRIC!" This last a great grunt of satisfaction as, through the piled corpses, Gaynor broke at last, to stand with his horrid eyes trained upon the face of his greatest enemy, the black-and-yellow sword, the ragged sword, flickering in his hand like lava fresh from some volcanic maw. "I did not think I would have need of this new power of mine, as yet. But here you are. And here am I!"

With that Gaynor lunged at Elric and the albino brought up Stormbringer easily to block him. At which Gaynor, surprisingly, laughed and lingered in the attitude of his failed stroke until, suddenly, the albino realized what was happening and tried to pull back, dragging Stormbringer free of the leechblade now seeking to suck all life from it. Elric had heard of blades which fed, in some strange manner, on the energies of such as Stormbringer—a parasite on whatever occult force emanated from the alien iron out of which these swords were forged.

"You resort to some ungentlemanly sorcery, it seems, Prince Gaynor." Elric knew that much of the power still remained in his blade, but could not risk further leeching of that energy.

"Honour has no place in my catalogue of useful qualities!" Gaynor spoke almost lightly, feinting with the black-and-yellow leechblade. "But if it did, I would say, Prince Elric, that you lack courage to face a foe, man to man—each with a singular sword to aid his work. Are we not fairly matched, Prince of Ruins?"

"Well enough, well enough, I suppose, sir," said Elric, hoping that the sisters would understand the urgency of their joint predicament. And, expertly, he made his horse sidestep another almost playful feint.

"You fear me, Elric, eh? You fear death, do you?"

"Not death," said Elric. "Not that ordinary death which is a transition . . ."

"What of that death which is sudden and everlasting oblivion?"

"I do not fear it," said the albino. "Though I do not desire it, either."

"As you know I desire it!"

"Aye, Prince Gaynor. But you are not permitted to possess it. You never shall suffer such easy release."

"Maybe." Gaynor the Damned became almost secretive at this and he turned to look over his shoulder to chuckle as he saw Princess Tayaratuka riding back towards them while her sisters and the other two women continued their fierce advance. "Are there, I wonder, any constants at all in the multiverse? Is the Balance no more than a pleasant invention with which mortals reassure themselves that there is some kind of order? What evidence do we observe of this?"

"We can *create* the evidence," said Elric quietly. "It is within our power to do that. To create order, justice, harmony . . ."

"You moralize too much, my lord. It is the sign of a morbid mind, sir. An over-burdened conscience, perhaps."

"I will not be condescended to by such as yourself, Gaynor." Elric let his body appear to relax, his expression become casual. "A conscience is not always a burden."

"O, murderer of kin and betrothed! What else but loathing can ye feel for your deficient character?" Gaynor feinted with words even as he feinted with the leechsword, and both were designed to deprive the albino of his faith in his own skills, his will to survive.

"I have killed more villains than I have killed innocents," said Elric firmly, though it was clear Gaynor knew how to strike at the very vitals of his being. "And I regret only that I cannot have the pleasure of slaying thee, failed Servant of the Balance."

"Make no mistake, my lord, it would be a pleasure for us both," said Gaynor—and now he lunged—now Elric must block the blow. And again the energy from the sword was drained in a great gobbling up of cosmic force, and the black-and-yellow leechsword began to pulse with dirty light.

Elric, unprepared for the power of Gaynor's sword, fell backwards and almost lost his seat, the runesword hanging uselessly from its wrist-thong. The albino, slumping forward in his saddle, gasping for air, saw all they had lately won about to be taken back in moments . . . He croaked for Princess Tayaratuka, riding close now, to flee—to avoid the leechsword at any cost, for now it was twice as powerful as it had been . . .

But the princess could not hear him. Even now, with a grace that made her seem almost weightless, she was bearing down upon Gaynor the Damned, the golden sword whistling and ululating in her right hand, her black hair whipped behind her, her violet eyes alight with the prospect of Gaynor's doom . . .

. . . and again Gaynor blocked her blow. Again he laughed. And again, in astonishment, Princess Tayaratuka felt the energy draining from herself and her blade . . .

. . . then, almost casually, Gaynor had knocked her from her saddle with the butt of his sword, leaving her to lie helplessly amongst the mangled flesh and bone of the field, and on her horse was riding to where the others fought, still oblivious of the danger he brought . . .

Princess Tayaratuka lifted her eyes to Elric's as the albino strove to drag himself upright. "Elric, have you no other sorcery to help us?"

Elric racked his brains, considering all the grimoires and charts and words he had memorized as a child, and could put himself in tune with no psychic power at all . . .

"Elric," came Tayaratuka's hoarse whisper, "see—Gaynor has downed Shanug'a—the horse races with her, beyond control . . . and now Mishiguya is fallen from her horse . . . Elric, we are lost! We are lost in spite of all our sorceries!"

And Elric began dimly to recollect an old alliance his folk had had with some near-supernatural creatures who had helped them in the early days of the founding of Melniboné, but he could remember only a name . . .

"*Tangled Woman*," he murmured, his lips dry and cracking. It was as if his whole body were drained of substance and that any movement would snap it in a dozen places. "The Rose will know . . ."

"Come," said Tayaratuka, getting to her feet and grabbing hold of his horse's bridle, "we must tell them . . ."

But Elric had nothing to tell; merely the memory of a memory, of an old tryst with some natural spirit which owed no loyalty to Law or Chaos; of a nagging hint of a spell—some chant he had been taught as a boy, as an exercise in summoning . . .

The Tangled Woman.

He could not remember who she was.

Gaynor was disappeared again, into his own ranks, seeking out Charion Phatt and the Rose, for now he was armed with a sword four times more powerful than those which had come against him and he wished to test the blade on ordinary, mortal flesh . . .

Wheldrake, still watching, still praying, saw everything from his balcony. He saw Princess Tayaratuka sheath her golden sword and lead Elric's horse to where her sisters stood, also in attitudes of exhaustion. Their horses had bolted in Gaynor's wake.

Yet still Gaynor had not found the Rose, and Charion Phatt evaded him as easily as an urchin in a market, returning to the others and speaking with some heat to the prone albino . . .

. . . When, round a pile of corpses, rode the Rose, dismounting in a single movement as she saw the predicament of her friends . . .

Then she, too, kneeled beside the fallen albino and she took his hand . . .

"There is one spell," said Elric. "I am trying to recall it. There is, perhaps, a memory. Concerning you, Rose, or some folk of your own . . ."

"All my folk are dead, save me," said the Rose, her soft, pink skin flushed with the work of battle. "And it seems I, too, am to die."

"No!" Elric struggled to his feet. He held tight to his pommel while the horse shifted nervously, not knowing why it could not continue with its battle. "You must help me, lady. There is something about a woman, the Tangled Woman . . ."

The name was familiar to her.

"All I know is this," she said, and, with furrowed brow, she recalled some lines of verse . . .

> "In the first creative weaving of a world,
> In the time before the time of long ago,
> When neither haughty Law nor fractured Chaos
>   rules,
> Lives a creature born of foliage and flesh,
> Who seeks to weave her world a-fresh,

And weaves one fine, a woven womb,
A womb of bramble flowers strong,
In which to sing her briar-song,
And bear her thorny child, who grows
Into a perfect rose.

"They are Wheldrake's. From his youth, he says."

But then she saw that she had, in a way she might never understand, communicated something to the pale lord, for Elric's lips were
moving and his eyes were raised to look into worlds the others could
not see. Strange musical sounds came out of his lips, and even the three
sisters could not understand what he said, for he spoke no earthly
tongue. He spoke a tongue of the dark clay and the winding roots, of
the old bramble-nests where the wild Vadhagh once, legend had it,
played and spawned their strange offspring, part flesh, part leafy wood,
a people of the forest and forgotten gardens, and, when he hesitated, it
was the Rose who joined him in his song, in the language of a folk who
were not her own, but whose ancestors had mingled with her own and
whose blood flowed in her to this day.

They sang together, sending their song through all the dimensions
of the multiverse, to where a dreaming creature stirred and lifted up
arms made of a million woven brambles and turned faces which, too,
were of knotted rosewood, in the direction of the song it had not heard
for a hundred thousand years. And it was as if the song brought her to
life, gave her some meaning at a moment when she had been about to
die, so that, almost upon a whim, from something like curiosity, the
Tangled Woman shifted her brambly body, arm by arm and leg by leg,
then head by head, and, with a rustling movement which made all her
foliage shudder, she formed herself into a shape very like a human
shape, though somewhat larger.

And with that, she took a casual step through time and space
which had not been in existence when she had first decided to sleep,
and which she therefore ignored, and found herself standing in an ill-
smelling morass of corrupt flesh and rotting bone which displeased her.
But through all this she sensed another scent, something of herself in it,

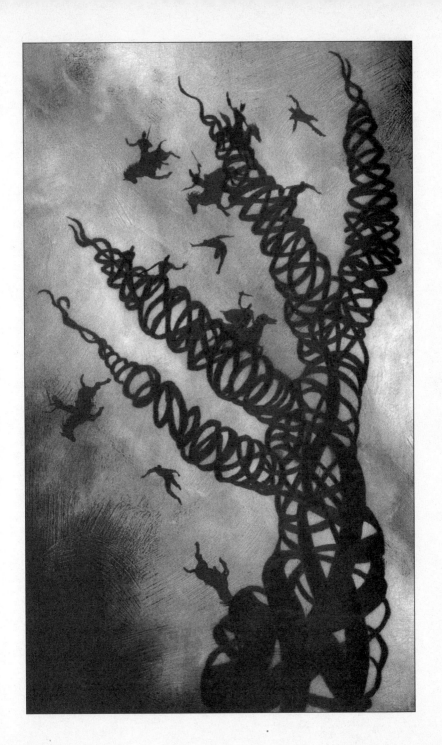

and she lowered her massive, woven head, a head of thick thorn branches whose eyes were not eyes at all, but flowers and leaves, and then she opened her briar lips and asked, in a voice so low it shook the ground, why her daughter had summoned her?

To which the Rose replied, in similar speech, while Elric sang his own tale to her, in a melody she found tolerable. It seemed that she concentrated her woven branches more thickly about her and looked with a certain sternness towards Gaynor and the remains of the Chaos army which had come full stop to stare at her before, at Gaynor's lifting of his black-and-yellow sword, a shard of raging energy, they began to race to the attack!

And the sisters clutched hands, linked with Charion and Elric and the Rose, and they held tight for security and power, for they somehow informed the Tangled Woman in her primitive soul—they directed her as she bent and reached a many-branched hand towards Gaynor, who barely yanked his horse aside in time and rode beneath her, slashing at the wood which, because the energy which enlivened it was of a kind that no power could suck out nor any mortal weapon damage, was scarcely marked and, where it was marked, healed immediately.

With calm deliberation now, as if she performed some unwelcome household task, the Tangled Woman stretched her long fingers through the attacking ranks of Chaos, oblivious to their hacking swords and jabbing pikes, their bitings and their clawings, and wove her fingers thoroughly amongst them, twining and twisting and bending and entangling them until every Chaos warrior and every Chaos beast still living was embraced and fixed by her bramble fingers.

Only one figure escaped, riding like fury from the bloody crystals of that battlefield, slashing at the horse's rump with the satiated leechsword.

Tangled Woman reached thin tentacles out towards the disappearing Gaynor but had little strength left; just enough to flick, with a thin, green branch, the sword from his flailing hand and bear it triumphantly up, to fling it away, deep into the forest where a black pool began to spread, turning all the surrounding crystal to the consistency of coal.

Then the leechsword vanished and they heard Gaynor's furious yell as he forced the sweating stallion up out of the valley and rode, without looking back, down the other side, to vanish.

Tangled Woman had lost interest in Gaynor. Slowly she withdrew her brambly fingers from the field, from the bloody corpses her thorns had pierced, from the flesh from which life had been crushed, her victims knowing a cleaner death than any Elric offered.

But now Elric pulled himself into his saddle and, while the others refused to look, he went about the business of slaughtering the wounded, letting the sword feast and renew his energy. He was determined to find and punish Gaynor for the evil he had done. And as he passed among what remained of the living, their imploring wails were ignored. "I must steal from you what your master would have stolen from us," he explained. And that killing had neither honour nor satisfaction in it. He did only what was necessary.

When he returned to his companions the Tangled Woman had gone, taking whatever payment she required, and all that were left were the dead.

"The Chaos army is defeated," said Princess Shanug'a. "But Chaos still dwells within our realm. Gaynor still has power here. He will soon come against us again." She had recaptured her horse.

"We must not *let* him come again," said the Rose, cleaning Swift Thorn upon a scrap of satin surcoat. "We must drive him back to hell and ensure he never more threatens your realm!"

"It is true," said Elric, moody with his own unquiet thoughts, "we must track the beast back to its lair and it must be confined, even if we cannot kill it. Can you find the way, Charion Phatt?"

"I can find it," she said. She had several minor wounds, which the others had helped her dress, but there was a kind of breathless pleasure in the way she moved, as if she were still exulting in her unexpected salvation. "He has returned, without doubt, to *The Ship That Was*."

"His stronghold . . ." murmured the Rose.

"Where," said Princess Mishiguya, settling herself in her saddle, "his power must be greatest."

"There is a power there, to be sure," agreed Charion, drawing her brows together—"a mightier power than any he commanded on this field. Yet I cannot completely understand why he did not use it against us here."

"Perhaps he awaits us," said Elric. "Perhaps he knows we will come . . ."

"We must go to reclaim the Rose's treasures," said Princess Tayaratuka. "We cannot allow Prince Gaynor to hold them."

"Indeed," agreed Elric with some feeling and a renewing sense of urgency. He had remembered that his father's soul remained in Gaynor's keeping and that very soon Arioch or some other Duke of Hell would try to claim it, whereupon it would flee to him and hide within his own being, forever united, father and son.

Elric drew off his black gauntlets and put his hands upon his horse's muscular flanks, but nothing would take away the chill that gripped his being. No ordinary warmth could comfort him.

"What of the others?" said Charion. "What of my uncle and my grandma, my cousin and my betrothed? I think they must be reassured."

They rode slowly back towards the cavern city, stabling their horses before beginning the long climb up the steps and walkways hidden within the walls, and when they finally reached the balcony where they had left the others, they found only Wheldrake.

He was distraught. His eyes were full of tears. He embraced Charion Phatt but his gesture was one of consolation rather than joy. "They have gone," he said. "They saw that you were losing the battle. Or thought they saw that. Fallogard had to consider his son and his mother. He did not want to leave, but I made him. He had the power to do it. He could have taken me, but there was no time and I would not go."

"Gone?" said Charion, holding him at arm's length now. "Gone, my love?"

"Mother Phatt opened what she called a 'tuck' and they crawled under it, to disappear—at the very moment when that vast thicket materialized. It was too late. They have escaped!"

"From what?" yelled Charion Phatt, enraged. "To what? Oh, must we begin this search all over again?"

"It seems so, my dear," said Wheldrake meekly, "if we are to have your uncle's blessing, as we had hoped."

"We must follow them," she said firmly.

"Not yet," said the Rose softly. "First we must ride to *The Ship That Was*. I have a small reckoning to extract from Gaynor the Damned—and from the company I suspect he keeps."

Chapter Five

*Concerning the Capturing and the Auctioning of Certain
Occult Artifacts: Reverses in the Higher Worlds; The Rose
Exacts her Revenge; Resolving a Cosmic Compromise.*

The little caravan came to a ragged halt as the cliffs were reached at last. Their remaining horses, sometimes carrying double, were almost completely exhausted. But they had found the Heavy Sea; dragging its dark and weighty waves upon the shore, then dragging them back again, all beneath a slow, morbid sky. They looked down now at the narrow entrance of a bay, where the sea seemed calmer. Its high, obsidian walls enclosed a beach of oddly coloured shingle, of bits of quartz and shards of limestone, of semi-precious stones and glaring flint.

Anchored in the bay was a ship which Elric recognized at once. Her sail was furled, but the great covered cage in the forecastle made her prow-heavy. Gaynor's ship and her crew had rejoined their master. On the far side of a spur of rock, which obscured their sight of the rest of the beach, there seemed to be activity—perhaps a figure or two—and now they must allow their horses to pick their way slowly down the narrow track from cliff to beach, threatening to slip on the shiny rock. Then at last the hoofs were grinding down upon the gleaming shingle, making a sound like ice being crushed, and the companions could see that the beach extended beyond the spur and that it was possible to ride along it.

Princess Tayaratuka rode a little ahead; then came her sisters (sharing a horse). Then came the Rose, followed by Elric and Charion Phatt, with Wheldrake's tiny hands about her waist. A strangely disparate party, but with many shared ambitions . . .

Then they had rounded the point and they looked upon *The Ship That Was*.

Before them stood one of the most grotesque settlements Elric had ever seen.

Once it had, indeed, been a ship. A ship whose score of decks rose higher and higher to form what had been a vast, floating ziggurat crewed by huge, unhuman creatures; a ship worthy of Chaos herself. Her lines had the appearance of something organic which had petrified suddenly after being tortured into unnatural forms. Here and there were suggestions of faces, limbs, torsos, of otherworldly beasts and birds, of gigantic fish and creatures which were combinations of all these things. And the ship seemed to Elric to be of a piece with the Heavy Sea which, like green quartz turned viscous and sluggish now, flung its spume upon that gloomy strand where men, women and children, in every variety of clothing, in rags and silks and shoes which rarely matched, in the filthy sables of some slaughtered king, in the jerkins and breeks of a nameless sailor, in the dresses and undergarments of the drowned, in the hats and jewels and embroidery with which the dead had once celebrated their vanity, moved backwards and forwards amongst those dreadful breakers, amongst carrion and flotsam brought here on the morose tide, the detritus of centuries, to scuttle with any treasure they might discover back to the warren of the ship, which lay at a slight angle on the beach, its starboard buried, its port a-tilt, where perhaps a mast had halted its complete upending.

A dead husk, the ship was infested with its human inhabitants much as the body of some slain sea-giant might be infested with worms. They stained it with their very presence, dishonoured it by their squalor, as the bones of the fallen are stained and dishonoured by the droppings and the debris of the crows which feed upon their putrefying flesh. Within the ship was constant movement, an impression of one writhing mass of life without individual identity or concerns, without dignity, respect or shame—wriggling, scampering, quarreling, fighting, squealing, roaring, whining and hissing, as if in imitation of that horrible sea itself, these were those humans pledged to Chaos but not yet transformed by Chaos; creatures who doubtless had had little choice in their masters as Gaynor carried the banner of Count Mashabak out into this world. They were wretches now, however, and they had only their shame. They would not look up as Elric and his companions rode towards the looming shadow of *The Ship That Was*.

They would not answer the albino's questions. They would not listen when the sisters tried to speak to them. Terror and shame consumed them. They had already given up hope, even of an afterlife, for they reasoned that the misery they suffered surely proved that the entire multiverse had been conquered by their tormentors.

"We are here," said Elric at last, "to take prisoner Prince Gaynor the Damned and to hold him to account!"

Yet even this did not move them. They were used to Gaynor's deceptions, the games he had, in his moments of boredom, played with their lives and their emotions. To them, all speech had become a lie.

The seven rode to where a kind of drawbridge had been built into the body of the upturned ship and, without hesitation, they cantered inside, to discover a nightmare of murky galleries and ragged holes, where crude doors had been carved between bulkheads, all strung with shreds of net and rope and various roughly made implements, drying bits of cloth and rag, of tattered clothing and ill-washed linen, where lean-to shacks and teetering shanties were erected, often on the very brink of an injured deck. Something large and strong had pierced this ship and brought her to her end, rupturing her innards.

Through the portholes from deck to deck poured a foggy, unpleasant light, creating a lattice of pale and dark shadows within the ship's serpentine bowels, making the shapes of the inhabitants equally shadowy, like ghosts, crouching, skulking, coughing, wheezing, tittering, too despairing to look upon the living without increasing their already unbearable misery. The floor of *The Ship That Was* was deep with human ordure, with discarded litter even they did not value. Wheldrake put a hand to his mouth and dropped down from Charion's horse. "Ugh, this is worse than the Stepney warrens. I'll let you go about your business. I have nothing useful to do here." And somewhat to Charion's surprise he returned to the comparative wholesomeness of that dark beach.

"It is true," said the Rose, "that he can do little that is practical. But his poetic inspiration is without parallel when it comes to tuning oneself to the harmony of the multiverse . . ."

"It is his most delightful quality," agreed Charion with a lover's enthusiasm, glad that what she admired in her beau was reflected in another's opinion—which went a short distance to disproving what lovers always suspect of themselves; that they have gone entirely mad.

Now Elric was losing patience with that conspiracy of the desperate and the dumb. As his warhorse stamped upon the filthy shingle, he drew the runesword out of its scabbard so Stormbringer's black radiance poured into that great, ruined space, and a dangerous murmuring song came out of it, as if it lusted for the soul of he who had tried to steal its energy.

And the warhorse reared up, pawing at the murky air; and the albino's scarlet eyes blazed through all that layered darkness, and he cried out the name of the one who had wronged them, who had created all this, who had abused every power, every responsibility, every duty, every treaty, every trust ever placed in him.

"Gaynor! Gaynor the Damned! Gaynor, thou foulest hellspawn! We have come to be revenged on thee!"

From somewhere high above, in what had once been the deepest and strongest parts of the ship, where the darkness was complete, came a distant chuckling that could only emanate from that faceless helm.

"Such rhetoric, my dear prince! Such bluster!"

Then Elric was finding a way for himself and his horse, crashing upwards into the shadows, through the trellises of misty light, up companionways which had once felt the feet of massive sailors and which were now all crowded and cluttered with the debris of these human inhabitants, knocking aside steaming pots and scattering fires, heedless of any damage, knowing that whatever materials constituted this hull it could not burn from mortal flames, the Rose close at his heels, shouting for the sisters and Charion to follow.

Riding through galleries of filthy darkness, where startled eyes stared for a second from a cranny or hunched figures skittered into ill-smelling holes; riding through this collection of hopeless souls, to seek their master and (all manner of entities and forces willing) free them from his tyranny! It was the Rose who now threw up her head in a clear, sweet song—a song which spoke, through its melodies, of lost love, lost lands and frustrated revenge—of a dedication to make an end to this particular injustice, this obscene perversion in the order of the multiverse; the Rose who drew out her sword Swift Thorn and brandished it like a banner. Then the sisters, too, had drawn their blades—one of ivory, one of granite, one of gold—and were joining in with their own harmonies of outrage, determined that the cause of their despair should perpetrate no further harm. Only Charion Phatt sang no song. She was an inexpert rider and had fallen behind the others. Sometimes she looked back, perhaps hoping that Wheldrake had decided to follow after all.

They reached at last a pair of massive doors, their carvings so alien that they were, right or wrong way up, indecipherable to the mortals. Once these doors had guarded the quarters of whatever beast had ruled the ship and had been deep at the vessel's heart, but now they lay close to the roof from beyond which could be heard the slow booming of the heavy breakers.

"Perhaps," came Gaynor's amused tones again, "I should reward such folly. I sought to bring you here, sweet princesses, to show off my little kingdom to you, but you refused to come! Now curiosity brings you here, anyway."

"It is not curiosity, Prince Gaynor, which brings us to *The Ship That Was*." Princess Shanug'a dropped from the horse she shared with her sister and went to push at one of the heavy doors, forcing it back a fraction—enough for them to pass through after they had all dismounted. "It is our intention to end your rule in this realm!"

"Brave words now, madam. Were it not for primitive earth-magic, you would be my slaves at this moment. Just as you shall be my slaves very soon."

The foggy air was thick with hot, unnatural odours and brands burned in it, scarcely casting better light than the flickering candles whose huge yellow stems dripped hissing wax upon what had once been an intricately carved roof but which was now covered in matted straw and rags. Webs were silhouetted in the air, hinting at the workings of enormous spiders, and from the deeper shadows came a scuttling that could only be of rats. Yet it seemed to Elric that all this was merely an illusion, a curtain which was being parted, for into view—and he was never sure how—came the fierce, rich, roiling colours of Chaos—a great sphere whose contents were in constant movement—and this displayed the dark outline of Gaynor the Damned, standing before it as if at some kind of altar on which he had placed some few small objects . . .

"Oh, you are most welcome," he said. He was half-crazed with delight at what he was sure must soon be their acceptance of his sovereignty. "There is little need for this display of challenges and insults, my friends, for I can surely solve our differences!" The helm pulsed now with a scarlet fire, shot through with veins of black. "Let us put an end to exuberant violence and settle these matters as wiser folk should."

"I have heard your reasoning tone before, Gaynor," said the Rose contemptuously, "when you tried to make my sisters bargain for their honour or their lives. I do not bargain with you, any more than did they!"

"Long memories, sweet lady. I had forgotten such a trifle and so should you. It was yesterday. I promise you a glorious rule in tomorrow!"

"What can you promise that we could possibly value?" said Charion Phatt. "Your mind is chiefly mysterious to me, but I know that you lie to us. You have all but lost your grip upon this realm. The power which aided thee, aids thee no longer! But you would make it aid thee, again . . ."

At this the great pulsing ectoplasmic sphere behind Gaynor flared and shivered and revealed, for an instant, three glaring eyes, tusks, drooling jaws and furious claws, and Elric realized to his horror that Mashabak was *not* free, that Gaynor had somehow kept control of the prison, appearing to do Count Mashabak's bidding while scheming to take the power of a Chaos Lord for himself!

Arioch had been banished from this plane, dragged through the dimensions by the last brave action of Esbern Snare, and Gaynor had been more audacious than any of them could imagine—he had determined that *he* should take the place of Arioch, rather than freeing his master! But though he held the Chaos Lord prisoner, he had no means of harnessing his power, of using it for his own ends. Was this why, with his leechblade, he had sought to steal the energy of Stormbringer and its sister swords?

"Aye," said Gaynor, reading his enemy's expression. "I had planned to gain the necessary power by other means. But I am a practical immortal, as thou must understand by now, and if I must bargain— why I shall happily go to market with thee!"

"You have nothing I need, Gaynor," said Elric coldly.

But the ex-Prince of the Universal was already mocking him, holding up one of the objects he had placed there and jeering softly. "Do you not want this, Prince Elric? Is this not what you have sought for so long? Across the realms, sir? With such considerable impatience, sir?"

And Elric saw that it was the box of black rosewood, its gnarled surfaces all carved with black roses. Even from here he could smell its wonderful perfume. His father's soulbox.

And again Gaynor jeered, louder now. "It was stolen by one of your sorcerer ancestors, given to your mother, then your father (who conceived his extraordinary deception once he understood what it was!), whose servant lost it! It was purchased, I believe, for a few groats by its owner in Menii. A pirate auction. Some small irony is to be enjoyed, I'd say . . ."

The Rose shouted suddenly, "You shall not bargain with us for that box, Gaynor!"

And Elric wondered why she had grown subtly more aggressive since they had entered those doors, as if she had rehearsed this moment, as if she knew exactly what she had to say and do.

"But I must, madam. I must!" Gaynor opened the box and drew out of it, between flickering blue finger and thumb, a great, lush crimson rose. He held it up by its dewy stem. It seemed to have been fresh-picked a moment earlier. A perfect rose. "The last living thing in your land, madam! Save yourself, of course. The only other survivor of that particularly enjoyable victory. Like you, madam, it has survived all that Chaos could do to it. Up to now . . ."

"It is not yours," said Princess Tayaratuka. "It is what the Rose gave us when she first knew of our plight. It was hers to give us. And ours to return to her. The Eternal Rose."

"Well, madam, it is mine now. To bargain with as *I* choose," said Gaynor with a hint of arrogant impatience, as if to a child who has not understood what has been explained.

"You have no right to those treasures," said Princess Mishiguya. "Give me back the briar rings, which are my part of our charge."

"But the briar rings are not your property," said Gaynor, "as well you know, madam. All these treasures were loaned to you, so that you could go onto the paths between the realms and seek Elric."

"Then give them back to me," said the Rose, stepping forward. "For they were, indeed, my treasures to loan or to bestow as I chose. They are the last treasures of my forgotten land. I brought them here, hoping to find peace from my tormented cravings. And then came Chaos and my hostesses' need was greater than my own. But now they have the swords they sought. They did not have to bargain, after all, with Elric. There's another sweet irony, prince. And we are here to reclaim those treasures. Give them up to us, Prince Gaynor, or we must take them by force."

"By force, madam?" Gaynor's laughter grew louder at this, and coarser, too. "You have no force to use against me! To use against Mashabak! I cannot yet control him, perhaps. But I can *release* him! I can release him into your realm, madam, and have him gobble it up in an instant, and all of us with it. Aye, and it would delight me to do so, madam, almost as much as it delights me to control such power. For would it not be *my* decision which brought about the conquests of unbridled Chaos? This blackthorn wand will set him free—with one tiny tap of its tip." And he revealed the thin, black branch that was bound with brass and elinfleur. "I repeat, madam, you have no force to use against me. While I remain here and my wand remains there, we are all of us safe as Arioch himself was safe when he made this cage . . ."

And suddenly there came a squawling and a roiling and a braying from the sphere and Count Mashabak's unlovely features were pressed there for a moment as he raved in response to his captor's name, at his absolute loss of honour in becoming the prisoner of a mere demi-demon. So vast and angry was the life-force imprisoned there that Elric and his companions felt driven back by it; felt as if they might be snuffed into non-existence by the very sight of it.

"And you, Prince Elric," yelled Gaynor the Damned above the cacophony of his recklessly captured prize, "you, too, have come to trade, no doubt. What? Will you have this? The skin your fierce friend left behind?" And he brandished the grey wolf's pelt that was all that remained of the tormented Northerner.

But to Elric it was no trophy Gaynor held. The abandoned wolf-skin meant that Esbern Snare had died a free mortal. "I echo all the sentiments expressed by my friends," said Elric. "I do not trade with such as thee, Gaynor the Damned. There is no virtue left in thee."

"Vice alone, Prince Elric. Vice alone, I must admit. But such creative, *imaginative* vice, eh? You have yet to hear your choices. I want your swords, you see."

"They are our bond-blades," said Princess Mishiguya. "They are ours by blood and by right. They are ours to conquer thee and drive thee from our realm. Never shalt thou take them, Gaynor the Damned!"

"But I offer you those treasures you borrowed and lost, madam. I'll speak plain. I want four swords such as the four you have between you. I have here *six* Objects of Power. I will trade them all for the swords! Is that not generous? Even foolish?"

"You are insane, Gaynor," said Princess Shanug'a. "The swords are our inheritance. They are our duty."

"But it's *your* duty, madam, surely, to give back what you have borrowed? However, think upon that for a little. Now I am going to offer

Elric his sweet old father's soul!" And he laid caressing steel upon the rosewood.

Angry at Arioch's betrayal of his secret, Elric could scarcely speak. Gaynor knew the true value of the soulbox and what it meant to Sadric's son!

"Would you be united—or would you be free?" Gaynor asked him, savouring every syllable of this temptation; understanding exactly what he offered the albino.

With a wordless oath, Elric lunged towards the altar but Gaynor motioned edgily with his wand and almost touched the ectoplasmic membrane where Count Mashabak roared and flexed his claws, his eyes seeming fierce enough to burn through those mystic walls and let him come rushing out, to devour, to warp, to make of this realm one screaming extrusion of tormented life.

"Your father's soul, Prince Elric, in return for that sword of yours. You know which you would rather have, surely? Come, Prince Elric, that's not a decision you must brood upon. Take the bargain. It releases you. It will free you from all thy dooms, sweet prince . . ."

And Elric felt the lure of it, the tempting prospect of being free for ever from his hellblade, from that unwanted symbiosis upon which he had grown to rely, of being free from the threat of his father's soul eternally merging with his own, of being able to help his father reach his mother in the Forest of Souls, where neither Law, nor Chaos, nor the Cosmic Balance had dominion.

"Your father's soul, Elric, for you to set free. The ending of his suffering and your own. You do not need the sword to live. You did not need its power to find it, to brave those ordeals, and others. Let me have the sword, Elric. And I shall give you all these treasures . . ."

"You want the sword so that you can control the demon with it," said Elric. "Do you have a spell which will give you such power? Perhaps you do, Prince Gaynor. But the spell alone is not sufficient. You must be able to frighten Count Mashabak—"

Again that raging din, that squawling and screeching and threatening . . .

"—and you think you can do that with Stormbringer. But you would need more than Stormbringer, Prince Gaynor, to achieve such control!" And again Elric reflected on the wild audacity of Gaynor the Damned, who sought to tame a Lord of Hell to his own bidding!

"True, sweet prince." Prince Gaynor's tone was softer again, and amused. "But happily I have more than your sword. The Rose knows of the spell I mean . . ."

And the Rose lifted her head and she spat at him, which made him laugh all the more merrily. "Ah, how lovers learn to regret those little confidences . . ."

Which brought a sudden understanding to Elric and a fresh sympathy for the woman, the last of her kind, and the particular nature of her moral burden.

"Give me the blade, Prince Elric." Gaynor stretched out the gauntleted left hand in which he held the soulbox. In his right hand, the blackthorn wand hovered near the ectoplasmic membrane. "There is nought to lose."

"I would only gain, I think," said Elric, "if you were to let me go free with that thing."

"Of course. Who would be harmed?"

But Elric knew the answer to the question. His companions would be harmed. This realm would be harmed. Many more would be harmed once Gaynor controlled Count Mashabak. He did not know exactly how the Prince of the Damned intended to use the weapon to control the Lord of Chaos, but it was clear there was such a means. Once, long ago, the Rose had confided her secret, her knowledge of such a powerful old sorcery.

"Or would you join your sire for ever, Elric of Melniboné?" The tone from within the helm was cooler now, more evidently threatening. "I would even share my new power with you. Your sword shall be the stick I'll use to goad Mashabak to my bidding . . ."

Elric yearned to agree with Gaynor the Damned. If he had been a true Melnibonéan, even one like his father, he would have thought no more of the matter and given up the sword in return for the soulbox. But through whatever ties of character, blood and disposition they were, his loyalty was for his fellows and he would not consign one more human creature to the mercies of Chaos.

And so he refused.

Which brought a yell of rage from the ex-Prince of the Universal and he cried out that Elric was a fool, that he might have saved something from these realms, but now they would be entirely devoured by angry Mashabak . . .

. . . when there came a creaking and a groaning and a scattering of plaster and bits of stone, of candle-wax and falling flambeaux, as some ancient bilge-system, some trap-door in the hull, began to creak open from above and through the gap came a questioning croak.

It was Khorghakh the toad. It was the navigating monster from the ship, pushing its way through. It sniffed and turned its head. It saw Charion. Whereupon it gave a grunt of satisfaction and began swiftly to clamber down the carved walls while Elric, taking advantage of Gaynor's inattention, chopped suddenly across the makeshift altar and struck the wand from the prince's hand, then thrust at him again, while Gaynor grabbed for his own sword and flung a blow at the albino's head.

But now Stormbringer sent up such a fearful keening, a sharp, specific utterance of rage, that there came a gasp of pain from within the helm—a helm that had not known pain for millennia. Gaynor brought up his sword to try to block the runeblade, but staggered.

Then Elric drew back the point of his hellsword and drove it directly at that place in Gaynor's armour which would have hidden his heart—and the Lord of the Damned howled with sudden agony as he was lifted upward, like a lobster on a spike, his arms and legs flailing, roaring his rage as Count Mashabak still roared his—suspended, helpless upon Stormbringer's point—

"Where is there a hell that could effect thy just punishment, Gaynor the Damned?" said Elric through clenching teeth.

And the Rose said softly:

"I know of such a place, Elric. You must summon your patron demon. Summon Arioch to this realm!"

"Madam, you are mad!"

"You must trust me here. Arioch's power will be weak. It has not had time to build. But you must speak to him."

"What good can Arioch do us in this? Will you return his prisoner to him?"

"Call him," she said. "This is the way that it should be. You must call him, Elric. Only by doing that can any harmony be achieved again."

And so Elric, with his enemy Prince Gaynor squirming like a spider on a stick in front of him, called out the name of his patron Duke of Hell, a creature who had betrayed him, who had attempted to extinguish him for ever.

"Arioch! Arioch! Come to thy servant, Lord Arioch. I beg thee."

Meanwhile the toad had reached the floor and was lumbering towards Charion, towards its lost love, and there was a kind of soft affection in its face as Mistress Phatt approached it, stroking its huge hands, patting its scales, while from above came a thin voice:

"We were in time, it seems! The toad found this entrance for us." And through the ruptured trapdoor came Ernest Wheldrake's head, looking down at them with some concern. "I was afraid we should be late."

Charion Phatt was patting the toad's enraptured head and laughing. "You did not tell us you had gone to bring extra help, my love!"

"I thought it best to make no promises. But I bring further good news." He looked at the route by which the toad had clambered, from carving to carving, to the floor and he shook his head. "I'll rejoin you as soon as I can." And he was gone.

"Arioch!" cried Elric. "Come to me, my patron!" But he could not offer blood and souls today.

"Arioch!"

And there, in one corner of this makeshift hall, a dark, smoky thing curled and shook itself and grumbled and then it had become a handsome youth, wonderful in his grace, but still not quite substantial. And the smile had all the sweetness of the hive. "What is it, my pet, my savoury . . . ?"

The Rose said: "Here is your chance to bargain, now, Elric. What does this demon own that you would have from him?"

Elric, his eyes moving from Gaynor to Arioch, saw his patron peering, almost as if he were purblind, at the leaping ectoplasmic sphere, at the writhing Gaynor.

"Only his lease," said Elric, "upon my father's soul."

"Then ask him for it," said the Rose. Her voice was vibrant with controlled urgency. "Ask him to give up his claim on that soul!"

"He will not agree," said Elric. Even with the sword's mighty energy, he was beginning to tire.

"Ask him for it," she said.

So Elric called over his shoulder. "My Lord Arioch. My patron Duke of Hell. Will you give up your claim on my father's soul?"

"I will not," said Arioch, his voice sly and puzzled. "Why should I? He was mine, as thou art mine."

"We shall neither be thine, if Mashabak is freed," said Elric. "And that you know, my patron."

"Give him to me," said Arioch thinly, "give me my prisoner, who is mine by right, whom I ensnared with the power of my occult subtleties. Give me Mashabak, and I will give up my claim."

"Mashabak is not mine to give you, Lord Arioch," said Elric, understanding at last. "But I will give thee Gaynor to make that exchange!"

"No!" cried the Prince of the Damned. "I could not bear such ignominy!"

Arioch was already smiling. "Oh, indeed, sweet immortal traitor, you shall bear it and much else besides. I know fresh torments that are presently inconceivable to you but which you will look back upon with nostalgia, as a time before your agony really began. I shall bestow upon thee all the tortures I had reserved for Mashabak—"

Then the golden body had streaked towards the bellowing Gaynor, who begged Elric in the name of everything he held holy, not to give him up to the Duke of Hell.

"You cannot be slain, Gaynor the Damned," said the Rose, her face

flushed with triumph, "but you can still be punished! Arioch will punish you and, as he punishes you, you will remember that you were
brought to this by the Rose and that this is the revenge of the Rose upon
you, for the doom you brought to our paradise!"

Elric began to realize that not all had been coincidence, that much
of what had happened was the result of some long-nurtured plan of the
Rose to ensure that Gaynor would betray no others as he had betrayed
her and her kin. That was why she had come back here. It was why she
had loaned the sisters the treasures of her own lost land.

"Go now, Gaynor!" She watched as the golden shadow embraced
the writhing prince . . . seemed to absorb the whole armoured creature
into itself, before flowing back again into its corner, and thence down
whatever narrow tunnel through the multiverse Elric had created with
his Summoning.

"Go now, Prince Gaynor, to your unsleeping eternal consciousness,
to all those horrors you had thought familiar . . ." She spoke with considerable satisfaction, while the face of Count Mashabak pressed for a
moment against the membrane and the fangs clashed and drooled as he
sought a glimpse of his rival, bearing back, with something close to
gratitude, his small prize to his own dimension.

"I have no claim now, Elric, to your father's soul . . ."

"But Mashabak?" said Elric as it dawned on him the responsibility
they had brought upon themselves. "What shall we do with
Mashabak?"

The Rose smiled at him, a gentle smile that was full of wisdom.
"There is something yet we have to do," she said, and she turned to
murmur to the three sisters, who took their swords—one of ivory, one
of gold and one of granite—and with slow care placed a black briar
ring upon the tip of each blade so that suddenly the swords were alive
with glowing, flowery light—a calm energy—Nature's energy balanced against the raging power of Chaos. Then they lifted these swords
in unison beneath the heaving membrane of that cosmic prison, so that
each tip stood lightly upon the skin.

And Count Mashabak growled and threatened and spoke some
words in a language known only to himself; made helpless by the very

act of being captured, for he was a creature that had known almost limitless power and had no means of existing with the shock of its own enforced impotence. He knew not how to beg or bargain or even to coax, as Arioch coaxed, for his nature was more direct. He had reveled in the unchecked force of his power. He had grown used to creating whatever he desired, of destroying whatever displeased him. He screamed at them to release him, he grumbled, he subsided, as the tips of the swords continued to support the ectoplasmic sphere. He was a crude, brutish sort of demigod and knew only how to threaten.

The Rose smiled. It was as if she were achieving everything she had dreamed of over the years. "He will take some taming, that demon," she said.

If Elric had been disbelieving of Gaynor's audacity, he was admiring of the Rose's. "You knew all along how Mashabak could be controlled," he said. "You manipulated events so that we should be here at the same time . . ." It was not an accusation, merely a statement of his understanding.

"I took the events that existed," said the Rose simply. "I did what I could in my weaving. But I was never certain, even as Gaynor bargained with you for your father's soul, what the outcome would be. I still do not know, Elric. Watch!"

She went to the table where Gaynor had placed his stolen treasures and she took the sweet-smelling rosewood box, advancing towards where the sisters held the sphere upon the tips of their swords, as delicately as if they balanced a soap-bubble, each woman concentrating upon her task while a strange, bubbling energy began to pulse along the blades. Down the ivory poured a smoky whiteness and down the granite a grey, curling substance; while the golden blade shook with light the colour of fresh-cut broom, all these colours spinning together and forming a kind of spiral which wound upwards again and back into the sphere.

Led by the Rose, the sisters began a chant, harnessing streamers of multiversal life-force and brought them together in a shimmering net of pale cerise light which surrounded them as they worked.

Then the Rose cried out to Elric. "Bring your sword now. Bring it quickly. It must be the conductor once more, of all this energy!" She opened the lid of the box.

The albino moved forward, his body making strange ritualistic gestures whose meaning was unknown to him.

He lifted the Black Sword even as it uttered a moan of protest, and he placed it between the other swords, at the very apex.

Carefully and slowly the Rose moved until she held the opened soulbox directly under the pommel of the runesword and cried: "Strike! Strike upwards, Elric, into the demon's heart—!"

And the albino yelled in terrifying anguish as the hellforce poured from the Chaos Lord in response to his single thrust. And Mashabak's unholy demon's soul poured with a gush of dark radiance which sent Stormbringer to shivering and howling again, down the blade and into the soulbox the Rose held ready for it.

And it was only at that moment that Elric realized what, under the Rose's direction, he had done!

"My father's soul," he said, "you have wed it to that demon's! You have destroyed it!"

"Now we control him!" The Rose's subtle pink skin glowed with her pleasure. "Now we have Mashabak. No mortal has the power to destroy him, but he is our prisoner. He will remain so for ever! While we can destroy his soul. He is forced to obey. Through him we shall re-create the worlds he crushed." She closed the lid.

"How can you control him, when Gaynor could not?" Elric looked up to where, oddly passive, the demon count peered from his prison.

"Because now we possess his soul," said the Rose. "This is my satis-faction and my revenge."

Wheldrake emerged from beyond the scaly back of his rival in love. "It is not a very dramatic vengeance, madam."

"I sought resolution to my grief," said the Rose. "And we learned, my sisters and I, that such resolution is rarely achieved by further destruction. These two, besides, could never be destroyed. Yet, living, we have seen to it that they have served some useful purpose, the pair of them, and that is all I wished to bring about. To do positive good

THE REVENGE OF THE ROSE   239

where positive harm had been done. It is the only possible form of revenge for such as myself."

And Elric, staring with growing horror at the soulbox, could not respond to her. He had been through all this, he thought, to fail at the very moment when he thought he had succeeded.

The Rose was smiling at him still. Her warm fingers were gentle on his face. He glanced at her, but he could not speak.

The sisters were lowering their swords. They looked drained and could barely replace the weapons in their scabbards. Charion Phatt, leaving the toad and Wheldrake, went to tend to them.

"Here." The Rose strode to the table and picked up the living bloom from where it lay upon the rosewood box which contained those three briar rings of power which had helped chain a demon's soul. She handed him the flower. There was dew upon the leaves as if it still grew in a country garden.

"I thank you for the keepsake, lady," he said quietly, but his mind was still full of the horror to come.

"You must take it to your father," she said. "He will be awaiting you in those ruins. The ruins where your people made their final pact with Chaos."

Elric did not find her humour amusing. "I shall be speaking to my father soon enough, lady," he said. With a deep sigh he sheathed his battle-blade. And he did not look into the future with any pleasure . . .

She was laughing. "Elric! Your father's soul was never in that box! At least, not trapped by it as the demon's is. The briar rings are for the bonding of a demon's soul. The box was built to *hold* a demon's soul. But the Eternal Rose is too delicate a thing to contain such a soul. It can only hold the soul of a mortal who has loved another better than itself. This flower protects and is nourished by your father's soul, Elric. That is why it lives. It is informed by all that is good in Sadric. Take it to your father. Once he has that, he can rejoin your mother as he longed to do. Arioch has forsworn all claim on him—and Mashabak has no power over him. *We* shall use the power of Mashabak. We shall force the Count of Hell to restore everything we loved. And so, by turning this evil into good, we redeem the past! And that is the *only* way by which we mortals may ever redeem our pasts! It is the only positive revenge. Take the flower."

"I will take it to my father, lady," said Elric.

"And then," she said, "you may bring me back with you to Tanelorn."

He looked into her quiet, hazel eyes and he hesitated for a moment. "I would be honoured, lady," he said.

Suddenly Wheldrake's yelling: "The toad! The toad!" And the creature is crawling, on massive hands and feet, through the door of the chamber and out into the galleries, the ruined decks, where all the wretches released from their servitude to Chaos are running and scampering and fleeing—out of the great hull, flushed rabbits from a warren, and Wheldrake runs behind him calling "Stop, dear toad. Sweet rival! For the sake of our mutual love, stop, I beg thee!"

But the toad has turned now, at the entrance to *The Ship That Was*, and looks back at Wheldrake, looks back at Charion Phatt who also follows, and pauses, as if awaiting them. As they come closer, it waddles out of the hull and into the light, the humans running like lice around it, escaping back into the land no longer ruled by Chaos. And then it squats, waiting for them . . .

. . . Where Ma Phatt, unsteady in her swaying chair, is borne along the beach by her son and grandson, the pair of them sweating and exhausted as she yells at them to increase their speed, then sees her grand-daughter and Wheldrake and shrieks for them to stop. "My dolly-joys, my sweety-hearts, my jammy, juicy jolly-boy!" She discards the tattered parasol with which she has protected her wise old head and licks her lips at him; she ogles him. "My rock, my tasty wordsmith! Oh, how happy my Charion will be! How happy I would have been, had I but known you were in Putney! Put me down! Put me down, boys! We have arrived. I told you they were safe! I told you she had a machination or two, a twist in the cosmic fabric, a little smoothing out of the tangled sleeves. Sweet-rumped little coxcomb! Tiny reveler in rhyme! Come with me. We'll seek the End of Time!"

"A confusing place, as I recall," says Wheldrake, but he basks in her approval, her celebration of him, her pleasure at his joining her family.

"I told you we did not go far, Father!" declared Koropith Phatt a little too triumphantly, so that Fallogard Phatt caught his eye in a stern glare. "Although you, too, were right, of course, when you recognized this beach."

The Rose and the three sisters were emerging now, to greet their friends, but they carried only the soulbox. The metaphysically filleted Count of Hell was left within, to think for a little upon the nature of his fate, in which he would be forced to create everything that was anathema to him. In her left hand the Rose carried, so that it hung loose and dragged upon the shingle, the grey wolf pelt which Gaynor had sported, not knowing that it was a sign that, in some manner at least, Esbern Snare had been released from his particular burden.

"What?" said Wheldrake, a trifle surprised. "Do you take that as a trophy, madam?"

But the Rose shook her head gently. "It belonged once," she said, "to a sister of mine. The only other survivor of Gaynor's treachery . . ."

And only then did Elric understand the full import of the Rose's fate-weaving, of her astonishing manipulation of the fabric of the multiverse.

Ma Phatt was looking at her quizzically. "You have your satisfaction then, my dear?"

"As much as is possible," agreed the Rose.

"You serve a powerful thing," added the old woman, clambering down from her rickety litter and hobbling across the shingle, her red face alive with a variety of pleasures. "Do you call that thing the Balance, by any chance?"

But the Rose linked an arm in Ma Phatt's and helped her to sit upon an upturned bucket and she said: "Let us simply agree that I am opposed to all forms of tyranny, whether of Law or of Chaos or any other power . . ."

"Then it is Fate itself you serve," said the old woman firmly. "For this was a powerful weaving, child. It has made fresh reality in the multiverse. It has corrected the disruptions which upset us so badly. Now we can continue on our journey."

"Where do you go, Mother Phatt?" asked Elric. "Where will you find the security you seek?"

"My niece's future husband has convinced us that we should discover the kind of domestic peace we value in the place he knows called 'Putney'," said Fallogard Phatt with a kind of hesitant heartiness. "And so we shall all seek this place with him. He has, he said, an unfinished epic, in two volumes, concerning some local champion of his people. Which he left in Putney, do you see. So we must begin there, at least. We are all one united family now and do not intend to be further separated."

"I go with them, lady," said Koropith Phatt, grasping the Rose's hand quickly and kissing it, almost as if embarrassed. "We'll take the ship and the toad and cross the Heavy Sea again. From there we shall follow the pathways through the realms until, no doubt, we shall come inevitably to Putney."

"I wish you a safe and direct journey," she said. Then she too kissed his hands. "I will miss you, Master Phatt, and your expert tracking through the multiverse. There was never a better psychic bloodhound!"

> "Prince Elric fled from that fateful strand,
>   Great hope had he in his heart,
> From the sweet rose blooming in his hand,
>   No mortal could dispart . . ."

intoned the red-headed poet and then shrugged by way of apology. "I was not prepared, today, for epilogues. I had hoped only for a noble end. Come toad! Come Charion! Come family all! We sail again upon the Heavy Sea! For far-flung Putney and the golden bliss of happy domesticity!"

And there was something in the proud Prince of Ruins that yearned, as he waved farewell, for the less dramatic adventures of the hearth.

Then he turned towards the Rose, that mysterious manipulator of destinies, and he bowed. "Come, madam," he said, "we have a dragon to summon and a journey to make! My father is doubtless a trifle concerned for the well-being of his much-bartered soul."

Epilogue

In Which the Prince of Ruins Honours a Vow.

Against the full heat of a harvest moon, Lady Scarsnout lifted her magnificent head to taste the wind, flapped her wings once to set her course and lifted away from that perpetuity of night where Sadric's ghost had hidden.

Elric had put the living rose into his father's pale hand. He had watched as the rose faded and died at last, no longer kept alive by the thing which had been hidden in it. And then Sadric had sighed. "I can hate thee no longer, son of thy mother," he said. "I had not hoped for so much as the gifts thou broughtest me."

And his father had kissed him with lips suddenly warm upon his cheek, with a momentary gesture of affection such as he had never made in life. "I will await thee, my son, where thy mother awaits me now, in the Forest of Souls."

Elric had watched the ghost fade away, like a whisper on the wind, and, looking up, he had realized that time was no longer stilled, and that Melniboné's bloody history, her ten thousand years of dominance, of cruelty and heartless conquest, was at the point of its beginning.

For a brief instant he had considered taking some new action—some action to change the course of the Bright Empire's progress down the centuries—to make of his race a gentler, nobler people—but then he had shaken his head and turned his back on H'hui'shan, on his past and on all brooding about what might have been, and he had settled himself into that natural saddle behind the dragon's shoulders and was calling confidently, with a new hope in his voice, for his mount to bear him skyward.

Then up they went together, dragon-leather slapping against the swirling clouds, up into the starry languor of a Melnibonéan night, into a future where, by a certain crossroads at the edge of time, the Rose awaited him.

For he had promised her that, when she first saw Tanelorn, she would be riding upon a dragon.

STORMBRINGER:
FIRST DRAFT SCREENPLAY

STORMBRINGER:
FIRST DRAFT SCREENPLAY
(1976)

The screen is dark:

URLIK (voiceover, echoing, melancholy):

"I AM
DOOMED
TO
LIVE . . ."

Shot 1. Exterior. Sahara Desert. Day.

The endless dunes of the Sahara at noon. We hear hoofbeats before we see mounted Arabs, swathed in flowing black robes, their faces hidden save for the occasional glitter of dark eyes, suddenly reining in their magnificently caparisoned horses. They stare in wonder at the sky. These Arabs are not armed—there is not a sword, dagger or rifle amongst them. The Arab leader is distinguished by a scarlet headband. The Arabs stare in silence but we hear a hint of sound, a faint rushing and fluttering from the sky which comes from—

2. Ext. Sky above desert. Day.

—a damaged airship drifting crazily towards the ground. Although its basic design is of a familiar pattern—gasbag above, gondola below—it is otherwise thoroughly bizarre. The gasbag is decorated in complex pictograms

very vaguely reminiscent of Sumerian or Babylonian styles, with many vivid colours. The gondola is of carved polished wood—the carvings equally complex and alien—though now much blackened from the effects of an explosion. The rails of the gondola, which is open, like the deck of a ship, are smashed and splintered in places. Fire flutters from the stern, where the twisted and useless propellers can be seen. Fire and black smoke boil from a section of the equally battered gasbag. We see a human arm dangling through a damaged section of the rail.

URLIK (*voiceover, booming and fading with a prolonged echo*):

"... FOR EVER!"

Titles now begin to appear over the following sequences:

3. Ext. Sky and desert. Day.
Suddenly the Arab leader lifts his arm in a signal and the Arabs are galloping on course with the falling airship. There is a great flurry of hoofs, flying sand, drapery, as they gradually speed up in pursuit of the ship which leaves a trail of black smoke behind it. As it drops lower in the sky, the smoke writhes around the riders.

4. Ext. Desert. Day.
The airship looms large on the screen as, with a crashing, tearing, scraping sound, it mashes into the dunes. Behind it the Arab horses rear and snort in terror.

5. Ext. Desert. Day.
After the noise of the previous sequence there is an uncanny silence broken only by the muffled sounds of the still-fluttering flames and by the Arabs who, on instructions from their Arab leader, duck into the wreckage to drag the ship's only occupant, Urlik, free. Urlik is as battered and smoke-blackened as the ship. His long almost white hair is secured by a headband of silver filigree. His clothing is torn and singed and there are livid welts where his naked flesh shows through—some of the wounds could have been

*made by the raking claws of an animal. Little remains of his silk shirt. His
vaguely Arabian-looking loose silk divided kilt, with its highly decorated
embroidery, is almost all in one piece as are his soft doeskin boots. Across his
broad bruised and blackened chest is a wide sword belt which supports an
ornate but empty scabbard. In haste, the Arabs drag him well clear of the
ship.*

6. Ext. Desert. Day.

*The ship blows up as they get clear and Urlik opens mad blue eyes, his
lips writhing as he tries to form words. He struggles feebly as the Arabs
gently but firmly restrain him.*

URLIK (*mumbling*): "Must go back . . . I love her . . . Oh, God—the
destruction!"

7. Ext. Desert. Day.

*The Arab leader signs for his men to take the raving Urlik back to their
camp. There is a general mood of rough sympathy about them. We still see
nothing of their faces except the occasional glitter of their eyes. Urlik is still
semi-conscious as he is swung over a saddle in front of one of the Arabs. They
ride back towards the fairly elaborate tents of their camp which is pitched
near an oasis.*

8. Ext. Oasis. Arab camp. Day.

*The Arabs erect an awning over Urlik. They wash his wounds and
make him drink some water while the Arab leader looks broodingly on.
Slowly Urlik begins to recover. His expression becomes less wild as he understands where he is and who he is with. A look of bitter resignation replaces
the previous expression, then he buries his head in his hands and we see his
shoulders shaking as he weeps silently. The Arabs withdraw and watch.
Another sign from the Arab leader and a small brass cup is put into the
leader's waiting hand. The Arab leader moves towards Urlik, taps him on
the shoulder. Urlik looks up, his eyes full of misery.*

End of titles.

9. Ext. Oasis. Arab camp. Day.

The Arab leader hands the cup to Urlik who accepts it, though his look is vaguely questioning. The Arab leader replies to the question in the look.

ARAB LEADER (*quiet, dignified*): "Herbs. To give you strength."

Urlik sips the brew and finds it palatable. He looks back at the Arab leader.

URLIK (*in resignation*): "I'm back, then? In the twentieth century?"

URLIK (*pauses, sipping again*): ". . . Punishment for my—treachery . . ."

ARAB LEADER: "A man should not be so full of guilt as you."

Urlik is bitterly amused.

URLIK: "No-one in the whole history of the world has had my burden
   of guilt . . ."

ARAB LEADER (*interrupting*): "A burden is lighter when shared."

The Arab leader sits down near Urlik, staring intently at him.

10. Ext. Oasis. Arab camp. Day.

Urlik and Arab leader are now in background. We see Arabs dragging some of the airship wreckage into the camp on the other side of the water hole. They hold up bits of twisted metal and carved wood. They talk quietly amongst themselves. We continue to hear Urlik and Arab leader conversing.

URLIK (*distantly*): "Reincarnation, prehistoric civilizations, an alien
   science, magic, monsters. A thoroughly incredible story . . ."

ARAB LEADER (*amused*): "We desert people are fond of incredible stories."

URLIK (*almost in hope*): "You couldn't believe in—in sorcery . . ."

ARAB LEADER (*shrugging*): "We believe everything and nothing in the desert."

11. Ext. Oasis. Arab camp. Day.

An Arab approaches the spot where Urlik and Arab leader sit. The Arab puts a broken piece of carving from the ship into the hand of the Arab leader. The Arab leader turns the carving over and over in his gloved hands as he talks to Urlik, who speaks a little more animatedly.

URLIK: "My name was once Colin Ericsson. I'm used to a different name now—Urlik ... For as long as I could remember I'd been fascinated with the legends of a time when all this desert was green and fertile, when a vast civilization flourished here, with a science and technology the equal to our own. Its centre was a city—Negrana—which vanished suddenly—yet sometimes appears as a mirage in the desert—an image thousands of years old. You know those legends?"

ARAB LEADER (*amused*): "We would call the stories *history*, rather than legend ..."

Urlik becomes excited, sensing a fellow spirit. He takes the piece of carving and brandishes it as he speaks with increasing animation:

URLIK: "Exactly what I believed! I was beginning to convince other people—got a grant for further research—into parts of the desert never before explored ..."

As Urlik speaks we fade from a close-up of the carving in his hand to—

12. Ext. Desert. Archaeological dig. Day.

—Urlik's hand holding a piece of stone with hieroglyphics on it. He is in modern desert gear. He holds a trowel and carefully brushes sand away from the stone. We pull back to see that we are at the site of a desert archaeological dig. Arabs have dug well below the level of the sand and are

handing up fragments of stone to others on the ground. Urlik is excited by his find.

URLIK (*voiceover*): "Some lucky finds brought more finance for more expeditions. I was looking for Negrana, of course, City of the Mirage. I sensed I was getting closer . . ."

13. Ext. Desert. Day.

An expedition led by Urlik in conventional tropical gear. Arabs lead pack camels after him. The desert seems endless. Urlik studies a map and compass as he goes.

URLIK (*voiceover*): "All my life I'd felt it my *destiny* to find Negrana. I felt it was my true home. As if I belonged nowhere else. It seemed to be *calling* me—as a mother calls her child . . ."

Urlik consults his compass and then puts it in his pocket. He points into the featureless desert. One of the Arabs shakes his head but shrugs as Urlik orders the expedition to turn in the direction he indicates.

URLIK (*voiceover*): "Still I found no signs. We'd been weeks in the desert. I began to give up hope. Then I started to hear a voice in my head. I was sure the sun was driving me crazy . . . The voice used a language I'd never heard—yet it was more familiar than my own . . . Then, the first night we'd set up camp . . ."

14. Interior. Tent. Night.

Urlik lies on his camp-bed. He is reading from an old parchment. The tent is filled with chests and boxes, with unfolded maps on almost every available surface. It is lit by a lamp that throws strong shadows everywhere. He sits up alertly as he hears a voice, distinct and clear, as if its owner is in the tent with Urlik. There is a very faint echo to the voice.

BELPHIG: "Champion—where are you? We sense your nearness. Come to us, Urlik . . ."

Urlik looks frantically around him for the source of the voice. Again it is obvious that he suspects his own sanity, his own hearing. He settles back to his parchment. The sonorous voice comes again.

BELPHIG: "Champion. Your destiny waits in Negrana. We need you now . . ."

Urlik claps his hands over his ears and mouth for the voices to go away.

URLIK (*voiceover*): "My mad obsession with Negrana had pushed me over the edge . . ."

15. Int. Tent. Night.

Urlik gets up, flinging down his parchment. As he does so he knocks the hanging lamp with his shoulder and the lamp swings crazily, sending shadows leaping everywhere. Shakily, Urlik takes a flask from his kit and drinks sparingly from it. He turns, close to panic, as the voice sounds again . . .

BELPHIG: "I know you are out there—spirit of our long-dead Champion—reincarnated somewhere in the future—you must find us . . ."

URLIK: "I'm not Urlik—please go away . . ."

BELPHIG: "Without you, we shall perish . . ."

As if pursued by the voices, Urlik stumbles from the tent and out into the desert night . . .

16. Ext. Desert camp. Night.

Moonlight throws the desert landscape and the light-coloured tents into sharp contrast as Urlik stumbles from his tent. A disturbed camel lifts its head, seemingly astonished by Urlik's behaviour.

URLIK (*voiceover*): "I couldn't rid myself of the—*knowledge*—they were calling to me from the remote past. Calling across Time—to an age where I had another identity—and a destiny that was mine alone. Yet still I resisted . . ."

Urlik whirls. He sees a hint of movement in the shadows. He calls out.

URLIK (*in panic*): "I can't come to you. There's nothing I can do for you . . ."

A ghostly figure can be seen for a moment in the shadows. It is Belphig, tall, portly, stately in rich robes, his sardonic face pale. He stares sightlessly out at Urlik, his lips moving, but no sound comes from them. Urlik moves towards Belphig.

URLIK (*in trepidation*): "Who are you? Why call me?"

Belphig turns to another (unseen) person and speaks.

BELPHIG: "He nears Negrana even now. We must work the ancient enchantments—bring the city to *him* . . ."

Urlik stumbles towards the image, reaching for him.

URLIK: "I'm here . . ."

As he reaches the image, it fades, and he is alone in the desert, some distance from the camp. He stumbles on, away from the camp.

URLIK (*voiceover*): "I had been awaiting that Calling since I was born. I *knew* their world—knew it my destiny to join them . . ."

17. Ext. Desert. Dawn.
Urlik stumbles on through the dunes. He is now completely alone in the desert.

URLIK (*voiceover*): "Still a small voice told me I was mad—but then, as the sun rose . . ."

The sun blooms over the desert. As it rises we see, shimmering on the horizon, a hazy outline which gradually becomes more and more concrete (though always just a little ghostly). It is Negrana, City of the Mirage. There are shining spires, minarets, crenelated walls, banners flying from turrets, strange designs in mosaics on the towers. A vast, fairy-tale city. Urlik begins to run towards it.

URLIK (*voiceover*): "Negrana. City of the Mirage. It was *real.*"

18. Ext. The city of Negrana. Day.

Urlik comes to the very edge of the shimmering city and stares at it in wonder. He finds a gate in the wall and hesitates before stepping through.

URLIK (*voiceover*): "We came together at the Crossroads of Time. It was inevitable. I knew I was going home . . ."

Urlik steps boldly through the gate—and vanishes.

19. Ext. The city. Day.

Urlik enters the City of the Mirage. It is beautiful, shadowy—still a trifle unreal—somewhat Arabian, with silver fountains, golden minarets, wide, tree-lined streets, some ruins. It is apparently unpopulated—a ghost city. He enters a square near the centre of the city and there he sees a monstrous Tomb, all in black-and-purple marble. There is an inscription on the Tomb which he tries to decipher, without success. There is an effigy which he stares at for some moments before realizing with shock that it is his own face he sees represented—though the stone is worn and old. The Tomb has an open entrance and he approaches it just a little hesitantly.

URLIK (*voiceover*): "I found a tomb in that deserted city—my own tomb—and it was my destiny to enter it . . ."

20. Int. Tomb. Day.

*Daylight enters the Tomb in a single swathe from the entrance. It illu-
minates a great slab of dark marble, carved with many cryptic designs. Upon
the marble slab is laid a scabbarded sword (the scabbard is the one worn by
Urlik in the opening sequences) with a huge black hilt, bizarre armour with
much fluting and elaborate engraving, dark shirt and baggy trousers, dark
boots and gauntlets—the complete war-gear of an ancient warrior. He fingers it in awe, he picks up the helmet and fits it over his head.*

URLIK (*voiceover*): "Inside I found all the gear of the long-dead warrior
   I had been. Sworn to return to Negrana when her need was
   greatest . . ."

*Urlik turns, detecting a movement from the shadows. Slowly he begins to
remove the helmet as we hear Belphig speak (as yet we don't see him). Belphig's tone is full of satisfaction . . .*

BELPHIG: "At last, Lord Urlik, you burst the bonds of Time to return to
   your people . . . To honour your ancient vows . . ."

*The scene is still somewhat dreamlike (perhaps in soft focus) but now Bel-
phig strikes a tinder and lights a torch so that the gloomy tomb is alive with
leaping shadows—the light reveals the sunken, suspicious eyes of gaunt
King Meliadus, grey in an iron crown. Both advance, though they are not
that distinct, even now . . .*

URLIK: "You can't be real . . ."

BELPHIG (*smiling*): "The world you've left is no longer real, Lord Urlik."

*Belphig seems to grow more solid as he moves into the shaft of sunlight, his
torch smoking. He puts the torch into a bracket on the wall and picks up the
huge sword from the marble slab. Although very grave and dignified, he is also
somewhat bland. There is always just a hint that he may be going through*

these rituals in a spirit of irony. The gestures, the tone, all hint at this. His eyes are very intelligent. They are colder than Meliadus's, whose eyes burn with fanaticism and suspicious of Urlik. Looking at the sword Belphig murmurs the first word almost to himself and then looks up to address Urlik . . .

BELPHIG: "*Stormbringer* . . . Champion, here's your Black Sword, your clothes, armour, preserved down the centuries. With them you'll vanquish the demon Eldren, as you predicted you would. We have followed the rituals, worked the enchantments, and have drawn you, body and soul, back to us. To make good your vow—to return as Humanity's Champion when our race was threatened with death. That threat is here . . . and you have come . . ."

Belphig suddenly drops to one knee, presenting the Black Sword to Urlik who looks frankly astonished, even slightly amused. Meliadus remains upright, refusing to make obeisance. Belphig's voice is sonorous.

BELPHIG: "Welcome, Lord Urlik, Eternal Champion, Hero of Humanity. With this you'll save us all!"

Urlik is startled, still amused . . .

URLIK: "I've never used a sword in my life!"

Urlik laughs, causing Meliadus to react with anger.

MELIADUS: "He mocks our traditions! I warned you, Bishop Belphig! Your meddling brings us more trouble!"

Belphig smoothly intercedes, rising again, raising a hand to stay Meliadus's temper.

BELPHIG: "The Champion is new-born and does not know our ways. He will learn . . ."

MELIADUS: "He has little time to learn. We sail against the enemy tonight. I like none of this, Belphig—it smacks of Eldren sorcery."

BELPHIG: "I but used the ancient rituals, as was ordained. He is our Champion. He could be none other!"

Urlik takes the scabbarded sword and speaks almost to himself.

URLIK: "Stormbringer—it's almost as if I can remember . . ."

Urlik makes to take the Black Sword from its scabbard but Belphig hastily stops him.

BELPHIG: "It is not yet time to draw Stormbringer from its scabbard."

Meliadus moves towards the Tomb's entrance.

MELIADUS: "Ready yourself, then, Sir Champion. The war-fleet waits in the harbour . . ."

21. Ext. Square outside Tomb. Day.

Now, side by side with King Meliadus, with Belphig close behind him, Urlik strides out—to find the scene utterly changed. Belphig hands him his helmet. He puts it on. The square is filled with cheering women, children and old men. A magnificent guard of honour salutes him as he appears. Baffled, half-amused, he hesitates—then he salutes the guards, the crowd. There is a huge response. Meliadus is impressed by this and wanting to make the best of it addresses the crowd. Grandiose, almost ridiculous:

MELIADUS: "As the ancient oracles predicted Lord Urlik returns to lead us in our great war against the Eldren—to wipe our ancient enemies from the face of the Earth!"

Another huge cheer goes up from the populace. The three begin to walk across the square, surrounded by tall guards. Urlik manages to whisper to Belphig, who replies with some amusement.

URLIK: "The city's suddenly alive!"

BELPHIG: "We've returned to our own time. What you saw was the illusion we sent to the future. The ancient power of our ancestors gave us that single means of reaching you."

22. Ext. Edge of square. Day.
Horses await them on the edge of the square. The crowd still cheers as they mount their horses. There are more signs of poverty, of something not being altogether right with the city. Suddenly, mounted Urlik takes the stance of a true Hero, smiling with self-mockery. Meliadus scowls at Belphig.

MELIADUS: "We waste time with all this ceremony. Even now the Eldren could be attacking . . ."

BELPHIG: "We owe the people a little ritual, my lord king. It is not every day a legend returns from the dead!"

MELIADUS: "I think you raise the dead to suit your own schemes. Your hand reached ever towards the sceptre, eh?"

BELPHIG: "My lord, I am content to rule the *spiritual* life of our people. I do not envy you your responsibilities."

MELIADUS: "Oh, truly, Belphig, it is only my privileges you covet!"

Belphig seems to treat this like the unfair suspicions of a burdened man. He accepts the king's accusations with holy patience. Meliadus spurs forward to the head of the party, shouting to them all:

MELIADUS: "Hasten, all of you, to the fleet! I lust to drown those demons in their own blood!"

Belphig rides alongside Urlik, shouting over the roar of the crowd.

BELPHIG: "The Eldren are without morality or mercy. They employ a terrible sorcery. Against it we should be powerless, but for you, Sir Champion. It is why we called you . . ." (*Belphig points ahead.*) ". . . We are almost at the river."

23. Ext. Harbour. Day.

A great harbour in which floats a score of bizarre sailing galleys, vaguely like Greek galleys, but with strangely painted sides and sails. The sailors—half-barbaric, sporting the finery, perhaps, of a more civilized age—cheer as the party arrives near the flagship and begins to dismount before going aboard. The general impression is of a great people reverting slowly to barbarism.

Meliadus, Urlik and Belphig go up the gangplank to the great flagship. Catapults, partially covered with tarpaulins, are mounted on the decks. The sails of the ship already billow as the wind rises. There is general activity as the fleet makes ready to sail. We see wounded cripples on the docks, some evidence of brutality, a general bustle, like some parts of India.

24. Ext. On board flagship. Day.

The three cross the deck and go towards Meliadus's cabin amidships. As Meliadus ducks his head just before entering the cabin he half turns to Urlik . . .

MELIADUS: "Summoning you, Sir Champion, was our last hope. I trust you prove your worth. This fleet—and you—is all we have left . . ."

BELPHIG: "Sword and Champion—they'll save us . . ."

Meliadus grunts skeptically as he disappears inside. Belphig claps Urlik on the back as Urlik is about to enter, just as jaunty Jarak, small, red-headed, cocky, charming, clad in plain war-gear, his hand on the hilt of his sword, presents himself to Urlik.

JARAK: "Greetings, Sir Champion. Captain Jarak . . ."

Urlik grins back.

URLIK: "Do you command the king's ship?"

JARAK: "I'm the best they can muster these days . . ."

URLIK: "The Eldren have been beating you?"

Jarak laughs ironically.

JARAK: "The Eldren? We humans have been destroying one another up
to now. Negrana's the last city still standing . . ."

Belphig's interruption is almost hasty.

BELPHIG: "You can meet your commanders formally, Lord Urlik—at a
more suitable time. Good day to you, Captain Jarak . . ."

*Jarak is sardonically amused, steps back with a bow as Belphig almost
pushes Urlik through to the cabin. Half-amused himself, Urlik calls back to
Jarak.*

URLIK: "I look forward to further conversation, captain . . ."

25. Int. Main cabin. Day.

*Meliadus's cabin is lavishly appointed, with charts and instruments of
alien design. Light falls through Gothic windows set close to the roof, so the
place has almost the atmosphere of a church. From outside we hear the
shouts and sounds of the sailors preparing to sail. The cabin rocks slightly as
the anchors are raised. Urlik and Belphig enter the cabin to find Meliadus
already studying a map.*

BELPHIG: "It becomes necessary to employ rogues like Captain Jarak—but I fear his respect for authority is not all it should be . . ."

Urlik is about to make an amused reply when Meliadus looks up. He speaks gruffly.

MELIADUS: "Here, Lord Urlik, we'll begin your education at once. By morning we'll be at sea—and by noon we'll have sighted Paphanal . . ."

Meliadus indicates a spot on what would be, more or less, the European mainland of the Mediterranean, though the coastline is very different and the sea itself is narrower.

URLIK: "The name's meaningless. I can't see what use I'm going to be . . ."

BELPHIG: "Paphanal is the Eldren's main sea-port. If we strike first we've a good chance of carrying the attack—before they can use their sorcery!"

URLIK: "How could we fight 'sorcery'?"

BELPHIG (*enthusiastic*): "*You*, Urlik, are our shield. You have the power of the Champion."

Meliadus shows resentment of this wholehearted enthusiasm for Urlik. He scowls.

MELIADUS: "We'd best leave our Champion from the reckoning—until he's proved himself . . ."

BELPHIG: "He will, my lord king . . ."

URLIK: "I wish I could agree . . ."

Belphig is more than anxious to reassure Urlik.

BELPHIG: "The combination will make us victorious—Sword and Champion together."

Urlik glances again at the Black Sword, now resting on his hip. A flicker of mystification crosses his face. Again he makes to draw it from the scabbard. Again Belphig stays his hand.

BELPHIG: "Not yet. That sword must not be drawn until we face Eldren sorcery . . ."

URLIK: "Sorcery . . ."

He shakes his head and Meliadus rounds on him.

MELIADUS: "For ten thousand years they've waited for this chance! Mankind's weakened to near-extinction. The Eldren live only to take vengeance on us. Long ago we defeated them—forced them back to their wilderness . . ."

BELPHIG (*almost sadly*): "Unless they're destroyed *we'll* not survive. You, reincarnation of our ancient Champion, give us the *power* to resist them—giving us the *spirit* to fight this last great fight. Without you, the race dies . . ."

Urlik has become more serious as he listens. He seems burdened by the information. He's about to ask a question when Iolinda enters. She is golden, beautiful, young and sweet, and Urlik feels an immediate attraction. Meliadus is surly but accepts the inevitability of the situation we'll learn about in the next scene.

IOLINDA: "Father . . ."

MELIADUS: "Iolinda, Lord Urlik asks me too many questions—since it's your destiny and his right—and I've no time—take him—eh—to his cabin, eh?"

Iolinda demurely bows her head and takes Urlik's hand. Astonished, somewhat delighted by this, he lets her lead him from the cabin.

26. Ext. Flagship. Sunset.

Urlik and Iolinda are walking along the ship which is now sailing towards the mouth of the river. They are close to Urlik's cabin at the far end of the ship. She hesitates as they near it.

URLIK: "Destiny? Right? Do you know what he meant—Iolinda?"

Demurely she stares at her feet, but she is quite amused.

IOLINDA: "I know, Lord Urlik. It is traditional . . ."

They reach the cabin door. Urlik pauses as she puts her hand to the latch.

URLIK: "Your destiny—my right?"

Iolinda pushes open the cabin door.

IOLINDA: "The right to wed the king's daughter . . ."

27. Int. Urlik's cabin. Evening.

Iolinda lights a lamp in Urlik's plainly furnished cabin. Urlik stares at her speculatively, hardly believing his luck. She is self-possessed, enjoying his surprise.

URLIK: "I'm not sure I understood you correctly . . ."

IOLINDA: "About our traditions?"

URLIK: "Well . . ."

IOLINDA: "It is true, I am afraid, my lord. I am yours, whether you desire me or not—it is what the legend foretold, you see."

She turns to him, presenting a mock-doleful face. She is close to him. She becomes serious.

IOLINDA: "If you could find it in you to love me a little . . ."

Urlik moves forward to take her hands. He is smiling.

URLIK: "I think, perhaps, I could . . ."

Iolinda seems satisfied. Urlik sits down on his bunk, grinning, as she moves towards the door.

URLIK: "Now I believe I've found my true identity—it all seems—right . . ." (*Urlik frowns as he unbuckles his sword and lays it on the nearby table.*) "Yet there's still something—a warning voice . . ."

Iolinda is at the door, now. She hesitates.

IOLINDA: "Perhaps a Hero, like a King, must lose his free will to follow his destiny . . ."

Urlik finds this idea sobering. He looks up at her, ready to continue this line of thought, but she changes her mood, becoming lighter.

IOLINDA: "Sleep well, Sir Champion. We marry as soon as the Eldren are destroyed."

Iolinda leaves, as if embarrassed by her own boldness, and Jarak enters almost immediately, staring with ironic curiosity after the disappearing Iolinda.

JARAK: "Forgive the intrusion, Lord Urlik. I'm not sure of the protocol due to a legendary hero brought back from the dead . . ."

Urlik is pleased to see him. He gets up, moving to a chest where wine and cups have been set.

URLIK: "You're the first to treat me as an ordinary man, so I'm glad to welcome you, Captain Jarak. Perhaps *you* can answer some of the questions Belphig avoids . . ."

JARAK: "I know nothing of high politics—or sorcery. If it wasn't for my skills I wouldn't be aboard at all. Until lately I commanded my own fate . . ."

URLIK: "More than I can say. Why serve King Meliadus now?"

JARAK: "There's no-one else left. Our wars were savage. Whole nations were destroyed. Negrana was the last city to survive. At least this new threat forces the remnants of mankind to unite. Meliadus won his victories at terrible cost—brutality, ignorance, superstition reign supreme . . ."

Jarak shrugs as if the list is endless. He is evidently something of a cynic. Urlik takes to him, pours him wine, smiling. He hands Jarak the cup.

URLIK: "So I'm called to unite the factions—represent the old ideals, eh?"

Jarak accepts the cup, appreciating Urlik's remark. It is evident a strong liking exists between the two.

JARAK: "True—they don't want a human being. They want a myth."

They drink.

URLIK: "They'll have to take me as I am . . ."

Jarak is skeptical.

JARAK: "It might be more comfortable to accept Belphig's talk of Destiny, Demons and a Grand Design. But I'll drink to the man— the legend needs more than luck . . ."

They toast one another with their goblets. We fade on the goblets and—

28. Int. Urlik's cabin. Dawn.

—we fade in on the empty goblets on the table and move from them along the length of the great black sword which lies beside them. The sword is pointing at Urlik who lies in his bunk, half-naked, tossing his head from side to side in his sleep. It's evident many strange thoughts go through his sleeping mind. Suddenly the door is flung open, the light strikes his face, waking him to panic. But it is Jarak standing there, dressed slightly differently, grinning at him.

JARAK: "Good morning, Sir Legend—join us on deck as soon as you've breakfasted. The enemy city's almost in sight!"

Urlik grunts and begins to rise. He stumbles from his bunk and his hand alights on the Black Sword. For a moment he pauses as he stares down at it. Then he dismisses the thought from his mind and goes to splash water on his face. From outside are shouts and yells as the ship comes awake.

29. Ext. Bridge of the flagship. Day.

Meliadus, Iolinda, Belphig and Jarak are already on the bridge as Urlik climbs up to join them. The whole fleet is stretched behind them. The four are staring at a coastline to starboard. Iolinda gives him a "special" smile as Urlik arrives. Meliadus grunts. Belphig points.

BELPHIG: "We have made good speed. It is Paphanal."

Urlik peers in the direction Belphig points.

30. Ext. Paphanal in distance. Day.
A long shot of Paphanal, the beautiful, ethereal city of the Eldren. It is a harbour town and we see the delicate, slender ships of the Eldren in the harbour.

URLIK (*voiceover*): "So that's the haunt of demons. They don't seem ready for war . . ."

31. Ext. Bridge of flagship. Day.
A close-up of Belphig looking extremely grave, more animated than usual.

BELPHIG: "Typical Eldren deception! You'll learn to recognize it. These Eldren are Masters of Sorcery."

32. Ext. Bridge. Day.
Iolinda moves closer to Urlik, as if in fear.

IOLINDA: "Bishop Belphig speaks only the truth. Since childhood we learn to fear their sorcery and cunning . . ."

33. Ext. Bridge. Day.
A close-up of Meliadus. His dark face is full of fear and anger. His lips writhe in hatred of his foes.

MELIADUS: "We attack at once. Give the order, captain."

34. Ext. Bridge. Day.
Jarak looks questioningly at Urlik who is, himself, uncertain.

JARAK: "With respect, my lord king, I agree with Urlik. The place looks undefended. Perhaps a parley . . ."

Meliadus is beside himself with rage. He seems almost at the point of cracking.

MELIADUS: "Is this mutiny? We were dolts to trust a pirate—and our so-called Champion turns our men against us!"

Belphig is placatory, as usual, trying to reconcile them all.

BELPHIG: "They are naïve, that is all. We cannot blame Urlik if he is skeptical. The town *looks* peaceful, but we know . . ."

Belphig raises his hand as if to pacify them all, but it is also almost as if, at a signal from him, that a tremendous disturbance comes from the water between the ship and the land. A sailor screams.

35. Ext. Ship. Sea. Day.

Suddenly, from the depths of the ocean, rears a Sea Stag. It is a monster with horns rather like a stag and a snout and teeth rather like a crocodile. It glitters with myriad shades of blue and green. Water pours from its huge bulk and its glaring eyes turn to regard, balefully, the ships. It is terrifyingly huge. Meliadus grabs Iolinda, snarling at Urlik as he, Meliadus, hurries the girl down the companionway to the deck.

MELIADUS: "Do you need further proof, sir? Iolinda—to safety . . ."

36. Ext. Ships. Sea. Day.

A huge wave buffets the flagship, flinging them about on the decks, as the Sea Stag snarls and turns on the ship nearest to it. It uses its horns to smash into the ship and, as the ship breaks up, diving at the survivors to snap them in its snout. Sounds of carnage fill the scene.

37. Ext. Ships. Sea. Day.

A longish shot to show Meliadus and Iolinda forced against the far rail of the ship, which is rocking dangerously, while on the bridge Jarak falls the length of the steps. Up above Belphig and Urlik cling to the rail, still managing to keep their footing. Belphig yells to Urlik.

BELPHIG: "There's proof of Eldren sorcery, eh? Only their power can summon Sea Stags from the depths!"

Even as he speaks, the Sea Stag is turning its attention on the flagship. Meliadus yells in terror, trying to help Iolinda to safety.

38. Ext. Deck of ship. Day.

Jarak picks himself up and begins issuing orders to his men to clear the tarpaulins from the deck-mounted catapults and bring the braziers, which stand close by, to life with torches.

JARAK: "Quickly—the catapults. Pray the beast fears fire!"

39. Ext. Ship and sea. Day.

Sputtering balls of green phosphorescent Greek fire are shot from the catapults towards the Sea Stag. Jarak makes for the rail closest to the beast.

40. Ext. Sea. Day.

The Sea Stag roars in some minor discomfort as the Greek fire begins to strike it—though most of the missiles miss it and fall hissing and bubbling into the sea. It is evident the fire hardly affects the Sea Stag.

41. Ext. Sea. Day.

The Sea Stag begins to swim towards the flagship, roaring and snapping its horrible teeth.

42. Ext. Deck. Day.

The Sea Stag lowers its head for the charge. Meliadus sees this and, forgetting Iolinda, dives for the safety of his cabin. The horns come nearer and nearer. Jarak makes some attempt to save Iolinda.

43. Ext. Ship. Day.

The Sea Stag's horn smashes into the rigging and brings down a mast. Jarak tries, ineffectually, to drag Iolinda clear of the tangled mass of lines and canvas and smashed timbers.

44. Ext. Ship. Day.

As the Sea Stag snaps its jaws at the ship, Urlik sees Jarak's and Iolinda's plight and vaults the rail to land squarely on the deck. He runs forward to put himself between Jarak and Iolinda and the Sea Stag.

45. Ext. Ship. Day.

Urlik yells at Jarak. He draws the Black Sword as the Sea Stag's head comes closer and closer. Instantly a strange, wild music comes from the sword and it flickers with a peculiar radiance.

URLIK: "Jarak—get Iolinda away. I'll do what I can!"

Urlik has time to glance once in astonishment at the enchanted blade in his hand and then the Sea Stag is coming for him.

46. Ext. Ship. Day.

The jaws of the Sea Stag open wide, dwarfing Urlik completely. But he slashes at the snout with the Black Sword and—by a miracle, it seems—draws blood. The beast draws its head back in astonishment—it has never been hurt by a mortal before.

47. Ext. Ship. Day.

Urlik leaps to balance on part of the rail still not smashed, steadying himself by means of a piece of trailing wreckage. As the Sea Stag snaps at him again he swings the Black Sword—and chops off one of its antlers. The beast snorts in astonishment.

48. Ext. Ship. Day.

Yelling, Urlik leans out from the rail, holding on only by the piece of *rigging, and plunges the Black Sword directly between the beast's startled eyes. The beast shrieks.*

49. Ext. Ship. Day.
Urlik readies himself for another attack from the Sea Stag. But the Sea Stag has had enough. Snorting, wounded, gouting blood, it sinks beneath the water. In relief, Urlik jumps back to the deck.

50. Ext. Ship. Day.
Iolinda runs up to Urlik and embraces him, thanking him for saving them all. Jarak hovers nearby, grinning sheepishly as he sheathes his sword. Urlik is startled. He is hardly aware of Iolinda or anyone else as he stares down at his bright black sword.

IOLINDA: "You prove yourself our Champion. You saved all our lives!"

JARAK: "A living legend has practical uses, after all . . ."

URLIK: "It was this sword saved us. I did nothing . . . Stormbringer— aptly named . . ."

51. Ext. Ship. Day.
Belphig moves into the scene smiling with satisfaction.

BELPHIG: "Now do you believe? Stormbringer allows only mankind's true Hero to wield her!"

Urlik looks at the sword in some distaste and, with a quick movement, returns it to the scabbard. The faint singing noise stops at once. Meliadus, a little shame-faced, approaches.

MELIADUS: "You saved Iolinda's life. I thank you—Champion . . ."

Urlik is grim, unhappy about what has happened, half-suspicious of them all.

URLIK: "You condemn sorcery—but this sword is sorcery! I am not sure I want its aid . . ."

BELPHIG: "The Sea Stag would have destroyed us all if you had not had Stormbringer. You must accept your destiny . . ."

Iolinda clings to him.

IOLINDA: "All this will not last long. Soon Earth will be cleansed of the Eldren vermin—and we shall be wed . . ."

52. Ext. Ship. Day.

A close-up of Belphig who has become unusually intense, his eyes full of fanatical fire.

BELPHIG: "Now swear your Oath. To serve Mankind without question for the rest of your life! Come—swear. Now that the sword is blooded—swear you'll always serve our cause . . ."

53. Ext. Ship. Day.

Urlik is still completely dazed, dumbfounded, under pressure from Iolinda on one side, Belphig on the other. Jarak looks as if he would like to interfere but cannot. Belphig lifts the hilt of the scabbarded sword to Urlik's lips. He murmurs to Urlik:

BELPHIG: "Kiss the sword and swear the oath."

URLIK: "Oath? What are you saying? Sorcery—vows—demons—I can't believe . . ."

IOLINDA: "Swear the oath, my Champion. For me—for the race!"

URLIK: "Swear? Very well—I swear . . ."

BELPHIG: "That you will serve mankind above all else. Swear it by the Black Sword."

URLIK: "I swear I'll serve mankind above all else . . ."

BELPHIG (*whispering*): "Swear it by Stormbringer—by the sword . . ."

URLIK: "I swear it—by Stormbringer!"

Belphig relaxes, satisfied.

54. Ext. Ship. Day.
   With a sigh of satisfaction, Belphig lets the sword drop. He begins to walk away, towards the bridge.

BELPHIG: "Good. Now Man and Sword are bound together . . ."

Jarak begins to shout at his men, as much to break the tension as anything else.

JARAK: "Clear this wreckage. Boats for survivors. Let's be ready before the Eldren send more sorcery!"

Urlik suddenly seems to wake up.

URLIK: "That beast was real—we've no proof of *sorcery* . . ."

IOLINDA: "We *know* the Eldren are sorcerers. Our stories . . ."

Meliadus, mollified by recent events, speaks more levelly than usual.

MELIADUS: "She speaks truth, Sir Hero. That was Eldren work."

Urlik refuses to be convinced, he turns and looks out to sea, towards Paphanal.

55. Ext. City. Day.
   The beautiful city of Paphanal. It is much closer now. We pan back to see . . .

56. Ext. Sea. Day.

The fleet of humanity is bearing down on Paphanal. The flagship is battered but still able to sail.

57. Ext. Deck of the ship. Day.

Urlik is on the bridge, talking to the men and officers who have gathered below. Iolinda is with him, but looks upset. Jarak, on the deck below, listens to Urlik while he continues to oversee the running of the ship.

URLIK: "We should parley with the Eldren. Give them a chance to make peace."

One of the officers replies from below. He is Mazak.

MAZAK: "Wipe out the dogs, Lord Urlik. *One* alive will destroy us!"

A number of the other officers, however, seem to be coming over to Urlik's point of view. Jarak, in the meantime, orders a seaman aloft, murmuring to him:

JARAK: "Get aloft. Warn us if they *do* attack . . ."

The seaman begins to climb the mast.

URLIK: "Unless we give them a chance we are no better than they are!"

58. Ext. Bridge. Day.

Urlik attempts to persuade the men who debate amongst themselves.

URLIK: "I'm your War Leader—but I'll not waste any lives—theirs or ours!"

Meliadus emerges onto the bridge and speaks in a low voice, close to Urlik, who only now becomes aware of him.

MELIADUS: "What's this, Sir Hero? More treachery?"

URLIK: "I speak logic!"

Even Meliadus is half-convinced. He fingers his jaw.

MELIADUS: "We're unused to logic nowadays—but perhaps a brief attempt at parleying . . ."

There is a cry from the rigging and they all look up.

59. Ext. Crow's nest of flagship. Day.

The lookout who Jarak has just sent up the mast is in the crow's nest. He is pointing into the sky.

LOOKOUT: "Eldren sorcery! We are attacked!"

60. Ext. Sky. Day.

We pan up, apparently from the pointing finger of the lookout, into the clear blue sky. And now we see a flapping winged creature coming closer and closer. It is the Man Bird—a flying monster, part man, part eagle, with huge talons. It begins to drop towards the fleet.

61. Ext. Fleet. Day.

The Man Bird comes dropping down on the fleet. It snatches the screaming lookout from his perch and drops him into the sea. It screeches in a peculiar kind of laughter and then begins to climb again.

62. Ext. Deck of ship. Day.

At Jarak's orders, several archers shoot long arrows into the sky.

63. Ext. Sky above ship. Day.

The Man Bird laughs again as the arrows whizz around it, most of them falling short. It cackles and points towards Paphanal. We pan towards the sea—and see strange lights flickering, apparently under the water, fairly close to Paphanal's harbour.

64. Ext. Bridge of ship. Day.

Urlik, Jarak, Meliadus and Iolinda crowd to the rail, looking towards Paphanal. The city is in the distance. The bright colours begin to swirl just above the waterline.

URLIK: "What was it pointing at?"

MELIADUS: "They call for supernatural aid. Are you still uncertain of the Eldren power?"

Urlik shakes his head, speaking to Jarak.

URLIK: "The catapults—more fire!"

Urlik looks back at the scene.

65. Ext. Sea. Day.

Now, as Urlik and Company watch, the bright coloured swirls of light begin to form themselves into several shapes, apparently standing between the fleet and Paphanal. These shapes are huge, glowing, greens, blacks, browns, blues, with glaring red eyes—fishy, jellylike monsters.

66. Ext. Deck. Day.

Belphig emerges on deck, pointing towards these Water Demons. He is triumphant, impressive in his authority.

BELPHIG: "Ignore those phantoms. They have yet to take material shape. You'll destroy them—if you destroy the source. Destroy Paphanal!"

Jarak awaits no further instructions. He yells to his men to begin the attack. He signals to the other ships to begin their attack.

JARAK: "Fire! Fire! Send fire! Loose the catapults!"

67. Ext. Sea. Fleet. City. Day.

A terrible rain of fire now begins to pour down on the city as the ships release their fireballs. The stuff whizzes though the air and almost immediately parts of the city begin to burn.

68. Ext. Paphanal harbour. Day.

Fireballs land on the city. Everything blazes. For the first time we get a sight of a helmeted Eldren, looking up alertly as the fire comes down. We hear the man shout an order.

69. Ext. Sea. Day.

Jarak turns to Urlik on the bridge. He points towards Paphanal.

JARAK: "The Eldren fleet attacks!" (*Jarak yells to his men.*) "Stand by! Stand by! Enemy attacking!"

Belphig seems satisfied, however.

BELPHIG: "As I predicted, the Water Demons grow weaker."

70. Ext. Sea. Day.

The delicate Eldren craft are riding through the water. As they come towards the human fleet the Water Demons do, indeed, begin to fade. The Eldren fleet passes through them as if they were smoke.

71. Ext. Ship. Day.

An Eldren ship sails close to the flagship. Eldren archers and lancers hurl their missiles into the flagship. Urlik narrowly misses an arrow in his arm. We catch glimpses of silvery Eldren helmets as the men of the flagship prepare to clash with the Eldren.

72. Ext. Ship. Day.

The Eldren grappling irons thud into the flagship's timbers and Urlik sends Iolinda below as he goes to help in the defense of the ship. Meliadus remains on the bridge. Urlik joins Jarak just as the Eldren swing aboard.

73. Ext. Ship. Day.

Two Eldren warriors swing from the trailing rigging and land directly before Jarak and Urlik. The Eldren have long-hafted war-axes which whistle as they whirl through the air. Urlik ducks a blade. He seems reluctant to draw the Black Sword. Jarak, now engaged with his opponent, shouts at him.

JARAK: "You'll need your sword now—no time for scruples!"

Urlik flashes a sardonic look at Jarak and tugs the Black Sword free. Immediately the singing begins and the sword glows with unearthly radiance. Urlik weighs in with it and again it seems to have a life of its own as the two Eldren go down before it.

74. Ext. Ship. Day.

The Eldren keep coming. Although more delicate in appearance than the humans, they have enormous courage and tenacity and we see them fighting bravely, against overwhelming odds, in all parts of the ship. We see little of their faces, because of their helmets, but they have a slightly Oriental appearance. Urlik and Jarak fight shoulder to shoulder, leading their men into the fighting. The Black Sword howls and time after time it cuts down the Eldren warriors. Urlik yells at Jarak as they fight.

URLIK: "Demons maybe—but they fight bravely!"

JARAK: "If it weren't for their sorcery, I'd relish this war with them!"

75. Ext. Ship. Day.

Suddenly all activity stops as they realize that all the Eldren are dead— save one. Panting, he is cornered near Meliadus's cabin. His war-axe is broken off at the haft. He has the appearance of a brave, desperate deer. Urlik confronts him. From the bridge Meliadus yells.

MELIADUS: "Kill him quickly—before he has a chance to work more magic!"

Urlik ignores Meliadus. He tries to put up the Black Sword.

ELDREN WARRIOR: "Aye—kill me. I've no taste for life now Paphanal burns. Oh, you are treacherous, you humans. Why attack us? We did not threaten you!"

URLIK: "I'll not kill a defenseless man . . ."

MELIADUS: "Strike!"

Urlik makes to sheathe his sword, but it twists in his hand and plunges at the Eldren, killing him.

URLIK: "The sword—it kills against my will . . ."

Jarak steps forward, speaking urgently.

JARAK: "Sheathe it! It lusts for death, that blade . . ."

Urlik sheathes the sword. Meliadus looks greedily towards Paphanal.

MELIADUS: "Now Paphanal is ours. Let's inspect our prize . . ."

76. Ext. Paphanal. Day.

Heavy smoke drifts across the scene. We see figures moving in it—Meliadus, Belphig, Urlik, Iolinda, Jarak and their captains . . . the outlines of ruined masonry—small fires flickering—for these are the ruins of once-beautiful Paphanal. As the conquering humans swagger in, some Eldren women and children scuttle away in terror. An appalling silence hangs over the scene. They enter a wide plaza, ruined by the fire, and Urlik looks around in horror.

URLIK: "It was virtually undefended. Is this what we feared?"

BELPHIG: "Their skill in sorcery more than compensates for the smallness of their number . . ."

Urlik glances around, seeing fearful faces of women and children.

URLIK: "These do not seem to be working much sorcery . . . We must help them."

Meliadus laughs.

MELIADUS: "We'll end their misery soon enough!"

Urlik takes his meaning but chooses to ignore him. Iolinda stares around her in distaste, holding on to Urlik's arm.

IOLINDA: "What wretches! It *is* hard to believe them so evil . . ."

Urlik is profoundly upset.

URLIK: "I've been fighting women and children and a handful of warriors! This isn't worthy of the trust you told me I bore—this is a massacre—genocide!"

Belphig is still persuasive.

BELPHIG: "It is all deception—*intended* to confuse you. I remind you again—these are cunning demons, not true men at all . . ."

Urlik turns on his heel.

URLIK: "The sight is sickening. The city's vanquished—let's leave now!"

MELIADUS: "And refuse our men their triumph? No, Sir Champion—
we *celebrate* our victory . . ."

*Dark smoke drifts over the scene again. We see hot, lustful eyes and lips
through the smoke. We see the terrified faces of the beautiful Eldren. The
smoke grows thicker and we fade on it.*

77. Ext. City. Night.

*We see Urlik bursting through a door into the plaza. Behind him it is
evident that Meliadus and the rest are enjoying themselves in a drunken
orgy. Urlik turns as Meliadus calls him from the interior. Meliadus lifts his
goblet, spilling wine. He has an arm around a shivering Eldren girl.*

MELIADUS: "You weary of our company, Sir Hero? Is this courtesy—to
your future father-in-law?"

*We pan so that we can see Iolinda staring with hurt baffled eyes at
Urlik.*

URLIK: "You sink into barbarism before my eyes. I'll fight with you—
but I'll not join in your pleasures."

*Meliadus stands up, glowering, almost toppling forward, the Eldren girl for-
gotten.*

MELIADUS: "You grow arrogant—you believe your own legend, eh?
You despise us . . ." (*Meliadus looks again at Iolinda who moves to his
side.*) "But you'll not despise her hand in marriage, eh? Belphig
seeks my throne, I know—but you'll defend me, Urlik—for the
throne when I die! Belphig would use you against me—but my
daughter is—is . . ." (*Meliadus flings his arm round Iolinda, leaning
heavily on her.*) ". . . my *security* . . ."

URLIK: "Nothing makes me war on defeated wretches!"

Iolinda supports her all but insensible father. She looks pleadingly at Urlik.

IOLINDA: "Let him enjoy his triumph—he has waited long—tomorrow the city burns . . ."

Urlik tries to reply, but he's too disgusted. He strides away from the open door, into the night, leaving Iolinda looking hurt and reproachful after him as she gradually lowers her father back to his seat. As Urlik plunges into the night, Jarak steps from the shadows. Urlik is relieved to see the only humane face in all that number. He smiles.

URLIK: "All your people seem to scheme against one another—or suspect schemes . . ."

Jarak is amused.

JARAK: "Mankind always has to have an enemy—even if it has to invent one . . ."

Urlik shakes his head in confusion.

URLIK: "And the Eldren are a fine new target, eh?"

Jarak is reluctant to agree to this, though it's evident he really does believe it. Urlik wants to press the matter but just then there is a harsh laugh from the shadows behind them and they turn, seeking the source.

78. Ext. City. Night.

Meliadus and Iolinda stand there, having followed Urlik from the Hall. Meliadus still very drunk.

MELIADUS: "I insist—finish—conversation . . ."

Before Urlik can reply Meliadus spots a movement in the shadows, lurches and catches a frightened, beautiful Zayad.

MELIADUS: "Aha! The gods send me a consort for the night!"

Iolinda is embarrassed, turns to Urlik for help. Then Jarak recognizes Zayad.

JARAK: "She's Zayad—the Eldren leader!"

Iolinda is curious and looks closer at Zayad.

IOLINDA: "Most notorious of all Eldren sorceresses! Halag Tharm's sister—rules the Eldren jointly with him . . ."

Urlik hardly hears Iolinda in his anger at Meliadus's brutality.

URLIK: "She's a prisoner of war—treat her with courtesy!"

Zayad looks at him in some astonishment, not expecting such words from the humans. She's cool and intelligent as she recovers some of her composure. Meliadus stares stupidly at Urlik, almost passing out. Meliadus, befuddled, protests, upset by what seems to him a breach of protocol.

MELIADUS: "She's mine by right! I am the king . . ."

Jarak senses that the situation begins to look dangerous, steps forward and speaks placatingly . . .

JARAK: "But no mere war-prize, my liege! A good bargaining counter in our dealings with the Eldren!"

Meliadus looks to Iolinda for help.

IOLINDA: "There's wisdom in that. Besides—she's safer imprisoned."

URLIK (*almost absently, suggests*): "See she's treated well in my quarters. We'll question her there . . ."

Jarak gladly leads Zayad away. Urlik looks after her, his expression brooding and troubled. Meliadus with a grunt of frustrated anger flings back towards the Hall, leaving Iolinda and Urlik alone. Urlik moves towards her, then looks to one side suddenly as he senses a movement in the shadows. He sees, for a second, the smooth, smiling face of Belphig—then the face ducks out of sight again.

IOLINDA: "You saved my father from foolishness. Thank you. She's beautiful, eh? The Eldren woman . . ."

Urlik shrugs and takes her in his arms.

URLIK: "In a way. I could easily believe her a witch . . ."

IOLINDA: "More beautiful than any human woman . . ."

URLIK: "Not more beautiful than you . . ."

It is what Iolinda has wanted to hear. She holds him close against her. She whispers in his ear. He smiles tenderly and nods. We fade to . . .

79. Int. Urlik's apartments. Night.

A large, beautiful room, sparely furnished after the elegant fashion of the Eldren. A few signs of Urlik's presence are here—his helmet—a cloak lying on the bed. Zayad stands by the window, looking out at the flickering fires. Jarak, watching her warily, stands by the door. Urlik enters. She bows to him sardonically, Jarak looks questioningly at him. Urlik nods for Jarak to leave. Now Urlik, still by the door, confronts Zayad. He is somewhat embarrassed, troubled. Zayad is almost amused. He moves towards the bed where his helmet and cloak lie.

ZAYAD: "You're the first of your race ever to address me with kindness. I'm grateful. When am I to be killed?"

Urlik is astonished. He turns.

URLIK: "Killed? I'm a warrior—making war on warriors. You're under my protection!"

Zayad is puzzled, but then she seems enlightened.

ZAYAD: "So you'll use me for advantage over my brother?"

Urlik has not considered this, but he regards it as an interesting idea.

URLIK: "It would be legitimate strategy . . ." (*Urlik pauses, amused. A relationship of mutual respect is steadily building up between them. Sardonically, he adds*) "I suppose I should ask for your word not to use your sorcery while a prisoner . . ."

Zayad smiles bitterly.

ZAYAD: "It's always suited you to believe us sorcerers. The Eldren were first on this planet, did you know?" (*Urlik is surprised, but he lets her continue.*) "You were driven from your own planet by one of your many wars. You came with death and destruction to claim this world for yourselves. To our eternal shame we retaliated . . ."

URLIK: "I've seen how you 'retaliate' . . ."

She turns her back on him as she continues.

ZAYAD: "We took pride in our respect for life—but we made weapons— to keep you at bay—so powerful you thought us sorcerers. You were ever superstitious . . ." (*Urlik cannot make up his mind if she is lying or not. He moves towards her, hoping to see her face and judge.*) ". . . we showed you our power—frightened you so badly you never dared attack us . . . until you were desperate for a fresh enemy—you had no-one left to fight—you knew we were weak . . ."

Urlik is disturbed, still trying to decide if she's lying or not. Her voice is low, persuasive . . .

URLIK: "Weak? Why not use the weapons? Why rely on sorcery . . . ?"

Zayad laughs openly at this.

ZAYAD: "We swore a great oath—never to use the weapons again—even if it meant our total downfall . . . As for sorcery . . ."

Urlik gestures behind him in the general direction of the harbour.

URLIK: "I witnessed sorcery today! If the Sea Stag was a real beast, what of the flying man? The Water Demons?"

Zayad speaks soberly, but, even as she begins, Belphig and Iolinda burst in. Iolinda has changed her clothes. She glances at Urlik, her look charged with intimate meaning. It's obvious their relationship has deepened . . .

ZAYAD: "I suggest you look to—"

Belphig seems anxious to interrupt her.

BELPHIG: "Excellent! Princess Iolinda told me about the Eldren vixen. Fear not—I'll protect you from her spells and summonings . . ." (*Zayad laughs at Belphig. She is contemptuous of him. Belphig's face grows stern. Iolinda looks bewilderedly from one to the other, her main interest is in Urlik and the impression made on him by Zayad.*) "Be certain, madam—you'll suffer the special fate reserved for all Eldren enchanters . . ."

ZAYAD: "Ah—human reasoning much more familiar to me!"

Iolinda glares at her.

IOLINDA: "Urlik—why did you come here to her?"

Urlik is taken aback by the implication. He's anxious to reassure her.

URLIK: "I came to collect my things. She was telling me her people's history . . ." (*Iolinda's features soften. It is evident that she regards Urlik as an innocent who has been deceived. Urlik moves to embrace Iolinda . . .*) ". . . and I think she'll be a useful counter in our war against the Eldren. Eh, Bishop Belphig?"

Belphig is reluctant to agree, but is thoughtful.

BELPHIG: "She could destroy us overnight. There's a great risk in allowing her to live . . ."

IOLINDA: "Urlik wants us to spare the lives of all the Eldren left—if a bargain can be made . . ."

BELPHIG: "We indulge ourselves, my lady—the Eldren must all perish!"

Belphig makes a movement towards Zayad—almost as if he will strike her. Urlik moves between them, speaking quietly and angrily . . .

URLIK: "I protect her, Belphig—sorceress or no. Let the king decide her fate!"

Belphig is openly contemptuous of the king, but adjusts his expression when he realizes that he shocks Iolinda.

BELPHIG: "The *king* decide . . ." (*He makes for the door.*) "You'll regret this flirtation with evil . . ."

Angrily, he reaches for the handle of the door.

IOLINDA: "Urlik says to show mercy is to show our power—the righteousness of our cause . . ."

BELPHIG: "One does not show mercy to a *disease* . . ."

Urlik and Iolinda are confused as Belphig storms off. Zayad goes to the window and looks out again, as if she hopes for rescue. Iolinda embraces Urlik. They kiss.

IOLINDA: "My father must make the decision—"

URLIK: "He's drunk with hate . . ."

IOLINDA: "He suspects Belphig seeks the throne. He might agree—to *spite* Belphig . . ."

Iolinda kisses him again and then looks towards Zayad who is still staring out of the window at the fires.

IOLINDA: "It seems she waits for rescue . . ."

Iolinda gives Urlik a meaningful look. We fade on Zayad looking out over the ruins of her city . . .

80. Ext. Rooftops. Night.
We see the Man Bird again. It has landed, apparently, on the rooftops of the city and is making its way stealthily towards a tower. We pan towards a lighted window in the tower . . .

81. Ext. Tower window. Night.
. . . we see through the window and into the room where Meliadus, recovered but ill-tempered, is talking to Urlik, who pleads urgently with him.

URLIK: "The women and children *must* be spared—they're much more use alive!"

Meliadus broods on this, looking sidelong at Urlik . . .

MELIADUS: "Iolinda agrees with you . . . ?"

URLIK: "It's sane logic . . ."

MELIADUS: "Belphig would hate it if I let them live. That fat priest does
nothing unless it brings him advantage over me. Yes, I might spare
them . . ."

*Meliadus glances calculatingly at Urlik as he, Meliadus, moves towards the
window, to the table with a jug of wine and a goblet on it. He looks up in
horror at the window at the sound of flapping wings.*

MELIADUS: "By the gods! More Eldren sorcery—"

82. *Int. Tower room. Night.*
*Meliadus stumbles back as the Man Bird attacks him. He is powerless
before its strength as it slashes and claws at him. Urlik flings himself on the
creature but is swept aside by a powerful wing. He stumbles up, tugging his
sword free. The Man Bird looks up from the now still Meliadus and eyes the
Black Sword. Evidently it knows the sword's power. Hastily it springs
through the window. Urlik rushes in pursuit and sees—*

83. *Ext. Sky seen through tower window. Night.*
*—the dark shape of the Man Bird climbs upward, screeching tri-
umphantly.*

84. *Int. Tower room. Night.*
*Urlik sheathes the sword and inspects the body of King Meliadus as
Jarak rushes in.*

URLIK: "Why should the Eldren wish to slay him?"

JARAK: "I saw the beast—Zayad, eh? Changing shape?"

URLIK: "Impossible . . ."

Frowning, he stares at the window.

85. Int. Tower room. Sunrise.
Soldiers bear the corpse of Meliadus away. Belphig, Iolinda, Jarak and Urlik remain. Iolinda wildly distressed. Belphig grim and grave. Urlik angry. Belphig comforts Iolinda.

BELPHIG: "Queen—now you rule us all . . ."

IOLINDA: "If we'd destroyed all the Eldren at once Zayad could never have killed my father . . ."

URLIK: "We don't know it was Zayad . . ."

JARAK: "Meliadus molested her—she could have summoned the beast—in revenge . . ."

IOLINDA: "The demons must die—now!"

URLIK: "There's no justice in that—not till we're certain!"

Urlik crosses the room to embrace Iolinda. She is grief-stricken and angry.

IOLINDA: "I can't listen—your advice caused my father's death!"

URLIK: "*If* the Eldren killed him . . ."

Belphig is dismissive.

BELPHIG: "*If?* Your reasoning's too tortuous for me. You were not summoned here, Urlik, to make decisions of State . . ."

Iolinda pulls herself together.

IOLINDA: "The queen makes those decisions—and I say kill them now!"

URLIK: "This is hysteria—not justice!"

IOLINDA: "It is my command!"

URLIK: "My conscience commands otherwise!"

BELPHIG: "I'd remind you of the oath you swore on the sword . . ."

URLIK: "Extracted under stress . . ."

BELPHIG: "But nonetheless potent—break it and you perish!"

URLIK: "Threaten me once more, bishop—and seek another hero!"

BELPHIG: "Threat? *Prediction* . . ."

IOLINDA: "Traitor! The Eldren die now—kill Zayad, Urlik—avenge your king!"

URLIK: "Grief clouds your mind. I beg you . . ."

IOLINDA: "You're entranced by the Eldren witch! I call you *traitor*!"

URLIK: "Call me what you will—I'll play no part in murder."

Captain Mazak bursts into the tower room.

MAZAK: "Halag Tharm's Eldren army. Attacking by land. They outnumber us."

JARAK: "A fresh army—and we are tired—weak . . ."

Urlik turns to Iolinda.

URLIK: "I beg you, Queen Iolinda—wait until after the battle. We'll need all the hostages we can keep."

Iolinda sees the sense of this. Belphig is angry.

JARAK: "There's no way to hold the city—too badly damaged . . ."

URLIK: "Then we'll meet them head-on . . ."

URLIK (*bows to Iolinda*): "With your permission—my queen . . ."

Iolinda inclines her head. She is confused. Suddenly concerned for him. Her sanity is returning. Urlik and Jarak leave for the battlefield.

86. Ext. Plain outside city. Day.

At the head of their men Urlik and Jarak ride forth from the city. The great part of their soldiers are weary infantry. They ride up an incline on the landward side of Paphanal, which is in ruins. Urlik almost cheerful.

URLIK: "This is more to my taste—at least we're free of madness and sorcery . . ."

Jarak is none too sure . . .

JARAK: "We may yet meet sorcery. The Eldren have strange wagons with them . . ."

Urlik and Jarak ride slightly ahead of Mazak and their men, to the top of the rise, where they can look down on the Eldren army.

87. Ext. Plain. Day.

At the top of the rise Jarak points out the Eldren army.

88. Ext. Plain. Day.

The Eldren army. Well-ordered, disciplined, mostly mounted. Their tall lances and war-axes make a forest of steel. They bring with them several large wagons bearing brightly coloured canvas (very reminiscent of the gas-bag of the airship we saw in the opening sequences—for good reason, as we'll see). At the head of this army is the noble figure of Halag Tharm.

89. Ext. Plain. Day.

Jarak and Urlik look back at their own somewhat disorganized army. It is pretty evident that they are outclassed.

JARAK: "The odds are too great—and they have sorcery . . ."

URLIK (*sardonically*): "But we have *ferocity*, Captain Jarak!" (*Urlik wheels his horse and gallops back to the head of his men. He draws the wailing sword Stormbringer:*) "The Eldren outnumber us—but we are wolves, with the courage of our race, to rend them, to devour them!"

His men cheer and begin to surge forward, following him.

90. Ext. Plain. Day.

There is a wild desperate look on Urlik's face as he waves the Black Sword so that its black radiance casts a shadow over his face. It howls, sings.

URLIK: "Here's our shield against sorcery—it makes us invincible!"

The men cheer again. Urlik spurs his horse forward.

91. Ext. Plain. Day.

The human army, roaring its bloodlust, pours down on the Eldren. Halag sees them—immediately orders his men to fall back. There is an almost comical pause in the events! Then as the Eldren appear to retreat, in good order, a jubilant cheer goes up from the humans and they charge on. Jarak comes into view. He looks amazed.

JARAK: "Are they such cowards? We drive them back!"

92. Ext. Plain. Day.

Urlik and Jarak continue to ride in pursuit of the withdrawing Eldren. Urlik bewildered by the tactic.

URLIK: "I think we follow too easily . . ."

93. Ext. Plain. Day.

The Eldren suddenly stand their ground and the human army virtually falls over itself as it clashes with them (again the scene has its humorous aspect). Soon Urlik and Jarak are in the thick of fierce fighting. It is then that Urlik notices what's happening with the wagons. They're rising into the air!

URLIK: "It was a trick—leading us away so they can bomb Paphanal to the ground. Iolinda, Belphig—they're doomed!"

Jarak makes no reply, but it's evident he's wondering how. They're almost surrounded by Eldren now. Urlik fights like a madman, his weird sword striking everywhere. He's in panic. Everywhere his own men are embattled.

94. Ext. Plain. Day.

Halag Tharm comes upon Urlik more or less from behind, as Urlik kills another Eldren. Urlik whirls to meet him.

95. Ext. Plain. Day.

Surrounded by fighting men, Urlik and Halag fight it out. Halag ducks every blow of the fearful black sword.

96. Ext. Plain. Day.

The two are locked in combat, their faces in close-up.

HALAG: "So you're the legend that gave courage to mankind—to come and destroy our land. Can you be killed, Sir Legend?"

URLIK: "As easily as I can kill you—Sir Demon!"

97. Ext. Plain. Day.

The fight continues. Halag falls, but Urlik struggles with his own sword to stop it killing Halag before Halag can regain his footing. Halag is bemused.

HALAG: "What's this? Human chivalry? You are a strange human indeed, Sir Legend."

URLIK: "And you're the oddest demon I've met!"

98. Ext. Plain. Day.

They fight on. Halag displays superb swordsmanship. Eventually, other Eldren swarm round and a war-axe strikes Urlik on the head, causing him to drop the sword. He is dazed, almost falling. Halag signs for his men to draw back. With a smile, he stoops to retrieve the blade, but pulls back his hand with shock.

HALAG: "It burns!"

Urlik is still dazed, answers groggily.

URLIK: "Only I can hold it. But I thank you for the courtesy, Sir Demon . . ." (*Urlik reaches down for the sword and falls to his knees. Halag immediately springs forward to support him. Jarak rides by. Urlik summons his failing strength to yell:*) "Get back to Paphanal! Save those still there!"

Jarak's face is panicky, but he sees the sense, wheels his horse, ordering the men back to the city. Urlik grasps the sword—it gives him strength and he fights on with such terrible ferocity he drives the Eldren back. His ferocity increases—the Eldren can't get near him.

99. Ext. Plain. Day.

Dazed, half-falling, he fights on, pushing them further and further back. They look at him in wonder. Then suddenly they all peer up into the sky and at a word from Halag they all stop fighting immediately. Again the wind is taken out of Urlik's sails. He fights shadows before he realizes that they have all withdrawn. Panting he slowly lifts his head and we follow his gaze up into the sky . . .

100. Ext. Sky over plain. Day.
The airships are returning from Paphanal!

101. Ext. Eldren army camp. Day.
The airships are being hauled back into the wagons. The gondolas contain the women and children who were trapped in Paphanal. Urlik sheathes his sword and approaches Halag. The rest ignore him.

URLIK: "I wasted my time trying to save them. This was your plan . . ."

HALAG: "We feared we'd be too late. Now we'll return to our ships— they're hidden in a creek back there. We retreat again, Sir Legend—like the cowardly demons we are . . ."

Halag welcomes the grateful women and children. It is Urlik who voices his fears first.

URLIK: "But where's Zayad?"

An Eldren warrior, one of those who has steered an airship, approaches Halag.

ELDREN WARRIOR: "She was too well protected, Halag—"

Urlik reacts impulsively.

URLIK: "Send a message—my life for hers—otherwise she's doomed . . ."

Halag responds at once to Urlik's advice, ordering a messenger to Paphanal . . .

HALAG: "Ride at once—Urlik's life for Zayad's—go now!"

HALAG (*turns to Urlik*): "I'm grateful to you—you're a strange human . . ."

URLIK: "You could take Paphanal—you've the strength!"

HALAG: "But not the will. We made a vow. We'll retreat again—hoping you'll leave us in peace . . ."

URLIK: "They are bent on your complete destruction . . ."

HALAG: "Then we'll perish with honour . . ."

We fade on Halag's sad, bitter face . . .

102. Ext. Eldren camp. Day.

The Eldren army, the wagons stowed, the women and children riding on top of them, begins to retreat. As it does so Jarak and the Eldren messenger come riding up at high speed. Jarak dismounts before the waiting Halag and Urlik.

JARAK: "Iolinda agrees—Zayad'll have a horse and be free as soon as Urlik's seen from Paphanal . . ."

Halag is satisfied. He turns to Urlik, who looks very gloomy.

HALAG: "Have I your word on it?"

URLIK: "You'll have my word."

Halag signs for Urlik's horse to be led forward.

HALAG: "Then go, Sir Legend. If there's to be no peace then our next meeting will doubtless be when you come to kill me . . ."

Urlik grips Halag's arm and mounts up. Without looking back he spurs forward, Jarak behind him.

103. Ext. Close to city walls. Sunset.
Urlik and Jarak riding hell for leather towards the city. Urlik is puzzled.

URLIK: "They can see us now. Zayad's not free. Why?"

Jarak says nothing, but looks miserable.

104. Ext. City plaza. Sunset.
Urlik rides rapidly into the plaza where Iolinda stands awaiting him. He flings himself from his horse and she runs forward to embrace him. He returns her embrace but looks around, demanding . . .

URLIK: "Where is Zayad?"

Belphig emerges from the Hall, smiling.

BELPHIG: "For once *we've* deceived the demons. We have you back—and we have Zayad, too. She'll be tortured to extract her confession . . ."

Urlik is furious.

URLIK: "I gave my *word* to Halag that his sister would be freed!"

Iolinda tries to placate him.

IOLINDA: "She killed my father. We must be revenged . . ."

Urlik even more angry.

URLIK: "There's no proof! The Eldren want peace. They could have wiped us out today, but didn't . . ."

BELPHIG: "What if all this was so? Our people must still have an enemy. Would you have them turn on you, or me, or Queen Iolinda . . . ?"

URLIK: "Your cynicism disgusts me. Release Zayad!"

IOLINDA: "She dies! You were summoned to serve us—now you speak for our foes!"

Urlik tries to speak rationally to her.

URLIK: "Belphig exploits your ancient terrors of demons and shape-changers . . . The Eldren are civilized, gentle . . ."

IOLINDA: "They killed my father!"

URLIK: "I do not believe they did!"

Iolinda begins to stride towards the Hall we saw in Shot 77. Evening is gathering in.

IOLINDA: "You saw the monster!"

Urlik makes to follow her into the Hall.

URLIK: "It could as easily have been sent by one of *us*!"

Iolinda storms into the Hall. Urlik is close behind. And behind him comes Belphig, shamming shock:

BELPHIG: "Treachery first—now he accuses *us*!"

Urlik enters the Hall.

105. Int. Hall. Twilight.
Iolinda has paced into the Hall which still bears the signs of last night's

orgy. Tied to a chair at the head of the littered table, with a guard on either side of her, is Zayad. She gives Urlik a peculiar smile when she sees him follow Iolinda into the Hall.

IOLINDA: "Begin the punishment!" (*Urlik strides forward to stay the hands of the guards.*) "Traitor! I am your queen. You have sworn loyalty! My father was right to be suspicious of you!"

BELPHIG: "Take heed, Lord Urlik—you face your own destruction!"

URLIK: "You revenge yourselves on the weak—because you, too, are weak. But your weakness is spiritual . . ."

Urlik begins to cut Zayad free. The ropes fall away. Iolinda is beside herself. Jarak hovers in the doorway looking upset.

IOLINDA: "Slay her now!"

URLIK: "The Eldren possess scientific power—to destroy all of us!"

BELPHIG: "Then why not use it?"

ZAYAD (*quietly*): "It's against our Code—our vow . . ."

Belphig is gleeful . . .

BELPHIG: "The Eldren have no will to live—so what matter if we kill them?"

Belphig signs to the guards who begin to draw their knives. Urlik gives them a warning glance, half unsheathing Stormbringer. They hesitate. Belphig steps in again.

BELPHIG: "Be reasonable, Lord Urlik. You are misguided, not disloyal. You'll share the throne soon—Rule the whole planet . . ."

Urlik glares at him.

URLIK: "A planet reeking of death and treachery? No! Release Zayad. I'll fight for you—but I'll not betray the innocent!"

Belphig pretends to be amused.

BELPHIG: "The innocent, say you? She killed Meliadus—and many more. She's enchanted you—she knows you're our main strength . . ."

Urlik dismisses all this.

URLIK: "I trust my instincts. I gave my word . . ."

IOLINDA: "And I trust my instincts! Jarak—cut her down!" (*Jarak, who has been happy to stay in the background, is confused . . . He hesitates, looking to Urlik. Iolinda is perfectly aware that she divides them.*) "Cut her down, Jarak!"

Belphig seems almost delighted by this turn of events.

BELPHIG: "The queen must be obeyed, Captain Jarak . . ."

Urlik is furious.

URLIK: "This is barbarous! You turn friend against friend! Stay back, Jarak!"

Jarak is thoroughly miserable, but continues to move forward, his loyalties totally divided.

JARAK: "I told you, Urlik. My first loyalty's to my queen. Zayad killed the king . . ."

URLIK: "Why?—He was going to spare her! Someone else killed the king."

Belphig comes in quickly.

BELPHIG: "Do your duty, Captain Jarak!"

Urlik shouts desperately at Jarak.

URLIK: "You can't!"

Jarak stares miserably around, drawing his sword. Urlik draws Storm-bringer. It whines and moans. Jarak turns to defend himself. The guards also rush forward. Belphig tries to stop Urlik, but Urlik smashes upwards, catching Belphig under the jaw. Belphig goes down, virtually unconscious. Urlik kills the first guard, parries a blow from the second and kills him. Then it is only Jarak and Urlik facing one another. Urlik is begging Jarak with his eyes to stand aside, similarly Jarak is begging Urlik. Both men are about to lower their swords when Stormbringer shrieks and aims itself at Jarak, taking him in the heart. Jarak falls.

URLIK: "Stormbringer—it killed him!" (*Urlik stares wildly around. He goes to Zayad's side and tugs at her to go with him.*) "Come—we leave!"

Iolinda is screaming for more guards. Screaming at Urlik and Zayad.

IOLINDA: "Guards! You'll pay with your life, Urlik. You betray your oath!" (*More guards arrive. Urlik, defending Zayad, moves towards them, clearing a path with his sword.*) "Take the sorceress—and welcome. You are both damned now!"

Belphig staggers up and follows in their wake as Urlik and Zayad pass through the door.

106. Ext. Plaza. Night.

Urlik and Zayad burst out of the lighted hall into torchlight as guards hurry forward. Urlik heads for the horses, cutting his way through, knocking torches out of the hands of warriors, seizing one torch. Into this confusion staggers Belphig, still dazed from the blow, calling after Urlik as he helps Zayad to mount and then mounts himself, sword in one hand, torch in the other.

BELPHIG: "You'll never be free of your fate! Stormbringer binds you to us!"

Urlik's eyes glow with torment. With a yell he hurls the Black Sword at Belphig's feet.

URLIK: "Take it! I want no further part in its destiny!"

Belphig's answering laugh as Urlik and Zayad ride for the gap in the wall is sinister.

107. Ext. Plaza. Night.

A close-up of Belphig, his face full of unholy glee, as he shouts after the disappearing couple.

BELPHIG: "You are Stormbringer's slave! Only *I* can free you! You *will* come back to us, Sir Champion! Without the Black Sword you cannot live . . ."

108. Ext. Plain. Night.

Urlik and Zayad gallop through the night by torchlight. Towards a rise where the silhouetted figure of Halag waits.

ZAYAD: "I know Belphig—there'll be truth in his threat."

Urlik ignores her, pointing towards Halag.

URLIK: "Your brother has waited for you."

109. Ext. Plain. Night.

Halag has a little trouble controlling his horse as he turns it towards the creek where his fleet awaits him.

HALAG: "Come with us—you have no choice."

Thunder begins to roll in the sky. Lightning flashes on the horizon. Urlik looks at Zayad and Halag and shrugs, spurring his horse forward with them.

URLIK: "I'm an outlaw—I've broken my oath—so lead on, Sir Demon!"

More thunder. It begins to rain—thick, driving rain. They ride through it. We hear, in the distance, Urlik's final remark . . .

URLIK: "Without a Champion, Iolinda might give up—perhaps it will mean peace for us all . . ."

110. Ext. Ice plain. Dawn.

The sun spreads a bloody glow over the great plain of ice over which the Eldren march. Time has passed. Urlik is dressed in basically Eldren gear, with a huge white fur cloak. Overhead drift the airships full of the women and children. The Eldren carry bundles, drag sleds—it is a general exodus to their last retreat—the Fortress of the Ice. Urlik, however, is weak and ill. Zayad and Halag help support him as they get him into a sled. Halag speaks to Zayad . . .

HALAG: "He weakens daily. What dreadful power reaches so far to claim his soul . . . ?"

ZAYAD: "Soon we'll be at the fortress. There I'll try to find herbs to cure him . . ."

Urlik has heard them. He looks up, smiling his thanks. He is very weak indeed. Halag shouts for the sled to begin moving. The last of the Eldren begin to move across the ice.

111. Ext. Ice plain. Day.

The ethereally beautiful Fortress of the Ice. It is predominantly black and white, with slender, tapering towers and a massive wall. It seems to grow out of the ice, which has a strong bluish tinge to it, reflecting the bright blue of the sky above. In all directions, for as far as the eye can see, is the great ice plain. On the horizon we see tiny dots moving—the Eldren move slowly towards their last retreat . . .

112. Ext. Ice plain. Day.

The camera is apparently moving amongst the turrets of the fortress, to the battlements. We look down to see the Eldren almost at the gates of the fortress, far below. We see the tiny figure of Halag gesturing towards the fortress, speaking to the fur-swathed Urlik in the sled.

HALAG: "There, Sir Legend—the Fortress of the Ice—our last retreat!"

113. Int. Tower room. Day.

A circular room in one of the towers of the fortress. We see an expanse of ice through the window. Urlik is moaning and tossing amongst the furs of his bed while Zayad and Halag stand over him. Zayad tries to make him take a steaming drink (in a brass cup not dissimilar to the one we saw in Shot 8 at the beginning). He sips a little and then falls back gasping onto his pillows.

URLIK: "Your skill can't help me. I bound myself to Stormbringer— now it drags my soul from me . . ."

Halag looks grave, speaking quietly to Zayad.

HALAG: "If we made him immortal—it might counter Belphig's sorcery?"

ZAYAD: "We can try—the only 'sorcery' we know!"

Urlik looks up at them, silent, puzzled, pleading.

114. Int. Tower room. Day.
Halag holds a tray on which rests a beaker of strangely mottled glass. Little lights seem to dance in the liquid in the beaker. Zayad reaches her hand to take it from the tray, cradling Urlik's pale head.

ZAYAD: "Drink every drop. This is our most precious secret—it will make you immortal . . ."

Halag turns a sad head to look towards the window. We move in on a close-up of him.

HALAG: "But not invulnerable—when the human army comes . . ."

We fade as Zayad's hand replaces the empty beaker on Halag's tray.

115. Int. Tower room. Night.
Urlik has recovered a little. Zayad still nurses him, though she's changed her costume, so we know some time's passed. It's plain that Urlik and Zayad have fallen in love.

ZAYAD: "You feel stronger now?"

URLIK: "A little. That potion—was I feverish—you said I'd live for ever?"

ZAYAD: "If you survive Belphig's sorcery. All the Eldren are immortal— which is probably why we prize life so highly . . ."

She speaks sadly. Urlik sits upright, still weak. He touches his temple with his fingertips.

URLIK: "The sword calls me—draining me, even as strength returns . . ."

ZAYAD: "You should go back. They need you—just as you need Stormbringer. Keep your oath . . ."

Urlik is grateful for her selflessness.

URLIK: "It was falsely extracted. Belphig is insane . . . If *he* were killed, this curse would go . . ."

Zayad turns away.

ZAYAD: "You think they'll attack us here, then?"

URLIK: "He'll play on Iolinda's jealousy—yes—he'll come."

Zayad whirls, flinging herself beside Urlik. He takes her in his arms. With the air of two who take what happiness they can while they can, they embrace.

116. Ext. Battlements of fortress. Day.

Urlik is still weak but he walks with Zayad and Halag along the battlements of the fortress, looking out over the endless ice plain. It is a grey day with heavy cloud in the sky. Halag looks up.

HALAG: "Snow comes soon. It will make a natural defense . . ."

Urlik leans heavily against the battlements. His breath steams from his lips, as if his life drifts away before their eyes. Zayad is anxious. She tries to steady him.

ZAYAD: "We must go inside . . ."

Urlik staggers. She supports him. Zayad and Halag exchange sad, significant glances. Then Urlik seems to sense something. He is baffled, glances around him, glances up. He has sensed the presence of the Man Bird.

117. Ext. Fortress. Sky. Day.

We move up from the battlements into the grey sky. And now we see, hovering like a great hawk over the fortress, the Man Bird. With a flap of its wings it moves into a cloud and disappears. We move down again to the battlements and . . .

118. Ext. Battlements. Day.

. . . down to where Urlik, Halag and Zayad are all staring up in trepidation. They have all seen the Man Bird.

URLIK: "That's the creature that killed Meliadus. Belphig said you created it . . . Maybe it serves neither humans nor Eldren . . ."

We move back into the sky and . . .

119. Ext. Fortress. Sky. Day.

. . . we see the shadow of the Man Bird in the clouds. We hear a faint, laughing screech, which echoes over into the following shot . . .

120. Ext. Ice plain. Evening.

. . . it begins to snow. We move down again and this time we see a blizzard. Slowly, through the driving, powdery snow, emerges the marching, menacing human army, all swathed in dark fur and iron, led by Belphig and Iolinda. Mazak is also there. Iolinda and Belphig also wear fur and iron—armour . . .

121. Ext. Battlements. Morning.

The blizzard continues, swirling around the battlements of the fortress. Eldren warriors are wrapped in their cloaks, clutching their weapons, peering down in silence at . . .

122. Ext. Ice plain outside fortress. Morning.

. . . the camp of the human army. The humans are laying siege to the fortress. There are siege engines, tents, guttering fires and torches. Smoke *drifts and mingles with the blizzard still falling. The dark, menacing figures of the human warriors come and go. Suddenly, out of the general confusion of this scene, come two bulky riders, making for the fortress . . .*

123. Ext. Battlements. Morning.

. . . the riders rein their horses under the battlements. Halag comes into close-up, peering down at them. The riders look up and are revealed as Belphig and Iolinda. Belphig calls . . .

BELPHIG: "Demons—release our Champion from his enchantment!"

Belphig brandishes Stormbringer by the blade. The thing moans and flickers. Iolinda speaks . . .

IOLINDA: "Without Stormbringer he will die!"

Halag is amused by this casuistry.

HALAG: "You'd steal his soul. But he must decide . . ."

Halag turns away.

124. Ext. Battlements. Morning.

Urlik is weak but he pulls himself together when he sees Belphig and Iolinda. A fierce pride and hatred for Belphig burns in him. Zayad hovers behind him. She is unseen by Iolinda or Belphig.

URLIK: "Kill me with your sorcery! I've made my decision. I fight with the Eldren!"

Belphig laughs.

BELPHIG: "Fight? Three more days and you'll be *dead*!"

Contemptuously, Belphig turns his horse. Iolinda looks up, crying out to him in desperation.

IOLINDA: "Urlik—I still love you. Rule Negrana with me! You made a vow!"

URLIK: "And I broke it. Now I pay the full price. As for your love—I cannot pay *that* price!"

Furious, hurt, Iolinda turns her horse to follow Belphig.

IOLINDA: "Then die! For a few scruples you throw away a world!"

As they go Urlik again falls back, supported by Zayad. He looks into her eyes. Fiercely, he kisses her. She looks beyond him, over the battlements, and gasps.

125. Ext. Battlements. Morning.
Through the blinding blizzard a huge dark shape rears. Gigantic, toad-like, with glaring red eyes and fangs. It reaches towards the battlements.

126. Ext. Battlements. Morning.
Urlik rallies himself enough to pull a spear from a nearby warrior's hand, who is fixed with fear, and hurl it at the monster.

URLIK: "This can only be Belphig's work!"

The spear strikes the monster in the throat. It tugs at it, not badly harmed, but shambles back into the gloom. Zayad is incredulous.

ZAYAD: "Do you think Belphig always controlled such sorcery—pretending it was ours?"

Urlik hurries her along the battlements, dragging strength from somewhere.

URLIK: "He uses this war to win total power for himself. Meliadus was killed because he suspected Belphig. Your ancient weapons, Zayad—they're needed now!"

Zayad shakes her head.

ZAYAD: "We cannot—our pledge . . ."

Urlik smiles grimly.

URLIK: "I made no pledge—let me make the decision!"

They descend the steps.

127. Ext. Battlements. Night.
An Eldren guard patrols the walls. Over the battlements pours a black, sentient smoke. It gradually takes shape behind him. It moves upon him. There is a dreadful growling noise coming from it. The guard is devoured. As other guards run up, the smoke pours back over the battlements.

128. Ext. Fortress. Square before gate. Night.
The Man Bird comes flapping down and carries off a screaming Eldren girl.

129. Ext. Fortress. Square. Night.
Halag has heard the scream and comes running, staring up into the night sky. His sword is in his hand. He looks desperate.

HALAG: "They use every form of sorcery—and they have hardly begun their fight . . ."

There is a grunting noise. He looks towards it.

130. Ext. Battlements. Night.
Over the battlements peers the baleful red eyes of the Toad Beast. This

is what has made the grunting. It tears at the masonry as guards strike at it with lances and axes.

131. Ext. Square. Night.
Halag shouts to his men as he watches the Toad Beast. Halag is aghast.

HALAG: "Ready the Sky Ships—we attack their camp—our only hope . . ."

132. Int. Tower room. Night.
Urlik and Zayad watch from the tower room as the airships rise into the night sky.

ZAYAD: "They can't succeed . . ."

Urlik evidently agrees. He holds her close. We fade on the climbing airships.

133. Ext. Sky. Night.
Clouds of sentient Thunder and Lightning, forming themselves into hazy, beastlike shapes, attack the airships. Those aboard fight bravely. The Man Bird flaps across the screen, screeching its triumph.

134. Ext. Airship. Night.
Halag, in the gondola of an airship, lashes out with his sword at a tendril of smoke. The airship is buffeted by thunder and lightning, half-seen beast-faces form in the air. Everywhere, it seems, is the screeching of the Man Bird. Everywhere airships are falling, destroyed by the Smoke Demons and other creatures of sorcery.

135. Ext. Airship. Night.
An Eldren warrior shouts at Halag above the scream of the wind and the mutter of the airship's engine.

ELDREN WARRIOR: "All the other ships are down. We can't defeat them this way!"

HALAG (*wearily*): "Turn back. We must think again . . ."

136. Ext. Fortress. Morning.

We see a fair bit of the fortress. Dead Eldren lie about here and there, the battlements have been torn down by the Toad Beast and other demons. There is a mood of desolation about the whole scene. Urlik, still weak, Zayad and Halag stand surveying all this in the square. Halag is battered, as we saw him in the last shot.

URLIK: "Use those weapons, Halag! You deserve to live—they do not! (*Halag shakes his head. Urlik persists.*) "Let me make the decision for you—as a human!"

Halag smiles sardonically.

HALAG: "Excellent logic, Sir Legend, but . . ."

Zayad interrupts.

ZAYAD: "It is destiny, Halag—fate. Let Urlik decide . . ."

Halag is too tired to argue. He shrugs. Urlik rallies himself, glad he can now do something.

URLIK: "Have the weapons brought out. Demonstrate their power—force Belphig to retreat . . ."

Halag calls an Eldren warrior to him and murmurs something.

137. Ext. Plain outside fortress. Day.

The siege engines of the human army creak and groan and move forward. The soldiers, too, move on the city. The blizzard continues. There is a whirring noise as Greek fire is flung from a catapult towards the walls of the fortress. Belphig grins in triumph, rides into the picture.

BELPHIG: "Weakened by my magic, they'll not withstand our attack!"

We see Iolinda. She looks disturbed.

IOLINDA: "I had not known you understood so much of magic, Bishop Belphig. Why have the Eldren used none against us?"

Belphig is openly mocking of her scruples.

BELPHIG: "These are not your concerns, madam!"

Iolinda bridles at this.

IOLINDA: "Remember your position, Bishop Belphig. You overreach yourself . . ."

She rides away, leaving Belphig glowering and thoughtful.

138. Ext. Fortress. Day.

As balls of Greek fire splash into the square, the Eldren bring up their bizarre-looking weapons from their vaults, supervised by a still worried-looking Halag. Urlik approaches one of the Flame Cannon—it is of brass and iron, baroque and ferocious-looking. He runs a hand along its sides.

URLIK: "Get them to the battlements. There's barely time . . ."

An intensified barrage of Greek fire obscures the scene. Two Eldren come running through the smoke carrying a brass-bound carved box—the heavy box has carvings of demons and dragons on it. Halag sees the box and starts forward, shouting urgently—

HALAG: "Not the Hell Weapon . . ."

Urlik is alerted. He turns.

URLIK: "What's that?"

Halag stands over the Eldren as they lower the box to the ground. Halag looks frightened.

HALAG: "It can destroy whole cities—a bomb . . ."

Urlik becomes thoughtful. He takes command.

URLIK: "We can frighten Belphig with it—take it to the airship—I have a plan . . ."

Halag is disturbed, but he lets Urlik have his way. More Greek fire. The scene fades in smoke and flame.

139. *Ext. Battlements. Day.*
With ropes and pulleys the Eldren struggle to get the Flame Cannon onto the battlements. They look up in terror . . .

140. *Ext. Sky over battlements. Day.*
. . . we see the Man Bird again. Screeching with maniacal laughter. We move down the sky to show . . .

141. *Ext. Outside fortress. Ice. Day.*
. . . the Toad Beast attacking, monstrous and fierce, the battlements.

142. *Ext. Battlements. Day.*
As the Eldren get two of the Flame Cannon into position the Toad Beast appears over the battlements. It snatches one of the Eldren and hurls him away, screaming.
Urlik comes running and staggering up the steps, to turn the Flame Cannon onto the Toad Beast. The Toad Beast reaches towards him.

143. *Ext. Battlements. Day.*
Urlik presses the stud of the Flame Cannon and a gout of fire bursts

from its snout to strike the Toad Beast full in the face. The Toad Beast shouts with surprise and pain and makes another grab at Urlik. Another gout of flame and the Toad Beast falls, crushing two siege engines.

144. Ext. Outside fortress. Day.
Iolinda witnesses the destruction of the Toad Beast. She is frightened. Captain Mazak rides up . . .

MAZAK: "A trap! They can destroy us in seconds with those weapons!"

Iolinda looks about her.

IOLINDA: "Where is Bishop Belphig?"

A fresh gout of fire from the battlements draws her attention back. Three more siege engines burn.

145. Ext. Battlements. Day.
The Smoke Demons appear. Urlik orders the Flame Cannon turned on them. Slowly the Smoke Demons are beaten back and dissipate. Everywhere is noise—fire, smoke, conflict.

146. Ext. Outside fortress. Day.
Belphig appears, riding close to Iolinda, as she attempts to rally the army, who are backing away.

IOLINDA: "Attack! Sorcery is of no use to us! Let us fight like real warriors!"

BELPHIG: "If we charge, we are finished. We must employ politics once more, my queen!"

IOLINDA: "Cunning and treachery, you mean!"

Belphig finds this moralizing out of place, considering their position . . .

BELPHIG: "We must put terms to them. Offer compromises—we still have Stormbringer . . ."

IOLINDA: "With no Champion to use it!"

Belphig spurs forward, dragging out the Black Sword.

BELPHIG: "Come, madam—we go to parley with the traitor."

He rides towards the fortress.

147. Ext. Battlements. Day.
A silence has descended on the scene. It is still snowing. Smoke drifts. Urlik, Halag and Zayad are on the battlements. Dismounted, below them, are Belphig and Iolinda . . .

URLIK: "Retreat now—and we'll never use those weapons again. We have the means to destroy you all—and Negrana, too . . ."

Belphig answers smoothly. He displays the Black Sword.

BELPHIG: "You are dying, Urlik. Without Stormbringer your fate's inevitable. Fight for us . . ."

URLIK: "You think everyone as corrupt as you. I'll die—knowing that the Eldren shall live for ever . . ."

Belphig scowls . . . Zayad comes forward, speaking urgently to Urlik.

ZAYAD: "Don't reject his bargain—I love you, Urlik—if I knew you lived, I could die happily . . ."

Urlik embraces her. Iolinda sees this and in fury and misery turns away, remounting—to Belphig's dismay a human factor has come to spoil his scheme again.

IOLINDA: "Come, Belphig. We'll fight on . . ."

Belphig, in some haste, follows after Iolinda.

BELPHIG: "Madam—think!"

She rides away. We fade on Belphig who reluctantly comes to a halt near the fortress, watching her go.

148. Int. Tower stairs. Evening.

Halag, Zayad and Urlik climb stairs of the tower. Halag murmurs to Zayad.

HALAG: "Are there other humans like this one—who can give up their lives for a principle . . ."

149. Int. Tower room. Evening.

Halag stares out of the window to where the airship is moored so that it is possible to step from the window into the gondola. Urlik is weak. Zayad tends him.

HALAG: "Iolinda will not parley now. She would rather she and her whole army perished . . ."

There comes a strange flapping noise from outside. It seems to go all around the tower. They stare at one another, bemused. The flapping grows louder, then stops. Halag strides to the door and is astonished to see Belphig, bland and self-composed, standing there.

BELPHIG: "Good evening, Prince Halag." (*Belphig bows to the others.*) "Lord Urlik is ill. I can help . . ."

ZAYAD: "You've worked sufficient evil, this day. How . . . ?"

Belphig ignores the question of how he got here.

BELPHIG: "Queen Iolinda is moved by jealousy now. She intends to prolong the fight. Now I accept that you have a considerable advantage over us and would discuss peace terms . . ."

ZAYAD: "But Iolinda will not make peace!"

Belphig dismisses this with a wave of his hand.

BELPHIG: "You have my word. She will not hinder us . . ."

URLIK: "Your word's worthless!"

Zayad calms him. Belphig looks hurt. It's obvious that Zayad will listen to anything if it means saving his life.

ZAYAD: "You'll lift the spell from Stormbringer—from Urlik?"

Blandly, Belphig reassures her . . .

BELPHIG: "I think I can do it . . ."

Urlik rises from his bed, gasping.

URLIK: "He plans further treachery. Kill him—if he dies, the spell is over!"

Belphig looks put out by this. He raises an eyebrow.

BELPHIG: "I'll give full proof of my sincerity in the morning. The battlements at dawn . . . ?"

He moves back through the door. Halag follows him.

150. Int. Landing outside tower door. Night.
Halag looks out the door—and to his astonishment Belphig has

gone. His gaze goes to an open window on the landing. We hear a faint flapping.

151. Ext. Battlements. Morning.
   The first shot is into the distance. Through the blizzard ride the massed human armies. Belphig and Iolinda ride forward after Iolinda has whispered something in Mazak's ear. We pull back to see Urlik, Halag and Zayad marshaled here. Urlik is in a very bad way.

ZAYAD: "He keeps his word thus far . . ."

Belphig calls up to them. He has Stormbringer again.

BELPHIG: "Greetings. Queen Iolinda wishes it to be known that—"

Iolinda glares straight at Zayad.

IOLINDA: "That we fight on and will show you no mercy!"

Belphig tries to silence her.

BELPHIG: "You are overwrought, madam."

BELPHIG (*turns to the people on the battlements*): "Madam—you force me to desperate lengths . . . I promised proof of my good faith. Queen Iolinda would prolong the fight, but I am a realist. Queen Iolinda would kill us all!"

Iolinda is plainly astonished by this. She has not been expecting anything like this from Belphig.

IOLINDA: "Treacherous Belphig—this is not what you said!"

Belphig smiles and begins to make passes around his face and body. His cloak spreads out and he seems to grow larger, growing within his cloak.

BELPHIG: "No, madam, but I needed you here—to show them . . ."

He begins to change . . .

152. Ext. Close-up. Iolinda. Day.

Iolinda gasps with terror at what she sees, for Belphig is changing into—

153. Ext. Belphig. Day.

—the Man Bird. He squawks with laughter and rises into the air. The Black Sword falls on the ice below him . . .

154. Ext. Battlements. Day.

Urlik and the others are horrified. We hear Iolinda scream. Urlik rallies his strength and leaps from the battlements . . .

155. Ext. Ice. Day.

. . . Urlik lands on the ice, sprawls, staggers, reaches for the Black Sword as . . .

156. Ext. Ice. Day.

. . . Belphig/Man Bird swoops on the terrified Iolinda, who lashes at it with her own sword. Man Bird grabs her in his talons and begins to drag her into the air. Urlik runs into the shot, bearing Stormbringer.

URLIK: "You'd kill her to prove your sincerity—you'll die yourself, sorcerer!"

He strikes at Man Bird who turns, dropping Iolinda, who falls heavily to the ice. The Man Bird shrieks into the air.

157. Ext. Ice. Day.

Urlik drops to one knee beside the dying Iolinda. She is weeping, begging him for forgiveness with her eyes.

IOLINDA: "If I die, the men will—attack. I told them . . . Ah, my love, this is a terrible thing. Belphig has betrayed—us—all . . ."

Iolinda dies. In fury Urlik stands up, searching the sky for signs of Man Bird. Then his attention is distracted by a huge, fierce roar from the human army. They are beginning to advance. It is as Iolinda predicted. Tenderly gathering up her body, Urlik retreats to the fortress, his strength restored with Stormbringer at his belt.

158. Ext. Square. Day.

Urlik enters the gate of the fortress which is quickly closed behind him. He hands Iolinda's body over to two Eldren soldiers. Zayad comes down the steps to embrace him. Urlik has now sheathed the Black Sword.

URLIK: "We can't stop her men now. It will be battle to the death!"

He embraces Zayad and they mount the steps again.

159. Ext. Ice plain and fortress. Day.

The human army in all its ferocity hurls itself against the walls of the fortress. This scene is short, sharp and largely obscured—flame comes from the walls of the fortress as if in one huge wave. It rolls over the army. When the flame and smoke are gone—so has the army. The ice has been turned to water, lapping at the walls of the fortress. This noise is the most significant sound—it is in sudden contrast to the huge volume of noise a moment since. It carries over into the next scene . . .

160. Int. Tower room. Night.

. . . and becomes the noise of wind slapping in the rigging of the still-tethered airship. Halag, Zayad and Urlik are all grim, looking sadly down at the body of Iolinda.

URLIK: "All dead, save for Belphig and those left in Negrana."

Halag turns away from the airship.

HALAG: "We must forget—rebuild—enjoy the love we have. Urlik, the Flame Cannon . . ."

Urlik nods, kisses Zayad, and follows Halag from the room.

161. Ext. Square. Night.

Urlik and Halag watch as the Flame Cannon are taken back to their underground vault. Halag is glad.

HALAG: "They'll never be used again. Oh—the bomb—the worst of them all—on the airship . . ."

They head for the tower. We hear a flapping—the sound of the Man Bird. They look up, knowing it is up in the tower. They hear a scream from the tower as they begin to climb the steps.

162. Int. Tower room. Night.

A terrifying scene. Bishop Belphig, mad, battered, has hold of Zayad and is forcing her through the window to the gondola of the airship.

BELPHIG: "With you as hostage I can still win the world!"

Zayad resists, clinging to the frame of the window. Belphig snarls and strikes at her.

BELPHIG: "My powers are weak—but I feel them return. Beware!"

Zayad bites him and he yells, beginning to make his mystic passes to change himself into the Man Bird, when . . .

163. Int. Tower room. Night.

. . . Urlik and Halag burst into the room. Cursing, Belphig dives into the gondola, abandoning Zayad, and tries to loose the mooring line. The gon-

dola sways badly. Urlik dives after Belphig just as Belphig gets the mooring line free and the airship begins to rise—with Urlik clinging to the outer rail. Belphig inches along the gondola towards him. Urlik cries back at Zayad . . .

URLIK: "Zayad, my love—whatever happens I'll find you again—I love you . . ."

164. Ext. Tower room window. Night.

Zayad looks up, calling something which cannot be heard. We move rapidly upwards, seeing her from Urlik's viewpoint as he is borne into the sky. A faint cry can be made out—

ZAYAD: "I love you, Urlik—I love you . . ."

165. Ext. Airship. Night.

Belphig has started the engine of the airship. The vanes begin to whirl and the airship moves rapidly forward. Urlik is trying to clamber over the side of the gondola as Belphig sets the wheel and drives a dagger into the shaft to fix it, drawing his own sword and meeting Urlik's attack as Urlik, the sword screaming and whining, finally flings himself into the gondola. Belphig scrambles away. The gondola sways and Urlik is flung backwards. Belphig begins to make his mystic signs and . . .

166. Ext. Airship. Night.

. . . Belphig changes into the Man Bird—shrieking, vicious . . . rushes at Urlik . . .

167. Ext. Airship. Night.

—who is ready to defend himself with Stormbringer. In its rush, the Man Bird smashes against the airship controls. Urlik swings the blade at the Man Bird—misses—hits the controls. Again the gondola swings wildly—and the box containing the Hell Weapon slithers across the floor, knocking Urlik off his feet. The Man Bird attacks again, perched on the rail. Urlik strikes, wounds it superficially and, with a shriek, it falls downwards into pitch dark. He peers into the night. The Man Bird seems vanquished. He

turns his attention to his engine, finding the controls are completely wrecked. He can't steer the ship or turn the engine off.

168. Ext. Airship. Night.

The night is filled with the puttering of the airship's engine. Urlik tinkers with the controls, evidently without success. We move up the bulk of the airship until we see the top—there—panting, exhausted, mad—but still very much alive—is the terrible outline of Belphig, in his human form as he recovers his sorcerous strength . . . The ship speeds on as dawn breaks. Belphig recovers all his strength and begins to make his mystic passes. We move down again as Urlik peers over the side. To his astonishment he sees the towers of Negrana (see Shot 17, etc.). He looks up at the sound of a flapping wing . . .

169. Ext. Airship. Dawn.

. . . and there is the Man Bird—more terrifying than ever.

170. Ext. Airship. Morning.

Urlik draws the Black Sword and fights a much more terrifying Man Bird which has recovered its strength. He slashes at the Man Bird. Wood splinters. One of the gondola's lines is half-cut away. It is a fierce, confused fight. The Man Bird flies off some distance and attacks again, ripping at the gasbag of the ship, shrieking. Urlik is flung backwards, near the box containing the Hell Weapon . . . The Man Bird alights on the rail, triumphant. It begins to move towards him. Urlik, possessed of the strength of the Black Sword, picks the box up and hurls it at the Man Bird. It picks it up lightly and raises it over its head to throw down on Urlik. Urlik scrambles up and ducks in with the point of the Black Sword. The Man Bird screams and loses balance, toppling over the rail. In horror Urlik grabs at the box—

URLIK: "No—not that box—it contains the bomb . . ."

We glimpse Negrana far below.

The Man Bird slashes at Urlik again. Automatically, Urlik aims another blow with the Black Sword and shears off part of a wing.

The Man Bird shrieks and begins to fall, the box clutched to its chest.

Urlik, loathing the Black Sword, hurls Stormbringer after him shouting:

URLIK: "Take your Sword—and your Sorcery—back for ever . . ."

Then Urlik realizes in horror what is likely to happen as . . .

171. Ext. Sky over Negrana. Day.

The Black Sword impales the box and the Man Bird which immediately changes back to Belphig—box impaled against his chest by the sword—as it falls. A glimpse of Belphig's terrified face, then . . .

172. Ext. Airship. Day.

Urlik stares down in horror.

URLIK: "The Hell Weapon . . ."

There is an enormous and evidently Atomic explosion which hurls Urlik backwards and the screen brightens to a blinding white . . .

173. Swirling colours.

Swirling, formless shapes and colours.

URLIK (*voiceover*): "I was sure I was dead—then I realized something worse had happened . . ."

174. Ext. Gondola of airship. Day.

Urlik is lying in the wrecked gondola as the airship, in the state we saw it in Shot 2, drifts on the wind, on fire, fluttering, ragged. One arm lies through a smashed rail. Urlik stares sightlessly down.

URLIK (*voiceover*): "That explosion flung me back to my own Time—separated from the woman I loved by countless thousands of years—

and I was doomed to live for ever ... perhaps a punishment ... Because of me, the whole human race had perished ..."

175. Ext. Gondola of airship. Day.

The sound of a crash. Arabs peer into the wreckage—we see them from Urlik's viewpoint—and begin to drag him out. We focus on a piece of carving ...

176. Ext. Arab camp. Day.

—we fade in on a shot of the carving Urlik was holding in Shot 11. And here is Urlik as we first saw him in those early shots, telling his story to the Arab leader, who takes the carving again, as if to inspect it, and gets up, signing to his men—who have packed their tents on their horses and are about to leave the camp.

URLIK: "That explosion *created* this desert where once all was green and lush ..." (*Urlik smiles bitterly.*) "It's a bitter price. Zayad was immortal—as I am—but there's no evidence that *any* of the Eldren survived ..."

The Arab leader begins to walk towards his horse and only now does Urlik realize that they are on the point of leaving. He is astonished. He begins to get up.

URLIK: "Can one man change history? Can the future itself be altered? The airship proves I wasn't dreaming ..." (*The Arab leader mounts his horse.*) "You don't believe me ..."

The Arab leader hands him a water bottle and some food; in a daze he accepts it.

ARAB LEADER: "I believe you, Urlik. What was legend to you is history to us ..."

An Arab leads a horse forward and puts the reins in his hands. The

Arab leader signs for his men to ride. They begin to ride away from Urlik.

URLIK: "But why are you leaving me here? I must find Zayad—look for Negrana again . . ." (*He stumbles a pace or two after them and then gives up.*) "Come back . . ."

177. Ext. Desert. Day.
A close shot of the Arab leader as he calls back to Urlik . . .

ARAB LEADER: "We cannot help you. You must find her yourself. For the moment, at least, you are truly alone . . ."

We hear music—the thin, mysterious singing sound of the Black Sword. The camera moves back with the departing Arabs, leaving Urlik a lonely, isolated figure in the desert he has himself created.

And now, for the first time, as he rides towards distant oil rigs, the veil falls away from the Arab leader's face. We close up on it. It is not a human face at all. It is the mysteriously smiling confident face of an Eldren. The mysterious music grows in volume.

The screen blanks.

The End

BLACK PETALS

BLACK PETALS
(2007)

CHAPTER ONE

The Apothecary in Horse Alley

FROM THE SEA the city of Nassea-Tiki was a mosaic of vivid colour, fluttering flags, gilded domes, red battlements, a busy market, tiny black figures. The harbour was vast, serving the trade of the entire South-Eastern continent. Foot forward in the prow of the Lormyrian cutter, peering ahead as the late afternoon sun set the great port on fire, Moonglum of Elwher remarked to his friend on the wealth of shining masts which stood at all angles, like the spears of embattled armies, casting a dozen reflections. The sails were furled for the most part, tightly rolled blues and loose-hung russets to match the gargoyles and grim seabulls decorating the hulls. These big ships were local. Others, such as their own, favouring black, dark red, white and silver, were from months away.

The ship's captain came to join them, staring ahead. "What a sight!" He drew in a breath, as if inhaling the entire vision. "After Melniboné they say she's the most beautiful city on four continents."

He looked at Moonglum's companion, as if for confirmation.

"After Melniboné," the passenger agreed.

Throwing back his thick, green cloak Moonglum turned his head, hands around the pommels of his twin sabres. "Who would have thought we'd find such a rich place after all those half-civilized villages we've seen on the way here?" He looked back at his friend, whose blazing crimson eyes seemed to find reflection in the effects of the sun. Set in an intensely beautiful face the colour of bone, the eyes were slightly sloping, like the lobes of his ears. His lips were full. His long hair was like poured milk. His eyes stared into a past and a future of equal tragedy. Yet there was a kind of amusement there, too.

Moonglum's own eyes were troubled as he contemplated his friend. Elric, last emperor of Melniboné, was breathing heavily, having difficulty moving along the edge of the deck, holding tight to the rail. He was hampered by the scabbard of a massive broadsword whose hilt was tightly wired to his belt.

Not for the first time, the Captain turned away, ostentatiously incurious.

"The drugs are ceasing to work, my friend," whispered Moonglum. "Were they the last?"

The albino shook his head. "Almost," he said.

Elric of Melniboné and his red-headed companion, refreshed to some degree, stepped towards the busy dock while over their heads swung goods of every description. Most eyes were on the cargoes rather than the passengers. Only a few noticed the two disembark, though most had no idea who they might be.

Nassea-Tiki was not merely busy. The vast port was in celebration. Her very palms seemed to dance. When the two adventurers stopped a passerby and enquired of the uproar seizing the city, the man said that the old system of peace-keeping had, on that very day, given way to the new. The two men were mystified until a passing ship's captain, dressed up in crisp blue silk and black linen on his way to meet a prospective customer, told them the capital city's notorious private, corrupt police force was being replaced by a trained band of municipal employees. These would be free from bribery and arbitrary brutality. "At least in theory," said the Tarkeshite, whose first impression of the albino's identity was now confused and who wanted to be on his way; a desire he indicated by glancing at the gigantic public hourglass of copper and greenish crystal dominating the busy quayside. A little amused, Moonglum wished him well and the two allowed him to continue.

Feeble as the young albino had become during his long, uncomfortable voyage, on Moonglum's arm he was still able to stumble beneath the blazing brass timepiece of timber and glass and reach the inn recommended by Captain Calder Dulk, master of the Morog Bevonia, as somewhere to find clean lodgings at little risk of being robbed. As they pressed slowly through the narrow streets, full of men and women enjoying a public holiday, he was noticeable as being taller and slimmer than the average. Though his cloak's high collar was raised about his face, it was clear to which race he belonged. The local people paid him no special attention but those from nations closer to his own gave him a respectful distance.

Paying for a quiet room, with two hammocks and a window overlooking the inner courtyard, Elric tipped the servant generously when hot water for baths was brought. Moonglum sighed. His friend was too generous with the little money they had remaining. After washing and grooming themselves, they donned fresh linen and went back downstairs. Looking around at the other guests, they judged Dulk's advice reliable. Moonglum's thieves' eyes brightened with curiosity when he saw that the main hall of the inn was full of well-dressed merchant seamen already engaged in the business which brought them half across the world and might take them still closer to the edge. Some men were running impromptu auctions with those who had waited days for ships, delayed by bad weather. Even Elric, who had traveled widely on dream quests over a hundred thousand years of history and seen much, was surprised by the amounts of money changing hands on speculative bargaining.

They sat together, under a window in the quieter part of the hall, drinking the local wine and studying a map they had bought in Thokora. The albino was having difficulty focusing. He muttered that the livestock the ships had brought in was in considerably better health than himself.

"Aren't you at all tempted to untwist those supernaturally intricate lengths of brass and copper which lock your sword to its scabbard?" Moonglum whispered, holding a blank scrap of vellum up to the light because he thought he might confuse a potential observer while he had the chance. Shaking his head, Elric seemed utterly unaware of what two men in a harbour tavern poring over a map might signify to the crazed, treasure-hungry denizens who hung around these merchants like carrion birds.

Moonglum knew that Elric feared his blade Stormbringer quite as much as any potential enemy. Indirectly, it was their chief reason for risking this long journey from the few remaining sources of Elric's drugs. In Melniboné's past, before such drugs were discovered, "silverskins" like himself had led short, painful lives usually ending in madness and self-destruction. Only by resorting to the darkest sorcery and trading their souls for supernatural aid, could the enfeebled creatures hope to live like others. While the drugs sustained Elric, they did not invigorate him as the sword had. Yet he wished never to draw it again and have more souls pay the terrible price so many had already paid for his own life. To that end, he must find the legendary *noibuluscus* plant.

For the first time in months, the pale prince, reassured that, in Nassea-Tiki, his reputation was no more than a distant legend, relaxed a little. Thankfully, the Bright Empire of Melniboné had never extended this far. And the *noibuluscus* could soon be his. He had bought the book and map in a market; they had been in the middle of a vast pile of manuscripts, any valuable decoration already removed, looted from somewhere by illiterate nomads who brought the stuff to market only in the faint hope someone would put value on it.

Map and herbal had told of the so-called "Black Anemonë" which grew in a temple's "*lunarium*" at the centre of an ancient jungle city, upriver of Nassea-Tiki. The plant had all the properties Elric needed to sustain himself. But, another grimoire he had consulted reminded him, the black flower only bloomed once a century; and in full moonlight. So he had gambled on finding it and forever protecting himself against the sickness brought by his rare form of albinism.

A dozen dark legends surrounded the Black Anemonë. Truth could not be told from fable. What all his sources agreed, however, was that the time of the Black Anemonë's blooming grew close. Their departure from Lormyr had been hasty. At certain moments, when the seas grew stormy, they feared they would arrive in Nassea-Tiki too late and Elric would be forced to fall back on the power derived from his sword. As it was, the ship had docked with only days to spare. Now they had to get upriver to the mysterious city marked on the map. Ancient Soom was now said to lie in ruins, deserted by its folk.

Relaxed and wearing the loose silks of Aflitainian gentleman captains, Elric and Moonglum completed their supper. Then, with his friend at his side, Moonglum at the bar enquired of his friendly, corpulent host if he knew the whereabouts of a certain apothecary with the unlikely name of Nashatak Skwett, said to reside in the older part of the port. This brought a broad smile to the landlord's face. "So old Nashatak's found another customer, eh?" Even here, so far from the Dragon Isle, they spoke a form of Low Melnibonéan.

Elric raised a white, enquiring eyebrow.

"Nashatak has a bit of a reputation as a quack in these parts," explained the innkeeper, "though I'll admit I've met a few wise medical men and women from abroad who seem to respect him. And you, no doubt, are one of them, sir. He wrote a much-copied book, I hear. It's often said that local wisdom gets no respect until it's traveled a ways. He's eccentric, I will tell you. He comes and goes a bit, but when he's here he's generally to be found at his shop in the Moldigore. That's the area sometimes called the old fortress. A fortress no longer, but it's where the robber-captains who founded Nassea-Tiki built a great stone keep and what became a self-sufficient village, for when the lords of Soom came a-visiting, impatient with their thieving. Long ago, when Soom was still powerful, the lords brought an army downriver. They razed the keep but, having no quarrel with ordinary folk, left the outer walls and the village standing. Anyway, it's in the Moldigore you'll find him."

To Moonglum's further disapproval, Elric put down generous silver. "But Soom, I gather, is itself a ruin. What became of her folk?"

"Nothing pleasant, sir, that's for sure. A few of her lords settled here and rebuilt the harbour. Some members of our present ruling council claim them as ancestors, for they were a learned and brave people according to legend. Others, however, say their blood turned bad with arrogant pride and they took to perverse teachings and strange practices. All we do know is that Soom is shunned by wise folk, not so much because of any supernatural curse upon the place, but because it is periodically occupied by a nomad tribe of cannibals during certain seasons of the year. I heard that the King of the Uyt was the last to go there, seeking some fabled treasure. Neither he nor his men are yet returned . . ."

Fearing that his loquacious landlord was about to launch into a series of local stories, Moonglum interrupted gently to ask the way to the apothecary's. The man raised a finger then led the pair back to his nook behind the bar, reached under a cupboard and unrolled a local map. "There it is—just off Horse Street." He waited patiently while Elric took a piece of charcoal and, borrowing Moonglum's scrap of vellum, made a quick copy of the map. Then, with a word of thanks, the exiled prince of Melniboné and his friend left the inn, pushing through still-celebrating crowds packing streets of multicoloured stone and brightly painted wood whose ornate frontages rose eight or ten storeys into the glaring, blue-gold sky. They followed the harbour wall until they found the turning into Moldigore's alleys and were soon at Horse Street.

The apothecary's sign was prominent at the far end of the narrow cobbled way, painted on the fading white wall of a tall old house whose black timber beams looked hard as iron. Now that they had at last found the apothecary's, the pair found themselves approaching with a certain reluctant caution. For too long Elric's quest for his ailment's remedy had ended in failure. Moonglum knew his friend had gambled everything, this time, on what he had read in Nashatak Skwett's *Herbal and Magical Remedies for Rare Diseases and Conditions* and was almost afraid to proceed. What did it matter that a few good folk had died to feed him their energy? After all, most of those his sword killed deserved their fate. But then Elric remembered his betrothed cousin Cymoril, who had died, albeit accidentally, on the point of that blade. His pace quickened. Slipping his silver-hilted dagger from its sheath, he rapped on the door with its hilt.

The door was almost immediately opened. A pink-skinned, bright-haired child of indeterminate gender opened its mouth in a question.

They gave their names. Moonglum asked for Master Nashatak. The child disappeared, then returned to hold out its hands to lead them through ill-lit halls and passages, up flights of crooked stairs. A mixture of smells struck their nostrils—chemicals, animal odours, a sweet stink reminiscent of rotten flesh. But, entering the room at the end of a long, twisting passage, they were impressed by its orderliness and the cleanliness of the relatively young man who rose to greet them. He was re-rolling a parchment and set this down as he opened his arms to them.

"I have your letter, my lord. Let me tell you how honoured I am to receive one as learned as yourself. And, of course, you, too, are welcome, Master Moonglum."

"Ah," said Elric, embarrassed, "such learning was commonplace in my homeland where we absorbed it on our dream couches. I can make no claims for myself . . ."

"As you please, prince." Master Nashatak's lank fair hair was pulled back from his lugubrious dark brown face and secured by a fillet of copper. He wore a long velvet gown which had been recently washed but on which the stains remained. He looked curiously at Elric. "We have an acquaintance in common. Doctor Cerlat Vog . . ."

"Who sent you this letter." The walk had tired him. Breathing with some difficulty, Elric reached into his purse and brought out a sealed packet.

"My old friend! Was he well?" Nashatak accepted the letter, breaking the seal. "His teeth?"

Moonglum answered. "They were little better when we left Noothar. But his feet showed some improvement. He enquired after the health of your wife." Still enough of a Melnibonéan noble to find such pleasantries at conversation irritating, Elric disguised his impatience.

"She is well. I thank you, Master Moonglum. Visiting her mother on the other side of the river. This is our child."

They still had no clue as to the little creature's gender. Its large, hazel eyes continued to regard them from the shadows.

Master Nashatak read the letter carefully, holding it close to one of the lamps and occasionally nodding to himself. "So you've heard of the *noibuluscus* by its true name. In your original letter you spoke only of a black flower. And you've come seeking it in the right season of the right year. But I fear there's another searching who has gone ahead of you. Do you know of Tilus Kreek, King of the Uyt?"

Moonglum shrugged. "We were told he died in Soom seeking a treasure."

"He has not returned, that's so. But I heard it from a friend that Tilus, too, sought the *noibuluscus*."

Elric turned, hearing the child utter a deep, throaty chuckle.

"The flesh-eaters caught him and ate him," it said. "And almost every one of his mercenary army was killed or captured."

Moonglum swore. "Where did you get such intelligence?"

"The streets. It's common knowledge."

Elric laid his hand on his friend's arm. "Nonetheless, I would go to Soom and find the Black Anemonë. Where can I employ a guide with a boat to take us upriver?"

"I suspect it will be difficult. There are other terrors, they say, in Soom."

"We've dealt with fierce beasts and men in our time, Master Nashatak," Moonglum told him gently. "And supernatural horrors, too."

"I believe you have. You are evidently soldiers of great courage and resource. Indeed, this letter speaks of your bravery and wisdom. You performed Cerlat Vog a considerable service, I gather . . ."

Elric restrained his impatience. "If he says so. I must have that boat and a guide, sir. I have little time remaining."

"If it's true," added Moonglum, "the black flower blooms only once in a century at this season when the moon is full, you will appreciate . . ."

The apothecary shrugged. "Nonetheless, it is unwise to go at this unprepared. I myself am curious, as you can imagine, but I could not afford the small army needed."

"Unless you can discover the whereabouts of the Uyt king's twin daughters and their escorts," murmured the child almost to itself. "I heard . . ."

"Heard? Where?" Its father frowned and Elric gave the child his concentrated attention.

"They came this morning, seeking audience with the Council. They met with one of your race, Prince Elric."

"A Melnibonéan?" asked Moonglum.

"Aye. And I heard that some of the same folk were in King Tilus Kreek's band."

They became still more intrigued.

"How could I find these sisters and the others?" Moonglum demanded.

"If the street speaks truth, then they no doubt lodge at the great Council House as guests of the city."

"Where's that?"

The apothecary interrupted. "Prince Elric, I would not have you go to Soom alone. I will write you a letter. My boy will take you to the Council House. Certain members of the Great Council are good customers of mine. You will need to be introduced. But first—" He crossed to one of several tables covered in all kinds of curios, many whose function was completely mysterious. He opened a box of ivory-inlaid cedarwood and took out of it a short string of amber beads which moved like sluggish flames in the lamplight. He handed this to the albino who, puzzled, turned it over and over in his long-fingered bone-white hands. The amber felt warm, almost like living flesh. It seemed to vibrate as if to the beating of tiny wings.

"You might not need it now, but you might need it some day. It is in acknowledgment of the service you did my old friend. Put it on," said the apothecary. "Place the beads around your neck."

To humour him, Elric did as he was asked.

"Wear it until you have the opportunity to use it," Nashatak told him. And when Elric sighed, he added: "I can tell that you are one who does not value his own life overmuch. But that thing might prove useful to you, for I know you have a destiny and a duty to live. I have no personal use for the charm. I wish you good fortune, sir, for I suspect you carry a weird which few would envy."

Elric's smile was thin. "My folk had lost any sense of sin they might once have had. It was my poor fortune to rediscover it. My destiny is a result of my actions, I suspect. Nonetheless, I value your good will. There are few in this world, I suspect, who share it. I thank you."

While Elric waited with growing impatience, Nashatak Skwett went to his desk and began to write. Meanwhile, the strange child continued to watch them through those laughing, hazel eyes until its father folded and sealed the letter, handing it to his offspring. "Go in peace, gentlemen." The apothecary made a sign to his child who again took their hands to lead them from the house.

Outside, the sky had darkened. Looking up, they saw a three-quarter moon above the rooftops and heard a distant sound, like the cawing of a crow. For an instant they saw black wings outlined in the moonlight, then they were gone and the city, which on their way here had been so raucous, was momentarily silent.

Chapter Two

Two Princesses—A Pair of Dukes

The city continued its celebration. The new peace-keepers had not had time to lose the citizens' good will. Somewhat cynically, Moonglum reflected on the many times in his journeying through the world when a change of government had been greeted with the same joy only to be followed by disappointment and anger when the new proved no better. "People hate real change," said the stocky Eastlander, "and are usually only satisfied with superficial and momentary differences. At least when Law controls the Balance. Remember how the Young Kingdoms, even as they recovered from their own terrible losses, took pleasure in the collapse of your Bright Empire. Now they grumble and curse their own leaders as they once cursed Melniboné. Some even long for the stability they knew under the Sorcerer Emperors. No doubt this republic's satisfaction will last as long."

The child led them deeper and deeper up the twisting, cobbled lanes of the port away from the sea until they looked back at the dark, crowded masts below and the glinting water, like ebony, beyond. To their left they followed the silhouettes of warehouses and other buildings on both sides of the river as it wormed out of sight into the distant jungle, seemingly impenetrably dense. They would have to go to those upriver docks in the morning, either alone or in company, depending on what transpired at the Council House.

The night stank of wine, burning wood and moss, of sweating bodies, roasting meat and other less identifiable things. Men and women linked arms and stumbled past singing. Although they had to pause occasionally while Elric rested, the three ignored the crowds and their friendly invitations, walking until the child brought them in sight of the gates of a vast and beautiful building, low and wide, with a tall irregular roof topped by masses of miscellaneous towers, drawbridges and battlements, all in different styles yet strangely unified, each patrolled and guarded.

"There," the child pointed to tall towers framing glittering gates. "The entrance to the Council House."

As they approached they saw that the entrance was festooned with a thousand flags and coats of arms. Again, Moonglum found himself marveling at the wealth and strength displayed. Before he could call out in Low Melnibonéan, to announce themselves, the child shouted something in the local dialect and instantly received a reply. A further exchange, followed by the slow rising of a great gate. At which point a liveried officer strode forward to receive the letter handed him by the child. The mismatched trio were left to stand in a circle of brandlight while the officer took the letter away.

A short while later a voice spoke from the darkness, asking their names and business.

"I am Moonglum of Elwher. This lord's companion. And he is Prince Elric, Sadric's son, of Melniboné. We seek audience with the Republican Council concerning a proposed expedition to the ruins of Soom."

And then the child had vanished. Surrounded by soldiers in rather intricate and impractical armour, with plumed helmets hiding all but their disciplined eyes, they were led into the depths of the great palace. They allowed themselves to be marched into a great hall. A celebratory banquet was clearly just ending. Diners fell silent as the two entered. The women in particular found them interesting. Male curiosity was warier. Rows of tables bore the remains of the elaborate meal. At the head of each table sat a man or a woman wearing identical blue-and-yellow robes. These were evidently members of the Council. A table at the far end of the hall was set cross-wise to the others. At its middle a tall, burly man, in the same livery but wearing a conical black cap, rose to greet them. "Good evening, Prince Elric. Forgive our hesitation. We heard you were either a legend or a ghost. Two such distinguished travelers are most welcome here. I am Juffa, privileged to be this city's Chief Councilor. Please come and be comfortable at our table. We'll have fresh meat and wine brought. Tonight we are graced with not a few people of high degree. Our nation, being a republic, still recognizes those of rank. You are not the first of ancient blood to honour us." He spoke as an habitual diplomat.

Two women sat to Juffa's right and two men to his left. From their clothing, they were clearly visitors. But it was not their dress which impressed the newcomers. For a long moment Elric stared into the face of the stranger furthest on the Chief Councilor's left. The man had risen from his seat, his face pale and his lips pursed, a gleam of hatred in his eyes. From his high cheekbones, slanting eyes and ears almost coming to points, he was clearly of Elric's unhuman folk.

Elric bowed first to the women, then to the Chief Councilor, then to the bearded man and lastly to the one who directed a look of terrible intensity towards him, raising a piece of meat on his table dagger. Placing it in his mouth he began to chew fiercely, taking his time swallowing.

"Greetings, cousin," Elric said. "I did not know you still lived."

The man controlled himself. At that moment he was almost as pale as Elric. He was Duke Dyvim Mar, one of the few Dragon Masters to survive Elric's betrayal of their nation to the Young Kingdom reavers. Trained from birth to betray no emotion, he barely kept the tremble from his voice.

"Greetings, Prince Elric. Sadly, I survived where my brothers and sisters did not."

"You are countrymen, I take it, from your appearance." The Chief Councilor seemed unaware of any tension. "Well met, eh?" He waved the letter the apothecary had sent with his child. "And with common interests, I gather."

The other male visitor, with thick blue-black brows, full red lips smiling from within a square, divided black beard, his oiled black curls falling to his shoulders, stared with some amusement at Elric and then at Dyvim Mar. He clearly knew more of Melniboné's recent history than did Juffa.

"Forgive me," said Councilor Juffa, rising a little unsteadily. "May I introduce Prince Elric? The Princesses Apparent of Uyt, Princess Nahuaduar and Princess Semleedaor." Elric and Moonglum bowed. "And this is Duke Orogino, Senaschal of the Shanac Pines, also of Uyt." Bearded Duke Orogino rose, his palm outward from his forehead in what was clearly the normal gesture of greeting of his people. The two princesses were both of exceptional beauty. Nahuaduar was pale-skinned, with wide black eyes and black hair curling to her shoulders. Semleedaor was of a rosy complexion, her auburn hair cut short against her oval face. Both were frowning, not quite able to understand what was happening.

Breaking this tension, two huge ginger dogs came to sniff at Elric, growling softly in an almost friendly way and wagging their tails.

Duke Orogino turned to Dyvim Mar and made a joke, but the young man did not respond. His eyes were still fixed on Elric.

Councilor Juffa continued. "The princesses are the twin daughters of Tilus Kreek, King of the Uyt, and these gentlemen are in their service. Duke Orogino was in the late king's household . . ."

"Last king," interrupted dark-haired Princess Nahuaduar in low tones. "We have no proof of his death." She stared steadily at Elric from beneath half-closed lids, her full, sensual lips curved in a sardonic half-smile.

The regent bowed his head, acknowledging his mistake.

"We have come because your countrymen failed to protect our father on their recent expedition to Soom," said Nahuaduar icily. "We had hoped to recruit other soldiers who might not have his portion of ill-luck. . . ."

At this, Elric's kinsman turned away, his eyes hardening. He had been insulted.

Duke Orogino cleared his throat. "But it seems only Dyvim Mar's

Melnibonéans and a few Lormyrians had the nerve to go to Soom. In spite of offering generous wages, we have been unable to raise soldiers for a second expedition."

Elric glanced at Dyvim Mar. His cousin spoke evenly, controlling any anger or confusion he felt. "I lost twenty-six brave Melnibonéans and seven Lormyrian archers. The jungle around Soom teems with dwarfish cannibals. We suspect more than one tribe has been traveling for weeks to get there. They attacked us. One Lormyrian and I escaped in the river, carrying our wounded, who died. I believe some of our men were taken alive. I suspect we were allowed to escape, perhaps as a warning to others not to attempt a further expedition. The Lormyrian is also dead. What brings my kinsman to Nassea-Tiki?" He clearly had some notion of Elric's intentions.

"I seek a flower said to bloom in Soom once a century under the light of the full moon."

"You are a botanist, sir?" This from an apparently innocent Princess Nahuaduar. "My father also studied plants."

"A curious coincidence." Elric inclined his head. There was still considerable tension in the air. "But what of these savages? I was told the city was deserted."

"So it is." The Chief Councilor was almost amused. "Unfortunately, the surrounding jungle is not. It is full of wily, brutal cannibals thought to be the stunted degenerate descendants of the Soomish people. Perhaps they regard the city as sacred. They appear to have been gathering all this year. We know not why. Usually the individual tribes war amongst themselves and offer us and the river traders no serious danger. But clearly I would fail in my duty if I did not keep all my people here to defend our own city against this horde, should it choose to attack."

"Aye." Elric drew breath to continue but was interrupted by a young man who rose from the end of the table. Like many locals, he had deep-brown skin and long black hair. He dressed simply, conservatively in black, while the collar and cuffs of his white shirt were exposed at throat and wrist. He carried a heavy, scabbarded sword of antique design.

"I am Hored Mevza, son of Councilor Menzi of the eighth ward. I have already volunteered to return with the new expedition, no matter how small."

Elric guessed the handsome youth to be enamoured of the sisters. Moonglum did not smile when he enquired: "How many do you command, sir?"

"None." Hored Mevza sat down again. "But perhaps a few of us can reach Soom where a larger party would be more readily detected."

"True." Elric looked enquiringly at the others.

"It's as good a logic as any other," said Duke Orogino. "I'm willing to put it to the test."

Princess Semleedaor rose suddenly. "Then shall we to our beds, my friends? Will you be ready to begin moving upriver in the morning, Prince Elric, Sir Moonglum?"

Taken aback, but impressed by her decisiveness, Elric smiled. "If there are no objections to my joining your party, my lady, at least until we are all arrived at Soom." Then he looked directly at Dyvim Mar, who said softly:

"I see no reason why you should betray us on this particular occasion, cousin. We have a good-sized boat in readiness. You will find us at the river harbour soon after sunrise."

Elric bowed his head again. "I look forward to it."

He fought to repress the sense of foreboding which filled him. Not since he had led the attack on his homeland had he felt so unwell. But he had no choice. He would free himself of the Black Sword's power or die in the attempt. Besides, he felt an obscure compulsion to aid his kinsmen if he could. He knew it was guilt that drove him, but this time he would allow his guilt to rule. Careless as he was of the opinion of the world, which could not hate him more than he hated himself, he would follow these most unMelnibonéan urges. Part of him was curious to explore such feelings. Moreover, he found Princess Nahuaduar singularly attractive. He guessed that, were he to succeed and choose to take it, the fruit of the black flower would not be his only prize.

As they turned to leave, Princess Nahuaduar's voice came sweet and clear from behind them. "Do you know what they call that black blossom, Prince Elric?"

"I have heard it called by several names, my lady."

"The Blood Flower. They say it yields a sap which can be dried and from which a drink can be distilled that will give a sickly silverskin the strength he naturally lacks."

When Elric looked back at her, he saw that she was smiling directly into his eyes. Again he offered her a brief bow. "I had heard that, too, madam. But, as one wanders the world, one comes across many unlikely tales. A man would be a fool to believe them all."

CHAPTER THREE

Upriver

Elric and a grumbling Moonglum arrived at the river dock in the cool air of early morning when dew brightened every leaf and gaudy piece of wood. Cocks still crowed and the languid smoke of breakfast fires rose from a thousand chimneys. Carrying a long bundle under his arm, Elric paused in surprise, seeing five figures standing near a big single-masted scarlet-painted boat anchored between several much larger inland barges which, they had been told, traded between Nassea-Tiki and the interior cities beyond Soom. Normally Soom was easily avoided, the river captains had said, but their traffic had stopped since news of the gathering savages had come. Now, said the landlord, only fools would risk the journey, or those whose greed outstripped their common sense. When Elric asked him "why greed?" he replied with some old, familiar tale of lost treasure.

Among the people waiting to go aboard the vessel, whose only shelter was a small deckhouse set amidships, were Dyvim Mar, wearing the formal light battle armour of the Dragon Master, and Duke Orogino, who had intricately carved wooden armour which made his body bulky and seemed cleverly designed to protect the wearer from

arrows and yet keep him afloat in water. The councilor's son, Hored
Mevza, had equipped himself in a coat of light brass mail and an elegant conical helmet. To Elric's mild surprise, the two princesses were
also present. Their armour was wooden, like their countryman's. Elric
greeted them with a bow. Princess Nahuaduar met his gaze with that
same almost mocking directness while her sister dropped her gaze and
seemed almost to blush. They greeted each other and, at a signal from
Dyvim Mar, who led by common consent, began to cross the narrow,
bouncing gangplank from quay to boat.

"We are grateful for your company, Prince Elric," said Princess
Semleedaor as they boarded.

"We are at your disposal until we reach Soom," he replied. "And
from then until the moon turns full. Then we have our own business to
follow."

She looked curiously up at him, clearly restraining herself from
asking him any further questions.

The tide and wind were in their favour. Within moments Hored
Mevza had untied the boat and they were carried by the current
towards the centre.

As the women watched, the men unshipped oars and set the single
sail, following the tide while it ran upstream.

Soon they had rounded a curve and the city was lost from sight
behind a curtain of lush palms and thick foliage. The rowing grew
harder. The familiar stink of the forest almost clogged their lungs. The
air filled with the calls of myriad birds and all the grunts, barks and
bellows of the diurnal jungle. The journey to Soom would take several
days. None showed the same impatience to reach the city as Dyvim
Mar, whose eyes never lost their haunted quality and rarely looked
directly at Elric. The titular Emperor of Melniboné felt an equal discomfort, though for opposite reasons. Dyvim Mar hated him for the
doom he had brought to Imrryr, a hatred Elric also felt; yet the Dragon
Master still knew respect for a name and lineage which had ruled the
Bright Empire for ten thousand years.

Dyvim Mar had no Phoorn to command and was by nature
laconic, when not speaking to his dragons. Phoorn and Melnibonéans,

it was said, had once been of the same race, in a time before time began, and still spoke the same language. But the dragons needed decades of sleep to restore their energy and their powerful venom. Almost all the dragons had been used in Imrryr's defense, destroying the invaders even as they fled with their booty, and none remained for a Master to command. This, Elric knew, was a further source of Dyvim Mar's frustration. The dragons slept in their deep caves, beneath the ruins of the city. The surviving Dragon Masters, Elric among them, yearned for the moment when they would begin to wake again. The very things which had once bound Elric to his cousin were those which kept them apart. He noticed that Dyvim Mar also tended to keep his distance from the others, as if he in turn considered himself guilty of betraying those he had first led to Soom.

In contrast, Duke Orogino and Hored Mevza seemed positively loquacious, talking almost to take their minds off the dangers ahead. Elric and Moonglum sat in the stern, taking the tiller whenever possible, and the two women, when not doing their share of the steering, sat near them. Princess Semleedaor, as she became used to the company, seemed direct and open compared to her twin, who was full of smouldering, secret humour and enjoyed baiting the men whenever the opportunity came to her.

At noon of the third day, as they lunched off local meats, breads and wine, Princess Nahuaduar turned her hard, sardonic stare on Elric: "A question I have been meaning to ask for some time, my lord emperor."

"Lady?"

"I wonder what it is that brings so many exiles from the Dragon Isle to these shores?"

Elric shrugged. As was common, Moonglum spoke for him. "I would imagine they need employment, my lady, and soldiering is the thing they know best, now they have no empire to defend."

"But the women? Are they soldiers, too?"

At this, Dyvim Mar growled: "There are few women. The reavers either slew them or took them as prizes. Then—" He lowered his eyes. "Then our dragons pursued the reaver ships."

"And?" She genuinely did not know the answer. Dyvim Mar turned away.

"They died aboard those ships," said Moonglum. Then Elric spoke: "My cousin would want you to know that it was as a result of my betrayal. They had sworn they would take only inanimate treasure. Perhaps we were all betrayed, one way or another, that day." Instinctively, his hand had gone to his black sword, Stormbringer, so tightly bound to its scabbard.

"We are from the Uyt, as you know, and have no direct experience of events surrounding your nation's sudden fall but I heard—a noble woman, was there not, to whom one of your princes was betrothed? I seem to recall a tale . . ."

"I doubt it's a tale my lord the emperor would care to hear retold," interrupted Dyvim Mar bitterly. And Elric stood up suddenly, finding some work in the bow of the boat. In spite of Moonglum's warning glance, Princess Nahuaduar called after him. "There's a sword involved in that story, too, my lord."

He sighed, his eyes clouding as he drew his brows together. "Lady, you'll have heard no doubt that my betrothed died by my own sword . . ."

"Is that why you keep it so thoroughly bound?" With slender fingers, she gestured towards Stormbringer.

"Oh, 'tis best you ask no more questions concerning this sword, your highness." He pretended further interest in the boat's equipment. On both distant banks of the river, under the blaze of the noonday sun, the dark jungle moved slowly by. "Indeed, it is in none of our interests for me to release this sword."

Enquiringly, she looked up directly into his own ruby eyes. "Then why carry it?"

"To placate my own patron, I suppose." His returning gaze was as direct as her own. "Be warned, lady. Few have ever been glad to have such questions fully answered."

Nahuaduar made to speak again. Then her twin called from where she sat in the prow. Semleedaor pointed to their left, to a long sand bar on which several large crocodiles basked. Among them was an object reflecting the sun. Metal washed by the river and polished by the sand. A large piece of armour. As they drew nearer, Moonglum recognized it as a breastplate of Melnibonéan workmanship, similar to that worn by Dyvim Mar. The two kinsmen turned away, frowning.

"Was it here?" Princess Semleedaor's voice was sympathetic.

Dyvim Mar shook his head. "Further upstream. It must have been dragged down this far by the current. And perhaps by those reptiles . . ." He lifted his head and stared into the middle-distance.

Duke Orogino murmured: "I never knew a people so racked by guilt. And yet which never knew a moment's self-doubt before their diaspora." He spoke ostensibly to an embarrassed Hored Mevza, who pretended to stare down into the water.

For some little time the party sailed on in silence. The heat had caused the men to discard much of their own armour. The sluggish water was thick with strange leaves, boughs and exotic, brightly coloured blossoms. The two women murmured together, but as evening came and the sun sat atop the silhouetted jungle, the atmosphere aboard became significantly more relaxed. Duke Orogino and Hored Mevza fell into a political conversation. The notion of a republic was foreign to the duke. He found it difficult to understand how such a thing functioned. He was used to the state embodied in the person of a king, reflecting and exemplifying his nation's virtues. A nation run by a set of institutions and elected officials seemed to him to be a strange, even sickly affair, no longer dependent on the virtue and honour of its hereditary leader; prey to the basest desires of people who would promise anything to an electorate in order to be placed in high office.

The princesses speculated on the wildlife to be found in the jungles and of the ancient, perhaps unhuman people who had built the city and ruled the land of Soom, occasionally asking Elric or Dyvim Mar for their opinion.

"The savages, though ugly and stunted, seemed human enough to me," Dyvim Mar said.

The women spoke of their father who had hired the Melnibonéans. Tilus Kreek had been obsessed with learning Soom's secrets, they said. He was convinced the city had been the centre of a wise civilization almost as old as Melniboné. Its treasure might have been knowledge or gold, he had not known from his reading. It might even have been the black flower, said to confer power on its kings. Ancient manuscripts had spoken of it in mysterious terms. Whatever form it took, that treasure could have revived his own nation's fortunes. The Uyt had suffered a great plague, taking a huge proportion of the population, making it weak and liable to being preyed upon by stronger neighbours.

"My father was obsessed with the stories he had heard of Soom," said Semleedaor. "He believed the older civilization would save ours. We belong to a race of scholars and it is our wisdom alone which has kept the worst predators at bay, even though we lost a number of our vassal states. Our war-engines are sophisticated, our magic, too, is feared. We have made none of the alliances which, by all accounts, made ancient Melniboné great. We believed that the crisis was over, that we had been able to resist the worst of the threats. There were other plans in place which did not depend upon discovering the secrets of Soom. But his curiosity, we suspect, began to drive him more than any immediate danger."

"You say he was a botanist, also?" Hored Mevza asked. "Perhaps this wealth he coveted was in the nature of rare spices? Our own city's fortunes were based upon the spice trade."

"Perhaps." Princess Nahuaduar was looking at Elric, as if to discover his reaction. Her own expression indicated that she did not welcome this suggestion.

Night fell for the third time since they had left Nassea-Tiki. The men drew an awning over the deckhouse and set up nets against the biting insects, tying up to a large tree trunk wedged where the river curved and the current ran slowly. They all slept soundly, save for the albino whose occasional groans and mutterings reminded Moonglum that his friend still relived those events surrounding the fall of that great capital. He had rarely slept in peace since the death of Cymoril, his betrothed.

Dawn came again and they rowed on upstream. By noon the sun was a throbbing, glaring eye gazing pitilessly down on them as they sweated to force their course on a river grown increasingly difficult to navigate, whose bends twisted and snaked, narrowing then widening unpredictably at every turn. Dyvim Mar warned them not to drag their hands in water now seething with poisonous reptiles and giant cephalopods. "And all are hungry for our flesh, or blood, or both." As he spoke, to illustrate his warning, a great coiling serpent leapt from the water to snap at a bird skimming the surface in pursuit of a giant dragonfly.

Moonglum murmured to his friend: "What could have possessed the Uyt king to leave his country and his daughters and mount an expedition here? You at least have a far better reason for seeking Soom."

Somehow, they survived yet another day and a night until at last Dyvim Mar stood up in the boat to point at something the colour of dried blood stretching out into the water. Clearly of sentient manufacture, it had the appearance of a ruined mole, of worn, red sandstone with rusted iron rings still set into slabs casting black shadows on thick, unpleasant water.

Moonglum, half-certain that intelligent eyes were watching them from the dark green jungle depths, made to draw one of his curved swords from its sheath. At any moment an arrow or a spear would come flashing out of the shadows and plant itself deep in soft flesh. Then a worse thought came to him—*What if they want us alive?* For what? For bait? In spite of all his experience, he caught himself shuddering. Now he wondered about more sinister projectiles. A net, perhaps? Or a poison dart?

Pulling on his armour, Dyvim Mar said: "If they act as they did before, they'll wait until we reach the city proper until there is little chance of escape to the river." He turned to Elric. "Others beside me have noticed how well secured that blade is, cousin. It might be wise to have it more immediately to hand."

Elric reached down and picked up the long bundle he had brought aboard. He raised his eyebrows. "You'd risk that?"

"No choice is palatable, but, having experienced what these savages are capable of, I'd take my chances with Stormbringer. Assuming you plan to remain on our side . . ."

This further stab at his conscience froze Elric's face into a familiar expression of hauteur. "Why, cousin, would you trust my word, even if I gave it?"

Buckling and knotting, Dyvim Mar peered into the forest. "Cousin, I trust nothing. But at least I know you . . ." With Moonglum at the tiller, he took an oar and, in unison with his kinsman, began to row towards the overgrown quay, murmuring: "It was no idea of mine to bring women here. But I was allowed no say in the matter. I understand why they want to find their father, but he is a fool. Haste and stupidity led us to that doom. Some of my own men might somehow have survived. I hope to save them. But you, Elric, what do you really seek here?"

"I seek to free myself from the weakness which made Yyrkoon believe he could usurp my power and put his sister, my cousin, into a trance."

Dyvim Mar nodded, adding: "Which led you to rely upon the stolen souls the Black Sword harvests."

Elric sighed. "The *noibuluscus* is the five-fingered flower whose petals are the colour of jet. It grows only in Soom. They say Soom's soldiers drank its distilled essence and thus imposed their authority upon the world."

"And do you recall the rest of that story?" his cousin asked.

"There are many versions."

"Most agree that the black flower poisoned the people of Soom, so that they relied upon it merely to survive."

"I should fear that?" Elric smiled more broadly than he had done for many years. "I should fear reliance upon a potion rather than upon a sword?"

His cousin shrugged. He could think of no suitable answer.

Chapter Four

Soom

Slowly, the thick foliage parted to the careful blades of the seven oddly matched men and women, each of whom carried a small, brass-studded shield. Duke Orogino exclaimed at what they saw. He was still the only one of the company not apparently affected by the atmosphere of danger. Elric unwrapped the long, simple Jharkorian blade he had carried aboard. A thoroughly practical weapon. Dyvim Mar was disappointed. "I would have preferred a bow or two or perhaps a javelin." If attacked from cover at a distance, they would be unable to reply.

"Gods! What minds designed such architecture?" Moonglum peered ahead.

Young Hored Mevza gasped. "Not human, whatever they say. Now I truly believe the stories are true and these buildings were raised even before fabled Melniboné thrived." He looked to Elric as if for confirmation.

Elric's expression had become sardonic at this reference to the fabulous nature of his homeland. Carrying slender scimitars like those of the Fookai pirates Elric had fought when employed by Ilmioran sealords, the women stepped onto a weed-grown pavement through which old trees now pushed up trunks, some grown almost as high as the great red ziggurats which stretched before them, carved with bizarre figures and shapes. Elric had some dim memory of this place. Perhaps he had visited it on one of his dream quests as a youth. But the association was in no way pleasant. On instinct, he turned suddenly to look backward. He saw nothing but the jungle through which, as silently as possible, they had trekked for the past few hours.

Duke Orogino lowered his own longsword and rested his gauntleted hand on the haft of a busily engraved battle-axe of silver-chased steel more commonly associated with cavalry fighting. He allowed a look of skepticism to spread across his bearded face and he shook back his head to rid it of the damp locks obscuring his vision. Dyvim Mar pointed a slender finger towards the centre of the ruined city and its crumbling pyramids. "That's where we were ambushed—as we entered yonder square overlooked by that ugly building—palace, temple, whatever it is. We had made too much noise and I think we were followed."

"You say you could not count them. A fair-sized tribe?" Princess Semleedaor pushed golden hair back from her damp forehead.

"A party of perhaps a hundred." With his soft doeskin boot, Dyvim Mar indicated fairly fresh bloodstains on the paving. "Perhaps a few more. We dispatched half that number—"

"Before you let them take you prisoner?" said Princess Nahuaduar sharply.

Dyvim Mar bridled. "I am a hired mercenary, madam. We followed the king's commands!"

"To do what?" The question was rhetorical. Elric suspected she had heard the answer before.

"As I said, lady, your father was anxious to reach that sandstone pyramid there, the one they have made some crude attempt to restore. He called it a palace, but I think it was some kind of temple. He took the majority of my men forward and left me to protect the rear with some Lormyrian archers, a few lancers and my chief lieutenant, Agric Inricson. The last we saw of the king he had disappeared into the palace. We fought off the savages for several hours until they fell back. Then we moved to try to rejoin the king and the rest of our men. We got as far as yonder house—the one with the walls still intact. A trap. They were waiting for us inside. Fresh warriors. I saw half my men butchered. Most of us were overwhelmed. Then we thought we saw a way free. We got almost to the river before they began shooting at us. We carried the wounded with us into the river. I now think they intended to let us go, maybe as a warning to any other expedition. That is why I think we have not been attacked. They believe no-one else will dare come to Soom."

"Or they have moved deeper into the jungle," said Moonglum, "taking their prisoners with them."

"Or they completed their business in Soom and returned to their tribal homeland further upriver," suggested Duke Orogino. "I agree it is most likely they would have attacked us by now if they were still in the city."

"Should we try to follow them?" Hored Mevza did his best to hide his disquiet.

"You may do as you please," replied Elric. "My business is in Soom."

"We need all the swords we can muster." Princess Nahuaduar glared at him.

"Indeed, my lady," Elric acknowledged. "But we agreed to lend you our aid until Soom and the rising of the full moon."

"There is some hope that Melnibonéans are still alive," said Dyvim Mar softly.

"And I hope to be again at their disposal once the moon has risen," said Elric. "A matter of hours." He reached into his pouch and drew out the map he had bought in Thokora. Beside what the king had called a palace was some kind of garden, perhaps the *lunarium*, what Elric's people had called a night garden, judging by the iconography on the map. The *noibuluscus* appeared to have a religious function. Perhaps the black flowers had grown there. While the others debated, he marked out the site in his mind. Timing was important. The flower had to be picked at the moment of its blooming. He and Moonglum moved away from the others. "This is where I guess the site to be," said Elric.

They had gone only a few steps when the brooding air was cut by a terrible sound—a high-pitched wail of agony which was suddenly cut off. The others stopped talking and listened carefully. Elric turned, questioning, into a sickening silence.

"It came from inside," Moonglum said. Duke Orogino began to cross the square at a run, heading for the huge pyramid, the women behind him.

And then, from out of a dark, ragged hole in the pyramid's wall, a scarlet figure came stumbling. Even Elric, versed in the refined tortures of his people, could not disguise his horror.

The figure might once have been a naked man. How it continued to move Elric could not guess, for every inch of skin had been flayed from scalp to feet. The red mouth moved. The throat gurgled with blood. Blue eyes, from which the lids had been removed, stared blindly before it. Every movement must have been a century of agony as it raised bloody hands before it, groping for unseen help.

The party stood stock-still as the flayed man approached. He screamed, leaving a trail of thick strings of blood behind him. Moonglum ran forward with the intention of helping the man. Instantly, an arrow thrummed from somewhere and took him in the shoulder. He fell to his knees, an almost ludicrous expression of surprise on his face. But the arrow had failed to penetrate his mail and dropped to the ground even as he raised his hand towards it. He stood up, sheepishly, drawing his long curved sword.

"Form a square!" Elric, Moonglum and Dyvim Mar took charge, showing the others how to raise their small shields to protect their faces and upper bodies. Moonglum ducked and picked up the long barbed arrow, darting a look of enquiry at Dyvim Mar. He nodded, confirming that it was the same kind of shaft which had killed so many of his men. Then a whole rain of arrows came from the same direction, thudding into their shields.

"I suspect they don't plan to take casualties or seek confrontation," said Moonglum. Elric nodded.

"They might even have released that flayed prisoner to encourage retreat."

Moonglum was puzzled. "Why, when they clearly outnumber us, would they avoid conflict?"

Still screaming, the flayed man stumbled on.

"Use the Black Sword, Elric! Use it now!" cried Dyvim Mar.

Everything in the albino told him to do as his cousin demanded, yet still he resisted. His hand fell to the scabbarded blade.

"No!" cried Moonglum. Then he murmured. "At least, not yet."

Dyvim Mar made to go after the flayed man. Elric stopped him. "No-one can follow him. If we break ranks we are dead."

"Then use the damned sword!"

Instead, Elric reached down and pulled a spear from his shield. Now he had a more useful weapon. Stormbringer stirred against his thigh. He heard it murmur but he deafened himself to its voice, to the tones of Arioch, Duke of Chaos, urging him to do as Dyvim Mar demanded. They were looking to him for leadership, even as the bloody figure, still intermittently screaming, disappeared into a jungle opening like a maw to swallow him.

Duke Orogino stood trembling, his eyes blank, maybe mad. The stink of the skinned man's bloody flesh was in their nostrils. Seeking the best cover, Elric made the small party fall back towards the pyramid and the high-walled annex from which the man had come. He had his own motives for investigating the compound. As they crowded in one of the women screamed and the lad fell back retching.

Princess Semleedaor turned her head away but her twin sister, pushing black hair from her face, forced herself to stare down at the blood-soaked ground. Laid out on it, like a suit of clothes, was the flayed man's skin, neatly separated from the body by an expert hand, including the hair of the head and the man's private parts. The operation would have taken a long time. Looking at the pelt they imagined the victim's horror and pain. But Elric saw something else, pushing its way through the dark mud created by the man's blood and urine. He barely resisted falling to his knees and staring at the small, dark shoot exactly the same as the one he had seen in a dozen grimoires and herbals. The *noibuluscus*. The Black Anemonë.

"So your instincts were right." Moonglum spoke so softly only Elric could hear him. They stood in Soom's ancient *lunarium*. From the histories and geographies Elric had read, he had expected something larger. Clearly, the compound, now roofless, had been roofed in crystal, perhaps even a great prism concentrating the moon's rays, used to grow the sacred flower which blossomed once every hundred years. And would bloom tonight, if the scrolls and books he had consulted told the truth. Then Elric was struck by a realization. The arrival of the savages was no coincidence. "The man's flaying, the draining of his fluids into the ground was a ritual. Those degenerates, doubtless descendants of ancient Soomians, were here to witness the black flower's blooming." The shoot was growing before his eyes, a tightly closed bud surrounded by black, spiky leaves.

Moonglum reached his hand towards it but his friend stopped him.

"The *noibuluscus* must be plucked at the optimum moment. We must wait until the moon is full. It's not even twilight. We must somehow hold out against the savages until midnight." He had waited so many months, he could feel the last of his strength ebbing out of him. He thought only of his own needs.

Dyvim Mar stared at his cousin in contempt. The princesses, too, knew what they had found, for their father had spoken of it, hoped to find it. Perhaps the *noibuluscus* was the treasure their father sought? Even Moonglum was troubled.

Elric cared nothing for what any of them thought. At last he need depend no longer either on herbs or hellsword. This, in turn, freed him from Arioch, from all those hideous pacts which had led, in his mind, at least, to the death of Cymoril. He knew a deep satisfaction. Everything he had hoped for was coming true. After tonight, his dependence on the supernatural would be over. All he had to do was survive . . .

"We're heavily outnumbered, Elric." Moonglum was reminding him. "We're trapped."

"This place can be readily defended," Elric replied. "The only entrances are that gap in the wall through which we came and that smaller opening—" he pointed to a small, square, regular opening in the main structure of the great pyramid itself. "It seems to be some sort of outlet, perhaps for water, used in the original construction." The battle leader he was trained to be, he positioned Dyvim Mar and Duke Orogino at the small, regular opening. The others were told to watch for activity beyond the wall. Any attackers could only come through one at a time. The walls themselves were too high to permit spears or arrows to be aimed at them.

When Elric turned to Princess Nahuaduar to explain this, she looked directly into his eyes and said firmly: "We are here to rescue my father, Prince Elric . . ."

". . . and to save any of my men who survive," Dyvim Mar added, peering down into the square opening and then leaning to look up, as if it was, indeed, some kind of sluice from above. "If only we could calculate the enemy numbers, we'd be better able to determine our strategy."

Elric ignored them. He had already told them his purpose. While their mutual interests coincided, he would work with them. If they conflicted, he would have to concentrate on the black flower's blossoming.

Moonglum went to stare through the gap in the wall at the horizon. The sun was already setting. He had long since accepted that Elric was driven by his own needs, but he had thought there was another quality in his friend, something which might just possibly on occasions put the greater good above his own. He shook his head, trying to clear it. Then he had a new thought. What if the savages, who had already demonstrated their sophisticated strategies, did not want to frighten them from the city at all? Perhaps the party had been deliberately offered this route. He whirled and as their eyes met it was clear Elric shared the same suspicion.

Elric cursed his desperation and need. "Is there time for a new strategy?" Hadn't he already found what he had come to Soom to take? Why not do, however, what the mysterious tribesmen least expected and attack the pyramid? Apart from himself, there were only two experienced soldiers amongst them. True, the women were brave and willing, even trained to arms to a degree, yet they were scarcely strong enough for an assault. Not unless most of the defenders were already dead . . .

Suddenly a shout came from above. Elric could not see who it was but Hored Mevza, furthest away from the main wall, looked up and Princess Semleedaor exclaimed: "Father! We are here to save you!"

A distant voice replied. "Fools! Now we are *all* doomed. Get out of here while you can. You men have brought my daughters into danger!"

"He lives!" Princess Semleedaor hardly listened to her father's words. "Oh, thank Yenob! He lives!" She and her sister stared upward with radiant faces.

"Great king!" cried Duke Orogino. "If they speak a civilized tongue tell them we'll pay any ransom they demand."

"Get out of that cursed compound if you can. Now! Get into the jungle. They do not want our gold. They want our flesh—ah!"

"Father!" Princess Nahuaduar was beside herself with emotion. "He's gone. They took him back!"

"He's right. We can't stay here." Dyvim Mar feared more for his men than for the king. "We must help them, Elric. Draw the sword! You are the greatest sorcerer in our history. You can help them! You owe them that!"

Moonglum said quietly. "Elric. Friend. You must."

"I am losing strength. It's almost gone. If . . ." But he realized he could not continue as he had. Every instinct was against it. Cruel his people might be, but they had loyalty one to the other. The last of his herbs were gone. His only hope now was that he could live until the *noibuluscus* bloomed. Even then, there was no certainty. A spell of the kind they wished him to cast would drain any vitality left him. If the spell failed, would he be too weak, then, to help his countrymen? Could he do nothing while another victim was flayed alive? Yet he had vowed never to draw the Black Sword again . . .

His cousin was yelling something at him. Beyond the tall, red walls of the ruin the blood-red sun was beginning to sink behind the dark jungle foliage. Twilight was coming. In a short while the full moon would rise and, if Elric's understanding was right, the black flower's petals would open and begin almost instantly to fall. At that point, they must be gathered. He must collect the seeds so he could grow fresh plants somewhere. Or was this red mud the only kind in which the plant would grow . . . ?

Still he hesitated. It would be worse than ironic if, only an hour or so before those petals opened, he lacked the energy to pick them.

"Elric! Do you not owe us *something*?" Dyvim Mar's bared sword almost threatened his cousin. "Do you want to see your remaining kin slain as—as that poor wretch—" and he pointed at the skin laid out on the wet ground—"was slain?"

Moonglum was silent, but it was clear he shared the Dragon Master's opinion.

Elric lowered his eyes.

"No," he said.

From somewhere above came another prolonged and terrible scream.

The albino drew a deep breath. His eyes stared as if into a vision. His lips began to move, silently forming the words of a tongue more ancient than that of Soom, more ancient than Melniboné's. Words he had learned in a dream quest, long ago, sleeping upon the dream couches of Imrryr, when he had forged a certain alliance. His mind began to travel out along the strange network of roads that had once taken him through the many dimensions of the multiverse.

He lifted his head, his eyes now shining with an alien brightness. And he shouted a word which burst like a blaze of voices upon the agonized ears of all near him. Yet the others could not make sense of the word they heard. They did not recognize the name. Only Elric heard and recognized it. And it drained his life-force from him even as it left his lips.

"*Saaasuurrasssh!*" he said.

CHAPTER FIVE

Kalakak

Somewhere *under* the river, in a dimension of waters and dank foliage, Elric's voice found a supernatural resonance, stirring the memory of a creature which opened its jaws a fraction and passed a long, leathery tongue between pointed teeth. Its eyes were shut in the sleep of centuries and would not open. The creature's curiosity was not yet aroused. Indeed, it still dreamed dark, sluggish dreams of death, of things devoured and things to be devoured. It was some time before it recognized the word which had awakened it and some further time before it recalled that Sasuras was perhaps one of its waking names, though not the name by which it identified itself. That name was Kalakak and it knew that somewhere it had kindred which spoke to it, called to it. But Kalakak still dreamed that it lay curled in the egg its mother had laid somewhere in the multiverse, so many millennia ago. Kalakak lay safely in the mud on the bank of a vast river, whose further bank could not be seen. The world river wound between mud flats and beyond the mud flats was the rich warmth of mile-high thick-boled trees, branches twisting and curling and full of living things, all of which tempted its appetite.

Kalakak remembered its appetite. It began to salivate. It remembered *Sasuras* . . . that name . . . the name which called it not to feed but to serve and it was therefore somewhat slower in its response . . .

Saaasuurrasssh

Kalakak's tail twitched. Its limbs began to sting and its eyes moved beneath heavy lids.

Saaasuurrasssh

Kalakak's nostrils moved and tasted murky, amniotic air. Something flickered in the darkness; veins of red fire, streaks of deep green and blue. And Kalakak took a massive breath.

Elric lay in Moonglum's arms. Dyvim Mar looked on, almost sympathetic. Somewhere, near the ruined gap in the wall, Hored Mevza thrashed and groaned and clawed at an arrow which had found a gap between his helmet and his throat. Princess Semleedaor stood beside him, trying to stop him from moving while she attempted to snap the head of the arrow from the shaft. It stuck out from the side of his neck. She spoke to him as soothingly as she could. Elsewhere Duke Orogino and Princess Nahuaduar peered around their shield rims. A makeshift brand in her hand cast sputtering light across the compound. Out in the square, shadows shifted, running swiftly here and there, shooting arrows, flinging lances. Only by accident had an arrow struck Hored Mevza. The young man dropped to one knee, his eyes wide with horror as the princess at last managed to get the haft out of him and staunch the blood with his own torn shirt. The arrow had not struck the jugular.

Weakly, Elric climbed to his feet, balancing with the spear, the steel sword in his right hand. From above, men's voices were shouting and it seemed to him that the captured Melnibonéans had broken free and were fighting their captors. Certainly, something was happening up there. He looked over to where the Black Anemonë grew, its tendrils pulsing and lengthening with every passing moment, the flower not yet opened. His mouth was dry, his arms and legs shook. He had difficulty breathing.

"Elric, you're too enfeebled." Moonglum spoke reluctantly. "The spell did not work."

Dyvim Mar was grim: "There is only the Black Sword now."

Still Elric shook his head. Trembling, he steadied himself with the spear and, sword raised with difficulty, turned to Princess Nahuaduar. "I led us into a trap, I admit. But I promise I will do all I can now . . ."

She cursed a soldier's curse and all but spat in his face. "I thought you, of all men, would be the one to help us. Now my father faces dreadful death and your own people, too. You carry an unhappy weird upon you, Elric of Melniboné. Oh, how I wish I had not let you join us . . ."

He managed to respond, his smile ironic, panting. "Madam, you must try to wait until midnight before you condemn me entirely . . ."

Another flight of arrows came pouring through the gap. By now they had taken cover. Hored Mevza had stopped screaming and now sat against a wall breathing rapidly, the rag pressed on his wound which no longer bled badly. Princess Semleedaor, sword in hand, darted a quick glance around the ragged gap. "I can see little in this blackness. It sounds as if they've gone back into the ruins or the forest."

Then, as if to contradict her, from above several spears rattled down uselessly. The object of both attacks was to demoralize them. Moonglum's attention was on the *noibuluscus*. "It's bigger! Look!" It reached towards the starlit sky now touched by the first faint traces of the rising moon. Even though Elric had studied all there was to study about the plant, its rate of growth astonished him. Was he going to die there, with the object of his quest so close? Watching it go through its entire cycle while unable to make use of its petals?

"Elric! Take the buds!" Moonglum helped his friend to his feet. "The attempted Summoning weakened you too much." Yet still he refused to untangle the wire binding his sword.

The long stem of the Black Anemonë stretched high towards the night sky and then curled downwards. It was only as it reached out towards the wounded Hored Mevza that Elric realized the thing seemed to be questing for something. Questing for fresh blood.

Moonglum cried "No!" and leapt forward, twin sabres whirling, slashing at the plant, which reared back, hissing.

Blood had stimulated the plant's growth. "It needs more blood! It's feeding." Moonglum's shout stimulated the albino, who cursed himself.

That was why they had been tricked into entering the compound. They were food for the black flower.

This knowledge seemed to stimulate the albino. Shouting an oath, his voice quavering, Elric shook his fist up at the window—to be answered by a haphazard rain of missiles. "Those savages want us wounded but not dead. That's why they took so many prisoners. To feed the plant!" A plant which drank blood and souls as thirstily as his runesword.

Above him scarred, wicked little faces glared down at them. Out in the night the other savages prowled, their only intent being to keep the party inside the compound.

As it had dawned on Dyvim Mar that they were the intended food of the black plant, he began to whistle an old, complicated Melnibonéan melody: "The Drowned Boy."

"What do you say, cousin?" Elric asked. "Would you wait like a pig in the slaughterhouse? Or would you die fighting these filthy little devils?"

His kinsman darted him a look of approval and began to move towards the ragged gap in the wall.

Before he could reach his object, he drew a startled breath and stepped backwards, staring. Turning sideways on to the plant, Moonglum peered into the gloom.

There was something else out there now. A much larger, heavier shadow. Some kind of beast?

And then Elric collapsed and Duke Orogino came blundering past them, screaming, to flee into the night. They looked back. "Gods! It's so fast!" Moonglum gasped. He tried to help, but he was already carrying Elric. The plant writhed and shifted on the ground. It had seized poor young Hored Mevza who now struggled in its coils. It was squeezing him so that his blood streamed from his orifices to be sucked up by the plant's tapering bud. "Ugh. The poor bastard's dead already!" What had been a thin stem was now a fair-sized trunk and as they watched, horrified, it thickened visibly, sucking the flesh and blood from the youth's now limp body. Then it dropped back to the ground, slithering into the spread-out skin of the flayed man, filling it.

A travesty of a human creature now swayed before them, its tendrils occupying the skin like legs and arms. And from each branch now, more tendrils sprang, like fingers and toes, reaching towards the five who remained in the compound. The plant, distinctly manlike in form, continued to grow.

And still, as Elric knew, it was not yet moonrise. Still the plant sought more sustenance.

With a yell, Dyvim Mar now flung himself forward and began to hack at the disgusting limbs. The sisters imitated him, their scimitars flashing in the growing light from the sky. Moonglum tried hard to hold his friend upright. Elric did his best to summon the last of his strength. He fell forward, stabbing at the monstrous thing. Anger and disappointed rage empowered him. He had wanted no more than a normal life of the kind enjoyed by others. Again and again he thrust the sword, but he made no impression upon the thing.

A noise behind them. Duke Orogino came shrieking back into the compound. His armour was pierced in a dozen places by arrows. His helmet had been knocked from his head which streamed with blood. He gibbered and pointed behind him and then fell to the ground.

They tried to pull him free of the Black Anemonë, but the gigantic plant was too strong. Its tendrils wrapped around the duke's body and dragged him to itself. He gave one last, long yodeling cry as he was lifted into the air and then suddenly the full moon rose above the high wall and illuminated the scene, the struggling Duke Orogino, the five figures, weapons in their hands, gathered around the swaying, manlike plant.

Then they turned to see what Duke Orogino had seen. What had caused him to flee back into the compound.

"Kalakak," said Elric.

And he smiled.

Chapter Six

The Black Flower's Blossoming

The two women stared in horror as the creature Elric called Kalakak pushed its massive bulk against the gap in the compound, breaking down the ancient brick, its cold green eyes glaring, its long snout opening to reveal teeth the length of swords and the thickness of a man's arm. In the moonlight its scales glistened with water. Its massive tail thrashed this way and that, scattering the corpses of the savages who tried to attack it. When it saw Elric, it lumbered towards him and from its vast, red throat something like language sounded. Only Elric could understand everything it said, but Dyvim Mar recognized a form of High Melnibonéan which he and the Phoorn dragons spoke between themselves.

The monstrous reptile looked down at Elric who was again supported on Moonglum's shoulder. Its eyes were full of profound memory, of old wisdom and a new thirst. "You summoned me, old friend?"

"I thought you had not heard me, Lord Kalakak. I called to you in the name of our ancient pact. I presumed you still slept." The thing looked like nothing as much as a gigantic crocodile, but its snout and tail were more slender, its legs and webbed feet longer. Like certain dragons, it had a tall, spiked crest on its neck and head. Its colour was neither green, nor black, nor brown. It was not an earthly colour. As it moved, its scales clashed softly, the sound of wind over drying leather.

"True it will be a millennium or two before I am fully rested. Now I am at your service. At least before sleep claims me again. Unlike our mutual kin, the Phoorn, I need rather more sleep than a mere century." The jaws clacked and smacked almost as if Kalakak joked. "Remember, I cannot kill for you. Otherwise, you must tell me what you need, before I return to the river below the river and close my eyes. There is a dream I need to continue."

As the manlike plant, distracted, began to devour Duke Orogino, Elric pointed towards the high window. "We need to reach that opening, yonder. Can you help us?"

"Use my crest to climb." Steadying his scaly bulk with his tail, Kalakak lifted himself on his huge hind quarters, his snout extending to the window from which the Uyt king, Tilus Kreek, had last called to his daughters. The black flower swayed in the background, unable to assess this new potential danger as if for all the world a sentient thing. The albino was dangerously weak, but he could still call out instructions to the others. They began to clamber up the reptile's massive back. Below them the black plant thrashed and screeched. Above them the dwarfish cannibals crowded to the window and stared in disbelieving consternation. With a yell as bloodthirsty as any warrior's Princess Nahuaduar led the way through the window, her scimitar taking off a head as smoothly as if she were cutting daisies in a field. Then she disappeared inside, Dyvim Mar and Princess Semleedaor behind her.

Elric and Moonglum were the last to reach the window. With a word of thanks to Lord Kalakak, the albino dropped into the room. The princesses and his cousin had already taken their toll of the savages. Bodies lay everywhere. Red revenge had been taken at last. The remaining savages scrambled into the outer corridors and scattered as fast as they could go. They left their prisoners bound but otherwise unharmed.

Weeping with joy, the princesses ran towards their straightbacked but naked father. As they cut his bonds he stared at them in astonishment. He, like the captured Melnibonéans, had not expected to survive this night.

Rubbing circulation back into limbs, King Tilus Kreek crossed to a corner of the room where weapons were stacked and found his own sword amongst them, returning it to his scabbard. He was a tall, old man with a short grey beard and long hair. He drew on a padded surcoat over mail and sweated in the heat of the night. Moonlight streamed into the room, showing Moonglum, Elric and Dyvim Mar the captured warriors, whom they set about releasing. Elric leaned beside the window taking great gasps of air, scarcely able to stand. Below, the ground shuddered. Presumably, Lord Kalakak had dropped back to all four gigantic legs. Looking down, Elric saw that oddly coloured tail disappearing from the compound. Out in the moonlight, the black flower still hissed and slithered and quested for fresh blood.

Swiftly, the released warriors recovered their weapons, then embraced their commander, Dyvim Mar. To Elric, they offered more formal thanks, clearly surprised by his ruined condition. Some showed concern as he leaned weakly against the window frame, still gasping for breath. The summoning of Kalakak had exhausted what was left of his strength and the climb had taken the rest.

"We owe our lives to our emperor," Dyvim Mar explained. "Without him, gentlemen, we should all be dead."

The fine-featured Bright Empire soldiers remained reserved in their greetings, but some were prepared to accept the truth of their captain's short speech and bowed briefly to the prince of ruins, best known as "Kinslayer," whose treachery had destroyed their homeland. Elric expected nothing from them, save acknowledgment of his rank, for none denied that he was their rightful emperor, named by his dying father as the true inheritor of the Ruby Throne.

"How easily can we leave Soom?" said Princess Nahuaduar. "We are still outnumbered by the savages. Has your reptilian ally departed the city, Prince Elric?"

"He was the best I could summon under present conditions. He helped us but he is forbidden to kill, which is the thing he yearns to do most. Like our Imrryrian dragons, he must sleep a year for every hour or so that he's awake. He returns to his rest."

"So we have no other ally against the savages?" asked Princess Nahuaduar, glancing significantly at his sword.

"Only our own courage and cunning, my lady." Elric turned again to glance through the window and stumbled suddenly backward. A thick, black tendril appeared. Next moment it was curling through the opening. Moonglum yelled to his companions. "Quickly. Back down the stairs. We'll fight our way through the savages to the river." Already the tendril had come snaking in as if scenting blood. Elric cocked his head. He could almost hear it sniffing out his remaining lifestuff.

Led by Dyvim Mar and Tilus Kreek, with the twin princesses following close behind and Elric leaning on his friend, the Melnibonéans poured from the room and down the broad deep winding blood-stained stone steps within the pyramid.

It was almost with a sense of anticlimax that they ran out into the open square to find no enemies. Warily, back to back, they moved slowly out through the alien ruins towards the jungle. Half-fainting, entirely dependant on the stocky Eastlander, Elric came last. From the darkness, spears and arrows flew. A Melnibonéan sobbed with pain as a spear took him in the arm. Without another sound, he pulled the arrow through and discarded it. The remaining Lormyrian archer gathered the arrows for his own quiver. Their shields absorbed the worst of the onslaught, protecting Elric and Moonglum. With a hissed curse, the archer fitted an arrow to his string and sent it back into the invisible pack.

Two more men were lost to enemy spears before they reached the edge of the jungle. In the moonlight they could retrace their original progress from the river. The undergrowth remained dense. With Dyvim Mar leading, they moved slowly on.

For the first time, the savages made a direct attack. Tattooed faces, white, glaring eyes, ochre skins and an assortment of cruel axes, spears, swords and lances suddenly surrounded them. No longer was the strategy to herd them into the compound to become food for the Black Anemonë. Now the cannibals sought only to kill the survivors, so that the man-flower would not devour the degenerate Soomians themselves. Their caution was gone. Moonglum, guarding Elric who was still barely able to hold his blade, did his best to fight back. Then Princess Nahuaduar took the albino's arm onto her own shoulder and helped defend him as they stumbled on. Mostly, the enemy's weapons fell on shields or were blocked by steel. Every so often one of Elric's party would groan and blood would flow. But they could smell the river now. If the savages had not destroyed their boat the remains of the two expeditions might still escape.

Then the remaining savages had fallen back. For a moment the jungle was still. No animals called, nothing moved. The brilliant moonlight cast deep shadows. Some of them seemed to shift and curl into alarming shapes. "Maybe," murmured Moonglum, "they've lost their stomach for the fight?" King Tilus Kreek let out a long relieved sigh—just as a huge, manlike shape loomed up behind them. A giant, with long, curling fingers waving as, momentarily unsteady, it balanced itself in their wake. The Black Anemonë lumbered relentlessly after fresh food. Any food so long as it pulsed with human blood. Then, suddenly, a dark arm shot into their ranks. The last Lormyrian archer shrieked and beat at the huge shape as he was lifted into the air.

They watched helplessly.

"We are finished," murmured King Tilus. "We cannot defeat that thing. I know its power. I should never have led my men here. Now my daughters will die obscenely, thanks to my folly. You go on. I will stay here and try to slow it." It was clear he had no hope of defeating the hugely bloated manlike tree. Only a few hours before it had been a tiny shoot. Now it came swiftly after them, gaining speed with every kill. Whenever it paused it plucked another man from the jungle. It was indiscriminate. Savages, too, were lifted kicking and shouting into its maw. They had no chance of reaching the river before they were caught and their lifestuff added to its size, speed and energy.

"We will fight together," said Dyvim Mar, coming to stand beside the king.

Moonglum drew his twin sabres. "Rest your back on mine, friend Elric. Sadly, we'll die disappointed deaths. Killed by the very treasure we sought."

"No," said Elric. He sighed. "Get the women and the rest of our fighters to the boat. I will stay to slow its advance . . ."

The savages had not fled after all. Realizing that they were now also food for the *noibuluscus*, they flung themselves again at the Melnibonéans, perhaps hoping their blood would satisfy the black flower. This time Princess Semleedaor gasped as a saw-toothed blade slashed her arm. Her father roared his anger and his sword took the attacker in the throat. Blood spurted. Another black tendril came out of the night and seized the slain savage.

"Go!" cried the albino, almost falling. "All of you! Go!" And his fingers began to fumble at the copper wire securing his sword.

Seeing this, Moonglum gripped his shoulder. "Elric. We may yet . . ."

"No. We'll all be slain. And for what? Take everyone and hold the boat for a little while. I'll try to join you. If not, well then, I'm missed by one friend, at least. And a debt will be partly paid."

Like five long fingers, black petals, a hideous, grasping travesty of a massive human hand reached for his arm. He drew back in horror, his own feeble fingers trying desperately to untie the thongs securing his sword's hilt to his belt.

Moonglum paused and helped the albino to untie the wire. Then he turned and with a shout began to run into the jungle, herding the little party of survivors before him.

The Black Anemonë rose up out of the tangle of silhouetted forest, the full moon outlining its writhing head, while moonlight revealed its broad, waving arms and hands. A thin, terrible whistling noise escaped the cluster of long leaves surrounding what resembled a mouth. From under its feet, a score of savages rose to surround Elric.

For a moment the tattooed cannibals stood there confronting him. The silvery light emphasized the whiteness of his skin. No doubt they saw him as some kind of phantom, the chief source of their plan's failure. With deliberate movements, they began to close in on him, watched by the creature they had created through their barbaric blood sacrifice.

Elric grinned.

Reaching for the great broadsword at his hip, he drew it from its scabbard. So finely balanced was the black blade, he could hold it easily in one hand, almost like a rapier. The sword murmured and whispered in his grasp and he felt a sudden rush of energy suffuse him. A thrill of ecstasy that others might feel in love-making.

Then he began his work.

Elric's eyes blazed with red, unholy light, reflecting the flickering runes which ran up and down his blade. He swung Stormbringer first one way and then another, as if to display its power. His lips twisted in crazy delight as he stepped towards the savages, now standing between him and the creature they had raised. His chest rose and fell with deep, strong breaths. He knew a pleasure he had all but forgotten. And, as that familiar black radiance poured from the blade and its song rose and fell in a melody that to him at least was beautiful, he remembered why the Black Sword had been so hard to put aside. Why his addiction had taken so long to conquer. "Aaaah!" Again he swung the blade, but this time it was not in display.

"Arioch! Arioch! Lord of the Seven Darks! Arioch! *Blood and souls for my lord Arioch!*" This time the black, strangely wrought metal sliced into flesh and bone. Heads sprang from necks like so many weeds in a hay field. Arms flew into the foliage. Legs buckled and torsos were hacked in half. Terrified savages tried to flee, but were now trapped between Elric and the Black Anemonë, drunk on the smell of ruined flesh. It was down on the jungle floor, sucking the blood which pumped from the remains of their bodies. It clucked and yelped with dreadful glee. A few men managed to scuttle past the monster they had brought into being, only to be snared by its pre-scient tendrils.

Elric yelled his mockery at the creature. "Come, Black Flower! Come to me. My blood is thin, but it is yours if you can take it!"

The *noibuluscus* paused, staring from its strange head, around which great, spiked leaves curled like a living crown. It bent, reaching out its long branches towards this laughing, white-faced, puny little thing of flesh and thin blood which challenged it and which, perhaps, it sensed as the agent of its own frustration.

Voicing the ancient battle-yells of his ancestors, Elric ran at the Black Anemonë. "Arioch! My lord Arioch! Blood and souls for thee and thine! I present thee with this sacrifice!" The life-force of all those he had killed seared through his veins, filling him with preternatural energy, with a wonderful lust he had almost forgotten, but always craved.

The tendril hands reached out to seize him. Elric dodged them, hacking at legs like two trunks standing across the path above him. The hands curled down to try to grasp him. A weird shriek escaped the monster as the black blade slashed at the writhing fingers, sending them flying into the undergrowth.

"Arioch! Blood and souls for my lord Arioch!" The albino's features were contorted in unhuman delight.

And from somewhere in the darkness came a low, mocking chuckle, as if Elric's patron demon had always known that he and the sword would feed again.

At last the black flower was down, but still the arms whipped and thrust and grasped for the albino. Still the Black Sword sang. Monstrous branches transformed themselves into snakes, coiling around his body, his arms, his legs. But too much energy now pulsed through him. He easily broke free, the blade rising and falling, rising and falling, like a woodsman's axe in the forest. Suddenly, he was tireless. With every blow the albino's energy increased, while the plant weakened. The head darted at Elric, the cluster of long, tough leaves spearing towards his face, trying to suck it from his shoulders, but he dodged it cleverly, still laughing with that wild, maniacal glee, as much in his blade's power as it was in his.

A huge blow. Another. Squealing and chittering, parts of the plant tried to escape now, slithering off into the undergrowth. From head to toe, Elric was covered in black sap, but still he hacked at the thing, finally pausing to reach out and rip the crown of leaves from around the ruined head. To snatch a handful of large seeds, beating like so many hearts, from the centre. He stepped back, panting. His body sang and thrilled with the force pouring through it. He lifted his head in exultation, shouting his mocking triumph at the moon.

"ARIOCH!"

A tendril began to curl itself around his leg. To his horror, he realized that the plant was re-forming itself. He stepped back and with the point of his sword threw the branch as far as it would go. Then he turned and ran towards the river.

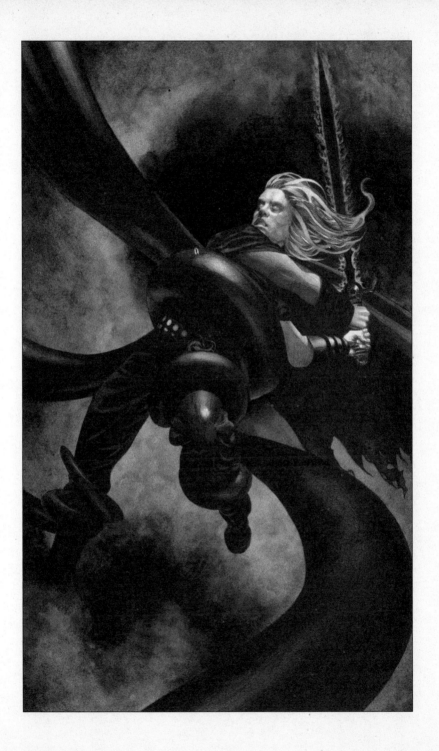

Epilogue

The full moon still brightened the dark waters as they rowed out into midstream and began to follow the current away from Soom. Dyvim Mar, seven Melnibonéans, the King of the Uyt, his two daughters and Moonglum. In the stern of the boat, taking no part in the rowing, sat a solitary figure, washed clean of the filth that had covered it, its pale hand resting on the pommel of a scabbarded black broadsword. Crimson, gloomy eyes stared into another world, seeing nothing of the others.

After some time, Tilus Kreek made his way to where Elric sat and placed a hand on his shoulder. "I must thank you, prince, for all you did tonight. I know from your friend and your kinsmen that it was no easy decision. You saved our lives. Perhaps, too, you saved our souls. I can only imagine the cost to you."

Elric turned those brooding eyes upon the Uyt. He nodded slowly. Then he reached into his purse, feeling what writhed there, almost like human flesh. He drew the stuff out. A bunch of already drying black petals which still moved with a life of their own. A few large pods which also had a fleshy look to them. "Here," he said. "I have no further use for these. I sought an impossible remedy for my condition. I should have known the only real remedy is the one I carry with me." He held the petals and spoors of the *noibuluscus* towards the king. But Tilus Kreek shook his aging head.

"I thank thee, Elric. We both sought to save something by the cultivation of the Black Anemonë. And both of us risked far too much in its pursuit. Perhaps we are lucky to have learned something and still have our lives?"

"Perhaps." With a sudden movement, the albino took the petals and scattered them overboard onto the murky, glistening water. For a moment they wriggled on the surface, like fish, and then sank out of sight. He threw the pods after them. It was just possible the current would carry them downriver and even out into the sea. One day they might even find fresh soil in which to take root. Whether they would ever again be nurtured by human blood, find form in human skin, however, was unlikely.

As the king moved discreetly back to join his other daughter amidships, Princess Nahuaduar came to sit beside Elric, her face flushing as she looked boldly up into his dangerous eyes. "And will you seek a substitute for the black flower?" she asked.

Taking her hand, he shook his head. "My lady, the sword will have to serve me for my usual sustenance. Meanwhile, I have other consolations."

Yet, even as she responded to his touch, he looked away again, as if still hoping to see something familiar in that dense, unpleasant forest.

ASPECTS OF FANTASY
(PART 4)

In this final article, Michael Moorcock explains his definition of the difference between fantasy and science fiction and ends with a tribute to Science Fantasy, *of which this will be the last issue to be published by Nova Publications Ltd.*

—*John Carnell,* Science Fantasy *No. 64, April 1964*

ASPECTS OF FANTASY
(1964)

4. CONCLUSION

FOR REASONS THAT are now obvious to you, I am forced to wind this series up faster than I should have liked. 1 shall have to draw conclusions which will not be as well-illustrated as I had hoped. In the planned discussions of books, themes and characters, I should like to have shown that whereas the form which I've loosely called fantasy is a creative and dynamic form (if not as important as I sometimes like to think) its more recent offshoot science fiction is on the whole a self-defeating, self-limiting form—that where it is good is usually in the elements which it has borrowed from fantasy or mainstream fiction.

A number of books have dealt with the development of science fiction from Verne or Wells, but none, so far as I know, has dealt with its literary development from earlier times. I have already partially described various aspects of fantasy which have gone to form many of the ingredients of modern science fiction, but before I go on to say why I think fantasy has it over science fiction, I'd like to deal with a couple of modern branches of fantasy which have developed from the Gothic phase of the eighteenth and nineteenth centuries.

One of these is usually termed the sword-and-sorcery story. The other has no name that I know of, perhaps because it is rarely published these days. This is the story dealing with what Harry Levin has described as the "haunted palace of the mind"—Otranto, Udolpho, Usher, Gormenghast, etc.

These two settings are connected in that they are both private worlds created from the author's imagination, having no evident connection with the history or geography of the earth we know, yet it is accepted that they *are* on earth. They are mythical worlds—worlds which the author's private mythology has created.

They differ in that one is boundless, horizonless, depending on adventure and supernatural marvels for its basic plot-ingredients, and the other is bounded, enclosed, oppressive, depending largely upon its interplay of characters.

The first is a development of the Gothic historical romance, the second is a development of the Gothic haunted castle story, the origins of which have already been touched upon elsewhere in this series.

It would be foolish to describe either of the outstanding modern examples of each stream as "Gothic novels," but they do contain many of the refined elements of the earlier type. They are both trilogies by British writers—namely Tolkien's *Lord of the Rings* and Peake's Titus Groan books.

I know that both authors have been surprised that people link their work. Yet there *is* a link in that both have created rich, closely detailed imaginary landscapes bearing little or no relation to the earth we know. Both, also, have used "innocents" as their central characters. Peake has used a child, Titus, while Tolkien has used childlike creatures—the Hobbits.

Peake's novels are, in other ways, far superior to Tolkien's, because Peake places emphasis on his characters, whereas Tolkien is content to write a classic tale of doom, marvels and high adventure. I find, also, that Peake's images stay in the mind, but I find it extremely difficult to conjure up distinct images of Tolkien's Middle Earth. Also Peake's characters actually develop as the story goes on, while Tolkien's characters do not.

*   *   *

The "haunted palace of the mind" was the dominant theme in Gothic fiction. Elements from this theme have been used in mainstream fiction (Murdoch's *The Unicorn* is a recent example), other branches of fantasy and science fiction.

Shortly after Walpole's *Castle of Otranto* was published (1764), a novel appeared which claimed to be influenced by *Otranto* and also called itself "A Gothic Tale." This was Clara Reeve's *The Old English Baron* (1777)—a story which yearned, like Walpole's, for an Age of Chivalry that never was and was influenced by Mediaeval Romance. Historical romances of this type did not share the same popularity, for a long while, that the "haunted castle" story had. These stories, of course, were tales of chivalry, nobility, adventure, knights, quests, dooms and naturally, the stock marvels of the Gothic—spectres, living portraits and the rest. As quite often happens, these rather poor tales influenced much better writers and there is little doubt that Byron, Shelley and other Romantics came, when young, under the influence of the Gothic fantasists and that the Gothic moods coloured their own ideas. It may be making an overlarge claim, but it is possible to imagine that we might not have had *Childe Harold* or even *Idylls of the King* without the first Gothic Romances. These Romances were much influenced by the stories of Arthur, Charlemagne and El Cid, as well as the Teutonic sagas and the later "fake" Romances such as *Amadis of Gaul* which Southey translated in the early part of the nineteenth century (see Introduction to this series). Compared to the haunted castle background, this theme was not, it seems, as popular, but it certainly encouraged Sir Walter Scott to write his Waverley Novels and in turn influence a huge body of historical novelists who doubtless, in turn, influenced the "sword-and-sorcery" writers of whom Lord Dunsany is recognizably the first.

Dunsany's sword-and-sorcery tales are rarely reprinted, these days. They were written in the last part of the nineteenth and early part of the twentieth centuries.

The Sword of Welleran is apparently one of the best, dealing with a youth who lives in a city once protected by a group of rather Charlemagnian paladins. When the city is attacked, he takes the sword of the chief hero, Welleran, and, disguised as the hero, drives the invaders back.

From my own limited reading of Dunsany's tales, they seem to be rather slight, depending largely on a deliberately archaic style used to evoke a nostalgic, highly coloured mood which tends to pall in even the shortest of the stories.

Dunsany seems to have influenced two later writers—Clark Ashton Smith (who doesn't have his demerits to quite the same extent) and J.R.R. Tolkien, who has Dunsany's demerits but compensates for them with other merits of his own.

Smith would appear to be one of Robert E. Howard's influences. Smith wrote of Hyperboria, Atlantis, of "prehistoric" civilizations of the past and civilizations of the future which seem exactly like them. His stories were, like Dunsany's, anecdotal and slight. Otherwise, Howard was influenced by contemporary writers of historical and oriental adventure, who had, in turn, been influenced by Scott, Conan Doyle and other historical novelists.

Howard's rough, erotic-exotic, violent prose had the archaicisms of Dunsany and Smith, but where they had built highly mannered "prose-poems," Howard told stories. Howard's style was a combination of the best and the worst in Poe, Edgar Rice Burroughs, Lovecraft and commercial hack-writers, filling the pulps of his day. His plots were involved, if not very original, and held the reader; in its rawness, its wildness and emphasis on physical strength and prowess, Howard's work was more of an "American" type than the others. Its hero was not the sensitive, delicate, shadow-creature of Dunsany's wish-world, but the virile barbarian, the iconoclast, the sneerer at authority and learning—in fact, Howard's Conan is the idealized American frontiersman in quasi-mediaeval clothing, with a sword instead of a long gun. Yet Conan, too, is essentially an innocent.

Fritz Leiber was the next important contributor to the growing body of stories in the sword-and-sorcery vein. Originally in *Unknown* and later in *Fantastic*, his polished tales of Fafhrd and the Grey Mouser owed influence to Howard, but harked back to Smith in their use of understatement and sardonic dialogue. These tales combine the best of both kinds and have a very distinct flavour which I find most palatable. If Conan was the "frontiersman," then the Grey Mouser is the "sharp operator"—for me, a much more interesting and subtle character.

There is a quality which most of these stories share in their construction. Dominant in the Gothic Romances of the two previous centuries was the picaresque theme—the quest theme which has been used as an effective vehicle for storytelling since earliest times. It is still the dominant kind of plot in modern sword-and-sorcery tales. Dunsany used it, James Branch Cabell used it in his Poictesme stories such as *Jurgen*, Howard's overall theme for his Conan tales involves a wanderer with a curiosity to see all; Leiber utilizes the theme rather less frequently, though again the overall theme of his Fafhrd/Grey Mouser tales is on the quest pattern. Tolkien of course has a highly involved picaresque theme, and this also applies to many of my own fantasy stories—typical examples being "While the Gods Laugh" or "To Rescue Tanelorn . . ."

For all some critics have said to the contrary, I am not a great sword-and-sorcery fan and find Howard and E.R. Burroughs, in particular, virtually unreadable. One of my criticisms of all but Leiber is that the stuff is, like far too much SF and fantasy, emotionally unconvincing.

Fantasy writers are often called writers of "adult fairy stories." Most of them are not—they are writers of fairy stories for adults who still want to read fairy stories. There is nothing wrong in writing or reading fairy stories. There is something retarded, however, in the man who devotes himself wholly either to reading or to writing the stuff. The writer who merely recaptures the dream-worlds of childhood without adding to this what his adult mind has learned is an inadequate artist, if nothing else.

He may be an inadequate artist and a good stylist, like Dunsany or

Bradbury or Tolkien, but if, as in the case of these, he cannot do more than recapture the wonders and terrors of infancy, he deserves to be regarded as we regard an infant prodigy—with admiration but not too much serious attention.

The label of emotional immaturity is an easy one to attach and is often applied these days, but I think it will stick in this case. This may be the reason why the appeal of sword-and-sorcery is on the whole to younger readers whose emotions are, understandably, not yet fully matured. What good it achieves, if any, is that it forms a useful bridge between childhood sense of wonder and adult sense of surrealism. However, that bridge seems to be infrequently crossed. People, to prolong the metaphor, sit down halfway over and stay there for the rest of their lives. This is bad for them.

The good sword-and-sorcery story should have something of the function of a moving-belt, perhaps, carrying the reader with it. The dream-worlds of these stories are worlds to which writer and reader initially escape. They leave *everything* behind. The dream landscapes and structures the less limited writer discovers as he creates a story will soon be utilized for his own artistic purposes, if he has any. He will cease to be merely an escapist entertainer—he will apply his skill and understanding to making these worlds relevant to our own situation.

Few fantasy writers manage it. Peake has managed it in his Titus Groan trilogy and, I am pleased to say, so has Leiber in a slighter way with his ironic and delightful Grey Mouser stories. It is what I have tried to do in the Elric tales—evidently without much success since the less escapist themes I tried to carry on the sword-and-sorcery vehicle have escaped a great many readers. I shall have to try again with a fresh or altered vehicle.

If I had to list what I consider to be the best current developments of fantasy's various streams, they would be:

(a) *Titus Groan* trilogy by Peake (representing the "haunted palace").

(b) *Two Sought Adventure* by Leiber (representing sword-and-sorcery).

(c) *The Drowned World* by Ballard (representing SF).

(d) The *Naked Lunch* trilogy by William Burroughs (representing how the elements of fantasy can be developed to push forward the progress of the novel).

The fantasy form has been progressing and refining itself for centuries. It has gone through various stages of borrowing from or influencing mainstream fiction, and is currently starting a phase where it will once again both borrow and influence until at length it is absorbed, for a while, back into the mainstream. Fantasy (and in this I include science fiction) that does not do this—and most of it, of course, doesn't—will enjoy variations of ephemeral success but will finally wither, die and be forgotten. There are those who feel that fantasy fiction should remain an "inland sea," cut off from the mainstream. That "inland sea" will fast turn into a stagnant pool, unless it is nourished by and is allowed in turn to nourish the mainstream.

Science fiction, therefore, is an offshoot of fantasy. It has sub-categories in turn—many of its stories specialize in explaining away "supernatural" phenomena, just as the Gothic often did. Others are fables or moral tales—satires, if you like—set somewhere in the galaxy or in the future instead of in an "unexplored" part of the globe like Lilliput. Many of them merely substitute ray-guns and Super Science for swords and sorcery, far-off planets for "prehistoric" lands, and are, apart from their use of scientific instead of supernatural jargon, direct developments from the Gothic and earlier kinds of fantasy. If science fiction's purpose is, as some say, to prepare people for possible eventualities in the future by detailing the probable influence that our technical progress will have on new generations, then it has largely failed. On the whole, I regard this claim as unsubstantiated. Much as I enjoy reading science fiction, I enjoy it for its moods, images and the fresh moods and images which they, in turn, create in me.

The fact is clear that SF is a vein of fantasy which has been more or less worked out.

To claim, as many enthusiasts have done, that fantasy is a "branch" of science fiction is nonsense. This should now be obvious.

The limitations of science fiction nowadays are far greater than its possibilities. Today the better SF stories are largely defeated by *being* SF! On the whole SF themes are super-conventionally handled and this results in the ruin and "conventionalization" of whatever merit existed in the theme originally. Where else, for instance, would a story like Harry Harrison's *Streets of Ashkelon* be hailed as daringly unconventional, save in the super-conventional world of SF? With all due respect to writer and editor, this theme has been used in mainstream fiction in one way or another for years! The fact is, of course, that the best SF is not strictly SF. The themes of *Case of Conscience*, *Canticle for Leibowitz* or *The Streets of Ashkelon*, if handled well, would carry infinitely more impact if put in a present-day setting! SF readers, writers and editors comprise, it appears, one of the most shockable sections of the modern reading public!

"Pure" fantasy does not carry these limitations in anything like the same proportion. The "other planets" of SF possess, by definition, shape and dimensions. The fluid dream-worlds of the sword-and-sorcery tale, say, do not carry the same limitations. As a *potential* form, then, the sword-and-sorcery story is the better bet as a vehicle for unconventional ideas.

Admittedly, fantasy fiction does not have the technical information and quasi-sociological themes of its currently more popular offshoot and this is why, I think, its enthusiasts are not so numerous. With his escapism, today's reader appears to want "authentic" material information rather than the more abstract variety. He wants Defoe's laundry lists rather than Richardson's "analysis of the human heart." This is the only explanation, too, for the current popularity of an otherwise poor series of spy-thrillers which tell John Smith how to dress, what food to order, where to eat it, what kind of handmade spark-plugs, size, weight, diameter etc., etc., to have in his expensive sports car, assuming he has the money. This emphasis on gadgets and their accompanying jargon is distasteful. But it is the only explanation for the current boom in SF compared to the static or only gradually awakening interest in experimental fantasy. A reaction away from SF towards fantasy may already be taking place—but I could be thinking wishfully.

Now we come to what I think of as fantasy and what you may have been considering as science fiction.

First I dismiss all talk of "sociological" SF and "satirical" SF as (as one critic has termed my own work) a load of old codswallop. Sociological fiction or satirical fiction or even fiction about the changing nature of man in a changing environment is, if presented as SF, limited by the very great limits of its chosen vehicle. If a writer's any damn good he doesn't need a gimmicky vehicle to carry his ideas.

J.G. Ballard prefers to call his published work "speculative fantasy" and this, I feel, is a more apt term for the best of what is normally called science fiction. Yet Ballard's ideas about science are at best twentieth-century ideas—not the Victorian ideas involving machines and dials and plugs and pistons. They are in keeping with the experiments modern scientists are making in the realms of nuclear physics, neurology, psychology—experiments which are increasingly touching on the metaphysical so that to read the text of a modern scientific paper is sometimes like reading the sayings of some old Asian hermit. Yet Ballard prefers to think of his work as "speculative fantasy."

Speculative fantasy is also what Brian Aldiss, the other eminent British contributor to the field, writes. Aldiss is less interested in abstracts than Ballard. His exceptionally good style and above all sympathetic interest in the human plight have combined to produce some excellent short stories.

Nowadays there is something horribly depressing, and earnest, and *dull* about the main body of work termed science fiction. Ballard and Aldiss stand far above the rest. They have realized the form's limitations but have not accepted them, have taken strides to cast them off. They have come up with stories like *Faceless Card* or *A Question of Re-Entry* which, while no means being science fiction, are extremely good stories that utilize the possibilities of the SF tale without giving in to its heavy limitations. And, above all, these two writers are literate. No wonder they stand out.

Science fiction as we know it sprang from the main body of fantastic fiction and must now, by degrees, ease back in again if it is to survive. It is doing this, it is learning that it cannot survive as an independent form. Fantastic fiction must in turn fertilize and be fertilized by the mainstream if *it* is to survive.

In the field of the magazines there have been two which have acted as outlets for the "changeover" story. One in America, one in Britain. The British magazine is *Science Fantasy*, the American is *Fantastic*. After this issue, we shall be left with one.

Science Fantasy has published a proportionately higher number of good stories than any other magazine to date. The comparative freedom allowed to the writer for this magazine has been greater than anywhere else. I only wish I could have written better stories for it while I had the chance.

It was not only my opinion that *Science Fantasy* was achieving a more literary and less prosaic tone in its choice of material. To some extent it had always possessed a more literary "image" than any of its competitors.

In recent years with the publication of stories like *The Watchtowers*, *Where Is the Bird of Fire?*, *Same Time, Same Place*, *Skeleton Crew* and many others, it has shown the uses to which fantasy can be put, has done something more than entertain on an escapist level.

Perhaps this is why it was beginning to be thought, in this country and the States, the best of all the current magazines.

It has long been a maxim that the best doesn't sell as well as the worst.

Ironically, future analysis may show that *Science Fantasy*'s very death was due to its emphasis on literate and literary writing rather than on gadgets and gimmicks.

INTRODUCTION TO
THE SKRAYLING TREE

Introduction to

THE SKRAYLING TREE
(2003)

T EXAS SUMMERS ARE notoriously cruel. They sap the life out of
you. Anyone able to do so escapes. Sometimes we go west to Cal-
ifornia, sometimes we go north-east, to Maine, to the forests and endless seashores, whose lands are as drenched in myth and legend as
Texas.

An Englishman, a Londoner, I'm often asked why I chose to live in
Texas. I have to answer that I was attracted to the landscape, the stories,
the vibrant mythology of the Southwest. This can be sensed in Texan
mountains and deserts as readily as different stories and mythologies
can be felt in the stones and streets of London or the moorlands, limestone pavements and deep valleys of my ancestral Yorkshire.

I have always loved America, first as a fantasy inspired by Feni-
more Cooper, Longfellow, Joel Chandler Harris, Louisa May Alcott,
Bret Harte and Clarence E. Mulford, and later as a reality, when I wandered the woods of the Delaware Valley or explored abandoned min-
ing towns in the Rockies. I have crossed the US back and forth three
times and delighted in her infinite variety, the complexity of her people
and cultures. These cultures, blended in the great cities of America,
have entertained and inspired the world.

I began writing heroic fantasy before anyone had a name for it,
when my Elric books were as marginalized as Professor Tolkien's. I
drew inspiration not only from T.H. White (*The Once and Future King*)
and Mervyn Peake (the Titus Groan trilogy), both of whom I was privileged to know, but from American writers like Fritz Leiber and Leigh
Brackett, whose wonderful prose and extraordinary imaginations were

without equal and with whom I also later became friends. Poul Anderson's *The Broken Sword* and James Branch Cabell's *Jurgen* were other enormous influences. Indeed, I found Tolkien, when his trilogy began to appear in my mid-teens, a little tame in comparison! The Americans were always my own literary heroes.

Therefore it is probably not surprising that the time came to acknowledge these boyhood enthusiasms and to recall the inspiration of American landscape and literature. Many American writers of fantasy have retold the tales of Arthur, Lancelot, Guinevere—the Matter of Britain. Very few have looked to the Matter of America, their native myth cycles. Hardly any have written about Hiawatha, the great civilizer, the American King Arthur, or used the images which fired the dreams of their ancestors and brought them to these lands as explorers, traders, settlers, sometimes conquerors, seeking a thousand different fantasies of idealism, security and wealth.

In *The Skrayling Tree*, I wanted to write an homage to America and the great Americans. Not an uncritical, sentimental celebration, because that would be disrespectful, but a tale of blood and beauty, touching on this country's early history before she became a nation.

With that in mind, I have written of the desert dwellers of the Southwest. I've described the plains, lakes and mountains of America before she was settled. I've told the stories of north-eastern forest dwellers. I have written of the savage yellow-haired Teutonic invaders who first came to these shores from Europe, of the legends and tales which inspired Longfellow and the American transcendentalists. Indeed, I've even written about Longfellow himself in one chapter! Images, like the tree of life, common to most peoples, are blended with more typically American images, like the legendary City of Gold, which brought so many to their deaths as they sought to discover it.

How Elric, the albino quasi-human Sorcerer Prince from another age, fits into this, how he meets savage Vikings, a man and a woman from our own time, as well as the great Hiawatha himself, and how they come together to save the heart of America, perhaps the entire multiverse, I'll leave for you to discover—and, I hope enjoy—in the pages of *The Skrayling Tree*!

If, in telling this adventure, I've touched a little on the Matter of America and described my own love for this vast, rich, complicated country, then I will have paid back my debt, at least in some small measure.

INTRODUCTION TO THE FRENCH EDITION OF ELRIC

Introduction to the French
Omnibus Edition of

ELRIC
(2006)

I T IS NO secret that the inspiration for Elric came from a character in
the long-running pulp adventure series (of which I was later an editor) *The Sexton Blake Library*. Sexton Blake began his career in 1897,
but it was not until 1918 that his greatest enemy appeared in the pages
of the *Union Jack*, a weekly paper devoted to Blake's adventures. The
enemy was Monsieur Zenith (always "Monsieur," perhaps to show that
he was a Romanian aristocrat in disguise), a pink-eyed albino who
smoked opium cigarettes, played the violin like an angel, was waited
on by fanatically loyal Japanese servants, and was immensely strong
and agile, living only for danger and careless of his own life. He would
battle Blake in a series written always by Anthony Skene (real name
G.N. Phillips) until 1941 when, in *The Affair of the Bronze Basilisk*, he
would die in an air-raid. *The Sexton Blake Library* finished in the early
1960s, but not before it had published my first novel *Caribbean Crisis*
under a house pseudonym. Blake stories, however, continue to be written to this day.

Of course, as a boy, I had read copious amounts of Romantic fiction
and poetry, from Norse epics to *The Song of Roland*, various Peninsula
Romances and Gothic novels either by Germans or in the German tradition, including Carlisle's *German Romance*, Lewis's *The Monk* and
Maturin's *Melmoth the Wanderer*. I had read Lord Dunsany, Robert E.
Howard, Edgar Rice Burroughs, Fritz Leiber and Poul Anderson's
The Broken Sword, but I had not read Tolkien's *Lord of the Rings*,
though I had met both Tolkien and Lewis, who were also enthusiasts
of some of the Americans I enjoyed. By the time I was sixteen, in 1956,

the year I became editor of *Tarzan Adventures*, I had found my way to Paris, which was where every London boy wanted to go for his first solo trip abroad. There, I played my guitar outside George Whitman's *Mistral* bookshop (now *Shakespeare and Co.*) and made enough money to buy books from him. By then my great enthusiasm was for Sartre, Camus and other French existentialists. All of these would influence the Elric stories.

When I was first asked to write an epic fantasy series for *Science Fantasy* magazine in the early 1960s I already had some pages written concerning a hero who would continue M. Zenith's adventures in a fantasy setting. They were written in open homage to Skene's creation, though, of course, by the time I came to set Elric's adventures down on paper my hero was already undergoing something of a sea-change. Reflecting the zeitgeist of my generation, which made heroes of James Dean, Elvis Presley and the early Marlon Brando, he became the man you will find in the following pages. Instead of perfect evening dress, he generally wears black leather and iron. Like M. Zenith, he swiftly becomes an outcast, but where Skene's albino was mysterious concerning his origins, mine was very specific about the psychic burdens he bore, the events creating his nightmares, and, of course, he had acquired supernatural powers. The first story, "The Dreaming City," appeared in 1961. The first Elric stories were published in France in about 1965. Philippe Druillet, around the same time, began to draw an original Elric story for a short-lived magazine called *Moi Aussi*. The Elric stories have, therefore, been appearing in France almost as long as they have appeared in England and before they came out in the United States. Nowadays he appears in a considerable number of different languages, including Mandarin, Estonian and Hebrew, and is without doubt my best-known character around the world. I have a particular affinity for his French version, however, especially since Druillet, like the English illustrator Cawthorn, who first drew him, in turn inspired me. Elric soon appeared in lavish Opta editions, which remain probably the most beautiful books ever to feature him.

It was not long before Elric left his inspiration behind and became my own character completely. These days I can, if I wish, write about him without reference to anything I have previously done. He lives, three-dimensional, inescapable, in my imagination. I recall his adventures much as I might recall my own. I have reread very few of the stories here, yet have never been accused of any serious inconsistency. I wrote the majority of them rapidly. Short tales would take a day or so. Novels, until recently, never took much more than a week. This was rather a long time for me, for I wrote many of my other popular romances in three days. I was a busy journalist, musician, editor and father, and that was the time I permitted myself.

Of all my generic creations, Elric remains my own favourite. In my literary novels, Mrs. Cornelius (*The Cornelius Quartet*) and Joseph Kiss (*Mother London*) are probably closest to my heart, but I love Elric most of all my "eternal champions." He was not exactly my first-born – the Eternal Champion was conceived in a story I wrote when I was seventeen—but he was the first hero who truly came to life for me and has remained my favourite ever since.

Since I began to write his adventures, Elric has appeared in many graphic-novel versions, and versions of the albino himself have appeared in a number of UK and US comics, including his most recent manifestations in the *Michael Moorcock's Multiverse* series from DC and as a pirate chief in a Tom Strong adventure I wrote at Alan Moore's suggestion. His early escapades are featured in a very good French edition, *Elric: The Making of a Sorcerer*, published here by Éditions Soleil. At time of writing, the Weitz brothers are developing Elric for Universal studios in Hollywood. There are also audiobooks, figurines, posters and all the usual modern variations of his image, as well as websites, a Hawkwind rock album (and stage show) and role-playing games. There was even an Elric jigsaw puzzle.

Given this sort of exposure, I am surprised that Elric has for me continued to maintain his integrity and with the publication of the last Elric book in the US, *The White Wolf's Son*, I resolved to write no more fantasy novels, convinced that I did not want to risk "thinning him out" as I have seen happen to too many of my favourite series heroes. I have laid not only Elric to rest, but also the Eternal Champion. It might be that in future I will write the occasional short story should one occur to me or even produce an idea for another graphic tale. In all the ramifi-cations of my multiverse, of course, the cycle will never end. But as far as novels are concerned, I have written the last one. This omnibus seems as good a place as any to say goodbye to him and to thank old readers for their patronage while hoping new readers will find my moody, ruby-eyed and ivory-skinned creation at the very least enter-taining enough to give them a few hours' enjoyable escape.

ELRIC: A NEW READER'S GUIDE

ELRIC: A NEW READER'S GUIDE
(2009)
by John Davey

ELRIC OF MELNIBONÉ—proud prince of ruins, Kinslayer—call him what you will. He remains, together with maybe Jerry Cornelius, Michael Moorcock's most enduring, if not always most endearing, character.

The first version of this guide to the many and various Elric publications was adapted from *Michael Moorcock: A Reader's Guide* (1991/92), and attempted to provide a title-by-title breakdown of the books together with the omnibuses in which each appeared. While that is still the case this time, there has been such an explosion in Elric collections over the last sixteen years—of which these Del Rey editions are the most recent (and quite possibly the best)—that this version of the guide has had to be rather substantially revamped. It retains its chronological format, but deals with each omnibus as an individual title, rather than including them within the main books' descriptions.

Elric began life in response to a request from John Carnell, editor of *Science Fantasy* magazine, for a series akin to Robert E. Howard's Conan the Barbarian stories. What Carnell received, while steeped in sword-and-sorcery images, was something quite different. All in all, nine Elric novellas appeared in *Science Fantasy* between June 1961 and April 1964. During that time, the first five were collected as *The Stealer of Souls* (1963). These were later split up and re-collected in, or absorbed into, *The Weird of the White Wolf* and *The Bane of the Black*

Sword (both 1977) and were also, as a result of this assimilation, slightly revised. Collectors should note that the true first edition of *The Stealer of Souls* (subtitled by its publishers as "...*and Other Stories*," against Moorcock's wishes) was bound in orange boards; an otherwise identical but less collectable second printing had green boards.

Stormbringer (1965), conceived as a novel, was first published as such when abridged and revised from the four remaining *Science Fantasy* novellas. It was later restored to its original length and further revised, in 1977. The original abridgments basically condensed the first two novellas (plus part of the third) into one section, "The Coming of Chaos."

The Singing Citadel (1970) is a collection of four other novellas originally published in various periodicals and anthologies between 1962 and 1967. They were later split up and all but one were re-collected in, or absorbed into, *The Weird of the White Wolf* and *The Bane of the Black Sword* as their events interconnect with those of *The Stealer of Souls*. They were also, as a result of this assimilation, slightly revised. The unused novella, "The Greater Conqueror" (sometimes erroneously listed as "The Great Conqueror"), was subsequently collected in *Moorcock's Book of Martyrs* (1976, a.k.a. *Dying for Tomorrow*, 1978), *Earl Aubec and Other Stories* (1993) and *Elric: To Rescue Tanelorn* (2008).

The Sleeping Sorceress (1971) was expanded from a novella of the same name, although it was originally commissioned as a serial for Kenneth Bulmer's magazine, *Sword and Sorcery*, which never appeared. One of its sections retells, from Elric's viewpoint, a part of the Corum novel, *The King of the Swords*. In 1977, *The Sleeping Sorceress* was retitled, with minor textual amendments, as *The Vanishing Tower* (*q.v.*).

Elric of Melniboné (1972) is a prequel to all other Elric novels. **The Dreaming City** (1972) was a version of *Elric of Melniboné*, published with unauthorized changes. Collectors should note that, in 1977, *Elric of Melniboné* was one of three Elric books published as illustrated editions in slip-cases. This first (in a red case) also had a smaller, limited edition (in a brown case) signed by the author, artist (Robert Gould) and publisher. In 2003, *Elric of Melniboné* was the first novel of Moorcock's to become an unabridged audiobook.

Elric: The Return to Melnibone (sic, 1973) remains, despite its comparative irrelevance to the overall series, one of the scarcest and most sought-after of Elric books. This is the result of its somewhat checkered history, a saga complex enough to rival Elric's own. It is actually little more than a showcase for the exquisite artwork of Philippe Druillet, beginning life in the mid-'60s as double-spread colour illustrations for the first two issues of a French children's magazine called *Moi Aussi*, with text by Maxim Jakubowski. In 1969, Druillet illustrated an omnibus called *Elric le Necromancien*, and in 1972 some of this (and new) artwork was put into a twenty-one piece portfolio as *La Saga d'Elric le Necromancien*, this time with text by Michel Demuth. All of this work up until then was unauthorized, but when the portfolio was reprinted and bound (less one piece) in the UK as *Elric: The Return to Melnibone* (text by Moorcock), Druillet threatened to sue! Moorcock was forced to step in on behalf of the British publishers, pointing out that permission had never been granted for Druillet to draw Elric in the first place. In order to avoid messy litigation, it was decided to allow the small print run to expire, never to be reprinted. However, a republication was finally agreed, and the book made available again in 1997 as *Elric: The Return to Melniboné*.

The Jade Man's Eyes (1973) is a separate novella which, in order to bring it in line with the developing series, was revised and absorbed into *The Sailor on the Seas of Fate* as "Sailing to the Past."

The Sailor on the Seas of Fate (1976) originally slotted, chronologically, between events in *Elric of Melniboné* and *The Weird of the White Wolf*. One of its sections retells, from Elric's viewpoint, a part of the Hawkmoon/Count Brass novel, *The Quest for Tanelorn*. In 2006, *The Sailor on the Seas of Fate* also became an unabridged audiobook.

The Weird of the White Wolf (1977) is a chronological arrangement of selected contents from *The Stealer of Souls* and *The Singing Citadel*, compiled in order to bring them in line with the developing series. At the time of this writing, *The Weird of the White Wolf* is due to become the third unabridged Elric audiobook.

The Vanishing Tower **(1977)** is a retitling, with minor textual amendments, of *The Sleeping Sorceress*. Collectors should note that, in 1981, *The Vanishing Tower* was the second of three Elric books published as illustrated editions in slip-cases. This edition (in a pictorial red case) also had a smaller, limited edition (in a brown case) signed by the author, artist (Michael Whelan) and publisher.

The Bane of the Black Sword **(1977)** is a chronological arrangement of selected contents from *The Stealer of Souls* and *The Singing Citadel*, compiled in order to bring them in line with the developing series.

The somewhat misleadingly titled *Six Science Fiction Classics from the Master of Heroic Fantasy* **(1979)** is a boxed set of six American paperbacks: *Elric of Melniboné, The Sailor on the Seas of Fate, The Weird of the White Wolf, The Vanishing Tower, The Bane of the Black Sword* and *Stormbringer*.

Elric at the End of Time **(1984)** is a collection of short fiction and non-fiction which actually contains only three Elric-related items among its contents of seven (excluding the introduction). The title story was also published separately in 1987 as a large-format novella (*q.v.*) illustrated by Rodney Matthews.

The Elric Saga Part One **(1984)** is the first Elric omnibus, and contains *Elric of Melniboné, The Sailor on the Seas of Fate* and *The Weird of the White Wolf*. *The Elric Saga Part Two* **(1984)** is the second omnibus, and contains *The Vanishing Tower, The Bane of the Black Sword* and *Stormbringer*.

Elric at the End of Time **(1987)** is a separate, large-format novella illustrated by Rodney Matthews for whom it was originally written some years earlier. Collectors should note that it was published simultaneously in both hardcover and paperback formats.

The Fortress of the Pearl **(1989),** the first Elric novel for thirteen years, expanded the saga and slots, chronologically, between events in *Elric of Melniboné* and *The Sailor on the Seas of Fate*.

The Revenge of the Rose **(1991)** slots between events in *The Sleeping Sorceress* and the stories from *The Bane of the Black Sword*.

In 1992, Moorcock began an ambitious project of re-ordering, revising and republishing much of his back-catalogue in a large set of omnibuses in the UK under the collective title, "The Tale of the Eternal Champion." The first of these to feature the albino prince was *Elric of Melniboné* (1993), containing *Elric of Melniboné*, *The Fortress of the Pearl*, *The Sailor on the Seas of Fate* and selected contents from *The Weird of the White Wolf*. The omnibus was retitled in the USA, when the "Eternal Champion" series began to appear there, as *Elric: Song of the Black Sword* (1995).

The second British omnibus to feature Elric was *Stormbringer* (1993), containing *The Sleeping Sorceress*, *The Revenge of the Rose*, selected contents from *The Bane of the Black Sword*, and *Stormbringer*. This omnibus was retitled in the USA as *Elric: The Stealer of Souls* (1998), not to be confused with the Del Rey volume of the same name (*q.v.*).

Collectors should note that, in the UK, "The Tale of the Eternal Champion" omnibuses were published simultaneously in both hardcover and paperback formats. In the USA, hardcover editions appeared ahead of their paperback versions.

Elric: Tales of the White Wolf (1994) is an original anthology of Elric stories by Moorcock and others, edited by Edward E. Kramer & Richard Gilliam.

Michael Moorcock's Multiverse (1999) is a graphic novel illustrated by Walter Simonson, Mark Reeve & John Ridgway, originally serialized in twelve parts (1997/98). It contains three interconnecting tales (each illustrated by a different artist), one of which—Ridgway's—is "Duke Elric."

The Dreamthief's Daughter (2001) was the first volume of a brand-new Elric trilogy—in fact the only preconceived Elric trilogy—linking the albino with some of the many and various members of the Family von Bek. (When revising his books for the "Eternal Champion" omnibuses, Moorcock had the opportunity to change several character names in order to bring them in line with the developing "Von Bek" series, which had begun in 1981 with *The War Hound and the World's*

Pain, although the name's derivation goes back as far as Katinka van Bak in 1973's *The Champion of Garathorm.*) Collectors should note that, also in 2001 (after the true first edition), *The Dreamthief's Daughter* became the last of three Elric books to date published as illustrated editions in slip-cases. This limited edition, signed by the author and artists (Randy Broecker, Donato Giancola, Gary Gianni, Robert Gould, Michael Kaluta, Todd Lockwood, Don Maitz & Michael Whelan), was followed two years later—still dated "2001"—by a smaller limited edition which was leather-bound and tray-cased.

Elric (2001) is another omnibus, containing *The Stealer of Souls* and *Stormbringer,* as part of the publisher's "Fantasy Masterworks" series. In 2008, it was repackaged as part of the same publisher's much smaller "Ultimate Fantasies" sequence.

The Elric Saga Part Three (2002), another omnibus, contains *The Fortress of the Pearl* and *The Revenge of the Rose.*

The Skrayling Tree: The Albino in America (2003) is the second part of the trilogy beginning with *The Dreamthief's Daughter.* **The White Wolf's Son: The Albino Underground** (2005) is the third and last part of the trilogy. Although this supposedly—again—final Elric subseries can be read as a standalone adventure (as, indeed, can each volume), brief mention is made of events slotting, chronologically, into those described within *Stormbringer.*

The Elric Saga Part IV (2005), another omnibus, contains *The Dreamthief's Daughter, The Skrayling Tree* and *The White Wolf's Son.*

Elric: The Making of a Sorcerer (2007) is a graphic novel illustrated by Walter Simonson, originally serialized in four parts (2004–06), and is a prequel to the novel *Elric of Melniboné.*

Elric: The Stealer of Souls (2008) is the first volume of Del Rey's series of six Elric omnibuses published under the collective title "Chronicles of the Last Emperor of Melniboné," each containing fiction and non-fiction. The first volume's fiction includes *The Stealer of Souls* and *Stormbringer.* **Elric: To Rescue Tanelorn** (2008) is the second Del Rey volume, a collection of Elric (or Elric-related) short fiction. **Elric: The Sleeping Sorceress** (2008) is the third volume, including the novels *The Sleeping Sorceress* and *Elric of Melniboné.* **Duke Elric** (2009) is the fourth volume, including *The Sailor on the Seas of Fate*, the "Duke Elric" graphic-novel script and a novella, "The Flaneur des Arcades de l'Opera." **Elric in the Dream Realms (2009)** is the fifth volume, including *The Fortress of the Pearl*, the *Elric: The Making of a Sorcerer* graphic-novel script and a short story, "A Portrait in Ivory." **Elric: Swords and Roses (2010)**, the sixth and final volume, includes *The Revenge of the Rose*, a *Stormbringer* (unmade) movie screenplay and a novella, "Black Petals."

First Editions and First Appearances

The Stealer of Souls:
> "The Dreaming City," originally in *Science Fantasy* No. 47 (edited by John Carnell), UK, June 1961
> "While the Gods Laugh," in *Science Fantasy* No. 49, Oct. 1961
> "The Stealer of Souls," in *Science Fantasy* No. 51, Feb. 1962
> "Kings in Darkness," in *Science Fantasy* No. 54, Aug. 1962
> "The Flame Bringers," in *Science Fantasy* No. 55, Oct. 1962
> Neville Spearman hardcover, UK, 1963
> Lancer paperback, USA, 1967

Stormbringer:
> "Dead God's Homecoming," orig. in *Science Fantasy* No. 59, June 1963
> "Black Sword's Brothers," in *Science Fantasy* No. 61, Oct. 1963
> "Sad Giant's Shield," in *Science Fantasy* No. 63, Feb. 1964
> "Doomed Lord's Passing," in *Science Fantasy* No. 64, Apr. 1964
> Herbert Jenkins h/c (abridged & revised from the novellas), UK, 1965
> Lancer p/b (ditto), USA, 1967
> DAW p/b (full length & revised), USA, 1977
> Granada p/b (ditto), UK, 1985

The Singing Citadel:

> "The Singing Citadel" (novella), orig. in *The Fantastic Swordsmen* (anthology edited by L. Sprague de Camp), USA, 1967
>
> "Master of Chaos," in *Fantastic* Vol. 13 No. 5 (ed. Cele Goldsmith), USA, May 1964
>
> "The Greater Conqueror" (non-Elric), in *Science Fantasy* No. 58, Apr. 1963
>
> "To Rescue Tanelorn . . . ," in *Science Fantasy* No. 56, Dec. 1962

Mayflower p/b, UK, 1970

Berkley p/b, USA, 1970

The Sleeping Sorceress:

> "The Sleeping Sorceress" (novella), orig. in *Warlocks and Warriors* (anthol., ed. Douglas Hill), UK, 1971

New English Library h/c (expanded from the novella), UK, 1971

Lancer p/b (ditto), USA, 1972

DAW p/b (as *The Vanishing Tower*), USA, 1977

Archival Press h/c (as *The Vanishing Tower*, no dust-wrapper, in pictorial red slip-case [also limited in brown slip-case]), USA, 1981

Granada p/b (as *The Vanishing Tower*), UK, 1983

Elric of Melniboné:

Hutchinson h/c, UK, 1972

Lancer p/b (unauthorized changes, as *The Dreaming City*), USA, 1972

DAW p/b (unchanged, as *Elric of Melniboné*), USA, 1976

Blue Star h/c (ditto, no dust-wrapper, in red slip-case [also limited in brown slip-case]), USA, 1977

Elric: The Return to Melnibone (illustrated by Philippe Druillet):

Unicorn outsize p/b, UK, 1973

Jayde Design outsize p/b (as *Elric: The Return to Melniboné*), UK, 1997

The Jade Man's Eyes:
Unicorn p/b, UK, 1973

The Sailor on the Seas of Fate:
Quartet h/c, UK, 1976
DAW p/b, USA, 1976

The Weird of the White Wolf:
DAW p/b, USA, 1977, comprising:
  "The Dream of Earl Aubec" (a.k.a. "Master of Chaos")
  "The Dreaming City"
  "While the Gods Laugh"
  "The Singing Citadel"
Granada p/b, UK, 1984

The Bane of the Black Sword:
DAW p/b, USA, 1977, comprising:
  "The Stealer of Souls"
  "Kings in Darkness"
  "The Flamebringers" (a.k.a. "The Flame Bringers")
  "To Rescue Tanelorn . . ."
Granada p/b, UK, 1984

Six Science Fiction Classics from the Master of Heroic Fantasy:
Six DAW p/bs, boxed, USA, 1979, comprising:
  Elric of Melniboné
  The Sailor on the Seas of Fate
  The Weird of the White Wolf
  The Vanishing Tower
  The Bane of the Black Sword
  Stormbringer

Elric at the End of Time (collection):

NEL h/c, UK, 1984, comprising the following Elric-related items:

"Elric at the End of Time," orig. in *Elsewhere* (anthol., ed. Terri Windling & Mark Alan Arnold), USA, 1981

"The Last Enchantment," in *Ariel* No. 3 (ed. Thomas Durwood), USA, Apr. 1978

"The Secret Life of Elric of Melniboné" (non-fiction), in *Camber* No. 14 (fanzine, ed. Alan Dodd), UK, June 1964

DAW p/b, USA, 1985

The Elric Saga Part One:

Doubleday (Science Fiction Book Club) h/c, USA, 1984, comprising:

Elric of Melniboné
The Sailor on the Seas of Fate
The Weird of the White Wolf

The Elric Saga Part Two:

Doubleday (S.F.B.C.) h/c, USA, 1984, comprising:

The Vanishing Tower
The Bane of the Black Sword
Stormbringer

Elric at the End of Time (novella, illustrated by Rodney Matthews):

Paper Tiger large-format h/c & p/b, UK, 1987

The Fortress of the Pearl:

Gollancz h/c, UK, 1989
Ace h/c, USA, 1989

The Revenge of the Rose:

Grafton h/c, UK, 1991
Ace h/c, USA, 1991

Elric of Melniboné (omnibus):
Orion/Millennium h/c & p/b, UK, 1993, comprising:
Elric of Melniboné
The Fortress of the Pearl
The Sailor on the Seas of Fate
"The Dreaming City"
"While the Gods Laugh"
"The Singing Citadel"
White Wolf h/c (as *Elric: Song of the Black Sword*), USA, 1995

Stormbringer (omnibus):
Orion/Millennium h/c & p/b, UK, 1993, comprising:
The Sleeping Sorceress
The Revenge of the Rose
"The Stealer of Souls"
"Kings in Darkness"
"The Caravan of Forgotten Dreams" (a.k.a. "The Flame
    Bringers")
Stormbringer
"Elric: A Reader's Guide" (non-fiction by John Davey)
White Wolf h/c (as *Elric: The Stealer of Souls*), USA, 1998

Elric: Tales of the White Wolf:
White Wolf h/c, USA, 1994, comprising the following Moorcock
items:
"Introduction to *Tales of the White Wolf*" (non-fiction)
"The White Wolf's Song"
plus Elric stories by Tad Williams, David M. Honigsberg, Roland
J. Green & Frieda A. Murray, Richard Lee Byers, Brad Strickland,
Brad Linaweaver & William Alan Ritch, Kevin T. Stein, Scott
Ciencin, Gary Gygax, James S. Dorr, Stewart von Allmen, Paul W.
Cashman, Nancy A. Collins, Doug Murray, Karl Edward Wagner,
Thomas E. Fuller, Jody Lynn Nye, Colin Greenland, Robert Wein-
berg, Charles Partington, Peter Crowther & James Lovegrove, Nancy
Holder, Neil Gaiman.

Michael Moorcock's Multiverse:
>DC Comics large-format p/b, USA, 1999
>>"Moonbeams and Roses" (non-Elric), illustrated by Walter Simonson
>>"The Metatemporal Detective" (non-Elric), illustrated by Mark Reeve
>>"Duke Elric," illustrated by John Ridgway

The Dreamthief's Daughter:
>Earthlight h/c, UK, 2001
>American Fantasy h/c (in slip-case [also limited in tray-case]), USA, 2001

Elric:
>Gollancz p/b, UK, 2001, comprising:
>*The Stealer of Souls*
>*Stormbringer*

The Elric Saga Part Three:
>S.F.B.C. h/c, USA, 2002, comprising:
>>*The Fortress of the Pearl*
>>*The Revenge of the Rose*

The Skrayling Tree: The Albino in America:
>Warner h/c, USA, 2003

The White Wolf's Son: The Albino Underground:
>Warner h/c, USA, 2005

The Elric Saga Part IV:
>S.F.B.C. h/c, USA, 2005, comprising:
>>*The Dreamthief's Daughter*
>>*The Skrayling Tree*
>>*The White Wolf's Son*

Elric: The Making of a Sorcerer (illustrated by Walter Simonson):
DC Comics large-format p/b, USA, 2007

Elric: The Stealer of Souls: Chronicles of the Last Emperor of Melniboné: Volume 1:
Del Rey p/b, USA, 2008, comprising:
"Putting a Tag on It" (non-fiction), orig. in *Amra* Vol. 2
No. 15 (fanzine, ed. George Scithers), USA, May
1961
The Stealer of Souls
"Mission to Asno!" (non-Elric), in *Tarzan Adventures* Vol. 7
No. 25 (ed. Moorcock), UK, Sep. 1957
Stormbringer
"Elric" (non-fiction), in *Niekas* No. 8 (fanzine, ed. Ed
Meskys), USA, 1964
"The Secret Life of Elric of Melniboné" (non-fiction)
"Final Judgement" (non-fiction by Alan Forrest), in
New Worlds No. 147 (as "Did Elric Die in Vain?"), UK,
Feb. 1965
"The Zenith Letter" (non-fiction by Anthony Skene), in
Monsieur Zenith the Albino, UK, 2001

Elric: To Rescue Tanelorn:
Del Rey p/b, USA, 2008, comprising:
"The Eternal Champion," orig. in *Science Fantasy* No. 53,
June 1962
"To Rescue Tanelorn . . ."
"The Last Enchantment" (a.k.a. "Jesting with Chaos")
"The Greater Conqueror"
"Master of Chaos" (a.k.a. "Earl Aubec")
"Phase 1: A Jerry Cornelius Story," in *The Final Programme*,
USA, 1968
"The Singing Citadel"
"The Jade Man's Eyes"

"The Stone Thing," in *Triode* No. 20 (fanzine, ed. Eric
Bentcliffe), UK, Oct. 1974

"Elric at the End of Time"

"The Black Blade's Song" (a.k.a. "The White Wolf's
Song")

"Crimson Eyes," in *New Statesman & Society* No. 333, UK,
1994

"Sir Milk-and-Blood," in *Pawn of Chaos: Tales of the Eternal
Champion* (anthol., ed. Edward E. Kramer), USA, 1996

"The Roaming Forest," in *Cross Plains Universe: Texans Celebrate Robert E. Howard* (anthol., ed. Scott A. Cupp & Joe
R. Lansdale), USA, 2006

Elric: The Sleeping Sorceress:

Del Rey p/b, USA, 2008, comprising:

The Sleeping Sorceress

"And So the Great Emperor Received His Education . . . ,"
orig. spoken-word introduction to *Elric of Melniboné*
(audiobook), USA, 2003

Elric of Melniboné

"Aspects of Fantasy (1): Introduction" (non-fiction), orig. in
Science Fantasy No. 61, Oct. 1963

"Introduction to Elric of Melniboné, Graphic Adaptation"
(non-fiction), in *Elric of Melniboné* (by Roy Thomas, P.
Craig Russell & Michael T. Gilbert), USA, 1986

"El Cid and Elric: Under the Influence!" (non-fiction), in
Comiqueando No. 100, Argentina, Aug./Sep. 2007

Duke Elric:

Del Rey p/b, USA, 2009, comprising:

"Introduction to the AudioRealms version of *The Sailor on the
Seas of Fate*" (audiobook), USA, 2006

The Sailor on the Seas of Fate

"Duke Elric" (script)

"Aspects of Fantasy (2): The Floodgates of the Unconscious"
(non-fiction), orig. in *Science Fantasy* No. 62,
Dec. 1963

"The Flaneur des Arcades de l'Opera," in *The Metatemporal
Detective,* USA, 2008

"Elric: A Personality at War" (non-fiction by Adrian
Snook)

Elric in the Dream Realms:

Del Rey p/b, USA, 2009, comprising:
The Fortress of the Pearl
Elric: The Making of a Sorcerer (script)
"A Portrait in Ivory," orig. in *Logorrhea: Good Words Make
Good Stories* (anthol., ed. John Klima), USA, 2007
"Aspects of Fantasy (3): Figures of Faust" (non-fiction), in
Science Fantasy No. 63, Feb. 1964
"Earl Aubec of Malador: Outline for a Series of Four Fantasy
Novels"
"Introduction to the Taiwanese Edition of Elric," in *Elric of
Melniboné,* Taiwan, 2007
"One Life, Furnished in Early Moorcock" (by Neil Gaiman),
in *Elric: Tales of the White Wolf,* USA, 1994

Elric: Swords and Roses:

Del Rey p/b, USA, 2010, comprising:
The Revenge of the Rose
Stormbringer: First Draft Screenplay
"Black Petals," orig. in *Weird Tales* No. 349 (edited by
Stephen H. Segal & Ann VanderMeer), USA, Mar./Apr.
2008
"Aspects of Fantasy (4): Conclusion" (non-fiction), in *Science
Fantasy* No. 64, Apr. 1964
"Introduction to *The Skrayling Tree*," written for Borders,
Inc., 2003

"Introduction to the French Edition of Elric," in *Le Cycle
d'Elric*, France, 2006
"Elric: A New Reader's Guide" (non-fiction by John
Davey)

MINUTIAE:

In both of the variant omnibus editions called *Elric: The Stealer of Souls*,
the version of *Stormbringer* appears in a definitive, re-revised form,
retaining its full, four-novella length but also incorporating some of the
pertinent changes from its 1965 abridgment which were lost during its
1977 restoration to full length.

Non-Elric items contained within the *Elric at the End of Time* collection include "Sojan the Swordsman" (a composite of short tales featuring Moorcock's first ever fantasy hero), "Jerry Cornelius & Co." (two
essays on that character) and the short story "The Stone Thing."

The essay "The Secret Life of Elric of Melniboné"—between its
first fanzine appearance (1964) and its collection in *Elric at the End of
Time*—was also in *Sojan* (Savoy Books p/b, UK, 1977). That collection additionally contained another piece of non-fiction, "Elric,"
which originally appeared in the fanzines *Niekas* No. 8 (ed. Ed
Meskys, 1963, as a letter) and *Crucified Toad* No. 4 (ed. David Britton,
1974).

The French omnibus, *Elric le Necromancien* (Éditions Opta h/c,
1969), collected *The Stealer of Souls* and the full version of *Stormbringer*—plus the novellas "The Singing Citadel" and "To Rescue
Tanelorn . . ."—all arranged in correct chronological order some eight
years before any English-language equivalents. Most recently, in
France, the mammoth omnibus, *Le Cycle d'Elric*, collected in a single
volume *Elric of Melniboné*, *The Fortress of the Pearl*, *The Sailor on the
Seas of Fate*, *The Weird of the White Wolf*, *The Sleeping Sorceress*, *The
Revenge of the Rose*, *The Bane of the Black Sword*, "The Last Enchant-
ment," *Stormbringer* and "Elric at the End of Time"! There is also a
French anthology of Elric stories by hands other than Moorcock's

(although he introduces it), *Elric et la Porte des Mondes*, which seems unlikely ever to receive an English-language edition.

Many graphic adaptations of the Elric saga have appeared over the years, mostly starting as comics. Moorcock himself, together with James Cawthorn, plotted a two-part strip in 1972, in which Elric and Conan the Barbarian join forces ("A Sword Called Stormbringer!" & "The Green Empress of Melniboné" in *Conan the Barbarian* Nos. 14 & 15). Cawthorn also produced a one-off graphic adaptation of *Stormbringer* for Savoy Books (1976). Several other Elric one-offs have appeared over the years, drawn by various hands, but the most widely available series for some time were Pacific/First Comics' *Elric of Melniboné* (6 parts), *Elric: Sailor on the Seas of Fate* (7 parts), *Elric: Weird of the White Wolf* (5 parts), *Elric: The Vanishing Tower* (6 parts) and *Elric: The Bane of the Black Sword* (6 parts), all serialized throughout the late eighties. The first three sets were also compiled as bound graphic novels. The sequence was stopped by Moorcock before *Stormbringer*, due to deterioration in the quality of the artwork, although a new graphic version of the novel, adapted by P. Craig Russell, was finally serialized in the USA for Topps/Dark Horse Comics in 1997 (compiled as a bound graphic novel a year later). Most recently, of course, two new Moorcock-scripted tales, "Duke Elric" and *Elric: The Making of a Sorcerer*, have developed the saga further still.

Also heavily and ornately illustrated are the various rule books and supplements for Elric-related role-playing games from the American companies, Chaosium (whose best-known *Stormbringer* has itself been revised and massively expanded several times) and more recently Mongoose Publishing with their *Elric of Melniboné*.

Elric ephemera has become quite a major industry, and if the long-awaited Elric movie comes to fruition, such things can only be expected to blossom. There have already been collectable cards, die-cast miniatures, dolls, jigsaw puzzles, model-kits, posters, T-shirts and, of course, records.

Moorcock's musical involvement with several rock bands, including his own, is well known. He wrote an Elric-related song, "Black Blade," for Blue Öyster Cult, but it is Hawkwind who have used the albino prince to the best effect. In 1985, they released the album *The Chronicle of the Black Sword*, and went on an accompanying theatrical concert tour—sometimes featuring Moorcock on stage with the band—which also gave rise to a live album, *Live Chronicles*, and video/DVD, some versions of which include Moorcock performances.

Quite what the ever-taciturn Elric would make of all this attention, I am not sure. He has already endured far more than those first nine novellas would have had us believe possible. Have we really now seen the last of him? Only time will tell . . .

ORIGINS

*Early artwork associated with Elric's first appearances
in magazines and books*

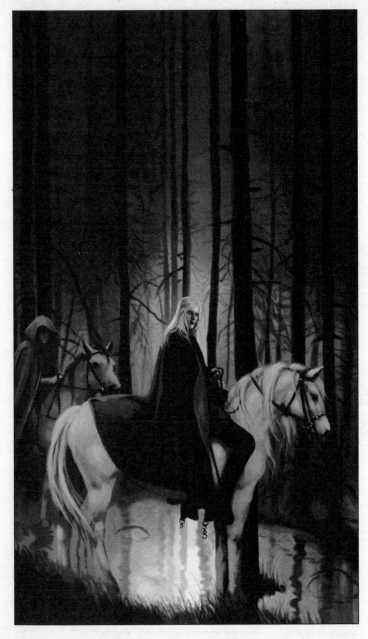

Original artwork by Marc Moreno, for *La Revanche de la Rose (The Revenge of the Rose),* French edition, Pocket Books, 2006.

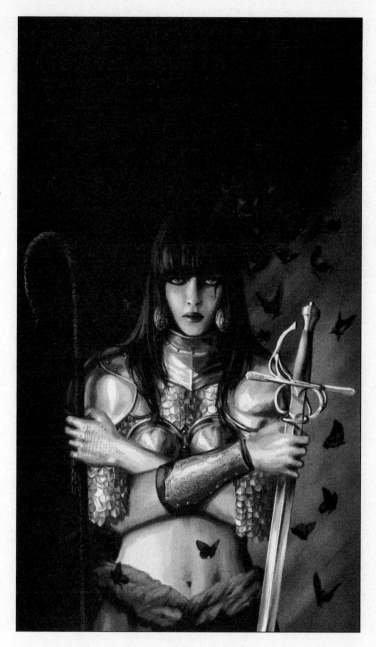

Original artwork by Marc Moreno, for *La Forteresse de la Perle*
(*The Fortress of the Pearl*), French edition, Pocket Books, 2005.

Original artwork by Guillaume Sorel, for *Elric et la Porte des Mondes* (*Elric and the Gate of Worlds*), first edition of an original anthology of new Elric stories in French, Fleuve Noir Books, 2006.

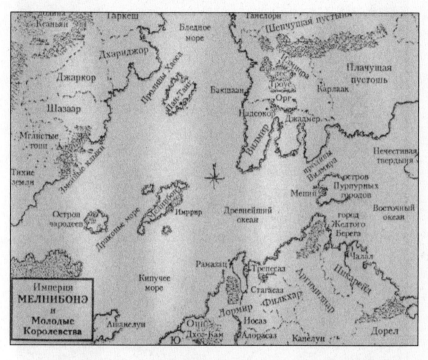

"**Империя Мелнибонэ**" ("Empire [of] Melniboné") map by **Н. Михайлов**,
1992, appeared in *Хроники Элрика* / *Приэрауhьiй Город*
(*The Dreaming City/The Sleeping Sorceress*), Terra Fantastica, 2001.

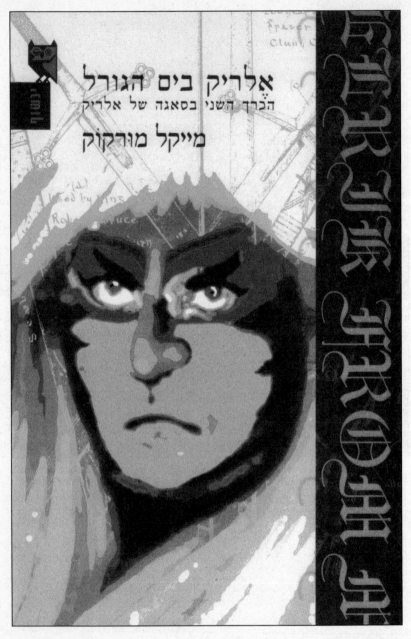

Cover artwork by Yael Bar-Dayan, for an Israeli translation of *The Sailor on the Seas of Fate*, Yanshuf Books, 2005.

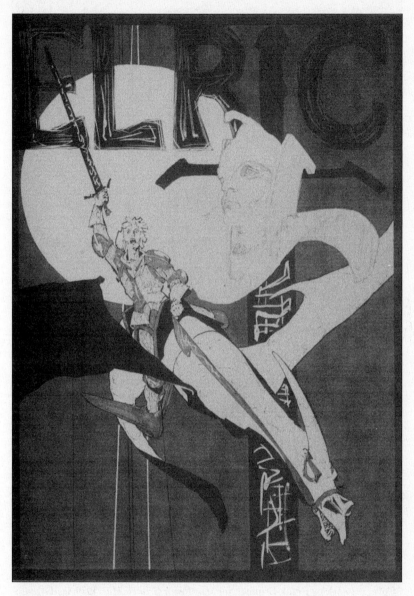

Cover artwork by Howard V. Chaykin, for *Elric*,
self-published portfolio, 1975.

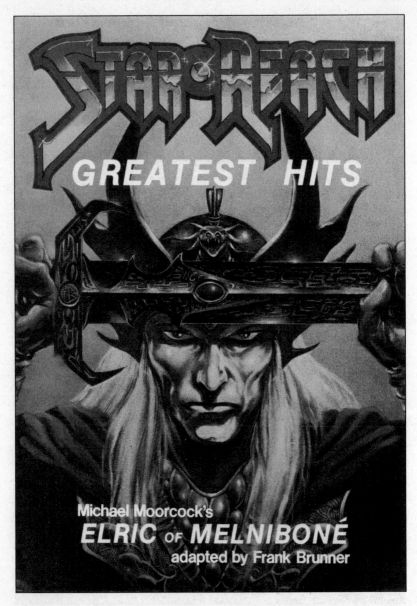

Cover artwork by Frank Brunner, for *Star*Reach Greatest Hits*, 1979; lead stories:
"Elric of Melniboné" by Brunner, and "The Prisoner of Pan Tang"
by Eric Kimball and Robert Gould.

A page from "The Green Empress of Meliboné," by Barry Windsor-Smith and Roy Thomas (plotted by Moorcock and Cawthorn), the second half of a story begun with "A Sword Called Stormbringer," first appearing in *Conan the Barbarian* Nos. 14 and 15, March and May 1972.

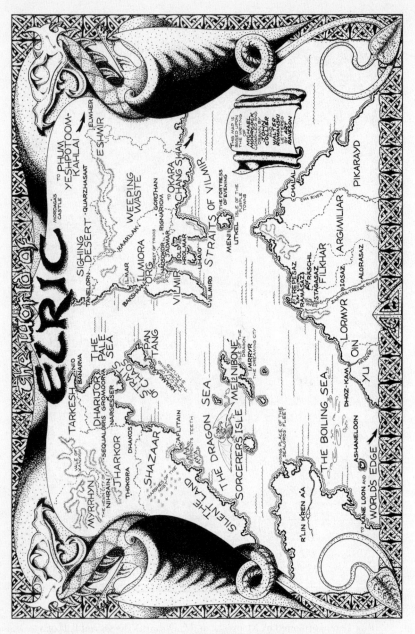

"The World of Elric" map by John Collier and Walter Romanski, 1976
(based on the map by Cawthorn and Moorcock), first published in
Elric of Melniboné (and all subsequent DAW Elric books).
This corrected version, previously unpublished, courtesy John Collier.

"Elric in the Young Kingdoms" map by John Collier, 2009.
This updated version, including placenames from the 2007 novella
"Black Petals," previously unpublished.

Interior artwork by Philippe Druillet, from *Elric le Necromancien*, Éditions Opta, 1969, later reproduced in *Elric: The Return to Melniboné* (1973).

"L'Ère des Jeunes Royaumes" ("The Age of the Young Kingdoms") map by Philippe Druillet, first appeared (loose-leaf) in *Elric le Necromancien*, Éditions Opta, 1969.

WORLD FANTASY AWARD-WINNING AUTHOR OF
THE FORTRESS OF THE PEARL

MICHAEL
MOORCOCK

THE REVENGE
OF THE ROSE

AN ALL-NEW NOVEL OF ELRIC—
HIS GREATEST ADVENTURE

Cover artwork by Robert Gould, for *The Revenge of the Rose*,
first American edition, Ace Books, 1991.

"Elric," 1992, first published as front-cover artwork for *The Time Centre Times* Vol. 2 No. 2, edited by D. J. Rowe, Ian Covell, Maureen Cuffe, and John Davey, August 1993.

"Urlik," 1976, a wash drawing to accompany the first-draft screenplay of an aborted motion picture, *Stormbringer*, previously unpublished.

Interior artwork, from *Elric of Melniboné*, DAW Books, 1976.

"Elric in the Young Kingdoms" map, 1992 (based on the map by John Collier and Walter Romanski), first published in *Elric: Song of the Black Sword*, White Wolf Books, 1995.

Interior artwork, 1978, from *Elric von Melniboné* (*Elric of Melniboné*), Heyne Books, Germany, 1979.

Interior artwork, from *Die See des Schicksals* (*The Sailor on the Seas of Fate*), Heyne Books, Germany, 1979.

Interior artwork, circa 1979, from *Der Zauber des Weissen Wolfs* (*The Weird of the White Wolf*), Heyne Books, Germany, 1980.

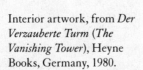

Interior artwork, from *Der Verzauberte Turm* (*The Vanishing Tower*), Heyne Books, Germany, 1980.

Interior artwork, from *Im Banne des Schwarzen Schwertes* (*The Bane of the Black Sword*), Heyne Books, Germany, 1980.

Interior artwork, from *Sturmbringer* (*Stormbringer*), Heyne Books, Germany, 1980.

"Jagreen Lern and Elric," 1963, one of the earliest Elric illustrations, first published in *A Serious Life*, by D. M. Mitchell, Savoy Books, 2004.

"Elric and Lord Horror," first published in *Hard Core Horror* No. 2, by David Britton, Savoy Books, 1989.

Two sketches, from an
undated series of six,
previously unpublished.

Dear Mike —
An Elric collection, and not a
headband in sight — Jim.

James Cawthorn & Michael Moorcock
DREAM OF A DOOMED LORD

As the beast foundered beneath him in blood and screaming metal, Elric of Melnibone hurled himself from the saddle. Iron feet stamped and slid, flailing blades ploughed the earth around him. He rolled and sprang erect, Stormbringer gripped in taut, bone—white hands. A spiked shape lunged, slashing with ragged claws. Storm—bringer smashed into the steel torso, shearing metal, tendons, bones, howling as it fed. Blinding blue sparks leaped crackling along the hellblade, burned in Elric's veins. The plain quivered under his feet, the air sang with power. He began to run, a raging white—masked demon, crimson eyes blazing in the black sockets of his helm. Storm—bringer lashed out, once, twice, and the way ahead was open.

He ran toward the castle.

. . .

They had combed the ruins of Melnibone, tower by ragged tower. Dyvim Slorm, inheritor of ten thousand years of brilliant and cruel Melnibonean culture, feared for his cousin's life. Moonglum, being merely human, had greater faith in his friend's ability to survive. When they eventually found him, he was standing at the sea's edge, where blue jade dragons brooded under the cloudwracked sky.

Dyvim Slorm quickened his steps. "Elric! We feared that —" He faltered as he looked into the albino's eyes of sombre crimson. For all his sorcerous learning, he flinched from the import of their fixed, unseeing gaze. He looked away. Moonglum, approaching, called out and pointed to an object in the surf. "What is that?"

Stooping, hands on swordhilts, they saw a sphere of crystal. Trapped in its intricate facets, violet light pulsed and flickered.

Elric ran, eyes slitted against the mounting fury of the violet sun that flared on the horizon. The quartz walls of the castle fed upon the light; shimmering, throwing off spectral rainbows that writhed above the plain. The quartz began to flow, melting and reforming, growing. Battlements soared in grotesque, mountainous conformations. Towers sprouted, bristling with deadly barbs of glass. And suddenly Elric knew, with a certainty which cut through his battle—madness like an icy knife, that there was no enemy in the castle. The castle, itself, was his enemy.

His limbs began to shake. Wrapping both hands about Stormbringer's hilt, he ran on, crimson eyes wide, staring into death.

. . .

For a day after Dyvim Slorm shattered the crystal with a single stroke of Mournblade, Elric lay, corpselike, in the Tower of D'a'rputna. To his friends' assertion that it had been a device of Chaos, he later assented, but without conviction. Throughout the little time which remained to him, he was haunted by the thought that, on some unknown field, he was doomed to live and fight again.

"Dream of a Doomed Lord," 1978, first published in
Something Else No. 1, edited by Charles Partington, Spring 1980.

FIVE

NINE

Two chapter-head sketches, 1989, from a series commissioned
privately to illustrate a copy of the first edition of *Stormbringer* (1965),
previously unpublished, courtesy Charles Partington.

Endpaper sketch, 1979, commissioned privately to illustrate
a copy of the first edition of *Stormbringer* (1965),
previously unpublished, courtesy George Locke.

Cover artwork
for *Crucified
Toad* No. 4,
edited by David
Britton, Winter
1974.

Title sketch, 1969, from an aborted graphic adaptation of
The Stealer of Souls, first published in *Crucified Toad* No. 4.

A page from *Stormbringer* graphic adaptation, Savoy Books, 1976.

Self-portrait, 2007, commissioned by Savoy Books,
previously unpublished.

Interior artwork (non-Elric), illustrating "Storm Bird, Storm Dreamer" by J. G. Ballard, first published in *New Worlds* No. 168, edited by Moorcock, November 1966.

Interior artwork (non-Elric), illustrating "Pale Roses" by Moorcock, first published in *New Worlds 7* (whole No. 208), edited by Hilary Bailey and Charles Platt, Sphere Books, 1974.

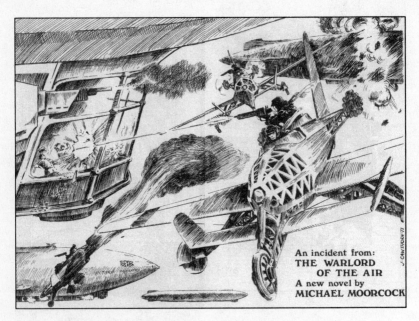

An incident from:
THE WARLORD
OF THE AIR
A new novel by
MICHAEL MOORCOCK

Interior artwork (non-Elric), promoting *The Warlord of the Air*
by Moorcock, first published in *New Worlds* No. 201,
edited by Moorcock, March 1971.

For further information about Michael Moorcock and his work, please send a stamped, self-addressed envelope to:

The Nomads of the Time Streams
P.O. Box 385716
Waikoloa, HI 96738

ABOUT THE AUTHOR

MICHAEL JOHN MOORCOCK is the author of a number of science fiction, fantasy, and literary novels, including the Elric novels, the Cornelius Quartet, *Gloriana*, *King of the City*, and many more. As editor of the controversial British science fiction magazine *New Worlds*, Moorcock fostered the development of the New Wave in the U.K. and indirectly in the U.S. He won the Nebula Award for his novella *Behold the Man*. He has also won the World Fantasy Award, the British Fantasy Award, and many others.

ABOUT THE ILLUSTRATOR

JOHN PICACIO has illustrated covers for books by Harlan Ellison, Robert Silverberg, Frederik Pohl, Jeffrey Ford, Charles Stross, and Joe R. Lansdale, among others, but his very first book cover assignment was for a Michael Moorcock work. Picacio not only illustrated the cover of the Thirtieth Anniversary edition of *Behold the Man* (Mojo Press, 1996), he also contributed interior illustrations and designed the entire book. Moorcock's early support and encouragement provided the right nudge at the right time, and that job energized Picacio to pursue a career as a book cover artist. In spring 2001, he left his day job in the world of architecture and has been a full-time professional illustrator ever since. He's produced cover art for major franchises, such as *Star Trek* and *The X-Men* among others. A three-time Hugo Award nominee for Best Professional Artist, he has won the Locus Award, two International Horror Guild Awards, the Chesley Award, and the much-coveted World Fantasy Award—all in the artist category. More than a decade after that first gig with Moorcock's *Behold the Man*, Picacio couldn't be prouder to work on this sparkling new Del Rey series of Elric editions. He lives in San Antonio, Texas, with his wife, Traci. For more information, please visit www.johnpicacio.com.